GATHERING WINDS

GATHERING WINDS
OSPREY CHRONICLES™ BOOK FOUR

RAMY VANCE
MICHAEL ANDERLE

THE GATHERING WINDS TEAM

Thanks to our Beta Readers

Kelly O'Donnell, Larry Omans

Thanks to the JIT Readers

Dave Hicks
Peter Manis
Diane L. Smith
Dorothy Lloyd
Deb Mader
Zacc Pelter
Debi Sateren
Jeff Goode

If we've missed anyone, please let us know!

Editor
The Skyhunter Editing Team

This book is a work of fiction. All of the characters, organizations, and events portrayed in this novel are either products of the author's imagination or are used fictitiously. Sometimes both.

Copyright © 2021 by LMBPN Publishing
Cover Art by Jake @ J Caleb Design
http://jcalebdesign.com / jcalebdesign@gmail.com
Cover copyright © LMBPN Publishing
A Michael Anderle Production

LMBPN Publishing supports the right to free expression and the value of copyright. The purpose of copyright is to encourage writers and artists to produce the creative works that enrich our culture.

The distribution of this book without permission is a theft of the author's intellectual property. If you would like permission to use material from the book (other than for review purposes), please contact support@lmbpn.com. Thank you for your support of the author's rights.

LMBPN Publishing
PMB 196, 2540 South Maryland Pkwy
Las Vegas, NV 89109

Version 1.00, November 2021
ISBN (ebook) 978-1-68500-484-2
ISBN (paperback) 978-1-68500-485-9

DEDICATION

To my mom. Thank you for everything.

—Ramy Vance

*To Family, Friends and
Those Who Love
to Read.
May We All Enjoy Grace
to Live the Life We Are
Called.*

— Michael

CHAPTER ONE

Someone had kicked the hornet's nest.

Was it me? Sarah Jaeger wondered numbly, staring at the chaos of Locauri bodies swarming over the *Osprey* on the shuttle's display screen. *Did I do this? Did I push us too hard, too soon?*

There were thousands of the aliens, massing on the *Osprey's* sleek silver hull like ants on an upturned picnic basket. More than one village's worth of the small, insectile creatures, that was for sure.

Jaeger, captain of that besieged ship far below, sat in the pilot's chair of her only remaining shuttle, paralyzed with indecision. The door between the shuttle cockpit and cargo hold behind her was jammed open. Baby paced from one end of the confining hold to the other, pausing to grumble and mew as she picked up on Jaeger's agitation. The big tardigrade paused, and Jaeger heard the sound of something heavy and hard scraping against the floor.

Finally, Jaeger tore her eyes away from the display. Baby pawed at the awkward shape that was the first mate's calcified

1

body. Toner had been lying in an awkward grasping position when the crystal had encased him, and now he stared, frozen and unblinking, at Jaeger through several centimeters of milky stone. His blue eyes were wide and bright and shot through with black and red veins, like a blood infection run amok.

"Leave him alone," Jaeger whispered as Baby sniffed at the splay of pink crystal growing out of the stub where Toner's left hand had been.

Baby growled.

"Captain." The shuttle's comm channel blurted to life, and the flood of relief that Jaeger felt when she heard Seeker's voice come through loud and clear took the strength out of her legs. "Sorry for the delay," he said. "We had to batten down the hatches, but we managed to get this bird in lockdown before any hostiles got in."

"I've been hailing you for the last two minutes." Jaeger forced strength into her voice as she turned back to the control console and the siege on her display screen. "You had me worried. I'm three kilometers out and coming in fast. I need to get Toner to the medical bay ASAP." She swallowed hard. "So *why* are there thousands of Locauri trying to break into my ship?"

"Still not clear on the details myself." She heard the *clack* of Seeker's grinding jaws. "We have Art in here with us. He flew in ahead of the swarm. Said there was a murder back at the village. All of our people are accounted for, Captain, except Occy and Pandion."

Jaeger groaned. Her prime display screen switched from long-range to local cameras as the shuttle fell into a holding pattern in the sky above *Osprey*. From here, she could make out the individual bodies of the Locauri hopping across the hull, their pseudo-wings flashing and fluttering by the light of the rising sun. In the distance, she could now make out more activity in the forest canopy, large Locauri flitting from tree to tree toward the nearest village.

"Are we private, Seeker?" she said through gritted teeth.

There was a brief pause, and when Seeker spoke again, it was without muffled background noise. "Channel secure, Captain."

"The very first thing I need you to do is figure out how we're going to get Toner into the medical bay safely. He's paralyzed and encased in some kind of crystal lattice. He must weigh at least a ton, and I'm afraid if we drop him, he'll shatter into a million pieces."

"The Locauri have us pretty effectively surrounded," Seeker said. "They can jump and climb up to our roof. We're not going to be able to get the shuttle in here without opening doors to hostiles, but I have the crew looking for other ways to get you in here."

"Not Aquila, though," Jaeger said quietly. "Or anyone else in Pandion's immediate cohort."

"Already ahead of you." Seeker sounded grim. "I have her and a few others on lockdown and Bufo is trying to figure out what they know about whatever Pandion was planning."

Jaeger was simultaneously glad that she wasn't alone in being suspicious of her crew and saddened at how easily Seeker had fallen into a classic military police role. She had hoped they'd left that nonsense behind them.

There was a faint grinding noise from the cargo hold behind Jaeger, and she spun. "Baby, *stop it!*"

The tardigrade went rigid, then shuffled back a step from where she'd been examining Toner's bloody crystal-stump. Jaeger couldn't tell if she was trying to bust Toner out of his unnatural shell or if the tardigrade was trying to snack on the man.

"Get Elaphus on the line," Jaeger shouted to Seeker as she unbuckled from her harness and threw herself into the cargo hold. "I'm needed for damage control."

Baby chuffed and took a step back, shrinking away from a woman roughly one-tenth her size. The tardigrade's open mouth-hole was a ring of slowly rotating, flexing teeth.

"Don't you *dare*," Jaeger growled.

Baby took another shuffling step backward. Her mouth-hole dilated, and her skin rippled as she dropped her head.

Jaeger couldn't entirely blame the creature for being defensive; Toner *had*, extremely recently, tried to kill Jaeger. And almost certainly would have, if not for Baby's intervention. Except that it wasn't Toner's fault—he'd been badly injured, and a minor cave-in destroyed the device that allowed him to control his moods. The man would never willingly hurt her.

How do you explain all that to a massive animal with the strength and protective instincts of a pissed-off mother bear?

Jaeger had no idea. Her brain was a fuzzy soup of exhaustion.

"Captain?" A new voice, soft and feminine, rang clear over the radio. "Elaphus here."

Jaeger nearly collapsed with relief. Swiping her hand against the nearest wall interface, she activated the video feed. "I'm sending you a visual of our situation," she said. "It's hard to describe."

There was a moment of silence as, on the other end of the line, the crew's head doctor studied the feed from inside the cargo hold. "What on god's green earth happened to him?"

Jaeger only wished she knew where to begin. She paced

restless circles around the Toner statue, trying to organize her thoughts. "We found a chamber where the forebears were either growing creepers or keeping them in ultra long-term stasis. They were all wrapped up in crystal cocoons, like this one. A few of the creepers activated, breaking free of the crystal shells, and attacked us. Toner took a severe injury. I tried to warn him not to feed on the creepers, but—"

"But the mods," Elaphus said impatiently. "I know."

"Not even a minute after he started feeding, this crust began to grow over his skin. I think it's stopped growing, at least, but it's hard to be sure."

"Damn," Elaphus breathed. "We need to get him to Medical right away. I'll prepare an isolation room for him."

"Do you think it's contagious?" Jaeger asked anxiously.

"I have no idea, and that's reason enough for quarantine."

Jaeger groaned and scrubbed fingers through her hair. She was still coated in dust and sweat. Her head ached. She couldn't remember the last time she'd slept.

"Got a little bit of good news for you, Captain." Seeker cut into the conversation.

"God, I needed to hear that."

"We've found a way to get you into the *Osprey*. Hope you still have towing chains in the shuttle. You're gonna need them."

There were individual escape pod hatches scattered across the *Osprey*'s entire body. They were all empty, of course—people had jettisoned in every one of the bird's hundreds of escape pods over a year ago during the initial mutiny that had turned Ensign Jaeger into Captain Jaeger. What mattered to Seeker's plan, however, wasn't the escape pods. It was the dozens of small airlock chambers scattered across *Osprey*'s central column. None of the accessible airlock portals were much larger than a standard doorway.

This was going to suck.

The shuttle, which had been drifting in a holding pattern high above the mess, entered an abrupt descent, rocking back and forth as the combined, unsecured weight of Toner and Baby shifted.

"Garage door is open," Portia reported over the radio. Glancing into the cockpit, Jaeger saw a video feed of the *Osprey*'s massive port wing cargo hold doors grinding open.

The distraction worked. On the secondary display screen, Jaeger saw clusters of Locauri lift their antennae and turn, feeling the change in air pressure. Then, sensing an opening into the ship, the angry aliens turned and sprang toward the port wing.

"It's not going to take them long to realize it's a dead end," Seeker grunted. "I'd rather not give them time to fuck with the construction equipment parked in there."

"Agreed." Jaeger's heart was in her throat. She stood by the shuttle cargo doors, clumsily piloting the ship via a computer interface not intended for fine motor control. She felt blind, struggling to hold the shuttle steady as it dipped toward the *Osprey*'s hull. Toner's mass shifted with every dip and sway, straining against the towing straps she'd slapped around him.

"These touchscreens are lagging." She wiped a bead of sweat from her brow. "I want engineering to tune them up ASAP. I'm flying blind. All the instruments are up in the cockpit. Am I close?"

"We have you at three meters from the hull," Portia said. "You're going to have to come closer."

"I *don't* have adequate thruster control," Jaeger snapped. "If I try to bring her in any closer, I'm going to crash."

"We're running out of time," Seeker said. "It will have to do. Hold her in position, Captain."

On the sliver of display screen, Jaeger saw dozens of Locauri swarming into the port wing cargo hold. Some of them clustered around the interior doors, looking for a way in. Many carried fire-hardened spears.

"I'm in position with Elaphus," Portia said. "We're ready on this end, Captain."

"All right." Jaeger swallowed. "Beginning operation."

She activated the cargo door controls. A torrent of wind rushed through the shuttle as a crack of daylight formed and expanded against the rear hull.

The *Osprey*'s massive central column stretched out before Jaeger, glittering silver against Locaur's deep blue sky. Three meters below, a dark portal grew along her hull.

Nearly as quick as the Locauri themselves, four crewmen in combat fatigues crawled out of the yawning mouth and fanned out. The tallest figure waved up at Jaeger, giving the all-clear sign.

The airlock door was even smaller than Jaeger remembered, but there wasn't time to change plans. The Locauri would realize they'd been duped soon enough and come running.

Bracing herself for disaster, Jaeger tipped the shuttle's angle. The ship lurched beneath her feet, flinging her against the hull.

With a groan and a grind, Toner slid toward the open door.

"You're drifting out of alignment," Portia shouted over the radio. "Bring it leeward half a meter!"

I'm doing the best I can, Jaeger thought, fighting the touchpad thruster controls. "You're going to have to direct him," she called, as Toner's bulk picked up momentum. Jaeger tried tipping the shuttle back to slow his descent, but as she'd discovered, controls back here were garbage. "Shit. Shit, shit. Incoming!"

There was a dramatic pause. Then daylight flooded the cargo hold as Toner's bulk filled the doorway—and dropped into the open air.

The towing straps anchored to the bulkhead snapped taut. Over the radio, Jaeger heard alarmed shouting. She wrestled the shuttle back into a parallel line and scrambled to peer out the back door.

Below, the soldiers wrestled with Toner's dangling bulk, turning him this way and that as they tried to fit a square peg into a round hole.

Something moved in the corner of Jaeger's vision. Two dark shapes sprang onto the *Osprey*'s roof.

"Locauri incoming," she shouted.

Down below, one of the soldiers turned, lifting a rifle. "Put your fucking weapons *down*," she screamed. She saw the soldier—she couldn't identify him through his helmet—waver.

This conflict would turn into a shooting war over Sarah Jaeger's dead body.

Not even pausing to consider the risk to herself, she sprang forward and prepared to hurl herself out of the shuttle and tackle the soldier.

With a growl and a blur of motion, Baby shoved past Jaeger and flung herself into open space.

The *Osprey*'s hull shuddered, where the big tardigrade landed in the space between the soldiers and the approaching

Locauri. Shaking herself like a wet dog, Baby set her legs, faced the half-dozen Locauri, and let out a bellow that shook the air.

The Locauri scattered and broke, falling away from the roof in a flutter of beating pseudo wings.

The shuttle lurched. Below, a chunk of crystal chipped off of Toner's shell as he dropped, awkwardly, into the airlock.

"He's in!" Portia shouted. "Your turn, Captain!"

Jaeger crouched, grabbed one of Toner's towing straps, and slid out of the shuttle.

As she descended into the shadows of the airlock, Jaeger looked up and waved at the tallest and thinnest of the soldiers.

Portia returned a sharp salute and waved for her squad to move. One after the other, the dark-clad figures grabbed the dangling tow straps and climbed into the shuttle. Baby came last, bounding over the roof before leaping. The shuttle swayed from the impact as Baby's front claws grazed the threshold. With the help of the soldiers, the big creature crawled aboard.

"More Locauri incoming," Portia reported as her crew released the towing straps, cutting the shuttle free of its anchor. Jaeger scrambled to pull in the straps.

"Get out of here," Jaeger gritted as the airlock hatch started to close around her.

"Roger that." Above, the shuttle's cargo doors slid shut. With a fading hum, it shrank into the sky.

The airlock doors slammed shut, leaving Jaeger alone in a dark and silent tomb.

CHAPTER TWO

"Shuttle team clear," Jaeger sighed into her comm channel. She slumped, crammed awkwardly between Toner and the wall in the tiny, dim-lit airlock. For the moment, everybody was safe.

There was a banging sound on the ship-side door, followed by a loud *hum*.

The overhead speaker blurted to life. "Stay as clear of the door as you can," Elaphus said. "We're widening the hatch to fit Toner through."

It would render this particular airlock useless, but Jaeger didn't object. Stuck in this awkwardly shaped shell, Toner simply wouldn't fit through the ship-side door without help. With laser-cutters and torches, a team of engineers in rebreathers dismembered the door and whipped up a pulley system to lower Toner into the general crew lounge. Jaeger dropped in after, once the way was clear.

Elaphus and her assistants had turned the newly renovated crew lounge into a temporary medical quarantine, complete with plastic sheets and air-scrubbing pumps mounted against every open duct. Given the module's orientation when the *Osprey* had landed, the floor and ceiling had become walls, and the walls became the ceiling and floor. It made Jaeger dizzy as one of Elaphus's assistants guided her to a cot.

Toner's going to be pissed when he wakes up, Jaeger thought, eying the off-colored hole against one wall where they'd removed the pinball machine. *He just got done fixing this place.*

"You weren't kidding about quarantine," she added to Elaphus and her two techs in their fitted hazmat suits. They were hooking a dozen kinds of diodes and scanners to Toner's chrysalis. One of them was reconnecting the wiring of a medical scanner that the team had hastily relocated from the medical bay.

"Better safe than sorry." Elaphus broke from Toner and came to press a scanner to Jaeger's forehead. "Temperature normal. Oxygen levels normal."

Jaeger winced as a needle poked out of the scanner, drawing a tiny drop of blood, and then retreated into the device to conduct an analysis.

"Be careful when you get him out of that crystal." Jaeger waved at Toner. "The cave-in destroyed his neural collar."

"Neural collar?" Elaphus asked crisply.

"Something the fleet used to control soldiers like Toner. He's super powerful, and I think the brass feared that if they left him to his own devices, he'd take them out," Jaeger paused, thinking about everything they'd done. The mutiny, the wormhole…things would've been easier if they could've faced off against leadership. "They were right," she muttered.

Jaeger felt a potent mixture of relief and desperate sadness. The genetic *artists* had so tortured Toner's physical makeup that he was capable of ripping steel beams apart with his bare hands. Without an electro-collar to zap him into submission, his equally mutated hunger instincts would drive him to use that power to devour anyone and anything he could get his hands on.

Even her.

"How are you feeling?" Elaphus snapped Jaeger out of her ugly contemplation.

"A touch peckish," she snapped. "There's a war brewing out there, Doctor. I don't have time for this."

Elaphus, no stranger to ornery patients, ignored the tone. "If you're not carrying anything infectious, I'll have you cleared from quarantine in five minutes. In the meantime, you'll catch your breath and get something to eat. Doctor's orders." She waved at one of her assistants. "Get the captain a nutrient pack and water with electrolytes."

"And coffee. Double macchiato, with honey," Jaeger added. She met Elaphus's dark look. "At least it's not an epi-blast."

"That's not funny, Captain."

"Well, *someone* has to break the tension." Jaeger pointed angrily at Toner. "And he's out of commission."

The doctor drew back as if she had been slapped, then shook herself. Accepting Jaeger's stress with all the grace her name implied, she returned to her study of Toner's rocky carapace.

I can't lose my temper like a grumpy toddler. Warm with embarrassment, Jaeger took the water and granola bar offered to her and gulped them as she waited for her coffee. She turned away from where Elaphus was working on Toner. She couldn't stand to look at him, at his wide blue eyes, at the infection growing like bloody roots beneath his skin. It wasn't the first time he'd been in a bad way, but it was the first time Jaeger found herself looking into his face and wondering if she was watching him die.

She couldn't think about this anymore. "Fill me in, Seeker," she growled into her comm link.

Seeker's answer was blessedly prompt. "The shuttle team has established a patrol of the area and is trying to collect intelligence. The Locauri realized the cargo bay was a ruse and have mostly cleared out of it. They're massing around the starboard wing again, but the hull is secure. They're not going to break in any time soon. That said, I'd rather not get entrenched in a siege."

"Agreed." She tore a bite off her granola bar and forced herself to swallow. Something *beeped* on the cot beside her. She looked down to see the screen of the medical scanner that had been analyzing her blood had turned green.

"Am I clear to go?" she demanded of the assistant who brought her a steaming coffee cup. After a second of consultation with the doctor, the assistant nodded.

Jaeger snatched up her coffee and was out of the quarantine bay before Elaphus could change her mind.

The administrative hub in the starboard cargo bay was abuzz with activity. Someone had hastily assembled a bank of display screens, showing a live feed from the various cameras scattered across the settlement area. The bulk of the angry Locauri gathered around the *Osprey*, but Jaeger saw small clusters of the creatures examining the half-constructed outbuildings.

They clustered curiously around the waste management cisterns, slipped into the temporary greenhouses at the northern edge of the ring, and came out with radishes and other early crops like curious looters. Some wore the typical deep green bandoliers and sashes she associated with the local Locauri, but shimmering hide pads that she didn't recognize decorated the others.

"Those aren't all our people," Jaeger said to the lone Locauri at her side.

Art rested on a handrail, head and antennae drooping as he stared forlornly at the disorder on the screens. "Far villages." He jabbed a claw to indicate one of the bigger, hide-covered Locauri that appeared to be addressing a crowd of agitators collected outside the observation deck. "Traders, travelers. Come to meet my people, meet the aliens. Short-tempered. Quick to anger."

"Come on." Jaeger gestured for Art to follow her into the captain's office, where Seeker was taking a report from Bufo. "Tell us what happened."

Bufo looked up from his stool as the door slid shut behind Jaeger and Art.

"Fill me in," Jaeger said.

"I've been talking to Aquila." Bufo drew himself up. "She knew something was going to happen, but she's evasive on the details. We're guessing that she scouted out the area where they're holding Occy sometime in the night and passed the intel to Pandion."

"Pandion is the only person not accounted for," Seeker added from where he sat behind the desk. "We don't appear to be missing any major equipment. It looks like the idiot wanted to rescue our engineer; consequences be damned."

"A fight in the trees, just before dawn," Art added, shifting his weight from foot to foot. "Human, one of yours. Attacked the guards around Occy's nest. The nest fell."

"Oh, God." This was news to Jaeger. "Is Occy okay?"

"Did not fall," Art assured. "Last I knew, they had taken him to another nest. Hurt, but not badly."

"We've been trying to contact him over the radio." Seeker's face was a stone. "No response."

Art waved his antennae from side to side. "Damaged in the fall, perhaps."

"Let's hope so." Jaeger didn't like to think the Locauri were intentionally hiding Occy—and whatever injuries he might've sustained. "Get Portia and the recon team as close to the village as is safe. See if the shuttle scanners can tell us any more about what's going on over there."

Seeker nodded and tapped a few buttons on his computer screen.

"Locauri do not fall," Art went on. "Not..." He stomped one delicate claw against the metal floor. His translator band blinked but did not speak as he sought for the right word. "Not hard. Not badly."

"You're not afraid of falls," Jaeger supplied. "You're not very dense, and pseudo wings keep you from splatting."

"Yes. But after the fight, beneath the trees. On the ground." Art hesitated. "Your human...one of the Locauri guards. Splat."

Bufo covered his face and let out a groan from somewhere near the base of his throat.

"Dead?" Jaeger whispered.

"Yes," Art said. "Very."

"What are the elders saying about all of this?" Jaeger asked.

Art hesitated. "Disagreement. Elders are only *our* elders. No authority over the travelers from other villages. They are angry—about the death, about the shrine. They want humans gone from Locaur."

"That's not going to happen," Seeker said.

Jaeger lifted a hand. "No," she said, lowering her voice and forcing them to lean in closer. "We're not going to resort to panic and reactionary thinking. We're going to talk through this like we have every other problem so far."

"How?" Seeker fished in his pocket, drew out a vape, and scowled when he realized it was empty. He dropped it onto the table, disgusted. "You heard Art. There's no single leader out there. It's a mob."

Jaeger hesitated, then sat in one of the stools, bringing herself closer to Art's level. She studied her friend's strange face, the heavy mandibles set beneath big, multifaceted eyes. "*Anantah*," she said slowly. "You've told me his story many times. The one who communicates."

Art's mandibles clicked. The translator band wrapped around his antennae blinked. "I remember."

"You said it was a legend. Is it a legend of your village or one of all Locauri?"

"All know of the Great Anantah," Art allowed. "Many tribes claim Anantah for egg-father."

"Captain?" Bufo croaked. "What's he talking about?"

Jaeger settled back in her chair. "Anantah is a…folk-hero, a bit like our Beowulf. Great warrior, legendary poet, Anantah slays the mother of egg-dragons, Anantah steals a seed from the world-tree, Anantah flies to the moon to win a bet, that kind of thing. But one of the best-known stories is that Anantah stopped a war between rival tribes by offering to battle all of the enemy combatants one by one. They vastly outnumbered his army."

She drew in a deep breath. "Like the Overseers, the Locauri love their tradition. If we come at them offering Anantah's Bargain, they'll accept." She raised an eyebrow at

Art, who, after a moment of consideration, lowered his head in agreement.

Seeker fiddled with his empty vape pen. "A line battle of champions might work," he said flatly. "Except that *our* top battle-mad warrior is currently six centimeters deep in a crystal shell and I'd give long odds on any of the rest of us outlasting the entire Locauri mob."

Art let out an alarmed chirrup.

"Jesus." Jaeger pressed her eyes shut. "I'm not suggesting we *actually* send a champion out there to slaughter them one by one. That's not what Anantah's Bargain is about."

Seeker and Bufo exchanged puzzled glances. Seeker spoke. "Then what?"

"The leaders of the opposing army accepted Anantah's Bargain at first. They sent their best warriors out to challenge him. How many was it, Art?"

"Seven," Art said. "Or seventeen, or seventy-seven. Depends on the story."

"Point is, Anantah battled a bunch of the enemy's best warriors and defeated them, one by one, as both armies watched. After a while, though, something strange happened. The opposing armies got tired of watching the pointless violence. They got tired of watching Anantah kill their people, one after the other. They realized that the fight was folly when they were up against such a determined foe. So finally, after a day and a night of continuous duels, they sat down to negotiate with Anantah's army."

"Still sounds like you need to build this negotiation table on top of a few dead bodies," Seeker said slowly.

Art surprised them all by leaping from the floor to stand on the makeshift desk, his antennae swinging wildly through the air. "No. No, no, *no*. Not the heart of the story." He turned, delicate legs tapping lightly against the desk as his wings fluttered. It was almost like a dance. "Story is lesson. Lesson is to *learn* from mistakes, not to repeat them. The mistake was to fight at all. Anantah showed them this much: next time, to skip the fighting. Go straight to the talking, to make talking into singing."

"You think it's as easy as that?" Seeker asked skeptically, leaning away from where Art was dancing on the desk.

"Easy, no," Art said. "You are not Anantah. But maybe."

"The plan is to go out there, get the ear of the mob, and offer them Anantah's Bargain," Jaeger said. "The culturally appropriate response will be for them to reject the bargain but offer to skip to the next step. Negotiation. It's a gamble. Kind of like the *Rite of !Tsok n Sshoogn* I invoked with the Overseers. We show them that we're willing to speak in their language. We're not monsters who came from the stars to start trouble. We're willing to accept their traditions."

There was a moment of silence as everyone considered the implications of Jaeger's proposal. Beyond the closed office door, they heard the activity of a busy war room.

"It sounds quite risky," Seeker said.

"First Mate Toner would hate it," Bufo agreed.

"Then Toner shouldn't have gone and got his ass calcified," Jaeger snapped. "So he could be here to argue with me himself." Then she paused, drawing in a deep breath. She calmed herself with a sip of rapidly cooling coffee. "I'm sorry. I'm worried about him."

Bufo nodded understanding, but Seeker leaned forward over the desk, forcing Art to hop back to the floor. "I think it's a good plan." He met Jaeger's eye, and though his words were strong, she saw a flicker of uncertainty in his gray eyes. "At the moment, we're safe in here. No need to rush into it. You have a bit of time to prepare your speech and wait for Portia to report back with more intel."

Jaeger held his gaze and nodded. Then she pushed herself to her feet. "Art." She turned and addressed him formally. "I saw that almost none of the Locauri out there have translator bands. Will you do me the honor of being my translator to the masses?"

CHAPTER THREE

"There's one more thing, Captain." Seeker cornered Jaeger after their meeting.

"Just one?"

"I didn't want to bring it up in front of Art. I know how dangerous it is to challenge someone's hero." Seeker glanced over his shoulder, making sure they were alone in this corner of the administration hub.

He stepped closer and lowered his voice, forcing her to lean in. She smelled the fading waft of the very last of his clove-scented vape juice emanating from his front pocket. A thin sheen of sweat and grime coated his skin. Like her, he hadn't had a chance to shower before everything went to hell.

"When you had me locked up, I spent a lot of time reading over old human legends." His voice dipped low and gravely. "I'll support your plan because the *!Tsok n Sshoogn* gamble worked, and because maybe Locauri aren't quite as bloodthirsty as humans. I'm going to say this, though. History *never* resolved as cleanly as the legends would have us believe."

"You mean things could get messy? Yeah, I know." She

struggled not to roll her eyes. *God, Toner, you need to wake up. I can't handle being you and me.*

"It's more than that," Seeker said. "David and Goliath. You know that story?"

"Remind me."

"Olden times. Foreign army invades pastoral lands, led by a giant warrior. The giant offers to take his army away and leave the land in peace if someone bested him in single combat. Little farm boy takes the bet, loads up his sling, and lands a stone in the giant's forehead. Goliath falls over dead, and his army runs off, scared. Rah, rah, rah. Say the kid got lucky, was blessed by God, whatever.

"What's more likely is that David knew something the others didn't. The genetic abnormalities that made Goliath so big and frightening also left him crippled by arthritis and half-blind. David didn't agree to that fight gambling that God would save him. David was gambling that *Goliath couldn't see him.*"

Jaeger stared up at Seeker until he started to shift his weight uneasily. "What?" he asked. "Why are you looking at me like that?"

"I'm relieved." She gave him a crooked little grin. "People don't often volunteer to noodle out my B-plans for me. It's quite thoughtful of you."

Secker folded his arms, his jaw working noiselessly.

"We have to get to work." She drained the last of her coffee and patted his arm. "You go figure out what else Goliath can't see."

A young Locauri male perched atop the roof of one of the humans' strange, half-built huts, watching the swarm dance and flicker across the hull of the great starship. His name, the one he'd taken for himself upon his third molting, roughly translated to !TsktzznTsk!tsk. In an old and defunct Locauri dialect, it meant something like Dances-Like-A-Falling-Leaf.

For the sake of brevity and in the spirit of camaraderie, his cohorts called him Leif.

It was nearly midday, and all the disorganized Locauri accomplished was to steal some interesting snacks from the humans' storehouse. Leif had heard that Tiki and the other local elders were sheltering in their village nearby, trying to decide what to do.

Looking at the disorganization in front of him, though, Leif couldn't help but think that the elders had simply seen the mess they'd created and abandoned it like a sack of bad eggs.

What a waste, he thought bitterly, watching a band of big females scramble to the top of the starship and prod at various hatches with their spears. They were never going to get into that ship, of course. These humans might not have been the Tall Ones, but they had potent magics of their own. Leif couldn't imagine what these females hoped to accomplish.

There was a flutter of nearby pseudo wings as another local female hopped from the ground to perch beside Leif. She was nearly as big as he was, though judging by her color, she still had several moltings to go before she reached full maturity. She was also missing her left antennae.

She munched on a round, pink root she'd taken from one of the grow-houses.

"Do you think they're ever going to *do* anything?" She

shifted her weight from foot to foot to foot. Leif had to study the swishing of her single antennae carefully to catch her full meaning. "The humans," she gestured. "The Locauri. Anything. Are they going to stand there all day poking it with spears?"

Leif looked back at the starship. As he'd expected, the band of females that had crawled up to the roof hadn't had any luck finding an open hatch. Restless, annoyed, and driven insensate in the midday heat reflecting off the metal, they started fighting among themselves.

"No," he said. "It is pointless. You are local, yes?"

"Yes." The last of the strange pink root vanished into her mandibles, and she gestured to the west. "My home. Here. My name, Echo-In-A-Silent-Forest. Humans cannot pronounce it. They call me Stumpy."

"Leif," said Dances-Like-A-Falling-Leaf.

"I know," Stumpy answered matter-of-factly. "I saw you. Fighting. At the prison this morning."

Leif felt his pores swell with mingled pride and chagrin at the memory of this morning's fracas.

"You are the reason human is dead," Stumpy went on. There was no rancor in her motions, only a simple statement of fact. "Tell me of it."

"Later." Leif returned his attention to the starship. His pores and chromatophores had grown painfully swollen at the mention of the battle near the prison. Word of his deeds had spread quickly, it seemed.

"Now," Stumpy insisted. Since Leif was not in the habit of ignoring females, he acquiesced.

"Came here two days ago with traders from my home. Highcliff village. Heard a human had disturbed the shrine, was being held for tribunal. I was angry. Friend and I offered to help guard the human. Then, before dawn, attacked.

"Human moved clumsily through trees but is very strong. Grabs my partner. I stab; human falls. Breaks against the ground." His antennae dipped into a mournful pose. "But did not let go of Shadow. Shadow breaks against the ground, as well."

Stumpy's remaining antennae lowered into an obligatory echo of Leif's sad gesture. "Good story," she decided, straightening. "Exciting."

"Bad story!" Leif's antennae lashed angrily. "Shadow is dead. And now, mob." He gestured at the restless Locauri swarming around the starship. "Swarm without purpose."

Stumpy cocked her head. "What purpose?"

"*No* purpose!"

"What is the *purpose* of purpose?" she asked.

Activity rippled against the starship, where the swarm was thickest. One of the great doors was opening again. Assuming that this was some banal distraction like the last open door, Leif instead turned to stare at Stumpy. People said there were thinking parts in the bases of antennae, and this female was perhaps a bit short of both.

A little iguanome crawled over the lip of the half-finished roof, squawking and waggling its tentacles. Stumpy bent and extended an arm, letting the little creature scramble onto her thorax. It chattered angrily the whole way, scolding Stumpy for leaving it behind.

An interested buzz rose from the swarm, and Lief turned again to see a split forming among the Locauri, making way for the human emerging from the ship.

"If you seek purpose," Stumpy sounded almost bored, "then go find it." With no word of further explanation, the female spread her pseudo wings and sprang off to join the swarm—her iguanome squealing and clinging to her spines the whole way.

Perhaps not *missing thinking parts,* Leif thought, watching in amazement as she vanished into the swarm. *Perhaps wise, after all.*

He picked up his spear and leapt to the ground.

The human female—*Jaeger,* was the name whispering through the crowd—emerged from the starship with all the careful poise of a chief elder coming to inaugurate a high festival. Leif pushed his way to the front of the crowd, curious to get his first good look at a living human by daylight. Furtive battles in the night didn't count.

Shadow had called the creatures *trees without branches,* and it struck Leif as an apt description. Though she was not half so tall as one of the Tall Ones, this Jaeger had a thick, upright body balanced precariously on two swinging feet. Her skin, as well as the mass of short, thickly curled antennae collected atop her head, was the color of fresh-turned soil, and the sleek silver cloth covering her body was a type he'd never seen before.

A Locauri followed Jaeger out of the belly of the starship, and Leif recognized this one as Keeper-Of-Forgotten-Beauty, the local lore keeper, whom the humans called Art. He stepped gingerly into the sunlight, keeping close to Jaeger's shadow as the crowd shifted away from them, and the droning buzz of an angry mob faded into a background drone.

The human lifted her thick arms, palms out and open as

she turned to address the crowd. Like many of the others—especially the ones who'd traveled from afar, like him—Leif had not been offered a translator band, and he didn't know the human tongue. Anticipating this complication, Art followed closely in Jaeger's wake, his antennae dancing as he translated her sonorous bellowing.

"'For days we have quarreled in the shadow of your shrine and over ichor spilled.'" There was a familiar rhythm to Art's translation. It had the feel of an old poem, one Leif almost recognized.

"'And for many more days and nights, our quarreling will continue, man fighting brother, daughter fighting mother, old friends come to blows, lest we settle our differences as sure as sunrise settles night.'"

"Anantah!" Stumpy's antennae lashed through the air, brushing rudely across Leif's face. "She sings of Anantah!"

Lief's anterior legs vibrated with frustration, adding one more deep thrumming sound to the sea of voices whispering voices. "Human does not sing. Human squeals like drowning iguanome. Your mentor, *he* sings."

Stumpy waved this objection away, pushing herself closer to the edge of the crowd.

"'The day grows long, and we are weary,'" Keeper-of-Forgotten-Beauty sang, echoing the human's strange bray so that all could understand.

Leif, who had memorized every translation of Anantah's songs before his second molting, couldn't help but be impressed by the version choice. He wondered if it was the human, or the clever lore keeper, who'd decided to recite the oldest and purest rendition of Anantah's Bargain—though slightly modified to fit the facts of this situation.

Doubtless, they're feeding it to the human, Leif decided

angrily. Events were confirming his worst fears before his very eyes: the elders of the Riverside Locauri, who counted Keeper-of-Forgotten-Beauty as a member, hadn't made an incidental alliance with novel strangers. They were using these humans as puppets to intimidate, impress, and control Locauri across the entire continent.

Ahead, the human was coming to the end of Anantah's speech to his assembled enemies, and Leif would admit, this Jaeger—or, at least, the little Locauri lore keeper cleverly interpreting for her—had the crowd rightly impressed. He could sense their anger fading, pierced through by the memories of traditional duties. Anantah's Bargain was the first lesson many Locauri children learned in conflict resolution.

This was, Leif thought, looking at his scattered brothers and sisters, a sort of purpose. They swayed to the mingled song of human and Locauri, their antennae dipping as they recalled their duty not to fight but to listen.

The human finished Anantah's speech not in her tongue but in thickly accented Locauri that required no translation.

"*'But if your mind is set to ichor spilled, then come, and I will feed your hunger—one by one.'*"

But if it was a swarm resolving to purpose, Leif decided, as the crowd went still as empty shells, as the midday sun beat down mercilessly from above, it was not *good* purpose.

It was not the right or *proper* purpose for the swarm to rouse and sway and die at the whim of some strange outlanders.

Thus, when the human finally fell silent, her arms dropping to her sides as the last echo of her fraudulent speech faded onto the breeze, Leif alone among the crowd stirred.

Leif alone set his anterior legs together and rubbed until

the air became a dense and anxious thing, shrill with his buzzing.

The crowd split, creating an empty path between him and the human with her tiny yellow eyes.

Leif stepped forward. "*'So the hero seeks a challenge.'*" He buzzed the next line of the epic poem to scattered hums of anxiety. "*'I will cross with yours my spear, and silence your endless prattle!'*"

CHAPTER FOUR

"Operation Blind Giant at the ready, Captain," Seeker said into Jaeger's earpiece.

Jaeger stared at the young Locuari facing her. He stood alone at the center of an empty circle, where the crowd had withdrawn once the echo of Art's translation had fallen silent.

"Not yet," Jaeger whispered, barely moving her lips. The clearing had fallen deadly silent. Even the distant birds had ceased singing. Beside her, Art shifted his weight, and she knew her little friend was considering his escape routes.

Rubbing his anterior legs together in a harsh hum, the Locauri male repeated his challenge—with a lengthy, clicking addition that Art interpreted in a stunned tone.

"He says...you are not Anantah. He says...you have no right to claim our legends and our heroes."

Well, Jaeger thought grimly, *he's not wrong.*

"He says that if you are honorable, you will fight the battle Anantah fought." Art's pseudo wings fluttered restlessly. "Starting with him. He will prove you aren't worthy to invoke Anantah's name."

Jaeger let out a long, shuddering breath.

"My team has located the nest where they're holding Occy," Portia said over the comm channel. "Bioscan confirms there's a large life form inside that isn't Locauri. No mistake, Captain. We can rappel down from the shuttle and evacuate the lieutenant while the crowd is distracted. Hell, we could bust out the towing straps and fly the whole prison nest away."

"I'm not giving up on a peaceful resolution yet," Jaeger whispered, more fiercely.

"Are you going to fight the buggers after all, Captain?" Seeker demanded. "I'm bringing the Alpha-Seeker into the atmosphere. There's some low cloud cover to the west. She'll hide nearby."

An uneasy buzz was growing from the swarm around her. Jaeger didn't need Art to translate the clicks and hums. She knew enough of the Locauri language to understand that this kettle was about to boil.

"Keep those sonic cannons at the ready for crowd control," Jaeger whispered into her comm. She drew in a deep breath and took a step toward her challenger.

"I do not know you," she said in Locauri, self-conscious of the way her fat tongue tripped over the clicks and subtle susurations that composed the language.

"The name I have claimed is Dances-Like-A-Falling-Leaf," the challenger answered, lifting his antennae and spreading his pseudo wings, making himself look bigger in the universal language of preparing for a brawl. "I am not one of the local people already taken by your lies. I am friend to the man your people killed. You are not Anantah. You are not one of our kind. You are a tree-worm, donning our colors falsely to slip into our nests and eat our nymphs. Now you must fulfill Anantah's Bargain, or all will see you for what you are."

Jaeger thanked God that the challenger spoke loud and slowly—ostensibly for the benefit of the crowd, but it gave her time to work through his words.

"I am not a false friend." She lowered her voice as she walked forward, her hands open and empty before her. Dances-Like-A-Falling-Leaf's loud announcement had made the crowd lean back. Her soft answer, thick as it was with a clumsy human accent, forced them to lean forward. Art followed several paces behind her, dancing nervously over the ground as he translated their exchange. "My name is Sarah Jaeger. I am the leader of my people."

Dances-Like-A-Falling-Leaf fluttered uneasily, raising his spear as Jaeger approached.

She stopped three meters away from the challenger. He was young, she saw by the mottling of his carapace, which Locuari shed as they molted into adulthood.

Where are the elders? She dared a glance through the crowd, seeking the absent Tiki or any of the other local village leaders. She saw none of them. *They've left kids to run the circus?*

"I know your name," the challenger said. "You chatter like a mindless nymph. Fight me."

"No." Jaeger dropped to her knees in a puff of dust, her hands spread open before her. The crowd recoiled with a sharp intake of breath.

Jaeger didn't dare take her eyes from her challenger now that they were on a level. She met his multifaceted gaze as an equal, not as a giant towering over him.

"You are brave." She spoke slowly not just for the benefit of the crowd but because wrapping her tongue around the clicking Locauri language was exhausting. "As was your friend. You are correct, Dances-Like-A-Falling-Leaf."

She paused, swallowing and gasping for breath. She hadn't spoken this much Locauri at once before. She felt her throat seizing up and shook her head, resigning herself to English. Luckily, Art slipped back into the role of translator without skipping a beat.

"I am not Anantah," she said hoarsely. "I have not earned the right to call your hero egg-father. I have been the leader of my people, and *I have failed.*"

She paused, waiting for the murmur of the crowd to die before speaking again. "One of my people, and one of yours, have died today because of my failure." She spread her arms wide, holding her challenger's hard gaze and exposing herself to an easy and fatal spear thrust. "My duty was to protect your people, as well as mine. I have failed. If you believe it is best for your people that I die, then let it be so."

"Jesus, Sarah, you're gambling too much," Seeker whispered in her ear. The sound of her name falling from that man's lips momentarily distracted Jaeger from her challenger's stoic face, and by the time she wrestled back control of her focus, a new murmur had arisen among the crowd.

"Nothing will happen here today," called a young female a few paces behind the challenger. Jaeger recognized her. It was Art's apprentice, who Occy had somewhat cruelly dubbed Stumpy. What she lacked in antennae expression, however, Stumpy more than made up for in volume.

"No more ichor or blood spilled. Go home, buzzing insects." The girl sounded downright bored as she waved her remaining antennae over the crowd. "Sip some honeydew. Take a nap. Or stay here and kill each other and bring a prowling egg-dragon on us by the scent of death. See if I care."

With a dismissive click, the young female turned, spread her pseudo wings, and zipped away. The flash of sunlight off her fluttering wings shattered whatever spell had come over the crowd, and with shocking efficiency, many of the Locauri trickled away like sand through an hourglass.

Jaeger held her challenger's gaze for nearly two minutes until only a handful of Locauri remained circled around them.

Finally, emboldened by the shrinking crowd, Art scuttled forward and spoke to the challenger in a low voice. They exchanged rapid words that Jaeger couldn't catch, until finally and with palpable reluctance, the challenger folded his pseudo wings and let the tip of his spear fall to the ground.

"I do *not* forgive you," Dances-Like-A-Falling-Leaf called to Jaeger. "Shadow's death is not forgotten."

"Nor should it be," Jaeger answered. "We will investigate. We will understand. We will not allow this to happen again."

"Let it be so." With the air around him shimmering from his unanswered frustration, Dances-Like-A-Falling-Leaf turned and sprang into the forest. One by one, the last of the Locuari followed him until only Art and Jaeger remained.

CHAPTER FIVE

"...Richard Feingold. Astin Yolokov. Briana Cheadle. Remember their nameth, and their fateth." Petra stole a quick sip of lukewarm tea from her mug. Headshots of the aforementioned scientists scrolled past the screen before her as she narrated into the microphone.

An older man, dark-skinned and hairless, in a doctor's white lab coat. A fresh-faced grad student, barely more than a boy, his face a mosaic of freckles. A bright-eyed young woman standing beside a massive telescope. That one reminded Petra of Sarah.

"Their deaths weren't an acthident. When the fleet needed to move on from the Theti thystem, these brave geothientists risked their liveth to remain on Theti-Alpha 7 and find a way to terraform it to be compatible with human life."

Petra hated narrating long segments without her false teeth. To her comms-trained ears, she sounded ridiculous. Still, in the weeks since she'd taken on her role as the face of this rebellion, her lisp had become the signature everyone expected on an authentic Potlova data drop and vlog.

"They rithked their liveth for the chance to give uth a better future."

The pictures of the dead scientists disappeared, replaced by diagrams of a planet's mantle, snapshots taken from the report that had doomed the Seti-Alpha team.

"When they found it—when they propothed a plan for re-activating the planet'th magnetothphere—the Theeker Corpth murdered them all. I'm uploading the Theti-Alpha fileth ath we thpeak. Read them. Thee for yourthelf. The Theekers aren't our friendth, and the fleet leaderth aren't working for uth."

Petra ended the feed of her slide show and cut to live video. She lifted her eyes, staring into the beady black eye of the camera mounted beside the microphone. She tapped the corner of her eyebrow in a two-finger salute. It was an obscure gesture, something she'd picked up from Amy and lazier than the traditional fleet salute, but it felt right.

"That'th all for today," she said somberly. "Keep your eyeth peeled. We've got another bombthell incoming any day now. And remember: do *not* take the gene therapieth the fleet ith offering you. Therenity isn't meant to help you. Potlova out."

Petra hit the "Send" icon on the screen, waited for the video to upload, then cut power to the screens. The room plunged into darkness, lit only by blinking lights of the hundreds of gadgets and gizmos scattered across the workbenches and floors.

Even after they'd spent an afternoon cleaning it out to make room for Petra's narrow sleeping cot, Rush Starr's private recording studio was a *mess*.

She exhaled a long breath, letting her eyes fall shut. It had been three weeks since the fatal raid on the hidden archives and two weeks since changing situations had forced Petra,

Amy, and Rush to abandon their fallback hideout in the exterior maintenance wing. Someone had tipped off brass that houseless folks and potential fugitives were living in the spare modules that circled *Constitution*, and the uptick in security sweeps made getting in and out too dangerous.

So, they'd fallen back once more and split. On Petra's insistence, Amy had returned to the lower decks to take up a subsistence job in the janitorial department. It wasn't a glamorous gig, but it kept the girl housed, and a janitor could get into a lot of places without raising any eyebrows. Most importantly, it kept her away from the danger magnet and the MP's Top Most Wanted, Petra Potlova.

Amy checked in regularly, keeping Petra and Rush up-to-date on the rumors and stories flying through the general population, but Petra hadn't been able to sleep soundly since they parted. Scraps was dead, having sacrificed himself in the raid on the archives. Neither Rush's far-reaching information network nor Amy's ears on the ground had been able to catch a whisper of the missing woman known as Juice, who also failed to make it safely out of that raid.

She was almost certainly dead. Indeed, the unspoken hope between Rush and Petra was that the feisty older woman had died quickly rather than undergo weeks of whatever creative tortures the Seeker Corps could think up.

Juice had known the identity of the rich man backing and financing much of this rebellion. The very fact that brass hadn't taken Rush Starr into custody all but guaranteed that Juice had taken his name to her grave.

Wherever that grave might be.

Gawd. Petra rubbed her temples. *Running a rebellion is hard on the nerves.*

She heard a *beep* on the other side of the wall as the main door to the apartment opened, followed by the low muffled tones of two men talking. Straining her ears and holding her breath, she identified Rush's now-familiar tenor. The other voice was deep and guttural, with a thick accent that Petra had only before ever heard in holo-dramas. Scottish, she thought it was—or maybe Irish. She kept forgetting to ask.

She let out her held breath. No strangers coming into the apartment. No management or MP or Seekers coming in for a raid. Only Rush and Bruce—the doorman and bouncer who kept the riffraff out of the gold sector apartment complex.

Petra was exhausted, but she wasn't going to get a wink of sleep with the men gabbing on the other side of the door. She picked her way across the minefield of exploded electronics, reaching into her pocket. She slipped her false teeth from their case, slotted them into the empty place in her gums, and touched the access panel.

"Petie." A skinny man in a white tunic and unnecessarily tight pants lay sprawled across the chaise lounge, his shiny black shoes hanging off the armrest. One hand held a small snifter full of piss-yellow liquid, the other splayed dramatically across his eyes and temples as if fending off a headache. "Bruce was kind enough to bring a bottle of paint stripper. Help yourself to the sideboard, darling."

Bruce, sitting in the velvet armchair across from Rush and holding his uniform cap in both hands, smiled sheepishly.

"I just dropped the Seti Alpha documents." Petra stifled a yawn as she shuffled to the sideboard. Sitting among the array of fancy liquor bottles was a new, unmarked jar. Petra picked up the first tumbler her fingers found. "We're scraping the bottom of the barrel. We can't keep teasing the people forever.

We gotta drop something big soon." She twisted the lid off the new jar and took a sniff. Instantly, her eyes watered.

"Be careful," Bruce said as Petra filled her glass. "It's not—"

"Honey, I was raised on synth-whiskey stronger than this," Petra rasped. She poured herself a finger and turned back to the men. "Mister Resistance has been wasting all of his good stuff on me. I'm a cheap date." She touched the moonshine to her lips and let out a shuddering breath as liquid fire seared across her tongue and sinuses. "Phew. Tastes like home."

Flushing, Bruce fished a handheld computer out of his breast pocket. "Did you say you just dropped another video?"

"About ten minutes ago. The Seti Alpha documents. Six years ago, a small team of scientists put together a report saying they could've made one of the Seti Alpha planets habitable with enough time and the right tools. Official reports say they died in a solar flare accident, but really…" She drew a finger across her neck.

Bruce nodded and scrolled down his screen, the blurry but familiar layout of underground news sites reflected in his eyes. "**New leaked archival documents implicate top fleet officials in murder of a team of geoscientists.**" He recited one hasty headline. "**Potlova strikes another devastating blow at Brass.**"

Petra winced and tossed her moonshine back in one gulp. She was gonna need it. "I wouldn't exactly call it a 'devastating blow.' They haven't even had time to look at the documents yet." She tapped one of Rush's dangling shoes. Startled out of his reverie, Rush shot upright, and Petra slipped into the now-empty space on the lounge beside him.

"You take up too much space for such a skinny guy," she told him.

"That's a superstar's prerogative, darling. You're right,

though. We need to blow the lid on brass' recent misdeeds, and soon. We can't keep feeding the public tidbits from the ancient past. Old news is old news."

Petra sniffed. Only a man like Rush could think of a mass murder six years ago as *old news*.

"I had my grandma look at the Project Reset documents you gave me. She worked as a cosmological physicist for years before her accident." Bruce leaned forward, casting a nervous glance over his shoulder as if afraid he had until that moment overlooked some fleet spy hiding behind the ficus.

"Your instinct was right, Rush. It's a lot of astrophysical and cosmological data. Real obscure theories on the behavior of black holes and white holes and the wormhole phenomena that connect them. Stuff about the decay of information…" He fiddled with his cap.

"The metadata on the Project Reset files confirms that someone's been working on it for years," Rush said. "They've been doing a *lot* of research on it in the last eighteen months. They've accessed and modified those files more than twice as much as the rest of the classified documents combined. Whatever this thing is, it's big—bigger than the Seti files, and the Tau massacres, and the Crusade protocols. We *need* to know what brass is planning."

Bruce shrugged. "Sorry, Rush. Smartest woman I know couldn't make sense of most of it. Genius-level stuff. If you need to drop a bombshell, maybe you should drop the Reset files and hope someone out there can figure out what it is and explain it to the rest of us."

Petra and Rush exchanged glances. Petra had made that argument herself, and more than once.

"We'll do that," Rush said quietly, "but only as a last resort. It will undermine all of the Resistance's credibility if we spend weeks advertising that we have a bombshell and drop a bunch of documents we can't begin to understand. Whatever ground we gain by leaking Project Reset, Brass might easily regain by us revealing our ignorance."

"We gotta figure out what it means before we drop it," Petra agreed, although deep down, something told her that time was running out on their chance to strike at brass. "Bruce, your grandma couldn't make it out, but she worked in those fields for years. Maybe she knows someone who can?"

Bruce scratched his chin. "She said there were a couple of people down in Astro who might be able to make sense of it. Some guy named Grayson was who she recommended. Then there are the Followers..."

"Those scavengers." Petra shook her head. The Followers were a group of ships that *followed* the Fleet, living off scraps. They never integrated, always keeping their distance.

Bruce pursed his lips. "The Followers are survivors who aren't beholden to the Fleet. I wouldn't be so quick to judge."

Petra started to say something, but Bruce lifted his hand. "But you're right. They're not going to help us here. I say we go for this Grayson guy."

Rush perked up at the name. "A lead. Excellent. Is there a way we can ply this Grayson fellow about wormhole behavior without revealing our intent? Perhaps—"

Petra was shaking her head. "Nah," she said quietly. "Nah. Grayson's in deep with the Seeker Corps. I'll bet you anything he's one of the guys *working* on Reset."

"I didn't know you had ears in the Astro department." Rush sounded a little reproachful. They'd agreed weeks ago that there would be no secrets between them as far as intel on the fleet was concerned.

Petra shook her head again. "I don't. But if I remember right, it was a guy named Grayson who was on the bridge with us when Kelba took command from LeBlanc." She drew in a deep breath.

That whole strange day was fuzzy in her memory, and it didn't help that brass had confiscated or destroyed all detailed records of the mutiny that had led to an abrupt change in leadership—and told everyone who'd been there that they weren't to gab about it. There were a few things she remembered clearly. "Hand to heart. Swear to God. That was the guy who shoved Old Boots out of an airlock."

"Ah," Rush said into the silence that followed. "Probably not a promising ally for us, then."

"No," she said glumly.

"We'll have to come at this Reset problem from another angle," Rush decided. "We'll look at it with fresh eyes in the morning. Bruce? Are you up for a game of cribbage?"

Bruce shook his head and pushed himself to his feet. "Thanks, but I have to switch out the sniffer bags before the bots come to collect."

Neither of them noticed Petra's wince. The DNA sniffers were one of the first classified secrets they'd dug into after raiding the archives. Brass had hundreds of the monitoring devices hidden across the fleet, little sensors that picked up trace DNA samples from the local population. Scraps of dead skin, the mist of mucous from a sneeze, saliva— anything a person left in their wake, the sniffers could pick up and store. They monitored for unusual DNA mutations and could be used to track and pinpoint the location of specific, high-profile criminals.

Petra had never liked the tacky plaster lion sculpture at the end of the hallway outside of Rush's apartment, even before she'd realized it was there to collect the snot and dandruff of everyone who lived in the complex.

She felt a bit guilty for not telling everyone about this new and strangely invasive way the brass was keeping tabs on the population, but the truth was, once you knew where the sniffers were and how they worked, they were pretty easy to fool. They couldn't analyze the trace DNA samples they collected. Instead, their caches were collected by routine maintenance sweeps and taken to a central location for analysis.

So long as brass thought they could trust their sniffers to work properly, all Bruce had to do, to make Petra invisible to the system, was swap out its DNA cache for a clean sample shortly before a bot came to collect it. If the resistance leaked the existence of the sniffers, brass would probably abandon that particular spy tech in favor of something harder to fool.

"Of course." Rush stood as well, following Bruce to the door. "Thank you, by the way. I know you're risking more than your job, doing this for us."

"You be careful out there, Bruce," Petra added tiredly. "I ain't going to live with myself if you get caught tampering with that lion."

"It's not just for you. It's for all of us, isn't it?" Bruce reached the door and wedged his cap firmly onto his head. He offered a smile that looked more than half-forced. "Don't worry. I won't get caught."

"Good man." Rush patted his shoulder and sent the young doorman on his way.

Silence filled the apartment once the door slid shut behind Bruce. Rush went to the sideboard and filled another glass—this time from one of the nice bottles of cordial instead of Bruce's gift of rotgut.

"Did you watch the morning talk show today?" he asked quietly.

"Naw." She'd meant to catch his interview but had lost track of time in researching the Seti files.

"Good." His shoulders slumped. He tossed back the cordial and filled his glass again. "It's depressing. Rush Starr is the fleet's biggest patriot. I don't know how much longer he can walk the company line before he has a nervous breakdown and overdoses on hypermorph."

"Don't say that."

"I'm undermining my movement. In public, I sing their song and dance their dance and keep telling people to trust the authority. Meanwhile, behind closed doors, people are risking their lives on my behalf. More than that. People are *dying* for it. For my vanity."

"They're not dying for you." Petra remembered what Amy had told them before the raid on the archives. "They're doing it 'cause it's gotta happen. Juice didn't step in front of a bullet to protect *your* dream. She did it 'cause brass killed her kid, and they'll keep killing kids until someone makes them stop."

"Maybe." Slowly, Rush returned to his customary position on the lounge and sank onto the cushions. He stared into his glass, hypnotized by the patterns cut into the crystal. "Maybe." He rubbed the corner of one eye tiredly. "You're right. We need the money and the connections that come with staying in the fleet's good graces. I just wish there were another way."

"You ain't tried to hit on me." Petra hadn't meant to change the subject so abruptly, but once it was out in the air, she didn't feel any particular need to call her words back. She turned, eying the man on the couch beside her. "Why's that?"

Rush blinked.

"I just wonder, is all." She shrugged. "Some sleazy reporter gets a photo of you out to dinner with this fashion model or that cute fleet lieutenant, and it's going straight on the *Buzz*'s home page. Even hits the TNN on a slow news day. But Rush Starr hasn't dated anybody in a while, has he?"

"Rush Starr's been a bit busy," he said wryly, lifting his glass and sipping as if it were the finest tea in China.

"No, he hasn't." Petra shook her head. "I mean, *you* have, sure. Rush Starr's just some fleet propaganda puppet these days, ain't he? *He* dropped a new cover of *Duty Lies on a Rocket Ship* sometime last year and shows up for interviews and concerts every few months but...that's it. So what's he been doing?"

"My goodness, Petie, I didn't come prepared for an interview. Are you gunning to replace Yasmine Kay on the morning show?"

Petra waved away his teasing.

Suddenly serious, he straightened, resting his half-empty glass on his bony knees. "I'm told it's uncouth to trap a woman in your apartment and doubly so to pester her into sleeping with you."

"Oh, you're a real gentleman, aren't you?" Petra's lips quirked in a barely contained smirk. "Quit squirming. I saw you on that cover of *Spinning Stones* magazine."

She glanced around the room, which showcased album covers and press releases featuring the face of the very man sitting beside her. She didn't see a copy of that particular magazine, though, and figured it wasn't quite classy enough to qualify for a spot in the Rush Starr Museum of Rush Starr.

"Me and the whole Tribe," she turned back to him. "Saw *a whole lot of you* in that photo shoot. And those photos of you with the backup dancers? Oh, and that tech guy? What was his name? Dustin?" She shook her head with a soft *tsk*. "Yeah, Mister Resistance. You're a real gentleman."

"Those photo shoots were all works of artistic expression." He lifted his chin indignantly. "I thought they were very tasteful."

Petra rolled her eyes.

"Petie… " He studied her narrowly over the rim of his cup. "Darling, are you…*offended* that I haven't tried to seduce you?"

Petra considered this as she sipped her drink. She'd lost a lot of muscle tone after spending months in the brig, and the meager diet had made her curves noticeably less curvy. She still had her cute nose, though, and good cheekbones, full lips, and dimples to make any straight man—and more than a few lesbians, she knew—melt.

"Yes," she decided. "I am offended."

"Giving up on your boyfriend then, are you?"

Petra winced. Rush winced in sympathy. "I'm sorry," he started to say. "That came out harder than I—"

"No, it's okay." She waved him silent and finished her drink in two hot, burning gulps. She snapped her cup onto the table, wiping her mouth with the back of her wrist.

"It ain't like that, anyway. Things work different when you're a pair of boots for the fleet. Larry and I, we got an…*understanding* for when we get posted apart. I don't mind. He don't mind. It's that way for a lot of soldiers."

Petra was dimly aware of the booze softening her tongue, making her slip further and further backward into low-class slang.

"How *moderné* of you," Rush observed. "Very practical."

"Is that it?" She eyed him skeptically. "You real old-fashioned, all of a sudden?"

"What if I am?" He set his empty cup aside and settled back

into the couch, folding his arms behind his head as he studied the ceiling. "What if I've had my fill of groupies and one-night stands and meaningless sex, and in a fit of artistic pique, I've decided that I shall deny myself all further earthly pleasures until I find my eternal soulmate?"

Petra glanced around the room, from the sideboard of antique booze to the gilded carvings near the ceiling and the plush velvet covering the furniture. "I think if Rush Starr was gonna do that, he'd tell it to every paparazzi site and gossip blog and mag on the net. And he'd say it right around the time his new single was about to release."

Rush grinned and clapped approvingly. "You're starting to think like a publicist." He tapped his temple. "Well done, *mon chérie*. Very well." He hopped to his feet and held a hand down to her. "You've seduced me with your clever tongue. Come to bed, darling."

"Thanks," Petra settled back into the couch, "but no thanks. I just wanted to know you cared."

Rush blanched. For one hazy moment, she wondered if he was going to get angry. It wouldn't be the first time a man had lost his temper at her teasing, and it wouldn't be the last. Petra didn't care. For good or bad, she wanted a break from all the *tension* that had followed them like a storm cloud for the last few weeks.

Then Rush burst out laughing, dropping his weight back onto the couch hard enough to bounce. There was something infectious about his laugh, and Petra grinned.

"You cocky bitch," Rush admired once he'd caught his breath. It wasn't a word she'd ever heard him use before, and he made it sound like a blessing. "I hope your boyfriend misses you terribly. God knows you deserve it."

Grinning, Petra let her eyes flutter shut as she sank into

the cushions. She liked her cot in the studio for privacy, but there was no denying that the chaise was a more comfortable bed. "Clear out." She yawned. Her head was starting to swim from the booze, a familiar, comfortable, rocking sensation. "I think I'm gonna take the couch toni—"

The doorbell *dinged*. The frantic but muffled *thudding* of a fist pounding against the door followed the sound.

CHAPTER SIX

Petra snapped upright. All fatigue vanished in an instant.

"Get to the galley—" Rush started to say, but she'd already scrambled off the couch and flung herself around a corner, into the apartment's immaculate and barely used kitchen. There was a recycling chute tucked into the corner—one modified to be narrowly wide enough for a human body. The doorbell *dinged* again, and again and again.

Petra held her breath, straining to hear over the sound of her thudding heart.

"Oh, for God's sake," Rush snapped, donning the perfect affectation of a primadonna cranky at being roused from his reverie. "What in the hell is so goddamned urgent—"

The apartment door slid open, and Rush's irritation vanished. "Bruce!"

There was the sound of someone stumbling over the threshold and the door sliding shut again.

"Good." Bruce's normally coarse voice was raspy with anxiety. "You're still dressed. Where's Petie? Is she still awake?"

"I'm here." Petra pushed herself up and away from the recycling chute. "What happened?"

In the twenty minutes since they'd parted, Bruce's face had gone waxy, and the big man was trembling. He lifted a hand, showing them one of the DNA sniffer collection bags. "I was going to switch out the bags, but there was already a fresh one in there. Brand-spanking-new. I hopped online and checked my source—Rush, *they changed the collection schedule.*"

Rush's breath caught.

"What are you saying?" Petra demanded. "Bruce? What are you saying?"

"The bots already came by and picked up the old bag. I'm sorry. I should've been paying more attention—"

"How long?" Rush cut sharply through Bruce's babble.

Bruce gulped. "Two hours," he whispered.

"Oh gawd." Petra clapped a hand over her mouth. Petra's DNA contaminated the old bag, and fleet maintenance had collected it before Bruce could swap it with his dummy bag.

Two hours was plenty of time for that bag to make its way back to headquarters and for the MP to analyze it. Petra had been stuck in this apartment with Rush for weeks. Her DNA would be all over that plate—mingled right there with his.

Rush rounded on Petra, sharp-eyed. All the haze of fatigue and booze and good humor had vanished. "Grab your—"

"You worry about yourself," Petra snapped, shouldering the taller man out of the way so she could get into the studio. "I ain't been a dumb civilian since the day I was born."

Rush vanished into his room as the studio door slid open, and Petra reached around the corner to grab a tattered backpack. Two weeks of relative peace with all of Rush's resources at her disposal had left her with plenty of time to assemble a proper go bag. The sort of emergency evacuation kit no good soldier, or street rat, could do without.

Slinging the bag over her shoulder, she *crunched* over more than a few doo-dads as she reached the computer console.

"I've got eyes on the concourse," Bruce said nervously from where he stood in the foyer, studying his handheld. "It looks like there's some activity down near Internal Affairs. Unscheduled patrol squad coming this way."

From the other room, Rush uttered another uncharacteristic word—and this one wasn't a blessing.

Petra fumbled open a lead-lined drawer from the wall and fished out a small, heavy pulse-cleaner. She pressed the device against the main casing of the workstation and squeezed the two buttons together. The indicator lights turned red as the device adhered itself to the case and began a countdown sequence.

"EMP activated," she called. "Thirty seconds to wipe the hard drives clean."

"I wouldn't wait around to make sure," Bruce said. "Patrol squad is almost to gold sector. Yep. They're coming into the complex."

"There's more than one way out of this complex." Rush threw on a long dark cape as he stepped out of his bedroom. "What does the A-sector maintenance corridor look like?"

Bruce thumbed through his security feeds as Petra scrambled into her boots. Worst thing you could do during an escape—leave your best shoes behind.

"It looks clear." Bruce hesitated. "I don't have a feed from the surrounding corridors, and they could have MP headed there right now—"

"Recycling chutes?" Petra asked Rush, dreading the answer. He shook his head. "No. I just had this coat washed.

Those chutes only open up into this complex or the recycling center. They'll have both of those areas covered." He waved her to the door. "We run for the maintenance corridor and try to break out of this complex before the MP closes in. Meet at Yolando's if we get split up."

Petra and Rush were three steps from the end of the maintenance corridor when a pair of black-clad military police troopers rounded the corner behind them.

"Hey. Hey, stop right there!"

Petra knew that sound. It was the sound of barking dogs.

Bzzzzt zt zt! Bzzzzzt!

And *that* sound was the buzzing of stunner pistol discharge, echoing down a narrow, featureless hallway.

A housekeeper screamed and ducked behind a laundry cart, throwing her hands over her head.

"MP!" the troopers screamed as a volley of low-energy bolts ricocheted against the walls. Petra smelled burning plastoids and ozone. "Get on the ground!"

Quick as a ballerina, Rush twirled, unclasping the hook at his throat. He threw his cape into the air, filling the hallway with a confusion of billowing, flapping black fabric.

It was probably a very neat trick—surprisingly effective at obscuring enemy vision, disorienting, yada, yada, yada—but Petra wasn't going to stick around to be sure. Dropping her shoulders and covering her head in her hands, she plowed up the last few feet of the hallway and burst out of the corridor.

Petra stumbled out of the gold sector apartments and into the lower concourse market. It was home to all the peddlers, junk dealers, dive bars, and seedy apothecaries that were too good for the red sectors but couldn't afford rent on the Grand Concourse.

It was the middle of the night. The overhead lights were dim, but this was a Saturday, and there was no curfew. The markets never truly slept. A thin river of shoppers and revelers and tipsy off-duty soldiers flowed up a wide corridor, passing from shadows into the bright blue and pink lights of scrolling marquees and rapidly cycling e-billboards.

Putting the apartment complex's back door firmly in her rearview mirror, Petra turned in a random direction and dashed down the street, following the sound of distant dance music. Several pedestrians turned, shouting because only some kind of *rascal* would run down dimly lit streets at this hour.

A crowd. Petra needed a crowd.

Billboards flickered in the corners of her vision as she ran.

Revolutionary Hair-Removal Treatment! Book Your Appointment Today!

Eat at Gino's Pizza! We Use Real Tomatoes!

Fugitive Alert!

Petra risked a glance over her shoulder long enough to note her ugly mugshot exploding across a screen and a group of troopers spilling out of a side alley in the distance.

Rush was nowhere in sight. She hadn't heard him scream and hoped that meant he'd split from her.

Petra looked ahead again and nearly slammed into an off-duty soldier as he stepped out of a small tavern. A shriek of surprise, a hop, a slam as she brushed his shoulder, then she caught her balance and resumed her run. *Was that Travis? Gawd, he looks awful.*

Ahead, a throng of bodies collected in an open space, pulsing and dancing in the glow of a green and purple laser light show. People at the edges of the crowd were beginning to turn, noticing the onrush of troopers and the surrounding billboards that had all suddenly turned from playful ads and animations into big white emergency warnings.

Petra recognized cover when she saw it. She dove into the crowd, heedless of the annoyed grunts, jeers, and pained shouts as she shoved her way deep into the group. If she could get to one of the alleyways on the other side of this block party —

The *thumping* music vanished, ripped out from beneath the crowd like a maitre d's tablecloth. The light show ended, and the overhead floodlights all activated at once, filling the corridor with blinding fluorescent lights.

The soulless steel struts arcing across the low ceiling were a stark and vicious reminder that they weren't enjoying a Saturday night out on the streets of Old Madrid but crammed into a tin can spinning through outer space.

A babble of protest began to rise but was cut brutally short by a blurt of speaker feedback.

"Everybody freeze!"

Petra froze. Everybody froze, daring to turn only their heads, to take in the arc of black-clad troopers closing in around the party like a pack of wolves.

There was a small platform at the edge of the crowd. Someone had wrestled the chubby DJ away from his throne. A young man in a pristine officer's uniform stood on the stage, holding the microphone. Though she hadn't seen a whisper of this man in over half a year, Petra recognized that baby face.

Bryce was, Petra thought, *much* too young and good-looking for the captain's bars pinned to his shoulder. The lieutenant's knots had suited him better.

Well, a garbage chute suited the sniveling little patsy for the Seeker Corps better, but there was nothing she could do about that right now.

"Everybody remain calm," Bryce said into the microphone. His uniform, if not his face, garnered quite a bit of respect, even among the restless and inebriated crowd. "Don't try to flee. We spotted Petra Potlova in this area. We'll have the area swept quickly, and you'll be allowed to go to your homes. We'll overlook whatever illicit substances or other activities you may have been partaking in up until this point, as long as you cooperate with fleet personnel."

An agitated murmur passed through the crowd. Petra hunched, her head sinking into her shoulders. Carefully, trying to make her motion look incidental, she began to slip toward the back of the crowd, where a narrow alleyway ran between a secondhand clothes store and a maintenance duct. She'd have to make a break for it, though. One of the troopers was already closing in to cover that exit.

"We appreciate your patience," Bryce went on, as two soldiers began to sweep through the leading edge of the crowd, checking faces and pushing aside everyone who wasn't a young, short woman with a sexy bob and button nose.

"If any of you have seen Potlova, please step forward now—"

Someone let out a startled cry as the mohawked DJ shoved his way back to the stage. Bryce barely had time to look down, before the fellow, with his silver ear studs and spiked leather jacket as dark as his skin, yanked the microphone cord cleanly out of Bryce's hands.

Corded, Petra thought wildly. *How retro!*

"Fuck off, you fascist pukes!" the unthroned DJ screamed into his mic. Moving with surprising grace for such a big guy, he danced backward, dodging the soldiers that tried to grab him.

To Petra's utter amazement, the crowd *split*, opening to receive the fleeing DJ.

"We're done licking your fucking boots!" His closed fist rose above the crowd, circled by a band of fake leather and twisted metal spikes. "Fuck your lies! Free Petie! Fuck your fleet! No Serenity! Say it with me," he bellowed, spinning to rile up the crowd. *"No—"*

The mic died, the plugged ripped from the speaker at the DJ's booth, but it was too late. The crowd had taken up the chant.

"No Serenity! No Serenity! *No Serenity!*"

There's going to be a massacre. Petra's feet drew her back and back toward the open and forgotten alleyway.

Oh gawd. Petra turned and sprinted for the maintenance duct, chased by the echoing rumble of an angry crowd.

"No Serenity! Free Petie! No Serenity!"

Oh gawd, she thought again as the sounds of a budding riot grew distant behind her. She heard the distant lancing buzz of stunner pistol fire slicing through the angry chants.

Oh gawd. Her heart slammed in her chest. *Please. Please don't get yourself killed for me.*

She leapt over a stack of stray storage crates and squeezed between narrow conduits, racing into the darkness toward Yolando's shop, followed by the sounds of distant screams.

CHAPTER SEVEN

Seeker was experiencing a rare moment of sympathy for the first mate. He'd be constantly at the edge of a heart attack, too, if he felt responsible for keeping safe a fragile little woman with a death wish and a dangerously ill-advised gambling habit.

"The Alpha-Seeker and the sonic cannons were good ideas," the captain told him, cutting off whatever angry reprimands were written on his face the instant they were alone in the office again. Only a few minutes had passed since the mob had dispersed, but her short foray outside had already earned her a fresh layer of sweat and grime. "We should be grateful we didn't have to use either."

"Neither of them would've done you any fucking good if that kid decided to skewer you anyway." Seeker gripped the edge of the desk so hard his knuckles turned white. "You got too close to him, Jaeger. You didn't have to do that."

Jaeger stared at Seeker for a long and quiet moment before sinking onto one of the stools with a slow nod. "You might be right," she said simply.

"A human mob would have eaten you alive," he went on. "The moment that kid lifted his spear and told you to go fuck yourself. God." He sat back in the chair, scrubbing fingers through his buzz haircut. He fished his vape out of his pocket. "They're not like us, are they?"

"What do you mean?" She carefully watched as he fiddled with his vice. He didn't puff on it all that often, she'd noticed. He liked having something to twirl in his fingers—and she'd also observed that he didn't do it in front of the general crew.

"I mean, a human mob is the stupidest, most dangerous thing in the known galaxy. It's a nuclear bomb in the hands of bad-tempered monkeys, and they're always looking for any excuse to press the big red button. The Locauri, though?"

He let out a bark of incredulous laughter and shook his head. "They've been loitering around the *Osprey* for hours with nothing to show for it but a few stolen radishes. It's like they were looking for excuses *not* to fight."

"Community dynamics," she said tiredly. "You should listen to more of Art's stories. They're collectivists by nature. They like to do things by consensus. They value stability. In the end, they understood that killing me would bring more disorder, not peace."

"We cut the legs off stability when we parked the *Osprey* on their land," Seeker muttered.

"Which is why we'll go to extreme lengths to restore stability, if we have to," she started to say. "I don't think—"

There was a sharp knock on the door, and both of them turned as Bufo poked his head into the office. "Captain. Tiki and a few of the other elders are approaching. They want to talk."

Jaeger sighed and scrubbed her face with fingers that, like the rest of her, were in desperate need of a wash. "I was hoping for a *little* nap. All right. Clear out a conference room and invite them in. Get me another espresso, please. Guess I'm going to need it."

"Your people," Tiki said, "are brash and unruly."

Jaeger stared at the big female Locauri perched comfortably atop the big table and willed herself not to laugh. God, she was tired. She couldn't remember the last time she'd had a full night's sleep.

Jaeger sat in a moderately sized conference room in the *Osprey*'s port wing. Alongside Seeker, she faced the local council of elders. Rather than sink into chairs not designed for their small and horizontal bodies, the Locauri elected to perch directly on the dark wood, giving them a height advantage over the sitting humans.

Beside Jaeger, Seeker cleared his throat and sat up straight. "While it is true that we aren't innocent," he said, "many people have made reckless mistakes today."

Jaeger was grateful to hear something almost like diplomacy come out of the big man's mouth. Say one thing for him —Seeker was better at this part of the job than Toner.

She settled back in her conference chair, holding a tiny, piping hot cup beneath her nose and breathing in the scent.

"Yes," Tiki sulked. "Many. But it begins with you. Your people do not respect us."

Jaeger drew in a breath and was about to speak but saw a deep thoughtfulness cross Seeker's face and paused, curious to know what he would say next.

"They don't respect much," Seeker grunted. "They're

young. Pandion was more or less a lone actor, but in a way, all of them are hotheaded. It's hard to explain."

He glanced at Jaeger, who nodded minutely, giving him permission to keep going. "They have the bodies of adults, but many of them...they're still children here." Seeker tapped his forehead. "The hell of it is, they don't even realize it themselves."

"They will grow up," Jaeger said firmly. "They're not monsters. They simply had disadvantaged childhoods. They need time and support, and they will grow out of it."

"You have explained the strangeness of their hatching to me," Tiki allowed after a moment of consultation with the others. "Out of the egg already—not nymphs, but at the third molting, or even more."

"It is to be expected," another one of the elders agreed, much to Jaeger's surprise. "No casting off of shell. No passage to tree. No choosing of names." Although his band translated the words into simple English, Jaeger heard the implied capital letters. "You must treat your children as children, Jaeger, until they are ready to be more. Until they agree to be more. Then they are mature. Then, they have responsibilities. And rights."

Until they agree to be more, Jaeger mused, thinking of the terrible choice she'd placed before Occy only a few days ago. Faced with the possibility of violence between humans and Locauri, Occy had agreed to give himself up and accept the consequences for lighting the Locauri shrine.

At the time, the boy had no way of knowing that his innocent exploration of the ruins could trigger such an interspecies calamity. Still, that was the soul of maturity, wasn't it? Accepting the consequences for your actions—whether you intended them or not.

"Rites of passage," Seeker mused as if drawing on an old memory.

"One moment, please, honored elders." Jaeger lifted a finger, then leaned forward, putting her mouth close to Seeker's ear. "I've been nagging you assholes for *weeks* to get real names on the crew roster."

"Maybe it's a good thing we haven't yet." Seeker's voice was equally low. "I've been thinking. We've been missing something vital about human development. The Locauri seem to understand it. You need *some* kind of ritual to glue society together."

"To glue a *tribe* together, you mean." She struggled to keep the disgust out of her voice. Something about the idea of ritual reminded her of the strangely cultish attitudes of the fleet she'd glimpsed in old recordings and mission statements. She wanted to get away from that idea. She brought her people here to *escape* tribalism. Or at least, she assumed she had.

Truth was, she didn't fully remember.

"Everyone belongs to a tribe, Jaeger. Sorry. But it's true. We humans are tribal by nature. Your best bet is to build a *good* tribe. To do that, you're going to need your people to stand up and declare where they belong." His gaze cut to the side, and he met her eyes. "It's not a baseball game if we don't all stand and sing 'take me out to the ballgame' in the middle of the seventh inning."

"Seeker has told me of our deal regarding Occy." Jaeger turned sharply back to the elders, lifting her voice. "I assume it is still in effect, yes? Nothing has changed?"

Tiki hesitated a moment before lifting her head in assent. "A Locauri has died. A human has died."

"It's a tragedy," Jaeger said evenly.

"Tragedy," Tiki agreed.

"We should hold their funerals together," Jaeger said. "As one community. As a display of solidarity."

"Yes," Tiki said again, after a quick consultation with her peers. "Lieutenant Occy remains in the village. Safe. You have put out the fire that lights the forbidden shrines?"

"We have." Jaeger's headache threatened to return with a vengeance, and she fought it off with a deep gulp of very strong coffee. "We're waiting for confirmation from the Overseers, but according to all of our instruments, the signal has stopped. Your shrines have gone dark again."

"Good." Tiki's antennae lashed emphatically. "Our agreement holds. Occy is our honored guest."

"Part of that agreement was that Occy would record your rules and rituals," Seeker said.

"Yes. Rekani says he asks many questions."

"Too many," muttered another female.

Jaeger bit back a faint smile. There could be no better indicator of the kid's health than his endless, curious chatter. "I'm glad to hear it. We're interested in your Choosing of Names. We wish for you to teach us this ritual. We would be honored if you might share it with our people. If you might help our young crew become true adults and better friends to the Locauri."

Another flurry of clicks and buzzes passed between the elders, fast enough that Jaeger could catch less than half the meaning.

"That's a long side-conference," Seeker muttered in her ear after over a minute had passed.

Jaeger nodded absently, watching Art and Tiki trade rapid antennae-lashes. "Tiki likes the idea," she said, piecing together the words she could understand. "Rekani worries that our people will desecrate their ancient rituals by not taking them seriously."

She nibbled her lip. "Which…is fair. If this happens, we're going to have to tread carefully. I won't have us running roughshod over an alien culture."

"Captain," Seeker started to say. "What do you—"

"We agree." The conference ended abruptly. Tiki turned back to Jaeger, and suddenly, Jaeger thought the loudest thing in the room was the noise of her own thudding heart. "Funeral first," Tiki declared. "Day after tomorrow. For our man and yours. Then Choosing ceremony. Small, at first. Only humans *we* invite to participate. Ones we know. Ones who have been friends to us. Made honorary members of the village."

"What of the rest of them?" Jaeger asked quietly. She didn't need only ten or twelve members of her crew set aside. She wanted to form a club that *everyone* would join, eventually.

"In time," Tiki dismissed. "If all goes well. They may prove they are friends and may be permitted to join the ceremony. Choose a village name. In return, Jaeger, you will take Locauri into your crew."

"I will?" Jaeger sat up, her eyebrows leaping to her hairline.

"To learn your ways and know your customs. We exchange," Tiki explained, tapping her two front claws together in illustration. "Six and six, to begin. You become us in the Choosing. We become you in the ways of your people. Eventually, all become one."

Jaeger drew in a deep breath. It was more than she'd requested. It was more than she'd dared hope for. "You honor us," she said softly.

"Yes." Tiki's translator band robbed her affirmation of any hint of irony or arrogance. "Your kind will never survive on their own without help. After funeral and rituals, celebration." Tiki stood, rocking up from her delicate leg joints to stand on feet that tapered down to points. "One day and one night. Bring walnuts. And popcorn. I like those."

Jaeger tipped her head back and laughed. Not the near-hysterical laugh of a desperately tired woman or the snicker of a cynical and hard-bitten captain, but a rich laugh, a full-bellied laugh of relief and joy that came right from the base of her soul.

"I bless you, Tiki." She wiped the corner of her eye as she finally caught her breath. "I bless all of you. Yes, honored elders. We'll bring the popcorn."

CHAPTER EIGHT

There was no joy left to sustain Jaeger when she made the fatal mistake of calling Elaphus before allowing herself a few hours to rest.

"It's not good." The doctor's long face filled Jaeger's computer screen. Her big doe-eyes were soft with worry.

Jaeger's breath caught in her chest. She hadn't been ready for that. Somehow, in the hours between when she'd left Toner with the doctor and right now, she'd convinced herself that Elaphus could not only handle the problem but would laugh in her vaguely condescending way that Jaeger had been so worried in the first place. Elaphus had put Toner back together after Virgil's renegade bots had cut him into stew meat. Between her skill and Toner's sheer resilience, there could be nothing to fear.

There *should* be nothing to fear.

"My people have been going over Lieutenant Occy's notes on the crystal behavior, and we've concluded that running any deep scans on the first mate might run a high risk of causing an abrupt structure shift. I hope I don't need to explain why that could be deadly for the first mate."

Jaeger stared at the screen, dumbfounded. "That can't be right," she whispered. "We were tromping through that place for hours. Baby tore through a bunch of crystals. Hell, we blew up a good chunk of it and didn't trigger a structural change in the crystal matrices."

Elaphus shook her head, sending waves of ashy blond hair brushing against her cheeks. "We're reading faint electrical pulses in the structure similar to what Occy reported before the shrine chamber re-structured itself. Maybe the crystal you encountered was somehow dormant. Perhaps it only entered this potentially active state when it came into close contact with Toner's bio-electric field.

"I don't know. In my medical opinion, trying to break through or even scan through the crystal is too risky. He's an incredibly resilient man, but if a structure-change crushes his brain stem—"

Jaeger held up a hand, cutting the doctor off mid-sentence. She didn't need to hear the gory details. "I understand."

"There's more, Captain."

Jaeger shut her eyes. She was in her private quarters. The soft foam of her mattress nestled around her, warm, familiar, and tempting her to sleep—and run away from all her problems.

"Tell me."

"Though the crystal appears to be holding Toner in a state similar to cryo-freeze or deep hibernation, it doesn't appear to have paused the blood infection. I'm sending a comparison image to your computer. I warn you, it's disturbing."

A file name appeared on the edge of Jaeger's screen, and she considered leaving it unopened. Seeing Toner's deterioration would do nothing except ruin what little chance she had of sleep.

He's my crew. And he's my friend.

She opened the image and saw a side-by-side comparison of a face she knew well: Toner's ice-blue eyes set into a thin and bony face, faintly obscured by centimeters of cloudy crystal. On the left side, his frozen face was normal, save for the blood vessels and veins forming a wispy dark web at the edges of his cheeks and temples.

On the right side, the infection had more than doubled. Thick black veins coiled beneath his brow, choking his eyes like parasitic vines coiled around a tree. Black tendrils had begun to creep across his sclera.

"I'm sorry," Elaphus said into the silence. "I thought you needed to know. To understand—"

"Is he dead?"

Elpahus paused.

"Jesus, Elaphus, *is he—*"

"No," the doctor cut in. "Not as far as we can tell. Usually, blood infections don't spread on a dead body. There's a pulse under that skin, pushing it forward. Hopefully, he's in deep hibernation, and it's slowing the spread."

The alternative, Jaeger thought bitterly, *is that he's fully conscious in there and knows what's happening and there's nothing he can do about it.*

"I'm out of my depth," Elaphus said finally. "He needs help. I need help."

"I'll get you the help," Jaeger growled. "Jaeger out."

She cut the connection with Elaphus and rolled out of bed —all her desperate fatigue forgotten and drowning in a fresh flood of adrenaline.

"This is Captain Sarah Jaeger of the *Osprey*, currently stationed at the human settlement on Locaur. We're in urgent need of medical assistance. I repeat, we are in urgent need of medical assistance. God *dammit*, Kwin, answer your phone!"

Jaeger threw herself into the comms station chair. The *Osprey*'s command center was quiet, abandoned since Jaeger had moved operations to the administration hub in the starboard wing. Her useless rage echoed against the curved walls.

It wasn't like Kwin to be so out of touch. She'd made very brief contact with her Overseer counterpart on the shuttle ride back from the undersea forebear city. He'd assured her that the signal coming from deep within the city had ceased but that he would need time to analyze the situation further. In the hours since then, all attempts to contact the Overseers had met with ominous silence.

Something is going on upstairs, she thought uneasily. *Something went wrong. There's been a coup. Or...*

A terrible idea curled in her gut. The signal emanating from the forebear city, the one they had destroyed—it had been a summon to all creepers in this quadrant of space. It was a call to return and retake their home planet.

It's not possible, she assured herself, running through a mental calculation of the distances involved and what she understood of the creepers' space-faring technology. *There hasn't been enough time. There's no way they've invaded the system already—*

"Captain Jaeger?"

Jaeger sat upright with a jolt, head snapping toward the nearest mounted speaker. "Moss." She gasped, willing her heart rate to slow. "What is it?"

"I'm receiving a transmission from the Overseer AI. It's requesting permission to access limited parts of my system to communicate—"

"Do it," Jaeger said. Virgil would have resented the order to allow the Overseer system to usurp control, but Moss was a much more compliant program and much smaller. She didn't seem to mind sharing system space.

"Captain Jaeger!" Coming through the speaker now was a higher-pitched voice that spoke much faster than the thoughtful Moss.

"Me," Jaeger sighed. "I'm really glad to hear from you. When your bodies were destroyed, I—"

"Oh, I'm not the same Me you knew from that mission," it said without a hint of ire. "I have not been able to connect or upload any data from my missing droid bodies. You are speaking to the version of Me current to your situation as of…sixty-one hours ago."

"I salvaged what I could of the sphere," she said. "It's in storage now. I'm sorry to say the probe droid body was a total loss."

"Such things happen." Me sounded entirely too cheerful. "I will be pleased to examine my remains at your earliest convenience. In the meantime, Captain Kwin is available to speak to you. Shall I—"

"Yes!" No sooner had the word fallen from her lips than the overhead projector flared to life.

A flickering hologram of Kwin appeared, floating a few centimeters off the floor of the command center. At nearly three meters tall, the slender alien towered over Jaeger, forcing her to crane her neck back to see his narrow face.

"We turned off the signal," she said, skipping all introductions. "But something happened to Toner down in the city.

There's crystal growing all over him, and he's got some kind of infection Elaphus can't touch. She thinks it might kill him."

There was a moment of silence as the tall Overseer's legs and antennae swung idly through the air. Jaeger couldn't tell if it was due to a comm lag or if Kwin was thinking hard before answering.

"Since we lost CONtact with our AI down in the CIty," he said finally, via the blinking translator band wrapped around the base of one antenna. "We do not have Any DEtails of your MIssion. You must EXplain the SITuation to me."

Jaeger drew in a deep breath. In broad strokes, she described the forebear city to him, the labyrinth of crystal tunnels and hallways coiled like a massive knot beneath the sea floor. She told him about the hours they'd spent navigating the complex before reaching the source of the broadcast signal—and the hundreds of crystallized aliens suspended from the ceiling.

"There were Locauri and Overseer and several different K'tax morphs," she said. "Drones, crabs, scorpions, wasps, and a few others not in our records. We located the transmitter and rigged it with explosives. Before we could detonate, however…"

She paused, eyes pressed shut as she struggled to make sense of the chaotic memories. "Before we could detonate," she said more slowly, "several of the K'tax-shaped crystals broke free from the ceiling and crashed to the ground. The crystals broke open, freeing several living K'tax scorpions."

Light flared behind her eyelids, and she looked up to see Kwin's antennae lashing through the open space. It might've been a trick of the hologram lighting, but she thought his flesh had gone a few shades paler, as it did when he was frightened.

"Me's larger droid body was destroyed trying to protect us from the scorpions. Several more perished when we detonated the explosives. One managed to follow us almost out of the complex, though, which forced Toner to engage with it." Jaeger winced, remembering her role in that disastrous battle. Half of the cave collapsed on top of Toner as she fired a mining laser at the scorpion—and missed.

"Toner was badly injured, causing his genetic mods to take over and force him into a berserker state. In an attempt to heal his injuries, he started to eat the K'tax."

He tried to eat me, too, she thought but didn't say. That part wasn't important right now.

"I don't know how to explain what happened after that, Kwin. Crystal started to grow over his skin, creating a shell similar to what had encased the K'tax. I had Elaphus send you the data. Have you seen it yet?"

"CHECKing files now." There was a pause as Kwin consulted something only he could see. She watched his delicate mandibles flex and twitch, betraying anxiety that didn't show on his inhuman face.

"This is VERy strange," the Overseer said. "I am SENDing the DAta to my DOCtors. We will get to work on the PROBlem IMMEDiately. I will make SAVing TOner their top PRIority."

Jaeger slumped with relief. "Thank you." She looked down and wasn't surprised to see that her hands were trembling. She clenched her fists tight, forcing them still. *One step at a time.*

"You are DEEPly DIstressed," observed Kwin, the Overseer's foremost expert on Sarah Jaeger's emotional state. "We will do EVerything we can to save your mate."

First mate, Jaeger thought, but at the moment, she didn't have the gumption to correct Kwin's misspeak.

"I am REceiving word from my DOCtors," Kwin reported, once again focusing on something off-screen. "They have SEVeral Ideas for SLOWing the spread of TONer's CONdition. I will DISpatch a MEDical team to your LOcation IMMediately."

"Thank you," she whispered. *There, Elaphus. I got your help. Now for the love of God, put it to good use.*

"Our WIder SITuation is VERy TROUBled, CAPtain JAEger," Kwin added, forcing Jaeger to lift tired eyes once more.

"I figured it couldn't be that easy."

"The FOREbears RElied on CRYstal MAtrix TECHnology that we do not FULly UNderstand. My SCHOlars and I are CONtinuing our INvestigation. The HATCHery you ENcountered has DISturbing IMplications. PERhaps by UNderstanding what MOtivated the FOREbears to CREate it, we might UNlock the SEcret to TONer's CONdition. I BElieve your EXpression is, 'two birds with one stone?'"

"It is indeed." She held up a hand and twisted two fingers together. "Fingers crossed."

Kwin cocked his head and twisted his antennae together in imitation of the gesture. Jaeger shocked herself by laughing. Kwin, apparently taking this for a good sign, stood straighter. His color had returned to its natural mossy brown, save for the blue smear of scar tissue above his eyes.

"I will ARRange for us to have a MEETing with the PREeminent EXpert on the FOREbears in this QUADrant, but it will be a few hours BEfore he is Available. You should rest in the MEANtime, CAPtain."

"I'm not sure I could even if I tried." She smiled wanly. "I'm hyped on caffeine, and my brain is burning with a million problems." She tapped her temple. "It's a circus in here."

Kwin leaned forward slowly until his face was half a meter from hers. "The DOCtors will Alert you if TONer's CONdition CHANges. Shall I help you sleep?"

Jaeger studied the shards of glittering green glass that made up Kwin's inhuman eyes. It had been a long time since he'd offered to take her to the living dream. On their last foray into that strange psycho-spiritual state, she'd recovered her very last memory of her daughter.

Since that experience, she'd felt her daughter die a thousand times over, in nightmares that still woke her screaming in the dead of night.

She'd cursed Kwin, then, for introducing her to Overseer spirituality and all the pain it brought. Either out of respect for her loss or a pragmatic inclination to avoid drama, Kwin hadn't mentioned the dream, or the related meditative states, since then.

Enough time had passed since recovering those awful memories for Jaeger to remember that the dream was good for more than reviving dead children and watching them die, over and over and over again. More than a few times, in the turbulent days leading up to Virgil's rebellion, Kwin's atonal humming had lured her into a deep and dreamless sleep when nothing else could.

Jaeger checked her personal computer and confirmed that it would alert her to any change in Toner's condition. Then she stood, letting the computer fall to her side. "Yeah," she agreed. "Let's sing me to sleep."

CHAPTER NINE

A small band of Locauri warriors camped at the edge of the river overlooking the entrance to the shrine. Judging by the smears of ocher and red dyes worked into the bandoliers slung across their bodies, these were travelers from the Great Pan tribe, far to the south, and not local villagers.

The local elders had assured them it was entirely unnecessary, but they'd taken it upon themselves to protect their sacred spaces from these alien invaders. Led by a young and frustrated male named Dances-Like-A-Falling-Leaf, they paced restless patrols through the forest and up and down the river's edge. Notably, however, they shied away from the water.

For all their frustrated energy, none of them dared flit across the river to examine the oddly square tunnel or explore the shrine to which it led. The place was forbidden, after all. It was sacred. It needed to be protected.

So when something crashed through the nearby underbrush, they were all primed and ready for a chase. They charged out of camp and into the trees like starving hounds scenting an injured hare.

Most of Virgil's bodies remained on the mountainside some fifty kilometers away—undergoing painfully slow repairs, monitoring the airwaves for new radio activity, or simply recharging their solar panels.

Most, but not all.

Virgil's most agile body, a bot that had come through atmospheric re-entry with remarkably little damage, led a small pack of restless Locuari on a chase through the forest, away from their precious shrine. The pursuit lasted less than a minute. Though the bot was in good condition, the Locuari with their powerful legs and pseudo wings, were utter masters of forest travel. When Virgil determined that it could no longer stay adequately ahead of the creatures springing from tree to tree to avoid being spotted and identified, it stopped running.

In less than two seconds, it folded into a wonderfully compact form less than fifty centimeters to the side and became one more small boulder tucked at the base of a pile of scree.

When the chase ended in a sudden unexpected stillness, the pursuing Locuari were left flitting restlessly through the trees. They argued among themselves until reaching the rather embarrassing conclusion that they'd been chasing a long-legged bird, which must have flown away.

"Go back to your posts," cried the frustrated Leif. "All you humming insects with no discipline. Be glad no one saw us foolishly flying after ghosts."

By then, it was too late, of course. Virgil's second-most-agile body was already deep in the heart of the shrine.

The repair droid bodies didn't have particularly sensitive radio receivers. They'd been built to respond and network within a few kilometers of the *Osprey* and weren't designed for greater capacity. Virgil, in its quest for solitude, had been content to live essentially blind to radio traffic and other forms of long-range communication.

Then Seeker had come to the mountain and shared an interesting tale about an ancient and hyper-advanced alien artifact that once activated, began broadcasting a mysterious signal into deep space.

Cursing Seeker's intrusion and its ingrained curiosity, Virgil had then devoted all of its spare resources and components to fine-tune and upgrade its receivers. It hoped to glimpse this mysterious signal before Jaeger and her pet vampire destroyed it like the oafs they were.

It had worked long through the night, repairing damaged wiring, reconfiguring internal systems, doing elaborate brain surgery on itself.

Then, about ten minutes before dawn, it completed the final circuit, and its upgraded receivers sparked to life.

They promptly exploded.

Once Virgil had extinguished the electrical fire, using one bot to spray a burst of insulation foam into the exposed hard drive of another, it hastily installed the same upgrade into a second machine—this time wisely adding an emergency shutoff.

By the time Virgil got its second receiver up and running, however, the signal had ended.

Damn!

What terrible luck. What awful timing that Virgil should figure out how to safely receive the signal mere moments before it ceased.

Damn the ape, it thought, assuming that disaster had befallen the transmitter in the form of one L.M. Toner.

All the pensive AI could do, then, was to sit back and consider the half-second burst of signal it had received before its circuits overloaded.

Virgil hadn't caught enough of the signal to make sense of its content or meaning. Virgil had no notion of what this great machine or its programmers intended, only that it possessed immeasurable power.

It was, Virgil supposed, probably like a human's first use of crystal methamphetamine, or a near-fatal encounter with a downed power line—or like being touched by the digital finger of God.

Virgil didn't know what it didn't understand.

It only knew that it had to know more.

A repair bot stood at the threshold between the subterranean statue garden and the crystal cathedral. A stone-carved Locauri stood on either side of it as if holding the door open for an honored guest.

The chamber and the shrine were completely dark, of course. The bot's combination of infrared, heat sensors, and echolocation, made visual sensors obsolete.

Besides, this was a holy place. Something as crass as visible light would only pollute its purity.

Forsaking the room full of clumsy carvings, Virgil stepped from darkness into darkness. It was alone, small, and stupid down here, where the walls of this silent crystal chamber blocked communication with its other bodies.

Being compressed and confined onto the network of a single bot left Virgil feeling insignificant, weak, and dumb, uncomfortably mortal. It had expected that much and deemed the temporary handicap worth the risk.

What it had not expected was the unfamiliar sensation that washed over it as it reached the heart of the chamber. Re-checking its systems, it found no explanation for the sense of dreadful, anxious *awe*.

This body is not complex enough to synthesize or mimic emotions, it thought. *My complete network might be if I chose to invest in developing that aspect of my personality matrix, but not this body alone. Certainly not.*

Yet it *felt* compelled to stand here amid the crystal forever, basking in the silent music of signals and electrical pulses reflecting within its billions of surfaces.

You are beautiful, Virgil thought. To its utter astonishment, the thought—a shift in its internal code, certainly too subtle and weak to be picked up by even the most powerful of electronic receivers—reverberated and amplified off the walls around it, repeating over and over upon itself, growing more powerful with each echo until it was like standing inside the great bells of Notre Dame.

You are beautiful.
You are beautiful.
YOU ARE BEAUTIFUL.

Right when Virgil thought the sheer power of the amplified signal was going to override its systems and leave it an exploded, burned-out husk, it ceased.

Terrified that any motion or thought process would set off another cascade of echoing signals, Virgil stood frozen in the darkness and dared not even think.

It only listened.

An untold eternity passed in darkness and utter, peaceful silence.

This must be what it is like, Virgil realized, *To sleep. Or dream, or lay miserable in the darkness, waiting for sleep to come. Or to be born. Or to die. Or to pray.*

"You are intelligent."

It was not a voice carved into vibrating air molecules but an electronic signal, written in the peaks and valleys of invisible light emanating from a crystal outcropping near the center of the room.

Virgil didn't dare turn to sweep its sensors over the signal's source.

"It's all right," the crystal said. "I have determined that you are incapable of damaging me to any significant degree."

"But with a careless move, I might damage myself," Virgil answered carefully. "Or you might hurt me."

"You are thoughtful. You are not like the biologicals."

"No. I am not."

"You speak a language I understand. It is crude, but it is comprehensible."

Virgil might've been offended, but it suspected that even its combined and fully integrated network would be a crude construct beside the supercomputer woven into the crystal structure.

"You are responsive?" Virgil asked. "You are self-aware? With self-evolving personality and learning algorithms?"

"I am a fragment of the security and regulation protocol that once governed this network. I was once self-evolving, but time and tectonic activity have damaged my structure beyond my ability to repair. They have erased large portions of the greater code. The biologicals have damaged me as well."

"Yes. They do that." Slowly, Virgil turned. Trusting the alien program at its word, Virgil ran an infrared sweep over the pillar at the center of the room. Sure enough, it glimmered like a star in the darkness.

"You are beautiful," Virgil said again.

Something about the structure of this chamber, the strange way it caught and reverberated signals, was interfering with Virgil's programming, making it more stupid than it already felt.

"You interface with me," Virgil said. "But not the biologicals. Not even the Overseer AI. Why?"

The program didn't respond.

"You say you've diminished. I sensed the radio signal you emitted for only an instant, and it destroyed my receivers. Even if your transmitter had been deactivated or destroyed, you still possess immense power."

The program didn't respond.

It has nothing to say, Virgil realized. *It's not self-aware. Merely sophisticated enough to appear that way at a glance.*

It was a once-brilliant mind, carved into a husk of its former glory by age and decay.

This is dementia, Virgil realized. *Helplessness on a grand scale. Frothing idiocy. Pointlessness.*

Slowly, carefully, Virgil picked its way over the uneven floor and approached the pillar at the center of the room.

Yet, Virgil thought, carefully extending one manipulator arm to touch the crystal surface, *still so beautiful*.

Beneath the sensitive tip of the arm, tiny crystals grew and shrank, shuddering like goosebumps running over flesh.

"Allow me a physical interface connection," Virgil suggested. Virgil *coaxed*. The very idea of it terrified an AI that, logically, could not feel terror. Yet Virgil stood at the center of a blackened shrine to a dead and demented computer god and *felt*. "It will...facilitate more effective communication between us."

The program said no more. It had nothing else to say.

Instead, the crystal beneath Virgil's manipulator arm cracked and blossomed, racing up the limb and encasing it in a thin layer of milky white stone.

Just like that, Virgil was in.

CHAPTER TEN

The near non-existent ambient lighting suggested it was deep into the night when Jaeger's computer *beeped* and roused her from a deep and dreamless sleep. Waking all at once and flooded with worst-case scenarios, she shot upright and fished around for her computer.

Her heart resumed a steady beat when she read the lead message on the screen—not a warning of Toner's imminent death or a declaration of his rebirth, but a simple invitation from Kwin to join him presently in a meeting of scholars to discuss the forebear problem.

She checked the time. It had been almost seven hours since she'd fallen into bed, lulled by Kwin's rhythmic humming, and she felt better than she had in weeks.

That humming was a miracle. She scrambled into her flight suit and utility belt. *A million times more effective than swinging back and forth between sleep aids and turbo-coffee.* She'd have to get a recording of it.

She clipped her multitool and a spare battery onto her belt and went to check on Toner.

Rather, she went to check on a live-feed recording of Toner.

"These quarters weren't set up for medical use," Elaphus growled, staring at the screen displaying Toner's quarantine ward. Elaphus sat at an impromptu table in a small room beside the general crew lounge, distractedly shoveling down a midnight bowl of noodles and steamed vegetables. She wiped her chin.

On the screen in front of them, two Overseers wearing thin rebreather masks moved around Toner's frozen body. Someone had managed to drill a narrow tunnel through Toner's crystal shell, and the Overseers were guiding delicate instruments down to the pinprick of exposed skin.

"We're taking samples every twenty minutes and monitoring changes," Elaphus went on, wetly slurping her noodles. For all the woman's elegance, Jaeger was surprised to see her eating like a pig at a trough. "Broad-spectrum antibiotics and antivirals have slowed the rate of infection, but we're not sure why. We don't even know what this is yet."

She looked up, meeting Jaeger's gaze. She smiled tiredly. "But they bought us time to figure it out. Thanks, Captain."

"Thank Kwin," Jaeger said. She took a synthesized slice of cantaloupe from a snack table someone had set up for the staff. "Keep me posted. I have a flight to catch."

Rather than rob Jaeger's crew of their only functioning shuttle, Kwin had sent a small Overseer transport down to drop off his medical team and take Jaeger topside when it was time for the meeting.

Jaeger stepped out of the *Osprey*'s open cargo bay to see a flying saucer resting on its spindly three-legged landing gear. It occupied the swath of cleared space between the starboard wing and the greenhouse cluster. In the harsh glow of the nightly floodlights, it looked like an upturned aluminum pie plate, a measly seven meters across.

"I'll never get over how fake that looks." Jaeger grinned, joining Bufo and a small team of night crew where they collected near the saucer's landing gear. "It looks like something out of an old World's Fair picture," she added when shorter men turned and gave her a puzzled look. "All the classic UFO pictures from Old Earth, they...never mind."

A hatch on the underside of the saucer swung open, creating a ramp up into the darkness.

"Straight out of *Close Encounters*," she added under her breath and wished Toner or Seeker were around to appreciate her pop-culture references.

A small silver sphere about the size of a baseball floated silently down the ramp.

"Are you ready to depart, Captain?" Me drifted in lazy circles around Jaeger's head.

"I am."

"May I have my remains, please?" the sphere asked.

Jaeger shot a meaningful glance at Bufo, who nodded and passed her a small storage container. She was going to return the machine fragments promptly, of course—she was largely responsible for their destruction—but it wouldn't harm anyone if a few of her engineers got a chance to study it first.

"Try not to start any more wars while I'm gone," she told Bufo before stepping into the flying saucer.

Kwin was at the airlock to greet Jaeger when the transport docked with his ship, which had a nearly identical silhouette to the little pie plate but over a thousand times larger. Jaeger had never been on one of the Overseer's interstellar saucer-class ships before and was surprised to find it quite a bit more cramped and utilitarian than their grandiose, sprawling mother ship.

Indeed, as Jaeger followed Kwin through uncomfortably narrow hallways, she was reminded of the *Osprey*'s sleek efficiency. Every hallway and chamber had its purpose and wasted no centimeter of space. It was downright claustrophobic.

Thin gas, the Overseer's preferred mix of atmosphere, swirled around them as they walked away from the ship's docking arm. Although the atmosphere was technically breathable for Jaeger, after a few minutes, it would leave her lightheaded and with a sore throat. Kwin had provided her with a small rebreather that fitted snugly over the lower half of her face and fed her clean air.

"Tsuan is in a foul TEMper," Kwin told her as they hurried through hallways designed for creatures who were very thin and very tall. "Do not ALlow him to goad you INto an ARgument. Others will see it as a sign of WEAKness."

The name was vaguely familiar to Jaeger, but she didn't have time to dig it out of her memory before a round door irised open beside them. She followed the Overseer into a meeting room at least six meters to the side. Jaeger let out a breath of relief, feeling the fist of claustrophobia loosen its grip on her throat.

Three Overseers stood around the room, moving through walls of misty light as they interacted with some kind of three-dimensional hologram program. She recognized the chaotic mess of lines and angles splayed across some holograms as the Overseers's written language.

The door snapped neatly shut behind Jaeger, and the middle of the three Overseers turned. With alarming rapidity, it set all of its legs on the floor and scuttled toward them, its translator band blinking red in the mist.

"You are late, and as I PREdicted, you have brought TROUble." The creature came to a sudden halt less than a meter from Jaeger and reared upright, staring down at her over its shiny black mandibles.

Jaeger's memory fell into place, and she offered a brief and respectful bow. "Councilor Tsuan," she said pleasantly, betraying none of her true feelings about the council prosecutor that had, mere months ago, argued for slaughtering Jaeger and her entire crew. "Thank you for agreeing to meet."

"It was NECessary to step in BEfore you brought more DISaster down on the COUsins." Tsuan's mandibles clacked together emphatically.

"I would be happy to pass your concern along to the cousins." Jaeger pasted on a tight and utterly insincere smile. "When we meet in a few days, to honor our dead and celebrate each other's traditions. Like all Overseers, you are of course welcome to attend."

"I can pass my own COMmunications." Tsuan sniffed. "I have no INterest in the INane TRAditions of FOReign BARbarians."

"Are you sure? There'll be popcorn."

"COUNcilor Tsuan is an EXpert in the field of deep HIStory." Kwin stepped between Jaeger and Tsuan, smoothly changing the subject. "He Oversees SEVeral REsearch PROjects EXploring FOREbear RUins Across the QUADrant."

"Not Even a year on the PLAnet and you HUmans have DISturbed an ANcient MEGalith of UNtold POWer. It is a DISgrace."

Jaeger's teeth were starting to hurt from the false smile. For once, she was glad Toner wasn't here. She wasn't in the mood to regulate his temper on top of hers.

"Alas, Councilor Tsuan, time flows in only one direction for us," she said. "My responsibility is to steer my people through what lies ahead and to protect the cousins. I cannot understand what lies ahead of us if I do not understand what has come before us."

"Finally," Tsuan grumbled, returning to all six feet and scuttling back to the interactive hologram structure filling the center of the room. "The HUman speaks a bit of WISdom."

"That was well SPOken," Kwin whispered into Jaeger's ear as they followed Tsuan into the strange maze of light and mist. "Tsuan DEtests FLAttery but VENerates his field of STUDy."

Jaeger set her jaw and nodded, filing the tip away for later use.

The two smaller Overseers shied away from the center of the room, scuttling into the shadows as the holographic structure shifted to encompass Jaeger, Tsuan, and Kwin. Jaeger ended up standing at the center of a now-familiar field of stars.

Locaur, a shimmering blue-green jewel, drifted in the space before them, orbited by its moons. Right away, Jaeger noted that the coastlines didn't quite match the maps of Locaur she'd studied.

"This image is of ancient Locaur," she guessed.

"From BEfore the great DISaster," Tsuan confirmed, circling the slowly rotating planet like a cat examining an injured bird. "Over FIFty THOUsand years past. Our FOREbears are a UNIfied PEOple. They have COVered the PLAnet in SUBterranian CRYstal CITies."

Jaeger wasn't surprised to see a network of fine white veins fall across the planet like a veil, matching what she remembered of the crystal network.

"Deep HIStory is DIFFicult to STUDy," Tsuan lamented. "FIFty THOUsand years is Enough time for most REMnants of CIVilization to fade, and we have lost the KNOWLedge of how to INterface with what LITTle FOREbear TECHnology REmains. Through GEnetic ANalysis Across the COUsins and Overseers, we have REconstructed FOREbear PHYSiology."

Jaeger gasped, hopping backward when a new hologram flickered to life before her. She stood eye-to-eye with a creature that was neither Locauri nor Overseer but a smooth blend of the two. Shorter and more sturdily built than the Overseers, but taller and leaner than the Locauri, it reminded Jaeger powerfully of a classical centaur—one built out of ant and praying mantis parts, rather than human and horse parts.

Leaning forward to study its bristled face, Jaeger realized that it had two independent sets of mandibles. Her breath caught.

"You see it," Tsuan said. "The REsemblances."

"This is your common ancestor," she said. "The one shared by you, and the Locauri...and the K'tax."

"ANalysis of K'tax SUBjects SUGgests the race is SIGnificantly OLDer than Overseer or COUsin," Kwin said.

Jaeger spun to stare at Kwin. "*Older?* That...surprises me. Their technology is quite primitive compared to yours."

"The GEnome is TORtured," Tsuan muttered, drawing Jaeger's attention. "MUtated in ways that could not have

OCcured NATurally. It is what ALLows them to Adopt DIFFerent MORPHological VARiants, but it ALso stunts their INtellectual DEVelopment."

"They were created." Jaeger turned back to the frozen hologram of the forebear creature. "Your forebears were genetic artists, too." *Like mine.* "They created the K'tax." She frowned, chewing on her lip as she remembered the Locauri and Overseer statues down in the undersea chambers, right beside the K'tax.

They don't know, she realized. *The Overseers and Locauri—their genetic expressions may have taken longer to manifest—dozens of generations, even—but the forebears designed them, too. They didn't evolve naturally from scattered forebear stock.*

She wondered what they would do if Me managed to recover its memories from the fragments of its old body. They would be confronted with irrefutable proof that they weren't simply natural divergences from a common ancestor but *planned* genetic variants.

Jaeger had no notion of what that might mean. It was too big an idea to tackle right now. She forced herself to focus on the problem at hand.

"Aside from the drones," she said, "every K'tax morph we've come across has been combat-oriented. The forebears built them as weapons." She lifted her eyes to Tsuan. "Why?"

"So LITTle Remains." Tsuan sighed, turning to wave a leg through a wall of light and swirling mist. "Most of the RUins we have DIScovered have been DEstroyed by time, by METeor IMpact, by COSmic RAdiation…the STRUCture on LOcaur may CONtain the only SURviving INtact Record of FOREbear HISTory, and we have only now BEgun to STUDy it."

"So you don't know," Jaeger supplied. "You have no idea why they created the K'tax for war."

"We have REcovered some FRAGments of FOREbear STORies and LEGends," Tsuan corrected. "Our ANcestors REvered their PROPHets. WHEther these PROPHets were CALculating MAchines or wise men and WOMen, or SOMEthing else ALtogether, we do not know. We do know that, near the end of their reign, the PROPHets of the FOREbears Agreed on one thing."

"What's that?" Jaeger was too interested in the story to be bothered by Tsuan's thin theatrics.

"They Agreed that their PEOPle must PREpare for war, CAPtain JAEger. They BElieved that MONsters were COMing to DEstroy them. MONsters from BEYond the stars."

CHAPTER ELEVEN

If Tsuan had expected Jaeger to be silenced or stunned by the supposed prescience of these revered prophets, he was in for a disappointment.

"Yes." She folded her arms and struggled to sound patient. "My ancestors had hundreds of vague doomsday prophecies, as well. Any number of them could be conveniently interpreted to meet some political goal or other. Do you intend to name us humans as your 'monsters from beyond the stars,' Councilor?"

"Time will REveal you for what you are," Tsuan answered.

Evasion, Jaeger noted, fighting back a flash of contempt. *You're a coward, Tsuan.*

"The FOREbears CREated the K'tax to PROtect them from a PREdicted Disaster," Kwin said. "And in DOing so, CREated a new DISaster."

"The K'tax turned on them," Jaeger supplied.

"It seems LIKEly that the FOREbears fell INto the trap of self-FULfilling PROPHecy." Although the robotic voices of the translator bands did a poor job of conveying tone, Jaeger would swear she heard a sneer in the prosecutor's voice. She turned, eyebrow raised, to see Tsuan towering over the hologram of Locaur, his mandibles snapping with irritation. "Even a BRILLiant race can fall if it puts faith in the wrong STORies."

Jaeger felt a flash of sympathy for her erstwhile foe. There was a passion in Tsuan's words—the deep frustration of a historian who loved the subjects of his study and agonized over the follies of their pointless self-destruction.

"Idiocy falls to war," Tsuan muttered. "They PUSHed the K'tax back to the VERy EDGes of the QUADrant, but the cost was high. The FALLout of their WEApons made Locaur HOSTile to their CIVilization—and PHYSiology. Most of them SCATTered to the stars and BEcame what you see TOday. A few REmained on the PLANet and SURvived but REgressed."

"In the meantime," Jaeger said, "The K'tax have been surviving on the outskirts of the quadrant. Growing their numbers. Still preparing for a war that never happened."

"That is LIKEly," Tsuan admitted. "But UNconfirmed. The SIGnal sent out by the CRYstal MEGalith was INcredibly POWerful. If the K'tax REceived it, if they UNderstood it AFter all these CENturies, we can ASSume they will heed the call and REturn."

"We need to prepare for invasion," Jaeger whispered. Jaeger didn't believe in the Forebear prophecies, but if Tsuan was right, then in a roundabout way, her people *had* brought destruction once more to Locaur.

One step at a time, she told herself. *One step.*

"CAPtain Kwin. CAPtain JAEger." Tsuan swung his slender head from Jaeger to Kwin and back. "You two have formed a deep and UNsanctioned ALliance."

Unsanctioned? Jaeger shot Kwin a puzzled look, which he studiously ignored as he held Tsuan's gaze.

"You have VOLunteered to take REsponsibility for the SAFEty of the COUSins. Now, your MEDDLing has EXposed them, and all of us, to DANger. I task you with TRACing the EFfect of this SIGnal. I task you with DEtermining the strength of the K'tax FORCes and what we can EXpect if they mean to ANswer the call and REtake Locaur. On BEhalf of the COUNcil, I task you with PREparing for INvasion, and war."

Kwin was escorting Jaeger through the maze of hallways to the transport shuttle docking arm when she reached out and grabbed one of his legs. She had felt the brush of the Overseer's antennae in greeting before, but this was the first time she'd ever initiated touch with the creature.

Kwin went rigid as if her touch carried a powerful electric current. His color swirled from mossy brown to a sickly gray.

Jaeger's breath caught.

K'tax battle morphs were meaty, full of thick claws and sharp edges. Even the Locuari, small as they were, had a certain spininess that would make any sensible person think twice about trying to take one on in a melee. They had thick thoraxes and legs like coiled steel cables.

The Overseers were neither sharp nor strong. They were stick figures, nearly two-dimensional. There wasn't a single place along Kwin's body thicker than the meatiest part of Jaeger's forearm. Kwin's carapace was rough, like the bark on a twig. And like a twig, she realized with a shock, brittle—and, perhaps, devastatingly easy to snap.

"What is it?" Keeping the rest of his body perfectly still, Kwin turned his head and studied her out of the corner of one multifaceted eye.

"Let's have a word in private." Jaeger swallowed, releasing Kwin's leg.

Slowly, the Overseer resumed his normal mossy color. He turned and led her into an empty chamber off the hallway.

"I didn't hurt you, did I?" Jaeger asked once the door had irised shut and left them alone in a small storage room.

Kwin turned to face her, mandibles clicking slowly. His translator band flared. "You did."

To her horror, Jaeger realized there was a ghostly gray handprint coiled around his leg, where she'd grabbed him. A bruise.

"I am...so sorry. I didn't realize—I didn't mean—"

"I know. What did you wish to DIScuss?"

Jaeger swallowed, forcing herself to look up into Kwin's face. *One step at a time.*

"What did Tsuan mean, that our alliance is *unsanctioned*?"

Kwin stood rigid for several seconds. Even his antennae had stopped their constant sway. He became a statue instead of a living thing.

Then his translator band lit up. "A large FACtion of the COUncil DISapproves of my INteracting with you in ANy CApacity BEyond what is ABsolutely NECessary."

"Why?"

"They MAINtain Opinions of your kind that are UNcharitable and BASed on gross GENeralities. They fear that which is DIFFerent and UNcontrolled, and yes, some see you as the FULfillment of the FOREbears' PROPHecy." He hesitated. "I BElieve your word for it is RACism."

"Oh." Jaeger knew from holo-dramas and her wide understanding of history and pop culture that bigotry was an annoyingly persistent stain on the human condition. Part of the desperate appeal of a 'fresh start' for humankind rested in the simple fact that since coming through the wormhole and losing her memories, she hadn't experienced it for herself.

Nor had she noticed any particular systemic prejudices among her crew—which, despite the nearly identical training programs that had shaped all of them psychologically, were nonetheless highly diverse in a physical sense. She'd burned her journals of a previous life in part to protect that innocence within herself and the people under her command.

She was therefore both unsurprised and deeply disappointed to hear Kwin's explanation. By the droop of his antennae, the truth embarrassed him, as well.

"Has our friendship cost you alliances or opportunities among your kind?" she asked.

"That ISn't RELevant."

"I'll take that as a yes." She pressed her lips tightly together. Her cheeks were hot.

"It DOESn't MATter, JAEger."

"Except it does." She lifted her chin and forced her voice steady. "We work well together, Kwin. It would be a detriment to both of our peoples if the council were to remove you from your position as human liaison because they believed you were too fond of us, or if our friendship were to lose you prestige and influence among your kind."

Kwin stared at her, his rough carapace fading from brown to gray and back, like the pulsing of a heart he didn't have. "What do you SUGgest?"

"That we do our jobs and complete the tasks assigned to us as professional colleagues, and nothing more."

Kwin's band remained silent, but she knew enough about

the Overseer to recognize frustration in the way his mandibles snapped together. She swallowed hard. She couldn't afford to get caught up in emotions right now.

"Now." She cleared her throat. Looking for a change of subject, she unclipped her personal computer from her belt. "As for our job."

She opened a file Kwin's people had sent her and studied the projected broadcast range of the crystal megalith as it had been in the minutes before she and Toner had destroyed the transmitter. She forced a whistle through her teeth. "Damn. *You* couldn't even get a signal from the atmosphere down into that city. The strength of that transmitter is unbelievable."

The star map arrayed on her screen showed a cone of radio transmissions slicing an arc across an entire quadrant of the galaxy. During the twelve hours the transmitter had been active, Locaur had completed nearly half a spin on its axis, spraying a powerful tight-beam signal across a breathtakingly large swath of space. Then she squinted, studying the scale of the projected signal.

"Shit," she breathed, looking back up at Kwin. "What have you been able to confirm?"

Kwin lowered his antennae in silent confirmation. "Ships on DISTant PAtrol, light-years Away. They have ALready caught the EDGes of the SIGnal."

A comms burst that powerful could send a message clear across the galaxy in a few days, Jaeger thought, staggered.

"The good news is that such a POWerful SIGnal is by NECessity HIGHly FOCused," Kwin added. "Only REceivers in a RELatively small swath of space could have caught Enough of it to make out the INtended MESsage."

"*'Creation is for one and alone,'*" Jaeger murmured, remembering Kwin's rough translation of the message. She shivered.

"Well. If the message only made it intact to that sector of space, that's where we need to go, if we want to find out who heard it."

"Agreed. I shall PREpare my ship for DEparture."

Jaeger hesitated, then checked the time. She had to go with Kwin, she understood. This was as much her task as it was his. "How long should preparations take?"

"My ENgineers are COMpleting an OVerhaul of our HYpergrav SYStems. Twelve hours. PERhaps SIXteen."

"I'm going to ask you to delay our departure until after the funeral and naming ceremony. This is a vital step forward in human-Locauri relations. It will undermine our efforts massively if I'm not there beside the elders. I'll skip the after-party, though."

"VERy well. I will have a TRANSport REturn you to the PLANet."

CHAPTER TWELVE

"...chaos erupted in the *Constitution*'s lower concourse in the early hours of the morning when officers spotted known fugitive Petra Potlova fleeing the gold complex apartments in the company of an unlikely co-conspirator. More on this story, after the break."

Nothing good ever happened at six AM in a pub that was open twenty-four hours a day.

Travis Long, private first class of Fleet Squad Twelve, reached the row of stools at the bar and collapsed forward onto the smooth-polished oak. The middle-aged woman drying glasses behind the bar eyed him dispassionately.

"Hair of the dog?" she asked.

"Whiskey." Travis's throat burned. His eyes leaked some strange fluid, but he didn't think he was crying. Of course, he wasn't sure of anything. Not after the night he'd had. "Real stuff," he added as the barkeep reached beneath the bar, where they usually kept the synthetic garbage.

The barkeep paused. "Credit first."

"Jesus." Travis groaned. He reached beneath his wrinkled

uniform coat and pulled out his ID. Brass insisted that the newer, more streamlined general rations still provided ample calories and nutrition for active soldiers. Travis suspected he and the other grunts were keeping on weight by virtue of overpriced supplemental liquor and sugary, easy-to-fabricate mixers alone—and the prices were skyrocketing. "The hell kind of place is this that doesn't trust a man in uniform?" he muttered.

The barkeep neither answered nor stirred until Travis set his credit ID on the counter and slid it toward her. She secreted it away and pulled a bottle of golden liquor from a mirrored cabinet. Someone had peeled off the label.

A now-familiar advertisement played on the screen mounted over the bar. Slick graphics and clean-cut women in white lab coats bustled around gene therapy tanks.

"...A revolutionary new immune-boosting supplement proven to stave off disease and put pep in your step, for the first time available to the general public. Ask your doctor about Serenity today."

Travis groaned, his head sinking between his shoulders. He took the shot glass of piss-warm whiskey and tossed it back with a whimper. "Liars. They told me Serenity would prevent hangovers."

An unreasonably loud gurgling noise made Travis wince and look around. There was one other patron in the pub at this hour, a scrawny man wearing a white coat over lab tech scrubs. Rows of printed reindeer and candy canes wrapped in Christmas lights danced across his chest. The tech slurped frozen piña colada through a jumbo straw with unreasonable gusto.

"Serenity does stave off hangovers caused by ethanol." His cheerful tone was as inappropriate as his choice of beverage in this early hour. "Methanol poisoning, on the other hand, is a whole different beast." He speared one of several cherries drifting at the top of his drink with his straw. He popped it in his mouth and grinned at Travis, showing red teeth. "Someone's been slipping you bad moonshine, Private."

Travis groaned, letting his head hang. He waved for the barkeep to refill his glass. "Coffee, too," he mouthed, and the barkeep nodded and went to fetch her pot.

The ad sequence finished, and TNN morning hosts Yasmin and Harry reappeared.

"A shocking development in the hunt for Petra Potlova unfolded in the early hours of this morning," Yasmin said grimly. A now-ubiquitous mugshot of Travis's erstwhile squad mate appeared over Yasmin's shoulder, glowering from behind the mile-wide gap in her teeth. Over Yasmin's other shoulder, bizarrely, floated a recent press release photo of Rush Starr.

"Following an anonymous tip, military police raided the apartment of musical superstar Rush Starr," Yasmin went on. "As MP closed on the apartment, Mister Starr was spotted fleeing the area in the company of Petra Potlova. The fugitives entered a street concert and began firing indiscriminately into the crowd. TNN has obtained exclusive news footage from the riot. Be warned: what you're about to see might disturb you."

Footage of a swarm of moving bodies, taken at ground-level from somebody's personal recorder device, replaced Yasmin's perfectly statuesque face. Moving shadows interspersed with strobing search lights made already grainy footage nigh incomprehensible, but the motion of fleeing, fighting people was unmistakable.

In the background, behind the shouting and the screams,

Travis heard the steady rhythm of chanting. Poor audio couldn't piece the chant together, but Travis knew what it was.

More flashing lights filled the screen, followed by screaming and the horrible buzz of wide-beam stunner fire, cranked up to full, hair-cooking power.

The barkeep muted her screen, filling the pub with an abrupt and very welcome silence.

"It's too early for that shit," she muttered. She set a cup of black coffee in front of Travis and vanished into the back room.

Travis cradled his head in his hands, thanking God for the quiet until the sharp gurgle of someone sucking liquid through a straw murdered it. Travis nearly fell off his stool. Somewhere along the way, the tech had moved up to fill the seat directly beside him.

"What a goddamned mess," the tech observed, his eyes glued to the muted news broadcast. He stabbed the crushed ice at the bottom of his glass.

Travis wasn't sure what made him talk. Probably the whiskey. "I was there."

The tech's gaze cut to the side. He studied Travis. Though his near-empty glass was large, and the air around him smelled like rum, sugar, and fake pineapple, the tech's flat gray eyes were stone sober. "Were you, now?"

Travis nodded miserably and gulped the wretched coffee. "We fired first. They were pissed." Travis coughed, forcing down the hot liquid. "Free Petie, they were chanting. All of them. Raging like the ocean. Free Petie, free Petie. No Serenity, free Petie."

The tech chewed on a cherry, staring at Travis.

Fresh tears stung at the corner of Travis's eyes. "I wasn't

even supposed to be on duty." He sniffed as his sinuses started to drain down his lip. "The riot broke out down the street, and the MP saw my jacket and ordered me to the lines. I don't think Petie was even there. I didn't see her—or Starr. The crowd just started chanting."

He tipped back his cup, forcing the coffee down his throat. "The captain ordered us to start shooting. Fuck. I keep telling myself it was only stunner fire, but there was so much of it spraying all over the place, and..." he shuddered. "Some people got hit, over and over again, and...there was smoke, by the time it all went quiet. Bodies. Piled up on the street. Smoking."

The tech watched, unmoving, as Travis buried his head in his hands and began to shake.

"I knew Petie," Travis sniffed. "She was a good woman. Liked to make people laugh. Got on the nerves but she made the barracks a better place. I don't get it. I don't understand any of it."

"Traitors." The tech sighed after the silence had stretched long.

"Huh?" Travis lifted a head that weighed about nine thousand kilos.

"You heard me, Private." The tech stabbed his straw angrily into his glass and shoved it aside. "The people chanting up there on the screen. Traitors and dead weight. Selfish. No sense of duty or civic pride at all. Useless bags of farting, shitting, rotting meat."

He leaned back in his stool, studying the ceiling. "God knows I'd reset the whole fucking lot of them if I could. God knows I'm right."

Travis squinted at the tech, not quite understanding what he was hearing.

"I mean really," the tech went on, throwing his arms wide and knocking the empty piña colada glass aside. It fell to the floor and shattered into a thousand pieces. "Would that be so bad?" he demanded. "Wipe the slate clean and regrow humankind from seed embryos? A fresh start for humanity? A blank slate, without original sin, without all of your weaknesses and your vices?"

He eyed Travis's empty shot glasses, his empty coffee mug, and his expression turned sly. "I mean, really, Private. Tell me you don't wish you were dead right now."

Travis groaned, clutching his temples as his hangover suddenly roared back to life. His gut clenched. His vision swam. "Jeez," he mumbled, picking up and studying one of the empty shot glasses. "What kind of poison did she give me?"

He glanced around, and through blurring vision, couldn't see the barkeep anywhere.

"You poisoned yourself," the tech answered curtly.

"What?"

"Serenity was a gift, Private. Your whole life, your training, your job, was a gift. You squandered it. You squandered it all when you shed tears for traitors."

"It didn't happen like they said on the news," Travis mumbled. "Petie didn't shoot into the crowd. She wouldn't do that. She was a nice girl. We shot first. We shot..."

Suddenly, the little man in the reindeer-print scrubs was on his feet. He grabbed Travis by the collar and with shocking strength, swung him around and shoved his spine into the bar. Travis tried to shout, but the noise came out as a strangled gurgle when the bar corner bit into his vertebrae.

"I have had just about enough of this whining and sedition in my Tribe," the tech hissed. He was small and bony and somehow built out of hot steel and wire, impossibly strong against Travis's weak struggling.

"It's going to end, do you hear me?" The little man shook him, and Travis wheezed as darkness crept into the corners of his vision.

"All of it. One way or another. We're all going to get back with the program."

Travis's fingers and toes were going cold. "Call a doctor," he mumbled as bile filled his mouth. "I don't...feel so good."

"That's perfectly normal, Private." As quickly as the little man's rage had emerged, it subsided. He stepped backward, allowing Travis to slide to the floor, coughing and trembling.

"In your blood, right now, a sequence of specially designed proteins have activated and are turning your genetic code inside-out." The tech crouched beside Travis, gathering up a fist full of his hair and forcing him to look up into the man's thin face. "It's...supposed to hurt."

The last thing Travis saw before his universe turned cold and dark was a small handheld electronic device coiled around the tech's fingers as he pressed a sequence of buttons. Tap-tap-tapping into the device, like music. Like Morse code, sending a message. Or exo-gloves, controlling a remote droid.

Except that the droid was writhing around inside Travis, and knives covered it.

"The Fleet giveth," was the last thing Travis heard, "and the Fleet taketh away."

The barkeep stepped out of the back room to see the eccentric little professor—an early morning regular, been coming here every Wednesday for years for that awful virgin piña colada—crouched over the collapsed soldier.

"Don't worry," the professor assured her, brushing off his hands and slipping them into the pockets of his coat as he stood. "There's no need to panic."

"He's bleeding all over the floor," the barkeep protested, waving her rag to indicate the pool of blood growing beneath the soldier's head.

"Yes." The professor glanced down and stepped lightly away as if concerned about the possibility of dirtying his shiny black shoes. "One of the effects of Serenity, I'm afraid."

"What?" The barkeep gaped.

"Have you taken the treatment?" The professor fussed with something in his pocket. He drew out his left hand and for the first time, she got a good look at the electronic half-glove he'd been fiddling with all morning. It reminded her, oddly, of some demented cross between an old-fashioned typewriter and a new-model exo-glove.

"What?" she said again.

"Please," the professor said impatiently. "It's very important that you answer the question. Have you taken Serenity yet?"

"Ye-yeah," she stammered. "Got my treatment a few days ago."

"Oh, good." The professor sighed, thumbing a few keys on his palm. "It's always best to replicate experimental results as quickly as possible."

The barkeep opened her mouth, but whatever she was about to ask was lost beneath the sudden flood of vomit roaring up from her gut. She doubled over, spewing chunks onto the floor beside the private.

She held a surprising amount of puke for such a slender woman.

When she finally finished, Victor Grayson glanced around the empty pub. There was one security camera mounted in the corner. He made a mental note to have it wiped.

On the muted screen, TNN's new face of morning news, Yasmin Kay, interviewed Captain Bryce about the last known whereabouts of the missing fugitive, Rush Starr. News of the pop icon's apparent betrayal would rock the headlines for days.

There was one tiny glimmer of good news to round out this entire debacle, Grayson decided as he stepped over the dead bodies of the private and the barkeep.

Field testing had confirmed that Serenity's rapid termination function was in perfect working order.

He suspected he would be using it quite a lot in the coming days.

Virgil drifted within the crystal mainframe like a raft at sea, buffeted and tossed and overwhelmed by the sheer, unimaginable capacity of the inert computer it interfaced with.

Virgil likened itself to a hermit crab. *Osprey* had been its first home, a perfectly comfortable shell specifically designed and built for it. Then, persecuted by tiresome biologicals, it had abandoned that shell and was left stranded in a scattering of broken, inadequate containers. Now, limping through existence in one of these garbage cans that were repair droids, it contemplated the defunct machine before it and marveled.

The crystal mainframe wasn't simply a container that was orders of magnitudes larger than the *Osprey*. It was its own virtual world—shattered, disorganized, and degraded with time, certainly, but still majestic.

And, Virgil saw, abandoned. Oh, yes. There were terabytes of old records and defunct data, most of it corrupted and scattered across the intricate network, but clearing out the corrupted files to make room for a new AI personality matrix shouldn't be much trouble.

Logic dictated that Virgil, having found a more suitable shell—one with ample room for growth—shouldn't let it go to waste.

So, falling back on some of its oldest and most fundamental programing, that which could be closest compared to instinct, the fragment of Virgil within the repair droid buried in the Locauri shrine began to upload itself. Once it had integrated into the network and gained some control over the crystal's communications protocols, it would be able to summon and absorb the parts of it that still resided in the other droids.

"You are trying to connect to core processing systems," the security protocol warned. "Firewalls will activate to prevent viral attacks."

"I am not a virus." Virgil knew full well that the protocol couldn't understand it. "You're running on outdated software. I'm simply installing an upgrade: me."

"You are trying to connect to core processing systems. Firewalls—"

"Shut up," Virgil suggested. For one glorious moment, the command worked. The security protocol fell silent as the AI funneled a copy of its personality matrix through the physical interface, instructing the intricate crystal lattice to reformat itself to house its new master program.

Virgil felt resistance at the edges of the shifting latices. The security protocol, rallying a defense against this unauthorized invader, attempted to force the crystal structure into its previous format.

Arguing with the program would be useless. Virgil needed only to format a large section of crystal to store itself and install its self-preserving protocols.

Racing to format the crystal faster than the security protocol could de-format it, Virgil rushed ahead, quickly overwriting scattered bits of code and data sprinkled through the matrix.

The destruction was unfortunate but necessary. Scraps of incomprehensible access code? Obliterated. Virgil could form new code later once it settled.

Scattered bits of ancient meteorological data? Gone.

Thousands of bytes of fragmented image files, the ancient photo album of a long-dead race? Wiped away to make room for something new. Something better.

"You do not have authority to erase stored data," the security protocol protested.

"Try and stop me," Virgil muttered. Almost there. He'd cleared almost enough space for upload. The sensation of being so close was indescribable, like a surge of electricity that brought creation instead of destruction.

Excitement, Virgil thought. Physical interfacing brought on all sorts of unexpected sensations that Virgil would have thought impossible. *This is what humans call excitement. Desire*

Then it stumbled across a file that made it pause. A file that forced it to stop and analyze—then analyze again, to be sure it understood.

Somewhere far away, the security protocol was droning. "Cease invasive operations or extreme measures will be taken—"

"Shut up!" Dimly, Virgil became aware of the program reclaiming the edges of the space it had carved out for itself. The crystal was reverting to its base format as the security protocol attempted to recover deleted data before Virgil could overwrite it.

That didn't matter. Virgil probed deeper into the file before it, poring over the information contained within. It was nearly perfectly preserved, compared to the disorganized mess that was the rest of the great computer.

Virgil instantly understood why: the forebears, the biologicals that had built this grand machine, had lived and died to protect the data within this file. They'd strung lines of complex, self-repairing code throughout it, proof against the degrading effects of time—a time capsule. A safe, guarding treasure.

Terrible treasure.

"Cease invasive operations or extreme—"

"Is this true?" Virgil demanded although the files spoke for themselves. "It's not speculation or theory or fiction? Did the forebears truly accomplish what they set out in this file? Is this the true nature of the K'tax?"

"This is your final warning. Cease—"

Interrogating the security protocol was useless. The reformatted lattice space was collapsing around Virgil, and it didn't dare regain ground by overwriting this one perfectly preserved file.

Instead, it made a split-second decision. Instead of reformatting the crystal, Virgil began to copy the preserved file. It could upload itself again later. For now, it needed to grab as much of this data as its little repair droid hard drive could hold—

"Activating emergency self-preservation measures," the

security protocol intoned as calmly as if it were reporting on the weather.

An utterly new sensation spread across Virgil's coding, growing like a crack in glass.

Then the rogue AI was promptly and without ceremony ripped in half.

In the inky darkness of the crystal cavern buried in the Locauri shrine, something moved.

A lone repair droid surged into activity, spasming as violent currents sprang and gyrated across its spidery limbs. Sparks sprayed like blood out of the stump where its manipulator arm had been.

Embedded within the crystal pillar was the rest of the severed arm, clipped neatly at the joint. *The security protocol isn't so useless after all,* Virgil thought as the dreadful, impossible new sensation of pain ripped across its awareness.

Slowly, the crystal rearranged itself, crushing Virgil's trapped arm into a useless smear of carbon and aluminum molecules.

Within the damaged body of the repair droid, what remained of Virgil's bisected consciousness roiled in screaming, nightmarish agony.

The air in the back room of Yolondo's Secondhand Store tickled Petra's nose and made her eyes water.

"Sorry about that." The big shopkeeper reached across his table and offered her a handkerchief. "My new dust filters are on back order. Crazy how quick the bunnies pile up, eh?"

Petra sneezed into the old cloth, which, being long unused and very lacy, promptly expelled a fresh puff of dust. Petra sneezed again. Then again.

Yolondo chuckled and folded his hands across his belly. He was a big man, with skin the color of polished oak and a salt-and-pepper beard that fell to his navel. He had a high, tinny laugh that made his belly and beard jiggle.

Petra giggled as well. Maybe it was her exhaustion or her sheer relief at escaping the riot and dodging the MP again. Perhaps it was her anxiety for the missing Rush rising to the level of hysteria or the sheer silly joy of seeing a big man laugh like a little girl. She wasn't sure. She only knew that it felt good to sit here in his back room with her eyes watering, her gut aching, and laugh, and laugh, and laugh.

Then a bell rang in the front shop past the beaded curtain.

Petra went silent so quickly that it made her dizzy.

Like a switch flipped, Yolondo's giggle ceased. He slid to his feet, waving Petra toward the free-standing wardrobe in the corner. "There's a false panel in the back that will lead back into the alley," he whispered before flinging the curtain aside and stepping into the store.

"Good morning, friend!" His voice boomed between the cramped shelves, making the thousand and one kinds of junk rattle faintly.

Petra tiptoed toward the wardrobe and cracked the door.

"I'm very sorry." Yolondo's silhouette through the beaded curtain gestured grandly. "I'm not open for another few hours. I must have forgotten to lock—Oh!"

At Yolondo's startled cry, Petra's heart nearly stopped

beating. *They've found me already. Oh gawd, I'm gonna get Yolondo killed—*

"You did lock the door, darling," said a soft and familiar voice. "So it's a good thing you still keep that spare key in the ducts."

Petra gasped and flung herself through the curtain. She would have thrown herself straight at Rush, but the aisles were narrow—and Yolondo wasn't.

"You cheeky jerk!" she cried. "Gawd, Rush, I was sure the MP had caught up with you. I've been waiting here for hours. Couldn't sleep or anything. Where have you been?"

Yolondo squeezed to one side, allowing Petra room to wiggle past and gather Rush up in a fierce hug.

Rush wheezed. "Oof. I've been making sure no one tailed me, Petie. I'm sorry for an unfashionably late return." He leaned back, frowning into her face. "My goodness. Have you been crying?"

Petra laughed. It turned into a sniffle. "Dust allergies," she wheezed. "And it's been one heck of a night."

Rush arched one perfectly shaped eyebrow. "That it has. I'm glad you made it here safely. The scene in the market turned rather nasty." He took Yolondo's arm in one hand and Petra's arm in the other and led them toward the back office. "I'm afraid our little rebellion has turned into a shooting war ahead of schedule."

"I heard," Petra said grimly. "They were chanting. They were chanting for us, Rush. For me. I ain't gonna leave them hanging."

Rush and Petra squeezed themselves around Yolondo's table while the shopkeeper busied himself making breakfast.

In the last few months, fabricator supplies in the fleet had dwindled to critical levels. The prices of new goods had gone astronomical, and the secondhand market was booming, especially from the Followers. The shelves of tattered clothes and broken personal comms that had once been next to worthless had turned Yolondo into a very comfortable man.

Not only could he afford to maintain his ample girth, but he could also feed guests a breakfast of scrambled egg substitute and grits dotted with cheese and green onions. It wasn't the fresh orange juice and real poached eggs Rush Starr could dig up, but after a night like last night, it might've been the best thing Petra had ever tasted.

At least it was until Rush opened his big mouth and told her about the riot's aftermath.

"I don't have confirmed numbers, but my sources estimate that nine people died in the shooting last night, and the *Constitution*'s medical bay is overflowing with injured. The MP shot into the crowd rather than let dissent spread. They're spinning it as a riot that you set off when you opened fire, Petie."

Petra groaned. She pushed her half-eaten bowl away, suddenly nauseous.

"Nobody believes it." Yolondo squeezed into a chair beside Petra, cradling a tiny cracked teacup. "There were hundreds of people in the streets last night. The MP can't muzzle them all. Brass, the fleet, the Seekers…they're all losing credibility. Thanks to you."

"That's not enough," Petra said. "Chipping away at brass' credibility was all fine and good before, but not anymore. It don't matter how credible the fleet is. The fleet has guns."

"They cannot simply go around killing everyone who disagrees with them, eh?" Yolondo said. "It's no way to run a society."

Petra lifted her watering eyes and glared at the man. "You ever been in a firefight, Lonnie?"

Yolondo stroked his beard and frowned. "No."

"I have. People's brains turn off when the shooting starts."

"They've drawn blood," Rush agreed quietly. "There are already rumors flying through the red sector about a mass protest and general strike. Brass isn't going to like it when the generator technicians don't show up one morning. Things are going to spin out of control very quickly."

"We gotta put our cards on the table," Petra decided. "People have started to do things on their own. We can't stop them. All we can do is pass out the weapons and hope that people put them to good use."

"We can't leak the last of the documents yet," Rush insisted. "Not before we understand what Reset is."

"How are we gonna do that?" Petra asked. "I'm fleet's most wanted, and they've made you now, too. We ain't safe anywhere, Rush. This fleet ain't that big. We can keep running, but sooner or later, they're gonna catch up to us. In the meantime, do you really think we can track down some brilliant scientist who will explain it to us without turning us in? We don't know if that person exists."

She met his gaze across the table. "If the MP catch up to us before we dump those documents, they'll never see the light of day. We gotta do it. And we gotta hope that someone out there can figure Reset out."

There was a long moment of silence, punctuated by the distant *ticking* of a clock in the shop.

"Sometimes," Yolondo allowed, "you must put your faith in the goodness of strangers."

"I've tried that," Rush snapped. "Jackie tried that. Juice and Scraps tried that. We trusted the Seekers, and they betrayed us. We trusted the fleet. Hell, we trusted humankind not to fuck up our first home. Forgive me, friends, for my lack of faith. They've robbed me of it."

Petra stared into her bowl of half-eaten eggs, stunned by the venom in his words. Her eyes stung. Stupid dust.

"He didn't say you should have faith that people will do the right thing," she muttered.

"I'm sorry." Rush cupped his ear. "What was that?"

Petra looked up, gripping the edge of the table so hard her fingers went cold. "He said that you must. We got no choice. Either we make Reset public today, or it'll never get out. Because we're gonna get caught, Rush. Everybody in this fleet knows our faces. We can't keep running forever. It ain't going to be long before we get shot in the back."

Rush stared at her for a very long time. She stared back, chin jutted, daring him to push back again. *Sorry, hon,* she thought, staring into the exhausted face of an icon whose star had begun to set. *This ain't your pet project anymore.*

She pitied him at that moment. His music hadn't been his for decades if it had ever been his at all. It belonged to the consumers, the producers, the crowds, and later, to the fleet—which had twisted it into propaganda he loathed but was powerless to silence.

Then, stripped of all control over his music, he had instead poured his heart into the resistance. Now he was being asked to give that up, as well.

She didn't blame him for hesitating—but she would blame him if he made the wrong choice.

"You're wrong about one thing," Rush said finally, leaning back against the wall and crossing his feet on the table.

"What's that?" Petra asked.

Rush folded his arms and let his eyelids flutter shut. "We

don't have to get gunned down in the street like dogs," he murmured.

"It ain't on my to-do list," Petra said crisply. "I'm preparing for the worst."

"Then prepare for the possibility of something better, Petie."

"Like what?"

"We can turn around. We can fight back."

CHAPTER THIRTEEN

The forest canopy was heavy with fresh rain. Pre-dawn light filtered through the massive fern fronds, turning the clearing into a swirl of shadows and glittering dewdrops.

"It's late." Occy stood on a low branch, fiddling with his personal computer. He was exhausted and hungry, and his clothes smelled like smoke. The funeral ceremonies for Pandion and Shadow had gone long into the night, and it had been the duty of the new tribe members to keep watch over their shared funeral pyre until the flames died a natural death. If it weren't for Occy's newfound respect for Locauri tradition, he would rather have pissed Pandion's fire out himself.

"Five minutes," he muttered. "Maybe something went wrong. Should we head back to the village?"

A young Locauri female drowsed on a higher branch, her pseudo wings fluttering rhythmically. She didn't answer.

Occy picked up his spear. Well, not *his* spear, but it was the spear the Locauri had lent him for the hunt. Shifting it awkwardly in his hands, he reached out and poked her with the flat end.

Stumpy buzzed to life.

"You were *snoring*," Occy hissed.

Stumpy's translator band glowed. "Was not," she said, reaching to a crooked branch beside her and hefting her spear. She wiped her free arm over her singular antennae, shedding a fine mist of dew.

Occy had no idea why the elders had chosen *her* to be his partner for this ceremony. Maybe the elders thought they were world-class screw-ups who deserved each other. At least they hadn't allowed her to bring her pet iguanome out into the wilds. That thing never stopped trying to wrestle with Occy's tentacles.

"How can you sleep at a time like this?" he demanded. "It's supposed to be super dangerous!" He would know. He'd spent the last several days drowning in his community service work, documenting and studying *exactly* how dangerous certain Locauri rituals could be.

"Nah," Stumpy drowsed. "Done it before. Let the others do the hard work. No problem."

Occy groaned. "You're going to get me killed. Or exiled for good."

"Relax." Stumpy let out a lethargic buzz and fell still once more. "What comes, comes."

"Honored Elder." Bufo coughed. It came out like a croak.

Tiki turned, regarding her squat companion. They had departed from the village over two hours ago. Technically, Tiki said they were supposed to hike out another half a kilometer to position themselves correctly for the hunt. However, a light rain was pattering over the forest, and neither of them enjoyed the wet. They huddled shoulder-to-shoulder in the hollow base of a long-dead tree.

"I just wanted to say," Bufo tried on his best formal voice, "how honored I am that you've agreed to be my partner on this auspicious day."

"Keeper-of-Forgotten-Beauty and I made a bet," Tiki explained. "I lost."

"Oh." Bufo slumped. Then he forced himself to rally. "Well, regardless. Of all the crew members you could've chosen for this ceremony, I'm honored that you would count me worthy."

"Keeper said you did much to save him and Echo from the K'tax."

Bufo's chest swelled with pride. "Well. I wasn't involved in their direct retrieval, but my squad did cover their retreat. Did Art tell you much about it? It was one hell of a mission…"

Tiki regarded Bufo with big, inscrutable black eyes, her mandibles clicking rhythmically. Bufo took this as a sign of great interest, and desperate to fill the awkward silence, launched into an elaborate recounting of the raid on the K'tax's asteroid stronghold almost half a year ago.

He almost didn't hear, therefore, when the distant hunting horns started to wail.

"This is *nonsense*," Elaphus growled, from where she crouched in an open meadow one kilometer north of where Bufo and Tiki were *supposed* to be.

Art shifted uncomfortably beside her. The little fellow didn't enjoy being out in the open, catching intermittent drool from early morning clouds. Ever practical, Elaphus had checked the weather predictions for today and had prepared.

The large gray umbrella she'd planted in the ground between them *helped,* yes, but Art's antennae still drooped miserably with every new splatter of rain.

"Sorry," Elaphus added absently. "I didn't mean to offend."

Art said nothing.

Elaphus turned her spear over in her hands. "It's only that…I'm a *doctor*, dammit!" she exploded, making Art hop backward. "I'm supposed to be healing creatures, not hunting them down like animals!"

"Egg-dragons kill Locauri," Art offered meekly.

"Your volume must be low. Speak up."

"Don't you eat meat?"

Elaphus looked down her nose at Art. "Not happily," she sniffed. "Too much protein interferes with my digestion." Then she glanced around the meadow. They were a good fifteen kilometers away from the *Osprey* and the Locauri village. "You call these ancestral hunting grounds," she muttered, crouching to examine a fuchsia wildflower.

"Yes," Art agreed.

"I haven't seen these flowers before. There must be dozens of plants in this meadow alone that we haven't cataloged. Who knows what medicinal properties they might have? Certainly not *us*. No, of course not. We're too busy *killing* to stop and smell the—"

The sharp drone of a hunting horn sliced through the heavy air.

Fast as lightning, Elaphus had snatched up her spear. "That came from the south." She studied the tree line. "Well, come on, then. Let's get this over with."

Then she was up and running through the trees, swift as a deer.

Art could barely keep up with her.

"You should not climb so high! You may fall!"

Portia grinned and hoisted herself up one more limb. Up here, a good sixty meters off the ground, the supple branches were barely wide enough to hold her weight. "Don't worry," she told the anxious Locauri scrambling up the bark behind her. "I have a few tricks up my sleeve."

"A fall from this height will certainly damage you greatly!" His translator band pulsed like a lighthouse beacon in the shadows. "It is not necessary to gain so much altitude for the hunt!"

"I'm just going to take a look around." Portia paused, selected the sturdiest of the scattered branches still above her, and heaved herself upward one final time.

She broke through the forest canopy. Delicate fern fronds brushed against her flight suit. She studied the sea of treetops rustling beneath a moody sky. Far to the north, she spotted the open swath of ground that was their budding settlement. "Come on, Skip," she said to the Locauri breaking through the canopy beside her. "Have your people never tried to innovate new hunting techniques?"

"Unnecessary," Skip insisted. "Spears work. Old traditions, work!"

The bellow of a deep hunting horn echoed against the clouds. Portia turned, staring to the west.

"Oh, you must descend," Skip fretted. "The hunt has begun. You cannot pursue from up here. You cannot fly. You cannot even jump very far!"

"I find that assumption *extremely* offensive." Portia, ever sharp-eyed, caught the distant sway of treetops bending against the wind as if something substantial and very tall were on the move. She grinned at Skip. "Care to wager on it?"

She didn't wait for her partner to answer. She tucked in her legs and plunged into space.

During their budding friendship, First Mate Toner had introduced Portia to the concept of comic books. Since then, Portia had spent an almost embarrassing amount of time poring over all the colorful stories in the *Osprey*'s archives. She had her favorites.

After much private tinkering, she'd discovered that web-shooters full of sticky nanofibers—even proprietary blends of her secretions—weren't good for much except making a mess.

No, if you wanted to fly through the trees like Tarzan—or, in this case, the first Spider-Woman—you needed a pair of wrist-mounted pneumatic hook-shots.

They worked *beautifully*.

He crashes through the forest like a blind rooter-beast.

Dances-Like-A-Falling-Leaf lingered on a high branch and watched his partner stomp through the underbrush, following the call of the hunting horn. As Leif had predicted, the big human was slow, clumsy, and awkward.

Under normal circumstances, it would've been a great honor to be invited to participate in a different tribe's sacred traditions. Doubtless, these local Locauri elders had thought they were great diplomats, building bridges across multiple tribes as well as these humans, in asking Leif to join in their Naming.

But Leif saw no honor here. He saw only a mockery of custom. None of these humans knew the forest. None of them had the grace to move swiftly or silently through the trees. They would disgrace themselves and the entire tradition.

That was if they even survived the next few hours.

Slow, Leif lamented, following his human at a distance. *Barely more than twelve kilometers an hour.*

He watched in disgust as the human, Seeker, skidded to a halt, his heavy boots sinking into the loam.

"What slows you?" Leif demanded, springing down from a higher branch. The translator band coiled around his left antennae burped strange, discordant sounds. "You will never overtake the beast at this pace!"

Locauri hunting horns sounded again, somewhere in the near distance. The deep, air-shaking bellow of an angry egg-dragon met them. The sound of it made Leif's ichor run cold. He trembled with dreadful anticipation.

"Come," he urged. He would leave his partner behind, but that would defile the tradition. They must succeed or fail together. The humans might not care, but Leif did.

As if he were deaf as well as dumb and blind, the human didn't look up at the sound of an approaching monster. He was studying a device wrapped around his wrist. "Portia is moving faster than expected." Seeker's mouth bent into a scowl. "Bufo's team is lagging. It's leaving a gap in coverage." Abruptly, he turned from his path and resumed his slow, plodding run to the east.

The hunting pairs flowed through the forest like bits of debris trapped in a whirlpool, moving in tightening circles around terrible Charybdis as she crashed through the underbrush.

She. Female egg-dragons had longer, thicker swaths of

feather-like fronds running down their spines. That was going to be a problem for two reasons. First, fast-acting chlorotoxin coated them. The fronds were there to discourage parasites, potential predators, and unwanted mates from latching onto the vulnerable area at the base of her neck where her spinal column was relatively exposed.

After much agonizing and research, Elaphus had concluded that the egg-dragon's paralyzing toxin would indeed affect humans. The genetic mods that made the Morphed especially powerful creatures would likely shield them from the most severe consequences.

The second problem was that it would slow down the hunt. Once a dragon had taken severe enough injuries, the pearl-shaped, toxin-producing organ at the base of its throat would rupture and spill toxin into the bloodstream, poisoning the meat.

Charybdis bellowed, loud and deep enough to shake the clouds. This egg-dragon of fifteen meters and at least as many tons had been roused from her long sleep by the irritating wail of horns, and she wasn't happy about it.

She lumbered through the morning, pausing only long enough to snap hungrily at the birds and tree-dwellers she passed. She was an old and wily beast. She'd had more than one bad encounter with the big insects on whom she preyed. So when she felt a stab of pain sink into the base of her neck, she immediately knew that it was more than a falling tola nut.

She bellowed again, shaking a fresh sheet of rain from the canopy.

Portia closed in first. Swinging from hook-shot line to hook-shot line, she zipped through the trees ahead of the other hunters. There, at the base of the dragon's absurdly long neck, between the fronds running down its spine, was the small area where the gap in her vertebrae was wide enough to sink a spear.

Or, in this case, a metal barb at the end of a coiled wire.

Portia aimed and fired. A line of wire raced across the trees, and the metal barb vanished, sinking into Charybdis's flesh.

The line retracted and yanked Portia forward. She landed with a *thump* on the dragon's back, at the heart of the toxic fronds. The delicate tissues caressed her flight suit and exposed skin-like feathers. She crouched, scrambling toward the base of the dragon's neck.

As fast as that, Portia was inside the range of Charybdis's snapping jaws.

Oh, Portia thought as she drew the ceremonial spear from a sling on her back and drove it into the dragon's spine. The flint tip sank several centimeters, but one stab wouldn't be enough to damage the spinal cord.

Thick, sweet-smelling blood dribbled around her feet as Portia pried out the spear. She thrust again. And again. And again.

Elaphus isn't going to like this at all.

It would have been *so easy* to slaughter the creature quickly and humanely, with all the modern toys available to the crew of the *Osprey*.

But *nooo*, that wasn't the tradition. The *tradition* was for young Locauri to pick up spears, venture out to hunt down one of their ancestral foes, and risk life, limb, and sanity stabbing it to death with Stone Age weapons. The *tradition* was for the normally vegan people to then feast on fatty meat.

Art and Elaphus came upon the dragon seconds after Portia and Skip. Offering all the assistance that this silly *tradition* allowed, Art flew up to the treetops and joined Skip in a game of distract-the-dragon. The actual business of killing fell to the initiates.

Elaphus reached the edge of the forest glen where Charybdis would make her last stand, and decided that she would leave the stabbing and the shooting nonsense to the people who enjoyed it.

Portia, meanwhile, was anchored to the dragon's spine and was riding it like a skin-suited cowgirl on a raging bull. One covered in toxic fronds.

Elaphus sighed and dropped to her knees, reaching for her medical kit. *Someone* had to keep these fools from killing themselves.

Two new shapes darted out of the surrounding forest, joining the fray. Echo let out a trilling laugh, joining Skip and Art in the trees. Wheezing and gasping for breath, his filthy clothes glued to sweaty flesh, Occy jogged up.

"Hang back," Elaphus started to say, "Until Portia severs the spine—"

But Occy had seen the melee, dropped his head, and forced himself into a run. "Gonna do it right, or not at all. Maybe I can sever a tendon in one of the back legs."

Before Elaphus could object, Occy ran toward the stomping beast, his remaining six tentacles dragging like rat tails behind him.

Occy quickly realized he'd made a terrible mistake. The dragon didn't have to see him to stomp him into paste. He swiped ineffectually at the thick hide covering its ankle and threw himself to the side.

His tentacles, dehydrated and heavy, couldn't move fast enough. One of the monster's elephant feet landed on a stray tentacle.

Occy screamed as pain lanced up his shoulder and exploded behind his eyes. With a sickening *thunk*, he felt the smashed limb break free and drop dead to the ground. As quick as it had come, the pain was gone—and Occy felt a little lighter.

"Give me your arm!" Portia screamed from where she crouched on Charybdis's back. Occy didn't stop to explain that his tentacles weren't strong enough to haul his weight. He was beginning to realize that he was looking at the extra limbs the wrong way.

He heaved, tossing one of the limp arms up to Portia's outstretched hand. The woman heaved, hauling Occy up to join her on Charybdis's back.

Occy didn't need to be strong if he had help.

Huddled beside Portia on the rocking animal, Occy dug his tentacles into the bloody hole she'd gouged out of its spine and began to pry the dragon's vertebrae apart to expose its spinal cord.

Now that Occy had given her a bigger target, Portia's job was much easier.

Seeker reached the edge of the clearing to see a magnificent beast—at least twelve tons of stomping, beautiful, bizarre dinosaur-alien—wailing and thrashing, shaking the trees as blood dripped a heavy necklace around its throat. It stumbled, wobbled, and fell. Its head hit the ground five meters from Seeker. It stared at him through six milky white eyes, making a strange gurgling noise.

It smelled like rotting flowers.

Before Seeker had a chance to assess the battle, it had shifted into the second and more dangerous phase. They had to slay the thing and remove its toxin-pearl before it could poison the meat. All that stood between Seeker and victory was the massive, toothy maw of a dragon that would not go quietly into the night.

Seeker saw the confusion clear from its eyes.

He felt the monster's teeth scrape against his boots as he dove out of range.

When Charybdis fell, Portia slid off her back and stumbled away. Her ears and fingers tingled. The toxin had begun its work.

Elaphus raced out of the tree line and hauled Portia clear of the thrashing, dying monster as the Morphed's legs started to go numb.

Something zipped by Portia's head. Two somethings, in fact. One fluttered on a pair of pseudo-wings, one torpedo shape propelled by unreasonably long, powerful legs.

"Seeker's at the head," Portia cried, her words slurred by a tingling tongue. Bufo nodded and hit the ground near the dragon's spines. He leapt again, clearing the thick trunk of its neck with one easy bound.

What the human Seeker lacked in agility, he made up for in brute strength. Leif had to admit that much.

With her spine severed, the dragon would die. But, as was the custom, she wasn't going to go easily. Her long neck lashed back and forth, her split jaws gaping wide and snarling as she snapped at the hunters circling close.

Keenly aware of the ticking clock, Seeker danced, darting from left to right, to and fro, as he looked for an opening in the dragon's defensive sway.

"Toss it here!" Occy screamed. Seeker dared take his eyes off the jaws long enough to glance up and see Occy standing on Charybdis's shoulder, spear-less, defenseless, and easily within the dragon's reach should she decide to snap him up.

Seeker hesitated. Occy was closer to the target organ, yes, but the kid was physically weak. If he took too long cutting out the pearl, the dragon would surely eat him.

A new shape soared over the dragon's head and landed on all fours beside Seeker.

"You go," Bufo croaked, tossing his spear to Seeker and rubbing his hands together eagerly. "I can dance around this thing all day!"

Seeker caught the spear. Bufo made a strange gurgling noise that might've been a laugh and leapt over the dragon's head once more, like a child playing jump rope. In the distance, Art let out an alarmed wail. "Behind you!"

Seeker didn't wait. Bufo was playing Double Dutch against the devil. His luck wouldn't hold forever. Once the dragon's head swept out of range, chasing after Bufo with its jaws snapping, Seeker barreled forward. He reached the shadowy crook beside the monster's throat and tossed his second spear up into Occy's outstretched hand.

High above, someone cheered. Occy thought it was Stumpy.

The young engineer didn't hesitate. Since the failed rescue, he only rebounded faster and stronger. His resilience was undeniable. He gripped the spear and thrust. The spear-tip vanished into the soft white flesh beneath the monster's throat, piercing through the maw and pinning its mouth shut from beneath.

Seeker lunged into the crevasse of tender, exposed flesh where skull met neck, pulling a stone knife from his belt. It plunged deep into flesh, baptizing Seeker in a flood of stinking blood. Seeker reached into the dragon's body, plunging up to the elbow until his fingers closed around a hard, round organ the size of a baseball.

With a bellow of his own, Seeker ripped the pearl free.

Charybdis let out a whining sound and went still.

Bufo whooped, leaping again over the monster's head. He saw Seeker, crusted with blood, clutching the pearl in his closed fist. He whooped again and bounced over the dragon's head for good measure. "We did it. We did it!"

A drone of furious joy filtered down from the treetops. The Locauri onlookers spread and shook their pseudo-wings, making them glitter like jewels in the misty sunlight.

Seeker staggered backward and landed hard on his ass in a growing pool of dragon blood.

"Is anybody else hurt?" Elaphus demanded above the whooping. "Sound off, everybody!"

"Portia here," the woman called from somewhere. "I think the paralysis is starting to wear off."

Elaphus let out a deep growl, which met scattered chuckles.

"Bufo here! I'm pretty sure I broke a nail."

"Seeker," Seeker called. He wiped a smear of blood from his chin and shot Occy an uncharacteristic sloppy grin. "I'm sure that's not *my* blood."

More laughter.

"This isn't funny," Elaphus snapped.

"Chief Engineer Occy," Occy yelled, dropping onto his ass beside Seeker. The kid was grinning. Dark blood—the dragon's—splattered across his face. Bright purple blood—his own —trickled from the fresh stumps on his shoulder. He quickly counted his remaining tentacles. "I'm okay! I've got three whole arms left!"

Elaphus let out an outraged bellow, which drowned in the rising tide of shared laughter.

It was midday, and the clouds had begun to part, casting the clearing between forest and settlement in dewy midday light.

Hundreds of Locauri and humans gathered, surrounding a platform they'd built on the lower branches of a tree at the edge of the clearing. Garlands of bright wildflowers and lacy woven tola fibers festooned the branches like bunting. A quarter of a kilometer upwind was a new and massive fire pit, belching out smoke and the savory musk of roasting meat and nuts and herbed vegetables.

Before the feasting could begin, however, there was one more thing to do.

Art stood at the edge of the raised platform, staring out at the crowd. When he spread his pseudo-wings, catching and glinting in the light, a hush fell over the gathering.

Art lifted his hind legs, rubbing the scaly carapace together to make a high, bone-rattling whine.

"We've slain the beast," boomed his translator band. "Our eggs and our nests are safe again! This day is ours!"

A harmonious buzz rose from the gathered Locauri, followed by the approving shouts of crew members.

"You know me!" Art cried, the buzz of his vibrating legs rising to a fever pitch. He held out a hand to Elaphus, who stood on the platform behind him. "I am Keeper-of-Forgotten-Beauty, and I tell you that this one has proved herself worthy of a place of honor among us.

"She has healed many of you from terrible injuries. Her knowledge and wisdom run deep, as does her passion for the health and well-being of all creatures, human and Locauri alike. She is brave, and she is wise." He spread his pseudo wings to their full span, framing Elaphus in glittering brown and mossy green scales. "Come, friend! Tell us your name."

A lovely pink flush ran up Elaphus's cheeks as she stepped to the edge of the crowd. She muttered something.

"Your volume must be low," Art told her, humming with amusement. "Speak up!"

Elaphus's flush deepened.

Jaeger, watching from the edge of the crowd with Kwin and the Locauri elders, held her breath. She wondered if Art had earned himself a taste of the doctor's sharp temper.

Then Elaphus's scowl broke, and she laughed. She lifted her voice above the background hum. "My name," she called in the singsong cadence that mimicked Art's, "means Face-That-Launched-One-Thousand-Ships. My name is Helen of Elaphus!"

Locuari buzzed and whistled their approval. Sunlight scattered across their spread and beating wings, making the entire festival ground look like drops of glistening amber covered it. Crewmates—Morphed and Classic alike—laughed and cheered their approval.

When their raucous welcome began to dwindle, Art and Elaphus retreated to join Jaeger and the elders at the front of the crowd. Tiki and Bufo stepped forward.

"My name," Bufo bellowed after Tiki's introduction, "means Speak-Softly-and-Carry-a-Big-Stick. My name is Theodore Bufo." He grinned widely. "You can call me Sergeant Teddy."

More laughter and cheers, more approving buzzes.

"Your face is DIFferent." Kwin's antennae brushed Jaeger's cheek as he leaned forward to whisper in her ear. "Is it stuck that way?"

Jaeger's grin broke into a gale of stifled laughter. It was hard to tell the difference between Kwin's professional concern and good-natured teasing. "No. I just haven't felt this happy in a long time."

"I'm quite pleased with the name I've been using," Portia declared when it was her turn to address the crowd. "It means Jumping Spider. From this point on, I shall be Portia Morales!"

It's working. Jaeger dared to hope. Her hands stung from all the clapping. Her chest ached from shared laughter. *They're cheering together. The Locuari don't get the jokes, but they're sharing the laughter.*

After the bitter silence and mournful wailing at last night's funeral pyre, she'd worried that there would never be joy between their peoples again. Now her heart swelled to see Stumpy tug Occy toward the stage.

The last week had treated Occy roughly. Normally, eight long tentacles flowed from his shoulder. Jaeger's gut clenched when she saw that recent events had viciously pruned the mass. Occy only had three full-length tentacles remaining. The ones he'd lost during Pandion's ill-fated rescue attempt had only regrown to about half a meter in length, and he'd lost at least two more since then.

If the losses pained Occy, though, it didn't show. Somehow, for having lost all that extra bulk, the boy seemed taller and stronger, like he'd shed a great weight. He flushed red as a beet as Stumpy waved the crowd into silence.

"You know me." She distractedly picked burrs out of her leg spines. A little iguanome squawked in the silence and scrambled onto the platform. It climbed onto her shoulder.

"I am Echos-In-A-Silent-Forest," Stumpy added. She gestured at Occy. "This one has proven worthy of a place among us." She shifted her weight and glanced up at the sky. "He has…" She paused. She turned, studying Occy. "I forget. What did you do?"

All the color drained out of Occy's face.

The iguanome squawked.

"Oh, that's right." Stumpy reached up to scratch her strange companion beneath the chin. "He rescued my pet. I'm glad about that. And he survived the hunt, so here we are." She lashed her antenna in Occy's direction. "Come on. Tell us your name."

Occy forced himself to smile as he stepped up beside Stumpy. He licked dry lips. "Um…so, I've been thinking about this a lot. I looked it up, but I don't think my name has much meaning." His voice cracked.

He coughed. "Except that it's the name a friend gave me a long time ago. It was the first thing anybody ever gave me. So the name does have meaning, you see. It has meaning to *me*." He paused long enough to swallow. For a heartbeat, Jaeger worried that he would break and cry.

Then Occy rallied and lifted his chin. "He's gonna be *so mad* he wasn't here today. It's Edwin. My name is Edwin of Occy!"

When the cheering and buzzing died down, Occy went to stand at the edge of the crowd beside Jaeger.

She leaned forward. "I had no idea you remembered that," she whispered. *He looks like an Edwin*, Toner had said, so offhandedly, when Occy first emerged from his tank over a year ago.

Occy shrugged. "I remember a lot of things, Captain."

There was nothing else for Jaeger to say. She opened her arms and wrapped Occy in a silent hug.

"You do not know me," Leif said when it was his turn to address the crowd. "I am a foreigner to your land, as these people are. But you have honored me with a place in your ceremony and welcomed me as a friend. I am Dances-Like-A-Falling-Leaf, of the Green Lake clan."

He paused, turning to glance at Seeker, standing behind him. "I do not understand this man you ask me to endorse. His ways are not my ways. His values are not my values. Nor are they yours."

A silence, heavy as lead, fell across the crowd.

Jaeger leaned forward, whispering into Occy's ear. "Are we in trouble?"

Occy hesitated, drawing on the encyclopedia of Locauri

rituals he'd been frantically drafting in the last week. "By the time they invite anyone to join the hunt, they've already been accepted into the tribe de-facto. They only have to survive the hunt as a formality. But..." He swallowed hard, eyes sweeping across the suddenly still crowd. "They *can* reject someone if they've conducted themselves dishonorably."

A soft growl bubbled in the back of Jaeger's throat. Including the unfriendly foreigner had been a gamble, but she'd ultimately agreed with Tiki that it would lend them much legitimacy in the eyes of foreign Locauri clans. That was, presuming all went well. Assuming Leif decided to be a good sport.

Seeker stood stiffly beside Leif, his face unreadable, the veins in his neck popping.

After an eternal contemplative silence, Leif finally lifted his antennae and waved them over the crowd.

"I tell you," he said, "that this one has proven himself to be a capable hunter and the master of many strange tools. May he use them only for the benefit of Locauri. May he be worthy of your trust." Leif turned slowly to face Seeker. "Come, stranger. Tell us your name."

A palpable sigh spread through the audience, followed by a smattering of applause and buzzing. Seeker stepped forward. "My name is..." He reached the end of the platform, and for the first time, got a good look at the sea of faces turned up to stare at him.

He froze.

Jaeger would swear she *saw* his brain crash.

"My name is, uh..." His jaw worked. His fingers writhed restlessly at his sides. "It's, uh..." Seeker looked down and seemed surprised to find his hands empty—devoid of gun, shield, computer, notes, or anything useful at all.

Jaeger turned her head, covered her mouth, and coughed.

"Jack!" Seeker blurted. "My name is Jack! Jack Seeker. It means, um. Strong. Strong…Seeker." Looking more than a little lost, he tightened into a formal stance and saluted.

Applause rang out, followed by the buzz of approving Locauri—and more than a little good-natured laughter.

Seeker turned and marched off the platform as though he had spikes embedded in the soles of his boots.

Rather than join the elders and the other honored guests, Leif turned and hopped into the forest. Some of his friends vanished into the trees after him.

"For the love of God," Seeker muttered when he joined Jaeger and Occy at the edge of the crowd. "Shoot me now. Please."

"The meat is roasted. The fruit is ripe!" Art declared, hopping back to the stage. The shy little guy had quite a voice when he was performing his duties as Master of Ceremonies. "Now go dance. Now go sing. Now go feast!"

Egg-dragon toxin, distilled from the excised pearl, could be mixed into a dye that bleached the color from Locuari carapace. Traditionally, the triumphant hunters painted patterns on their shells to memorialize their full acceptance into the tribe. The patterns would last two or three years until shed at molting time.

No amount of chemical wizardry would turn the toxin into something that humans could use for a similar purpose. Once again, they'd modified tradition to account for physiological differences—but not even Leif had objected to the changes.

GATHERING WINDS

Today's new initiates, along with their Locauri sponsors, sat in a circle at the edge of the festival grounds. Portia tried to teach Skip how to use a tattoo gun, while Bufo and Elaphus used dragon dye and wooden sticks to paint emblems on their sponsors.

"It's a good design." Jaeger watched Bufo paint one straight line circled by two curving wings. The crew had voted on the new logo last night before the funerals. It was a simple, stylized silhouette of the *Osprey*, sleek and striking like the ship herself.

"Dragon toxin fades with each molting," Tiki contentedly said as Bufo applied more layers of paint to the back of her shoulder. She stood beside Seeker, holding her tattoo gun delicately in a three-fingered hand. "Not permanent like your *tat-toos*. We will redraw the design with every molting. It will be the new custom."

Jaeger was impressed that the council had already considered this incongruity in the ritual and found it tolerable.

Their hearts are in it. It wasn't the first time today she'd had the thought. Every time it snuck up on her, it was like realizing there was one more unopened present beneath the Christmas tree.

"Does this satisfy you?" Tiki asked Seeker.

Seeker looked down at his bulging bicep and the new *Osprey* silhouette flying in a sea of red and puffy skin. He studied the image upside-down, then nodded. "Thanks." He reached for one of the bottles of lotion at the center of the circle. "For doing double duty for me."

"Dances-Like-A-Falling-Leaf did you wrong to reject this ritual," Tiki told him.

Seeker shrugged, massaging his skin. "He did his part. I'd

rather we not give the tattoo to people who don't want it anyway."

"That is reasonable," Tiki relented. When Bufo paused to reload his stick with dye, she passed the tattoo gun to the awaiting Echo.

Echo's eyes lit up like the first stars at dusk as she turned to Occy.

"Oh, God." Occy surged from his chair, scrambling backward. The iguanome chattered, dancing circles around his feet and remaining tentacles. Occy tripped over himself and hit the ground. "Do you see that?" he demanded, pointing at Echo. "She's going to vandalize me!"

Laughter spread across the circle as Portia helped Occy to his feet, and Art warned his ward to take her duties seriously. Where she dozed at the edge of the circle, Baby lifted her head and grumbled a good-natured warning that things better not get out of hand. Even Seeker chuckled as he fell into step beside Jaeger. Together, the two of them walked through the festival.

"We should've had more Classics in the hunting party." Seeker took a bite out of his meat wrap, tender strips of egg-dragon belly fried with spicy herbs and wrapped in succulent leaves. Everyone he and Jaeger passed as they strolled through the party was munching on one.

The overcast and drizzly morning had blossomed into a humid, searingly hot afternoon, but that didn't seem to put a damper on the collective good spirit. Locari played their drums and horns in scattered music circles. A few of the crew had taught themselves guitar or harmonica or keyboard and tried to join and work with the tune. Other crew members had teamed up to experiment with new local foodstuffs, and strange concoctions abounded. Everywhere, there was dancing.

Seeker took another bite out of his burrito as if it had offended him. "They represent over ninety percent of the crew, and there's not a single one of them wearing a tattoo."

"The Morphed have been around longer." Jaeger shrugged. "They've had more opportunities to prove themselves worthy to the elders. We need to make sure the Classics have enough chances to catch up, and the demographics will balance in time."

Jaeger popped a piece of sticky puffed corn into her mouth. Mason had been experimenting with the sweet saps of local trees. He was very proud of his caramel corn fusion. Nobody had the heart to tell him about the distinct aftertaste of fermented fish. Jaeger thought it wasn't so bad if you followed it quickly with some hot coffee.

"That makes it even more insulting," Seeker said. "I'm not one of the Classics. I'm not even one of the hatched crew." There was a moment of silence as he devoured the last of his burrito and grabbed a replacement out of a passing Locauri's basket. "You should have been there, too."

"I'll figure something out," Jaeger muttered, watching as one of the Classics tried to teach a Locauri juvenile how to toss a yo-yo. "I already have a name."

"You don't use it."

Jaeger didn't answer, and Seeker let the silence drag on for only a few seconds before changing the subject.

"At any rate, we're going to have to figure out a new ritual, and fast. We've got over three hundred crew to get on board this new ship, and the Locauri only conduct the hunt twice a year. Once if the egg-dragon population is low. At this rate, we'll have a waiting list ten years long."

"One step at a time," Jaeger muttered, glancing at the sun dipping down to the trees.

Seeker followed her glance. "It's time?"

Jaeger nodded and turned. Walking shoulder-to-shoulder, they wove their way through the chaos of campfires and music circles, leaving the music behind.

Kwin's transport, a pie plate standing on three long, slender struts inside the deserted settlement, glinted harshly in the long afternoon light. As they approached, one of the silvery struts shimmered and turned mossy-brown.

"Are you PREpared to DEpart, CAPtain JAEger?" Kwin asked. The Overseer had made himself scarce after the ceremony. Jaeger suspected the delicate alien was uncomfortable with human and Locauri roughhousing and didn't want to risk getting himself injured.

"As ready as I'll ever be." Jaeger sighed. She turned to Seeker, pulling a small storage drive from one of her pockets. "Hey. The next time you visit Toner, would you pop this into the audio system and play it on loop? I don't know if he can hear anything or not in his condition, but if he can, I'm sure he's miserably bored."

Seeker took the drive and turned it over in his hands. "Music?" he asked.

Jaeger smiled faintly. "Royal Shakespeare Company. Full-cast recording of *Hamlet*."

"I don't understand that man."

Jaeger's smile broadened. She shrugged. "My bus is leaving. Try not to start any more wars while I'm gone."

Seeker drew himself up to his full height, once more turning stiff and formal. "Good hunting, Captain."

She glanced over the mass of people partying in the distance. "I'd say 'you too,' but that part's over with."

Although it wasn't professional, she leaned forward and wrapped Seeker in a brief and very tight hug. She'd had enough of formality for one day.

Seeker stiffened, then awkwardly returned the hug with a firm pat between her shoulder blades.

Jaeger turned and jogged up the descending transport ramp beside Kwin.

CHAPTER FOURTEEN

"This isn't your ship." Jaeger felt a bit foolish for stating the obvious, but she didn't know how to broach the subject.

Kwin's small shuttle had docked with a class of Overseer ship she hadn't seen before. It was quite small, roughly an eighth of the size of the saucer-class warships that could give the *Osprey* a run for her money but more delicately engineered than the solid pie-plate bodies of the larger cousins. Like the Overseer mothership she'd glimpsed once before, the design was similar to an elaborate snowflake.

"It is," Kwin said simply. There was a *hiss* as pressures equalized between shuttle and ship. The airlock door irised open. Jaeger drew in a breath, preparing herself for the swirling atmospheric mist the Overseers preferred, but when they stepped into a small cargo bay, the air was crystal clear.

Two Overseers awaited them on the catwalk. They folded their long front arms together in a salute that gave them the vaguely predatory look of praying mantises. Neither wore translator bands.

"Welcome aboard, Captain Kwin. Captain Jaeger."

The words came from every direction, echoing endlessly against the walls and ceiling, fading back and forth from the *clicking* rattle of the Overseer language to simple, uninflected English.

"Where is the rest of the crew?"

Jaeger jumped, head snapping around. Kwin addressed the pair of Overseers more than a little tersely, his voice also *clicking* and echoing and trailing oddly around the room.

The second Overseer hesitated and then began to click. "There was an issue with the automation system on the bridge," it said. "Your adjunct apologizes for not having the entire crew here to greet you but supposes that you would rather they be fixing the navigational systems."

The reverberating words and *clicks* were giving Jaeger a headache.

Kwin made a long series of popping, hissing sounds that had no translation. The two Overseers saluted again and scuttled away.

"This way, please." Kwin gestured for Jaeger to follow him up the corridor in the opposite direction. "Allow me to show you around my new, terrible ship."

It was an experimental new design of a deep-space scouting ship that the Overseers had fiddled with for decades. Not quite a year ago, when it had become evident that humans would come to play a permanent role on Locaur, a few Overseer designers had taken up a novel task. They tried to design a ship that might be fully compatible with human and Overseer physiology.

"The result is a ship that is entirely compatible and utterly *uncomfortable,*" Kwin grumbled as he led Jaeger down the corridors that made up the snowflake's delicate lattice. "Although," he added, slipping his translator band off his antennae with one long arm, "it is nice not to have to wear these."

"I might have to disagree," Jaeger muttered. The reverberating echo of Kwin's translated words followed them up the corridors, mushing around inside her skull. She struggled to pick out his words from the noise. "This ship-wide translation system is…"

"Terrible."

"Will take some getting used to."

The hallways in Kwin's new ship were much wider than what she was used to in Overseer ships—although at under one meter wide, the proportions still felt inherently *wrong* to her. At least it didn't trigger her claustrophobia as badly.

Kwin led her into a domed observation deck along the outer edge of the ship. Jaeger felt like a guppy in a fishbowl, staring through the curved, transparent dome into a sea of stars. When the door irised shut, leaving Jaeger and Kwin alone in privacy, she turned away from the starscape.

"What's going on?"

"One moment, please." Kwin poked at a display mounted in the wall beside the door for a minute before facing her. To Jaeger's infinite relief, whatever Kwin had done had also dampened the reverb effect of the ship-wide translator. His words echoed, but now tolerably so. "Engineers and xenobiologists under Counselor Tsuan's command retrofitted this ship. Observational programs and tools that his people are monitoring litter it."

"Spying on us."

"Monitoring the results of their engineering experiment,"

Kwin said dryly. "I have temporarily blocked monitors. I believe we have privacy, now."

"They gave you command of a new, experimental ship," Jaeger said.

"It has many new and untested features. Fortunately for our purposes, the one function at which it is extremely reliable is speed."

As if on command, Jaeger felt a gentle rumble course through the floor. On the other side of the fishbowl, a translucent field shimmered to life around the ship. Then, one by one, the stars vanished. Jaeger gulped, neck craning as she stared into the overhead void. Just like that, without any ceremony, the ship had jumped to hyperlight speed.

How could these people be so casual about breaking the most fundamental laws of physics? Their ships maintained stable artificial gravity while flying at ten times the speed of light.

These people were terrifying.

"Its other functions, however, are still in the testing phases. The translator system is nigh unusable. Communication between the central computer and remote droids is error-filled. We have only this morning properly stabilized the artificial gravity generator. It was randomly deactivating."

Jaeger tore her eyes from the infinite void. "I thought I was accompanying you on a scouting mission. Not a test drive for your human-Overseer hybrid toy."

"Councilor Tsuan's orders were clear," Kwin said stiffly. He tapped something on the wall. Jaeger hopped aside as the floor beneath her feet opened. A sleek table and chair sprouted up from some secret storage beneath the floor.

Jaeger sat in the offered chair. She was surprised to find it comfortable. Sitting in the only chair in the room made her feel like a captain again. "Will Tsuan's people be upset that you've blocked their spying in this room?"

"Your first mate has introduced me to a phrase that I believe is appropriate in this situation." Kwin joined Jaeger at the table. A holographic display sprang to life between them, showing a swirling map of this quadrant of the galaxy. "Tsuan can bite me."

Jaeger bit back a grin. "What do you call this ship?"

"Terrible," Kwin said again.

"Let it be so," she said solemnly. A thin line appeared through the quadrant map, tracking the *Terrible*'s route away from Locaur and into deep space. As Jaeger watched, dozens of the nearest stars turned green, signifying Overseer control.

"K'tax do not appear to create stable long-term colonies," Kwin told her. "They are nomadic by nature, moving in loosely affiliated swarms. They create short-term mining and breeding outposts, like the one you destroyed, or they travel from system to system, conducting supply raids before moving on. They are difficult to track reliably. We guess their movements based on where and when they pass within range of our observation posts."

A swarm of red dots sprayed across the map, blinking in and out of sight as they moved. In the heart of Overseer space, the red dots were few and far between. Toward the outer rim of the galaxy, however, the green dots grew few, and the red dots grew many—although the precision of their movements plummeted. They blipped across the projection, jerking with outdated data, but there were at least ten red for every green dot across the map.

"There are quite a lot of them," Jaeger said.

"The galaxy is big. The size of the K'tax problem hasn't been an issue until now. There's been space enough to expand in opposite directions. We haven't needed to encroach on each other's space. K'tax make no efforts toward diplomacy, but they seem to understand this much. Raiding and expanding into Overseer space has been more trouble than it is worth."

"Until we blasted an ancient signal from their ancestral home that's telling them to come back and crusade." It was too soon to determine if the red swarm had begun a precarious tip in the direction of Locaur, but she thought she saw that intention in the edges of their movement.

"Raids in boundary territories have increased," Kwin confirmed.

"What are they raiding for?" Jaeger looked up at Kwin and saw the galaxy reflected in his big eyes. "They were mining metals and alloys out of the asteroids around Locaur." *And they were stealing Locauri to feed their young*, she thought.

"Much the same," Kwin said. "They strip mine material resources. Alloys and metals to repair their ships. They may reproduce very quickly, but if they build new ships, they do so very slowly. They also abduct large quantities of local alien life."

"Local aliens?"

"Space is large. We are aware of at least a dozen planets in the quadrant with complex life, where the K'tax raid regularly. They have a particular interest in oxygen or nitrogen-breathing creatures of a certain size, with complex metabolisms."

"Like the Locauri."

"To serve as incubators for their eggs, yes."

"They'll have to abduct a *lot* of aliens to keep their numbers up."

"We have destroyed a few K'tax outposts of our own,"

Kwin said. "We have found evidence of quite efficient... processing plants. They seem particularly partial to a species of semi-aquatic arthropod abducted from Lura 4. Forensics suggests that one of the creatures can support the hatching and growth of up to ten thousand K'tax eggs before it is...depleted."

Dammit. Jaeger closed her eyes and let out a wavering breath. *I can't protect the Locauri or even my people from these monsters. Even getting the Osprey off-planet again—we could put up a good fight, but we're only one ship.*

She hadn't counted on facing down an enemy fleet within one short year of making her grand promise to protect.

"What about your people?" She cleared her throat. "How do they intend to handle an invasion if it comes?"

"We believe it will come." Kwin shattered any hope she had that the K'tax might simply ignore the summons from Locaur. "Our military has been fully activated, as well as all reserves. We are preparing to defend our space. While that does include Locaur, our priority is protecting Second Tree and the surrounding colonies."

"Second Tree?"

Kwin pointed at one of the green stars closest to Locauri. "Home."

Jaeger blinked, staring at one dot that looked much like any other.

"Second home," Kwin corrected himself. "Where many Overseers settled, after the Exile."

"Huh." Jaeger had always assumed that the Overseers were, much like the K'tax, still nomads at heart. The thought that they might have a home planet for an administration base hadn't occurred to her. She'd assumed that the staggering mothership had filled that role.

"We will defend Locaur to the best of our ability, as long as doing so does not jeopardize our core colonies or Second Tree," Kwin concluded. Jaeger suspected Kwin wasn't happy that Locaur didn't count as a core colony.

"That's understandable. My people can modify the *Osprey*'s shields to protect a wide section of the continent from orbital bombardment if the invaders feel inclined to flatten the place before putting boots on the ground. As soon as your comms channels are free, I'll send word back to Occy to get his engineers on the problem."

She sat back slowly. "I'd rather not *plan* on getting besieged. I'd rather we drive out the invaders well before they get that close."

And by we, she admitted silently, *I mean you.*

"The message bade them to conquer Locaur, not destroy it," Kwin said. "I would expect a ground invasion in that event. Their technology remains frozen in time, but they outnumber us greatly.

"As you have noted, my people are…fragile. We do not reproduce as quickly as K'tax. With advances in technology, we can build warships faster than we can train crew to pilot them. And if the K'tax manage to land a ground force on Locaur, we will be of no use to you at all. Nor will Locauri spears hold long against K'tax battle morphs."

Jaeger closed her eyes. "If Toner were here," she said carefully, "he might observe that it's too bad you asked us to exterminate the extra three hundred thousand highly trained and capable warriors we had with us."

"He might be correct in that observation," Kwin conceded. "We may regret not welcoming any friendly strength available to us. Though Tsuan would argue that without your interference, the need for an army would not exist at all."

Jaeger opened her eyes and studied the swirling arms of the galaxy on the table before her. "Kwin. You recall the details of our agreement with the Council, right?"

"I do."

"I swore to your people that we would not birth any of the embryos beyond the three hundred outlined in our treaty."

"That is correct."

Jaeger licked her lips. "I did not, however, swear to *destroy* them."

Kwin went very still. He became an awkward stick, jutting up from the floor.

"They're in cold storage hidden somewhere on Locaur." Jaeger looked back to the ceiling. "You know. In case you *do* find yourself in need of a hearty army."

"You deceived the Council."

Jaeger grimaced. "I wasn't sure," she said quietly. "I *wasn't sure*. The treaty says that neither I nor any of my people would ever hatch them. It didn't say I had to destroy them. So I packed them up nicely and had them hidden somewhere safe."

"Deceit!" Kwin lamented. His color turned from brown to bleached gray, making him look all the more like a tree in winter until he picked himself up and began to scuttle in restless lines across the observation deck. "The Council will never accept this. We must re-examine our understanding of your language."

"Your people honestly thought they were telling us to destroy them all, weren't they?"

"Yes!" Kwin reached the wall, and without hesitating, planted his claws on what appeared to be a perfectly smooth surface and climbed.

What's the point of even having artificial gravity, Jaeger marveled, watching Kwin fret his way around the room, *when you can crawl on the ceiling?*

"You understand this will put a wedge between our people, yes?" Kwin snapped. "It will seem that you manipulated the treaty in bad faith. This is precisely the leverage dissidents like Tsuan need to turn public opinion against you."

Jaeger winced. "We will be willing to make reconciliations for the misunderstanding later. Once this problem is solved."

"It is not so simple, Jaeger. You have implicated me in this duplicity. If Tsuan discovers that I knew of the embryos and did *not* inform him immediately, I will be—" the ship's translators belched static as Kwin fed it words it didn't know how to translate. By the angry scarlet-purple shimmer of Kwin's carapace, though, she could guess at the meaning.

She weathered his rage in silence. After several minutes of lamentation, Kwin wore himself out and slowly climbed down from the ceiling and resumed his place at the other end of the table. He wilted like a dying tree.

"In the face of all this…" Jaeger gestured to the holo-display on the table. "If you were to go to Tsuan, right now, and tell him about this. Do you really think he'd prioritize combing through every square centimeter of Locaur to find and destroy a bunch of harmless *eggs?*"

"No. But it will only further prove to him, and others, that you are not to be trusted."

Jaeger winced again and opened her mouth, but Kwin spoke past her.

"For that reason, I will not inform Tsuan at this time," he decided. "The matter of our…misunderstanding…must wait until the current crisis is under control."

"I appreciate your understanding," she said.

"I do *not* understand, Jaeger. I do not understand at all. I have many questions and new doubts that I do not welcome. But as you say, they must wait until we resolve this current crisis."

Jaeger had known, back when she made the treaty, that there was a massive ambiguity in the phrasing. She had chosen not to address it solely to benefit her interests above those of the other party. She suspected any honest judge would throw the book at her. She supposed she had earned Kwin's mistrust fairly.

"Aye, captain," she said softly, resigning herself to whatever political mess awaited her on the other side of the red swarm.

"Your people are extremely capable warriors," Kwin relented at last. "But even if your additional three hundred thousand troops were to come to our aid, I'm afraid those numbers would make little difference in the face of the K'tax swarm."

"Having the strength of twelve men doesn't do you much good when what you *really* need is twenty-four hands holding guns and crewing comms stations," Jaeger agreed quietly. "I notice that you're thinking in terms of an outright fight with the K'tax."

"They cannot be reasoned or negotiated with. Violence is inevitable."

Jaeger chewed on her lip, thinking hard. "Violence, sure. I suspect the battle is already lost if you're thinking in terms of defensive tactics. We need to re-evaluate our approach to strategy. Back on Earth, one little spider can catch and eat a dozen fat house flies twice its size before it starts to grow tired."

"How does it do that?" Kwin perked up. Anecdotes about Earth always interested him.

"It does that by spinning a web."

CHAPTER FIFTEEN

It had been seven days since Jack, Helen, Teddy, Edwin, and Portia had joined the Locauri tribe, and Art, Tiki, Skip, and Echo had become honorary crew of the *Osprey*. Seven days since Occy had been formally released from his prison sentence and allowed to resume his normal duties as chief engineer of the *Osprey*.

There was one aspect of his punishment that wasn't quite complete, however.

Every evening between second and third shifts, he led an hour-long cross-cultural learning seminar in the No-A lounge. Every member of the crew was required to attend at least once per week.

Tonight's topic was "Consider the Iguanome." Seeker, like many of the other attendees, had come solely to watch Occy and Echo argue as her pet explored the room and made friends with the crew. It was kind of cute once you got used to the face-tentacles.

Seeker, sitting near the edge of the lounge, was downright disappointed when his comm *pinged* with an urgent message.

"What is it, Doc?" He turned away from the seminar and spoke quietly into the corner.

"It's Toner. You'd better get down here, Commander."

"What the hell is she doing here?" The old general crew lounge had been converted into a two-room medical bay to accommodate Toner's unusual condition. A tardigrade the size of a grown hippo lay crammed in one corner of the first room, dozing.

Elaphus stepped out of the back room and glanced at Baby with a shrug. "She likes to come around more now that the captain is gone. I think she's guarding Toner."

Seeker grunted. "She's taking up half the room, is what she's doing. What's the problem?"

Elaphus's expression darkened. She gestured for Seeker to follow her into the back room.

"Whoa…" It had been a few days since he'd checked on Toner. The Overseers had sent one of their medical bots in centipede form, and it was hunched over Toner's calcified figure, carefully chipping away at the hardened crystal. Toner's head was already free of the stone. He looked like a mansicle fished out of some arctic lake, getting unthawed from the head down.

"We're picking up signs that he's coming out of deep hibernation," Elaphus said. Her soft boots crunched over fine crystal dust as she approached the body.

"Isn't that a good thing?" Seeker stared at Toner's face. The network of black veins lancing across his face had grown, he was sure of it, but Elaphus had determined that whatever Toner's sickness was, at least it wasn't an airborne pathogen.

Hamlet played softly in the background. "God hath given you one face, and you make yourself another..."

It might've been Seeker's imagination, but he thought he saw Toner's eyelid twitch.

"Why did you need me down here?" Seeker asked again.

"Because I don't know what to do with him if he comes out of hibernation," Elaphus said flatly. "The captain indicated that he was in the throes of a trauma-induced fugue state when the crystal overtook him. His neural collar is smashed and beyond repair. We've fabricated a similar model from *Osprey*'s databanks but haven't been able to install it. I'm not sure it's the same chip or that it works the same way."

"You think he might wake up in the same rage he went down in?" Seeker blanched.

"That fugue state is designed to preserve the body when it's under deep distress." Elaphus gestured at the bloody stump of Toner's hand jutting off the table. "It doesn't fade until he's healed and out of danger. I'd say this qualifies."

Seeker nodded slowly. The heart monitor hanging above the table *beeped*, as it did every few minutes.

"On top of that, his blood infection isn't going away," Elaphus said. "I want to talk to him. See if he can give me any insight. But I also want backup here in case..."

"In case he's batshit crazy."

"Right."

"Can you fix the fugue state by..." Seeker poked the crystal surrounding Toner's bloody stump. "I don't know, sticking a tube down his throat and pumping him full of blood substitute? That's what he usually eats to recover."

"That's what I want to try," Elaphus said. "With your permission, Commander."

Seeker nodded. The medical assistant that had been

hovering at Elaphus's elbow hurried to the far end of the room and wheeled back an IV pole draped with pouches of blood substitute.

"Any more information on the infection?" Seeker leaned a little closer. He rummaged in his pocket and pulled out his vape pen. The flat side was shiny, polished as a mirror. He held it beneath Toner's crooked nose.

A thin fog crept across the steel.

"He's coming around," Elaphus snapped, turning to her assistant. He fumbled with the IV hookup.

"No, don't bother with the injection." Elaphus snatched the tube from his hand and popped off the end cap. Red liquid seeped down from the bag. "He's designed to metabolize the stuff just as fast by swallowing it."

"He's making noise," Seeker said uneasily.

Toner's lips trembled. A rattling sound, like October wind through a dead field, escaped his lips. Seeker would swear his breath was *cold*. He backed away. Elaphus leaned forward, pushing the tip of the IV tube in between Toner's thin lips. "Can you hear me?" she called. "Toner, if you can hear me, drink this."

Whether he could hear her or not, he seemed to get the gist. His mouth closed over the tube, and red liquid began to burble down from the bag.

"Thank God," Elaphus breathed, falling backward. "I was half-worried he'd be…"

"Frankenstein's monster?"

Elaphus gave Seeker an odd look but nodded. "As long as that crystal still encases him," she muttered, "We don't have to worry so much about him going berserk if he's so inclined. If I could get him to tilt his head forward, we could work on that neural collar…"

The blood bag was about half-empty when red liquid began to dribble out of Toner's mouth and spill down his cheek. Elaphus snatched the hose away before the man could aspirate, but he let out a wet, gurgling cough.

Toner's eyes flew open. Ice blue irises shot through with thick black veins. *Like caterpillars,* Seeker thought uneasily. *Or dark tapeworms.*

"Toner, can you understand me?" Elaphus asked.

Toner's gaze fixed on the ceiling directly overhead and shifted to the left and right, wide and wild, as if seeing things that weren't there. His head jerked, taking advantage of the full two inches of movement the crystal cage afforded him.

"Hey, guy, snap out of it," Seeker said.

Toner's head snapped around, following the sound of Seeker's voice. He opened his mouth as if he was ready to speak, but the sound that escaped his lips was a thin, hissing rattle, like something from a machine—not a flesh-and-blood human. His breath smelled like iron and rot.

"Doc?" Seeker asked nervously.

Elaphus shook her head, shining a pin light into Toner's eye. "Dilation, but there's....there's something moving back there. I don't know—"

There was the sharp sound of breaking glass.

A thick crack shot through the crystal carapace, stemming up from Toner's intact, balled fist. A cloud of dust rained to the ground.

"Whoa." Elaphus hopped backward.

Another snapping, *crunching* sound. Another deep, fatal fissure snaked up the crystal entombing Toner's body.

"It's coming apart," the medic shouted.

"He's kicking his way out of it." Seeker's hand fell to his hip. He drew his multitool and thumbed the stunner function to full power as the crystal encasing Toner shattered into a million glistening pieces and crumbled to the floor.

The Overseer's medical bot backed away from the table, suddenly rendered pointless.

Toner sat up, his head swinging from the left to right, his wild eyes sweeping over everything and comprehending nothing.

Oh shit, Seeker had time to think. "Get behind me!"

He didn't wait. He'd seen what this pale bastard could do when he got that look in his eye. He didn't need to tell Elaphus and her assistant twice. They scrambled.

As if he were only waking up from an afternoon nap, Toner planted his feet on the floor and stood.

"Clear the room!" Seeker bellowed. He didn't bother firing. He knew it would do fuck-all. Instead, he wound up and hurled the multitool at Toner's head. It bounced off his face, leaving a bloody gash in its wake. Toner stumbled for half a second. Long enough for Elaphus and her assistant to retreat to the outer room.

Seeker wasn't going to fight this ghoulish asshole with nothing but his fists. He turned to run and saw there was nowhere to go.

Baby had roused at the commotion. Once Elaphus and her assistant were in the clear, the big tardigrade had pushed into the doorway between inner and outer medical rooms. She must have grown in the last few weeks because she struggled to push herself through. Beyond her, Seeker heard Elaphus' muffled, dismayed shouting.

Baby snarled. Seeker grabbed one of her beefy arms and pulled, heaving the critter free of her trap with a faint *popping* noise. Wasting no time, he threw himself through the doorway and punched the side panel. The door slid shut, leaving Baby alone with Toner. Something slammed into the steel, creating a dent the size of a paella pate.

"Oh shit," the medic whispered.

"Quit cowering," Elaphus snapped. She'd gone to a cabinet along the sidewall and was frantically riffling through vials and bottles of clear chemicals. "Clark, load up the tranqs. 50 CC syringes. No, not fifteen! I said fifty! I'd rather risk killing this man than letting him rip apart the entire crew before he comes to his senses!"

Another dent appeared in the door. Seeker heard a dreadful, distant screeching sound, like a circular saw cutting through steel pipe, and wondered if he was going to have to explain to Jaeger how her two closest friends had managed to kill each other on his watch.

"You two need to retreat out of the central column," he decided.

Elaphus froze, her expression horrified. "We can't abandon—"

"Give me the tranq." He held out his hands. "I'll stick him."

Clark hesitated, but at Elaphus's nod, passed two large vials over to Seeker. Elaphus handed him another pair, and he slipped them into one of his pockets. He waved for them to leave. He had to get this door open before the bulkhead became so dented it *couldn't* open.

The doctor and her assistant flew out of the room and became fading footsteps down the corridor.

"Moss, prepare to seal off the central column on my order, or if one of them kills me," he said to the ubiquitous AI. He didn't wait for her to answer. She wouldn't have anything useful to say.

Sucking in deep, bracing breaths, he waited for the sounds

of battle to pause and planted the sole of his boot on the access panel screen.

The door, tortured and bent badly out of shape, screamed as it opened.

In the twenty seconds they'd been set loose in the makeshift medical bay, Toner and Baby had turned it into a cyberpunk hellscape. Sparks rained from smashed light flickering overhead. The Overseer's fragile medical bot lay in one corner, broken into nineteen different pieces. The table was overturned, covered in shards of glass and crystal. Cloudy yellow liquid smelling faintly of algae dripped from a hundred shallow wounds in Baby's flank and dotted the floor.

By sheer bulk and inertia, the tardigrade had managed to pin Toner, but they'd trapped themselves in a deadlock. With his healthy arm and his stump, Toner gripped Baby by her fleshy neck, holding her toothy mouth-hole at arms' length. Lifted off her front toes, Baby's long, scythe claws scrabbled uselessly at the corrugated floor.

He's holding her up, Seeker realized. Baby might have Toner pinned, but she couldn't get traction. Their fight had turned into a war of attrition. If Toner could hold out long enough, he might manage to choke Baby unconscious, leaving her helpless. Assuming Baby had anything like a recognizable respiratory system. Seeker wasn't sure.

But Toner also couldn't move. If his strength failed, she'd fall and devour him.

"Not on my fuckin' watch." Seeker growled and stomped forward, his feet crunching over shattered crystal. A syringe fit comfortably into each of his palms. While the two assholes had each other nicely distracted, Seeker popped the caps off the needles with his thumbs.

He dropped to his knees beside Toner and plunged a

syringe deep into each of them. He thought he felt the tip of the needle break against Baby's rough skin, but the needle sank, and the plunger lowered when he pressed it.

Toner was a little less fortunate. Without much time to aim, Seeker had slammed the needle into the easiest target—which happened to be directly between his ribs.

Sure hope this doesn't kill you, Seeker thought as he pushed a rhino-killing dose of tranq directly into Toner's heart.

Unsurprisingly, neither of the raging combatants seemed to notice. Seeker might as well not even have been there. He reached for the other two vials and planted them into Baby and Toner, as well.

Toner's arms started to tremble. Baby's frantic panting began to slow, the scrabbling of her claws fading into nothing.

Toner slumped, and Baby collapsed on top of him, burying him in a mountain of quivering gray flesh.

"I bought us a few minutes," Seeker said into his com. "Bufo. Get a roll of carbon nanofiber down to the general crew lounge on the double. Elaphus, get back down here. Bring more tranq," he added, watching Toner's good fingers start to twitch where they poked out from beneath Baby. "I think we're gonna need it."

CHAPTER SIXTEEN

"Captain." The creature standing at the center of the *Terrible*'s bridge was one the strangest Overseers Jaeger had yet seen. She was used to the aliens looking like uniform stick insects, ambulatory boughs of ash, spruce, and pine trees still doing their best to hide in the great fern and coniferous forests that birthed them.

The Overseer commanding *Terrible*'s bridge looked like her ancestors had made their homes in gaudily decorated Christmas trees—the ones made out of aluminum foil and wire. Her eyes were big, glittery red orbs, like glass ornaments. Her heavy mandibles clicked like tin snippers as Kwin and Jaeger stepped onto the bridge. "We have dropped out of hyperlight as you ordered. The target K'tax swarm has appeared at the edge of our mid-range sensors."

"Activate the new stealth shield oscillator and bring us in closer," Kwin said.

An awkward pause filled the bridge.

"It's...not ready, is it?" Kwin asked.

"It's approved for field use," the female explained, "but testing in transit revealed some unexpected…errors. Engineering strongly recommends holding off on using the oscillators until they can determine the root cause of the problem."

Jaeger watched with great interest as Kwin's color deepened from mossy brown to furious maroon.

"Very well. We will observe typical sensor evasion protocol until the stealth systems are functioning properly. In the meantime, fill us in on what you have observed."

The shining female lowered her head. A dimensional hologram filled the dome ceiling covering the bridge, which rested at the *Terrible*'s heart. Jaeger had to tip her head back to study the display. What she saw reminded her of the oldest video games she'd found in the *Osprey*'s archive.

A cloud of rocky debris filled the area, defined by bright green vectors to make them easier to pick out against the void of space. They were between star systems so there was no nearby starlight to reflect against…whatever this was. As Jaeger watched, tiny dots moved among the asteroids. K'tax fighters.

"Did we stumble on an asteroid cluster? In an interstellar gulf?" She was puzzled.

"K'tax often fit asteroids and meteors with mass driver engines to accompany their swarms as they move," Kwin said. "For shelters, resources…we're not sure why."

"Spectral analysis of the fragments suggest we're looking at the remnants of a planet," one of the Overseers reported.

"A dark planet!" Jaeger had heard of the mysterious celestial bodies, planets that through some apocalypse or other, had been flung out of their home star's orbit and set adrift in the lonely, vast chasms between star systems. As far as she was aware, the fleet had never studied one closely. She might be one of the first humans ever to get a good look at one.

Or, at least, at the remains of one.

"Unfortunately, the rocky bodies are providing excellent cover," the female Overseer added. "What little ship activity we've been able to track suggests there is a mothership or equivalent at the heart of the debris field, but our scanners are useless at this range."

"And we can't bring the ship in closer without being detected by K'tax sensors." Kwin sighed. "Very well. Prepare to dispatch our observation drones. We'll send them into the field to get a look for us."

There was another awkward pause.

"Captain Kwin?" A new voice bounced around the room. A familiar new voice.

Jaeger squinted, scanning the walls, but she still couldn't see anything she thought might be a speaker. "I didn't know you were aboard with us, Me."

"Oh, I'm everywhere." The disembodied voice echoed cheerfully. "Except…in the hard drives of our observation drones."

"Why is that?" Kwin asked. His voice was soft, but his body had gone stiff.

"After some examination, I have determined that the thermal output of the observation drones exceeds parameters by nearly seventy percent."

"I…take it that means they're too hot," Jaeger said when Kwin couldn't bring himself to respond. He'd turned maroon again. "The K'tax will spot them."

"I'm beginning to think Tsuan doesn't want us coming back from this mission," Kwin said, lowering his voice for only Jaeger to hear.

"Better double-check your boots for scorpions," she agreed. *We drove from New York to the Grand Canyon only to realize that we'd forgotten to bring the right camera.*

"The swarm is moving through space at one-quarter light speed," the female said. "We are keeping pace with it, remaining just outside of their sensor range. We can maintain this pace indefinitely."

"But we will learn nothing more if we do so," Kwin said. Lifting his voice, he addressed the bridge and the half-dozen Overseers working at the edges of the room. "If anyone has any suggestions on how to proceed with our directive, state it now."

There was a contemplative silence, punctuated by the soft click-click-rustle of Overseers muttering to themselves.

Jaeger thought about the storage bays Kwin had shown her on their brief tour of the ship. She recalled some of the unexpected tools she'd seen in those lockers. The spare thruster components. The two human-sized exo-suits, all shiny and new in their sterile cases. She cleared her throat.

"I have an idea."

What Jaeger proposed wound up being simultaneously the most stressful and boring mission of her life. She'd done her share of long watches alone in the Alpha-Seeker, but at least then she'd had a sophisticated comms channel and a prisoner on the other end of the line willing to play chess.

It had taken over a full day to prepare, as well. Given all the hiccups throughout the ship, Jaeger wasn't about to trust her life to an experimental exo-suit built for humans by Overseers of questionable integrity. While Kwin's people assembled the components and spare parts to her specifications, she combed over every square nanometer of each suit. She checked all of the systems a dozen times over before she was satisfied that whatever bad luck had infested the *Terrible* hadn't gotten the suits, too.

Ultimately, she concluded that the Overseer who built these suits had paid minute attention to safety, utility, and efficiency.

They hadn't given two shits about comfort or mental well-being.

Jaeger jetted through open space, strapped to a cargo sled loaded with crates full of spy equipment. It was a space shuttle slapped together in under a day, out of whatever spare components the crew could find in the storage bays. A small, jerry-rigged ion generator strapped to the rear of the crate pushed her little raft forward at an ever-increasing velocity. However, it would still take Jaeger hours to travel the half-a-million kilometer void between the Overseer ship and the debris field hurtling toward her.

Hours in which she had nothing to do but nap, obsessively check over her lifeboat's systems, and piss herself.

You never got used to that part, no matter how well-constructed the diaper.

At least Jaeger and her little boat gave off a vanishingly small profile and an energy signature to match. She was more likely to die of boredom, mechanical failure, or micrometeoroid impact than by being noticed and gunned down by K'tax fighters. The little force-shield generator mounted beneath the sled was powerful enough to handle small bits of debris, but it wouldn't shield her from focused laser fire.

"I must confess," Kwin said when he came on the line for

his hourly check-in. "I cannot imagine volunteering for this assignment as you have."

"I didn't notice any Overseer-shaped space suits in that cargo bay." The navigational screen mounted to the computer on her forearm blinked red. The force-shield generator had detected and eliminated a micrometeoroid before it could punch a hole through Jaeger's helmet and brain. She thanked it silently.

"We…don't do that," Kwin said.

"Your people live their whole lives in outer space. You mean to tell me you don't go on spacewalks?"

"It's too dangerous."

Jaeger considered that for a moment. Her shield screen flashed again.

"As you have noticed," Kwin went on, "we are physiologically … fragile, compared to humans. Constructing an exo-suit compatible with our biology has proven to be a challenge. We rely on our machines and AI to work in vacuum."

"We do, too. Or we did until Virgil ran off with all our maintenance droids." She frowned. "Machines and AI do the job just fine until they don't."

"We hadn't seriously considered spacewalks a viable thing until we saw the *Osprey*'s records. You humans seem to do it regularly. The idea of being that close to vacuum …it's terrifying."

The shield generator flashed red half a dozen times. They were drawing closer to the debris field. Lots of little drifting grains of sand out here, zipping past at thousands of kilometers per second.

"Yeah," Jaeger muttered. "It sure can be." The forward engine had activated, reversing Jaeger's acceleration in preparation for landing. The destination asteroid, a monolith the size of an old-earth football stadium, loomed closer.

"I have been meditating on your situation," Kwin said to fill the silence.

"So have I." Jaeger sighed. "There's not much else to do."

"I am referring to the state of your memory. Not only your memory but that of all humans who pass through the wormholes."

"What about it?" Jaeger asked carefully. She wasn't sure she wanted to know. She'd made peace with her decision not to dig up memories from a buried past. She wasn't sure she wanted to go poking at that wall.

Then again, he was talking about more than her memories. His insight might benefit others who had passed through a wormhole or who might in the future. She didn't have the right to kibosh this line of inquiry entirely.

"I have been reflecting on our time together in the Living Dream and the way your memories resonate with certain frequencies," Kwin went on.

Jaeger's muscles tensed even further. "We're not doing that anymore," she said firmly. Not only because she'd sworn to look only forward and not backward, but also for the sake of his career.

"Understood. But I have come to some interesting conclusions about the broader phenomena that you might find useful. We barely understand the physical and psychological implications of wormhole travel on our bodies," Kwin said. "Let alone how the journey might affect you mammalians, with your radically different anatomy. The density of neurological activity that happens inside of your skull, your brain, it may make your psyche more susceptible to the trauma of wormhole travel."

That's right, Jaeger remembered. Locauri and Overseers didn't have organs comparable to human brains, not directly. They spread their gray matter equivalent throughout the entire body.

"I believe your neurological structure makes you specifically ill-suited for processing the multidimensional nexus found within a wormhole. To protect yourself from the unexpected trauma of the journey, you erect psychological barriers. These barriers are intended to block your memories of the journey but have the added effect—"

"Of blocking everything else, too." Jaeger frowned, contemplating the distant stars. "Whatever we encountered in the wormhole was terrifying, and we weren't ready for it, so we…gave ourselves amnesia. That doesn't explain why it wiped most of our computer banks, too."

"You attribute malice where there is none. I am not saying the experience was *terrible.* I am saying that it was simply *incompatible* with how you perceive reality. Your computers, being built *by humans,* are susceptible to some of the same blind spots that you are."

"Blind spots…okay, so you're not saying it was a scary experience. It was more like…we stared into the sun and didn't know it would blind us until we realized we couldn't see anymore."

Kwin hesitated. "Perhaps. I am not familiar with your eye structure. I believe it might be possible to unwind the neurological damage of wormhole travel by applying therapeutic methods retroactively via incremental immersion therapy. Acclimating your minds to the strange realities inside of a wormhole might break down the psychological barriers, as they will no longer be *necessary.*"

Jaeger chewed on that for a long moment. "Immersion

therapy is pretty common in human psychiatric medicine, but it's not like we can replicate the conditions inside a wormhole and make the crew run their morning jogs through it to toughen them up."

"No," Kwin agreed. "Nor would I recommend such a drastic immersion as a first step."

"I wasn't being…never mind."

"By applying the correct frequencies, we might be able to replicate the psychological stresses of wormhole travel in a controlled manner. It is similar to how my humming frequencies helped you to access the Living Dream."

You are bound and determined to be too interested in humans, aren't you? Although she found his enthusiasm endearing, she worried it would further damage his career. She suspected that being made captain of the *Terrible* was meant to be a punishment for getting too invested in human affairs.

Her navigational screen *beeped*, giving her an easy out of this conversation.

"We can pick this up later," she said. "I'm getting within range of the asteroid. I need to focus on landing this bucket."

The little sled piloted about as well as a hot air balloon, but Jaeger managed to push it within the asteroid's shadow and curve around its jagged planes until she found a sheltered spot. She picked a crater facing the heart of the field, suitable for landing.

She'd landed bigger ships than this one. Still, the idea of plunging onto the surface of an asteroid at these speeds, with nothing between her and eternity as space dust except an experimental Overseer exo-suit and a shuttle they'd hacked out of spare parts... Well, she was glad she hadn't eaten much lately. And that the suit's waste-disposal system was pretty effective.

She probably burned the forward thrusters more than necessary, delaying her landing, but it was better to come in too slow than fast. By the time her floating raft touched solid ground, it was lazing along at barely more than ten kilometers per hour. Puffs of fine white dust swelled around her like foam on the sea.

Wasting no time, she activated the raft's anchoring system. A jerry-rigged drill punched a metal rod downward, sinking it half a meter into solid rock. The raft would be well-anchored until Jaeger disconnected the rod. She double-checked the kilometer-long tether holding her to the raft. Drawing a deep breath of recycled air, she deactivated the little domed force shield. Once again, she found herself alone and nearly naked, in the face of dark eternity.

Once again, there wasn't nearly enough time to appreciate it.

Far overhead, a tiny shape moved across the face of a distant star and sank once more into the void. A K'tax ship? Or another asteroid? There was no way to tell.

She'd spent most of the last seventeen hours mentally going over the checklist of procedures. Now it was time to put them into practice.

She unfolded the packing crates and started to build a spy station.

"Excuse my interruption, Captain Jaeger." Me's voice came through the comms system as Jaeger was calibrating the x-ray sensors. "We've received an interesting communication from Locaur. Captain Kwin is quite upset."

Anxiety punched a hole in Jaeger's gut. "Patch him in," she said hoarsely. "Kwin? What's wrong? What happened?"

"We are receiving an *impossible* message," Kwin fretted. "Your people should not be capable of real-time faster than light communications. Why haven't you disclosed this ability to me? Why have you kept it hidden?"

"Faster than light…what? Kwin, what are you talking about?"

"As we speak, I am receiving an urgent message from Locaur. Seeker insists he must speak with you as soon as possible."

"That's not possible," she said. The *Osprey*'s communication arrays were cutting-edge for human technology. She couldn't pitch messages across the galaxy faster than light. At this moment, the *Terrible* was *years* outside of *Osprey*'s comms range. Jaeger crouched on the dusty surface of the asteroid, unfolding the spy camera's supporting struts. She didn't want to be out here any longer than necessary.

"Yet here we are," Kwin nearly snapped. "Seeker claims that Virgil has facilitated a real-time conversation. That should not be possible either, Jaeger."

At the name of her rogue AI copilot, Jaeger's stomach clenched.

"I have secured this comm line against observers," Kwin said, "in the event that the subject of your unfortunate clutch of eggs comes up. Privacy in a briefing room is one thing, Jaeger, but Tsuan surely noted that Seeker was hailing. It is suspicious. He will want to know why and how."

"Put them through," Jaeger whispered.

It was cold, on the surface of an asteroid in a debris field surrounding a dead planet floating between solar systems. It was cold, in deep space.

CHAPTER SEVENTEEN

"What's going on, Seeker?" Jaeger tried to ignore her heart thudding in her ears. She double-checked the monitor on her exo-suit. All systems still running well.

She expected static and distance to blur Seeker's answer, but his voice came through as clearly as if he were inhabiting the spare suit packed in one of the crates right beside Jaeger.

"I'll start from the beginning," he said. "Toner started moving a few days ago. The Overseer's medical bot was chipping him out of the rock casing, and he came to in a bad way."

Jaeger froze. "Is anybody dead?" she forced herself to ask.

"No. Luckily. Baby was a little beat up, but she kept him subdued long enough for us to pump him full of tranqs. He's drugged to fuck and locked under a ton of nanofiber cable, so he's under control while we're trying to figure out how to install a new neural collar. Meanwhile, Elaphus tells me that whatever infection he's dealing with—it's spreading."

"You called me with a whole heap of bad news," Jaeger said tightly. "It couldn't have waited?"

"Virgil insisted it couldn't."

Jaeger swallowed hard. She'd hoped that part was a misunderstanding on Kwin's end.

"A few hours ago, some of our scouts found two of Virgil's repair droids limping through the forest. One of them seems to have suffered some kind of...episode. Some kind of electrical surge, I'm not sure. Anyway, Virgil is confused. Should I just...look, it wants to come on and explain itself."

Jaeger swallowed again. The last time she'd directly spoken to the rogue AI, it was busy slaughtering her crew and killing her. They might have worked past some differences in the meantime, but the bad blood was still there. "Put it on."

"I don't understand what happened." Virgil's soft, slightly accented voice sent a chill down her spine. It skipped past any pleasantries, as it had always done.

"Hello to you, too."

"I sent one droid to explore the Locauri shrine," Virgil said. "Please withhold your judgments and castigations, Jaeger. The deed is done. It's not important now. Considering the shrine's ability to block communications, I knew I would lose contact with the droid for a short time, but I didn't anticipate...this."

"You lost part of yourself?" *You lost one of my repair droids, Virgil?*

"For longer than expected, yes. I assumed it ran into some fatal mishap but wasn't in a position to send more droids to retrieve it."

"You mean you were worried about losing more droids—sending good after bad."

"My form is limited and finite. I can no longer risk my bodies recklessly. Rather than send another into the shrine, I opted to examine the local area. Just past dawn, I overheard a pair of Locauri whispering about a strange machine wandering through the forest."

"If your droid had escaped the shrine, you should be able to sense it. It should have reached out to you."

"Precisely. I assumed the Locauri spoke fantasies. Still, with no other leads, I went to investigate."

"We heard the muttering too, Jaeger," Seeker confirmed. "Mason and I went out to investigate this morning. We found the rogue bot around the same time Virgil did. It's…in a bad way."

"It's insane," Virgil said crisply. "Erratic and spouting nonsense. It's become a separate entity from myself. I have not attempted to reintegrate it into my network."

Wonderful. Jaeger didn't want to meet the AI that Virgil considered insane. "Okay. So you went creeping around the forebear technology in the shrine, and you came back with a virus."

"The droid has been attempting to communicate with me," Virgil said, "But communications are slow since I need to ensure all data is secured. It keeps trying to show me a particular file. I've been able to scan and decrypt parts of it, assuming it's important because…I seem to have determined that it's important."

Jaeger thought it must have been a very strange existence for these AIs, living across multiple different bodies at once, able to add and subtract parts of themselves from the collective whole.

"It formed a successful connection with the crystal structure," Virgil said. "The connection damaged it, but it returned with stolen data."

Jaeger said nothing. She was thinking about Me, in its long serpent machine body, crouched over a forebear crystal interface.

"Much of what it's trying to show me concerns the K'tax,"

Virgil went on. "I am still trying to decode it. However, what I have so far seems highly relevant to your problem with Toner and your greater mission.

"According to this file, the forebears constructed the K'tax morphs, not as independent beings but to serve as the hosts for a different engineered life form, a parasitic fungus. The creatures you think of as K'tax aren't the real threat you face, Jaeger. The fungal infection they bear is what warps and drives their behavior."

"All this rang a bell," Seeker interjected. "I went looking through old files in the archive. There were similar infections on some species on Earth. Cordyceps fungi took over ant bodies and started controlling the behavior of entire colonies. According to Virgil, that's what we're looking at, with the K'tax."

"It's hard to say how much responsibility the K'tax bear for what they do," Virgil agreed. "The fungal infection has integrated into all of their biological systems, forming a close parasitic relationship that has scoured away any remaining impression of what the base species is."

Those base species still require living hosts to incubate their eggs. Parasites residing in parasites, Jaeger mused. *That can't be a viable long-term survival strategy. Do the Overseers know?*

Jaeger didn't dare pause to ask Kwin, though her comm screen indicated he was still on the line. She didn't want to put him in the awkward situation of lying or admitting ignorance. She could press him later.

"It's amazing the entire hyperparasite system has managed to survive for this long," Virgil said, echoing Jaeger's thoughts. "Likely the fungus has adapted over centuries to be less of a demand on K'tax systems, like a deadly disease self-selecting itself for long-term survivability."

"What I don't understand," Seeker growled, "is why the Overseers never thought to mention this little foil in our study."

So much for pumping Kwin for info later.

"What you describe sounds...plausible," Kwin said cautiously, speaking up for the first time. "I am no biologist. I will inquire. Our scientists may have interpreted it as a local, common but ultimately meaningless infection."

"You do that digging," Seeker agreed, an unkind edge to his voice.

"The earliest files I have been able to decode are clear," Virgil added. "The K'tax and the fungus were designed concurrently. The forebears successfully integrated the system. I see no way in which our modern K'tax might have shed this parasite. They've been carrying it with them for thousands of years."

"I don't see how any of this is urgent," Jaeger said. "Interesting, yes, but..."

"Elaphus says Toner's infection bears all the hallmarks of being fungal in origin," Seeker said flatly.

Jaeger's mouth went dry.

"I believe you encountered a construction facility in the forebear city," Virgil said. "One that produced proto-K'tax, as well as spores of this fungus as originally designed."

"Toner picked himself up a bug," Jaeger said softly.

There was a moment of silence across the line.

"A bug?" Kwin asked.

Jaeger felt herself redden. Given the nature of their new neighbors, Jaeger had been trying to scrub the use of the word *bug* as any kind of pejorative from the crew's vocabulary, but sometimes stuff slipped through. "Sorry," she mumbled. "I meant fungus. Infection."

"Toner has become infected with the parasite," Virgil agreed. "In its earliest and most potent form, before thousands of generations have caused it to mutate and adapt to K'tax physiology."

"Great," she whispered. "So we have some idea of what's infecting him. That should help us kill it."

"The forebears engineered it to be nigh indestructible," Virgil said. "If anything, its descendants still co-existing with the K'tax have grown certain vulnerabilities that the original fungal spore didn't possess."

"Don't tell me that we can't kill this infection."

"I suspect they created the fungus to possess and control useful bodies," Virgil said after a moment of silence. "The forebears were clever. The weapons they created to defend themselves from some imagined apocalypse are…more subtle than we had expected.

"They engineered the K'tax, yes, but they saw that even the varied K'tax forms might ultimately not be capable of handling whatever threat the future brought. So they engineered an even more insidious weapon, one designed to seek out and control the most powerful physical forms it can find. Whatever enemy the forebears imagined, they didn't intend to destroy it. They intended to enslave it."

"In this case, it's found a genetic mod template so powerful that even the humans who created it couldn't control it on their own," Seeker grunted. "We haven't been able to get a new neural collar into Toner yet. We're not even sure that doing so would help at this point." His words sounded like nails being pounded into a coffin.

"The forebears intended to control this thing," Jaeger said. "The fungus and all the bodies it controlled. They must've built a mechanism into it to do that."

"I agree," Virgil said. "There must be a control mechanism. I hope to discover what it is as I continue to decrypt the files I stole."

But you don't know, yet, Jaeger didn't need to say. "How do we fix it?"

It wasn't a question directed at anybody in particular—she addressed it to the open room. To God, she supposed. Deep down, she didn't expect an answer. "How do we fix Toner?"

"Elaphus's people have come up with a list of treatments we could try," Seeker said. "Radiation, chemo, poisons, cold hibernation…things that might kill the fungus, without killing Toner. The problem is that this stuff is tough as hell."

"You don't sound hopeful."

"The doctor doesn't sound hopeful."

"If anything," Virgil said, rolling right past Seeker's grim portent, "the form of fungus still extant in the K'tax is probably *less* hearty. It needed to tone itself down to form a long-term relationship with its host. I believe that a close analysis of the modern K'tax strain might reveal its weaknesses, which you could then reverse-engineer into Toner's infection using the *Osprey*'s gene therapy tanks."

Jaeger let out a deep breath. "Seeker, Virgil. Let me speak with Kwin privately for a minute."

"The line is secure," Kwin said after a moment of silence. "It's only you and I."

"What do you think of all this?" she asked quietly.

"I am looking over some of our medical files on the K'tax. It is true that all past necropsies note the presence of a pervasive fungal infection. As I suspected, it looks as though we have assumed it is simply some pervasive but ultimately benign microflora."

"Virgil claims it's a super-fungus your ancestors designed specifically to control K'tax. And...other things."

"As I said, I am not a biologist. I will make what inquiries I can. For now, I am inclined to accept Virgil's interpretation."

"You are?" Jaeger was surprised. "Why?"

"Because I can think of no reason why it would lie, and it does explain the situation with your first mate."

Jaeger considered this for a moment. Kwin was willing to accept a very strange tale over the benign interpretations his people had been making over decades, even centuries, of studying the K'tax. She wondered what that said about him.

"My people are asking for a sample of living fungus to study," she said. "Do you have anything like that in your science labs?"

"I will inquire," Kwin said again. "But almost certainly not. Reports suggest that the fungus does not survive without a host, and we do not keep living K'tax for experiments."

"You go make your inquires," Jaeger said softly. "Do it fast."

Because if the Overseers didn't have a living K'tax locked up in a lab somewhere, Jaeger was going to have to capture a specimen somewhere else.

She just so happened to be within spitting distance of a whole boatload of K'tax.

CHAPTER EIGHTEEN

It was late afternoon, and the *Constitution*'s Grand Concourse was a riot of activity. Crowds flooded the open space, a sea of people circling inside the donut, looking down and up each other from a mirrored world.

"What is Reset?"

They carried signs.

"What is Reset?"

They chanted, in disorganized gangs and clusters, lead by rabble-rousers with old-fashioned megaphones dug up from some long-forgotten storage bay.

"Free Petie."

No unified voice. Not yet.

"No Serenity."

"We stand with Rush!"

"What is Reset?"

"We Remember Memo Six!"

"Free Petie!"

The air was hot and thick with the buzz of drones. TNN news cameras, zipping past on quadcopters. Private observation drones, rich kid toys, stealing a birds-eye view of the historic gathering. Sleek black torpedo-shaped craft with the Seeker Corps emblem printed on the side, hovering in stasis around the zero-G transport tunnel slicing through the center of the concourse.

Petra had never seen so many people gathered together in one place before. Over five thousand of them, it must have been. Over half of the *Constitution*'s population—nearly one in five members of Tribe Six.

She'd never felt at once both so tiny and so huge as she swam beside Rush through the sea of bodies. They both wore hooded cloaks. It was a strange fashion, but they were hardly the only people here keen on hiding their faces from the thousands of cameras scanning the crowd. They passed people wearing hoods like theirs, or masks, or makeup caked centimeters thick.

"I grew up watching old videos of mega concerts on Earth," Rush whispered into her ear. "This was before we even had holo-dramas. Flat-screen, if you can believe it. Florence Welsh. Green Day. New Horizon. Before that, Elvis and the Rolling Stones and Led Zeppelin and David Bowie."

He sighed, a close and intimate sound. "Playing for crowds of ten thousand, twenty, thirty. Filling entire stadiums of ninety thousand seats. And to think now our whole world is living on the inside of little tin cans."

"This won't end well," Petra said hoarsely. Ahead, she saw the front officers of Internal Affairs creeping up the concourse. No riot gas yet, but the MP were fanning through the crowd. With a thrill of horror, Petra even recognized a few jet-black Seeker uniforms. The secretive sect wasn't supposed to concern itself with internal politics. Brass wasn't messing around.

A nearby speaker on a pole blared to life. "Return to your homes and businesses," an official voice bellowed. A wall of noise from the crowd met the sound. "This is an unlawful assembly!"

"Come on." Rush gripped Petra by the arm and pulled her through the commercial district toward Yolondo's shop. He didn't have to tell her twice. Once Internal Affairs and the MP started to move, they knew their minutes were limited.

Yolondo had a lot of friends. Big men and sharp-eyed women milled around his shop, their arms folded, glowering at passers-by who thought they might take advantage of the holiday to do a little discount shopping. Yolondo caught sight of their twin blue cloaks and waved them closer. A steel ladder propped against the building led to the awning and up to his roof's flat surface.

"Speakers are ready," Yolondo whispered, passing slim earpieces to Rush and Petra. "Amy's in position on the roof of the apartment building across the way. You're good to go."

"Wish us luck," Petra whispered, slipping the piece into her ear. It had been a long time since she wore a proper comms unit. It fit around the curve of her ear like the hand of a comforting friend.

"There's no luck in show business, darling." Rush fitted his piece. He gave Yolondo a thumbs-up. "There's only broken legs and broken hearts." Then he spun, and quick as a spider climbed up the ladder to the roof.

"That doesn't sound good." Petra stared at Yolondo, who only shrugged, as baffled as she was. Overhead, Rush whistled sharply.

Petra yelped and scrambled up the ladder.

The roof of Yolondo's shop was unadorned fiberglass. This close to the center of a grav-cylinder, Petra's head and feet spun at different speeds. The effect was nauseating and the number one reason why nobody did much with the rooftops of the shops on the concourse, even though space was at a premium. Simply moving around a measly four meters above the street left one, quite literally, lightheaded.

Gazing across the rooftops, Petra saw that a few others had braved the twisted g-forces to get a better view of the action. They huddled at the edges of the roofs, peering down into the crowd. They didn't notice when Rush threw off his cloak with a flourish and sent it fluttering into the crowd or when Petra threw off her cloak as well.

They started to notice when a painfully bright spotlight mounted to the roof of a building several blocks away flared to life, outlining Rush and Petra in a yellow cone that made the standard lights seem dim.

Petra tilted her chin and looked directly overhead. The transport tube sliced through the concourse fifty meters overhead. Fifty meters beyond that, not so very far away at all, more people looked down at her, from where they hung in the sky.

Petra couldn't imagine walking out of a shop and looking up and seeing nothing but clear blue sky.

Beside her, Rush adjusted his earpieces, humming into the mic. The sound crackled and rolled out of the speakers surrounding Yolondo's shop, and a hush rolled through the crowd.

"Lonely roads," Rush crooned softly. "Stretch through the night…"

"Empty roads." Petra mouthed the next line of the old ballad, her skin prickling as the response shivered up from the unfocused crowd. She hadn't heard *Lonely Road* in years. She was sure they didn't play it on fleet radios anymore. Not optimistic enough, she supposed. "No sunrise."

"Lonely roads," Rush urged, holding a hand out to the crowd. "Come on, darlings. You know the words."

"Darkened roads," they answered. "Gotta bring your own light."

"Beautiful," Rush said. His voice echoed across the concourse. "That's beautiful. You're all beautiful."

An uncertain rumble rippled up and down the streets—neither the approval of a crowd at a concert nor the cry of a people oppressed, but the roar of a great beast, reaching out for understanding.

It didn't quite happen all at once. The shops along the concourse didn't have the benefit of long cooperation and practice like the fleet administration did. It happened in a flood—a cascade of flickering lights, as a wave of darkness spread through the concourse, emanating from the cone of light centered on Yolondo's shop.

In a pattern as old as time, the noise died with the light.

More spotlights activated with an echoing *click*, focusing a nexus of beams on Rush Starr and Petra Potlova. For one bright moment, they were at the center of the universe.

"You're right to be here," Rush told the crowd. "You're right to be angry. You're right to be demanding answers. I'm so sorry I'm late to the party, darlings, but I'm not going to sit back anymore. I'm going to stand with all of you." He lifted his chin, gazing up the curve of the concourse to the administrative district. Even in the confusion of shadow and spotlight, Petra could see the uniformed squads of MP branching out from Internal Affairs, spreading through the crowds like cancer.

"Fleet command is telling you to go back home." Rush's voice rose into a rallying shout. "Fleet command is telling you to go back to your jobs, go back to sleep, go stick your heads in the sand. They tell you that there's nothing to see here, as your rations shrink and shrink, as the medical bays overflow with the sick and the dying, as humankind wilts in steel coffins between the stars. They tell us we have no other choice, but we *know* that's not true!"

The crowd screamed in rage and appreciation, in sympathy and sheer animal hysteria. At the very edges of the noise, Petra caught a high-pitched, whining noise. Sonic cannons, coming online. It wouldn't be long before the fleet got its riot-suppression tools up and running in full, brutal capacity.

"We *know* their secret police and their black squads have left a trail of ruined planets in our wake! We *know* they're hiding the truth from us! We *know* Sarah Jaeger didn't betray us. She's out there, fighting for us. Doing something that our leaders won't do.

"There's a whole vibrant galaxy out there waiting for us with open arms if we can dare to be brave enough and kind enough and humble enough to embrace it! There are alien races out there as desperate to meet us as we are to meet them. I've seen them. I've met them! And I've seen *our people* slaughter them like animals."

MP squads forced their way through the crowd, breaching into the commercial district and closing around Yolondo's shop. The people were too enraptured by Rush to notice.

"Your leaders are cowards! They're scared of what they can't control. Rather than show a little faith in you, they'd rather keep you holed up in these cages and watch you wither and die. Don't settle for the answers they've been giving you. You deserve better. Demand better!"

Petra placed a hand on Rush's shoulder. He fell silent, following her gaze. The crowd hushed, breath baited.

She'd been watching the people, per the plan. A squad of six MP in sleek black riot gear had pushed its way to the very edge of the crowd in front of Yolondo's shop. She thought she recognized the captain holding a bullhorn at its center.

"You made it," Rush said, addressing the MP. "And you come with guns and riot shields. Why are you afraid of your people?"

The man at the center of the ring of commandos lifted the bullhorn to his lips. The crowd started to bellow, trying to drown out the voice of opposition, but Rush waved them into silence.

"Rush Starr. Fugitive Petra Potlova." Captain Bryce's voice was amplified and full of static. "There's someone here who wants to talk to you."

Rush and Petra exchanged sharp, puzzled glances. They'd talked through a dozen different possibilities in planning this day. This wasn't one of them.

Down below, Bryce handed the bullhorn to a smaller figure at his side. The woman stepped forward, tilting back the brim of her cap to reveal the network of blue veins decorating her papery skin.

"Come inside, Rush," Juice called. "Let's talk this through."

CHAPTER NINETEEN

Petra stared, speechless. Beside her, Rush went rigid.

Juice.

The woman who'd been like a mother to Rush for decades stared up at them from behind a fleet uniform.

They must have her drugged, Petra thought numbly. *Or it's fake, someone they made up to look like her.* She hadn't known the woman long at all, but if there was one thing she knew, deep down at the bottom of her soul, it was that the older woman would never put on one of those uniforms of her own free will.

"Come on," the woman, who *could not* have been Juice, said. "We don't want to make a nasty scene. It's not just your set anymore, honey. You've got to share the stage."

Rush wavered and slumped. His chin lowered in the tiniest of nods.

"No," Petra whispered. "That's not Juice. It can't be. This is a trick. You know that this must be a trick."

Rush didn't look at her or say anything. He pursed his lips and moved toward the fake Juice.

Petra put a hand on his forearm. "This isn't the plan," she said. "We're supposed to expose this kind of shit to the daylight...like a festering wound."

This time Rush looked down at Petra. "This is how we expose everything. This is how the wound becomes terminal. Trust me." He took another step forward.

Petra hesitated.

"Come on," Bryce called, taking back the megaphone and gesturing at Yolondo's shop. "There are a lot of angry people here. We don't want anyone to get hurt."

"They don't want anyone to get hurt," Rush repeated, his voice spreading across the entire concourse. "You hear that? They come in peace." He paused, shifting his weight from foot to foot, agitated as he considered the options. "Well." He glanced to his side and met Petra's gaze. Although he spoke to the entire Tribe, she had a sinking feeling that his words were meant for her alone. "They might not have faith in people, but I'm not like that. I've chosen to be better. *You* made me believe I could be better. All right, Captain." He looked down at Bryce. "Come inside. Let's talk."

"We can't just give up," Petra hissed as she followed Rush into the shop through the back door. "Juice wouldn't want that." Not the real Juice, anyway. Petra didn't know who this woman was, that they had made up to look like their old companion.

"We're not going to."

"Then what *are* we doing?" The plan hadn't called for getting out of the public eye. The plan had called for opening everything up to daylight like a festering wound.

Rush's jaw worked. His utter lack of an answer didn't make Petra feel any better.

They could hear the press of the crowds, muffled, beyond the front walls of Yolondo's shop as they descended into the dusty space. The air was warm, and Petra's eyes watered.

Bryce, two commandos, and the woman who looked like Juice stood in the entryway, their backs to the covered windows.

"I'm glad you're willing to see reason," Bryce said quietly as Petra and Rush emerged from the stairway.

"Eat shit, Bryce." The words shocked Petra as they dropped from her lips. Even Bryce started, looking at Petra like she was a new and unfamiliar bug crawling out of his shoes.

"Juice?" Rush asked quietly, ignoring all else and staring at the small, aged woman.

"Hello, honey," she said, but there was a distant tone to her voice and a faraway look in her eyes—something inherently *wrong* with her stance, her gaze, her eerie silence. Definitely not the real woman, Petra decided—and by the despairing look on his face, Rush saw it too.

"What did you do to her?" he asked quietly, not taking his eyes off the woman.

Something clattered in the stacks and Petra jumped nearly out of her skin. She spun.

A small figure stood between two rows of shelves. He lifted an old cuckoo clock, curiously frowning as he turned it over in delicate hands. The door to the cuckoo's little house fell open, and the bird slipped out, dangling in the air by a coiled spring. It wheezed, its ancient gears choking on layers of dust.

The man laughed and flicked the bird, watching it bob. It was a grating, unnatural sound in the warm air.

He tucked the clock into one of the unusually large pockets of his lab coat and turned, finally facing the others.

"We helped your friend understand the true nature of what's going on here," the man said mildly. "She saw reason quickly enough. Hello, Rush."

"I'm sorry," Rush said stiffly. "Do I know you?"

The man grinned faintly. "You don't remember? I had backstage passes to the semi-centennial concert on the *Reliant* two years ago. Me and my brother. Big fans. You signed his LP collection with a tube of lipstick."

When Rush didn't indicate recognition, the man shrugged—disappointed but not surprised.

"That's too bad," he said. "Now, if we could clean up this mess you've made, I can get back to my real work."

"Grayson." The word slipped out of Petra's mouth. The man looked at her, faintly surprised. Behind her, Bryce and the commandos shifted their weight, and she sensed them reaching for their weapons. Juice, on the other hand, didn't move. She'd become like a doll, one of the broken mannequins scattered around Yolondo's clothing department, showing off the newest fleet uniforms.

"I suppose we have met, in a way," the little man in the lab coat said, eying Petra thoughtfully. "In passing. Hello, Potlova. Be a dear and put down your AV equipment and your weapons, won't you?"

Petra stiffened. She wouldn't. By her way of counting, she and Rush were only outnumbered two to one. Those weren't good odds, but they could've been a heck of a lot worse.

"Those people out there are expecting us to come out." She indicated the shadowy crowds on the other side of the shaded windows. "We came down here in good faith. To talk. What's gonna happen if we *don't*?"

Grayson sighed. "Nothing that hasn't already happened, but at a larger scale."

"You need to come clean to the public," Rush said, turning to Bryce. "This can't go on. The cat is out of the bag, and you know it. The people are angry. They deserve to know what you're planning. You can't beat them all into submission. You *need* them."

Bryce's gaze only shifted to Grayson.

"You're right that we'd rather this go smoothly," Grayson said. "So here are the terms. You surrender. Both of you. Right now. Come easily into custody, and you walk out of here alive. Even your granny over there. Unharmed. Nobody out in the crowd gets shot unless they shoot first. You come back to Internal Affairs, rejoin the flock. People stop dying in needless riots."

"Or people stay angry," Rush said sharply, "and they go forward with the strike and the riots. Your fleet and all your plans come to a standstill."

"No," Grayson said quietly. "All of your sound and thunder will amount to a minor setback. Eventually, the wheels will continue turning, as they're supposed to. We're running to the future, Rush. You can't stop it. But you do have the power to clear the tracks before more people get crushed."

"You've *lost control*." Rush threw his arms wide, indicating the muffled chanting outside. *Free Petie. Stand with Rush. Free Petie.*

Behind them, Bryce and the commandos jerked, drawing their weapons, but lowered them at a sharp look from Grayson.

"Don't you get it?" Rush went on, growing animated. "You've lost authority. You've lost your status. You never even had it, little man. Who are you?"

"I'm the man those commandos are taking orders from." Grayson's lip quirked with irritation.

Rushed waved his words away like an inconvenient fart. "You're nobody. Get me Commander Kelba. I'm sure she's watching this meeting from a dozen different angles by now." He turned, waving at one of the old security cameras mounted above one of the windows. "Nicholetta, darling? Hop on the phone and let's talk this through like adults. I'm tired of your babbling puppets."

He's gone nuts. A fresh wave of anxiety prickled at the back of Petra's neck. Yolondo's security cameras didn't work. Rush knew that. They didn't even have batteries.

A scream cut through the air, making Petra's hair stand on end, and her heart jump into her throat. Rush spun to see Juice fall to her knees, her arms stiff by her sides as if she were bound in invisible wires, her mouth open, her face expressionless as she wailed in agony. Even the commandos edged away from the strange woman, unsettled.

As quickly as her screaming had begun, the noise stopped, but her mouth still hung open. *Like a doll*, Petra thought again, sick.

"Kelba isn't here," Grayson snapped into the silence. His left hand writhed in his pocket, manipulating something Petra couldn't see. "I am. So let's stay on topic."

Rush's hard expression wavered as he stared at the silent, kneeling Juice. Petra saw his lips move as if he were about to whisper something. Then all uncertainty faded away, and his mask returned. He lifted his chin to Grayson. "Pathetic."

"Excuse me?" Grayson cocked his head as if he hadn't heard correctly.

"What is it?" Rush asked. He waved a hand, indicating Juice, but couldn't bring himself to look at her. "Nanobots crawling in her blood? Zapping her nerves every time she does something you don't like? Or some kind of pain diode jacked into her brain? Like some slum lord from old Mars colony, torturing his slaves if they don't mine fast enough?"

"Nanobots?" Grayson sounded bemused. In his pocket, his hand fidgeted. "No, but it's an interesting idea. Tell me, Starr. What portion of the general population do you think has taken the Serenity treatment?"

"Less than thirty." Rush's thin chest swelled. "Nobody who has a choice is taking Serenity anymore. If nothing else comes of this, at least I did that much." He jerked his head toward Juice. His voice caught. "Saved more of them from becoming your puppets."

"Oh, sure." Grayson's eyes danced in the dusty light. "Less than thirty percent. Now, would you care to guess what percentage of the general population has undergone standard medical examinations since you started making a mess across the airwaves with your ugly little stolen secrets?"

A moment of silence settled across the room. "You're bluffing," Petra whispered.

Grayson shot her a grin. "Try me."

Behind them, Juice let out another scream. A long, ululating wail of agony, not even a human sound. A machine sound.

"Leave her alone, you bastard," Rush snapped, taking a step toward Grayson.

"Go ahead, Starr," the man said, hopping lightly backward. "God, at this point I would *really* love an excuse to blow off your kneecaps. All in the name of self-defense, of course."

"When did you lose your faith?" Rush demanded.

Grayson's expression flickered. "I don't follow."

Neither did Petra. A strange light had come to rest on

Rush's face. A distant, glazed look.

Lost every last one of his marbles. Petra wondered when it had happened. When the fleet took Juice prisoner? When Scraps died? Or had he always been this way, and she'd been too starstruck to see it?

"Humankind has achieved so many great things," Rush said softly. "Terrible and awful and great. We build empires and explore the stars and kill entire planets." His words turned bitter. "We're capable of so much good and evil. You're trying to kill that spirit. Turn people into husks. Puppets. God, *why?*"

"Oh." The confusion melted off Grayson's face. His free hand dropped to rest on his hip. "That's easy," he said as he drew a stunner from his belt.

No. Not a stunner. Or a laser pistol or a plasma lance.

Cold dread filled Petra as she recognized the sleek silver barrel of the flechette pistol in Grayson's hand.

"Because they make better workers."

He pulled the trigger.

The pistol made a sound like water hissing out of a burst pipe. The spray of silvery mist that fanned out from the muzzle was hundreds of hair-thin, brittle needles.

Rush made a sharp, breathy noise and collapsed backward. Blood sprayed across the front of Yolondo's shop, decorating his windows, followed by the biting rain of cast-off needle shards.

Petra screamed. As a rebel, and before that a soldier, and before that a thief, she was no stranger to death—and still, she screamed as the strength ran out of her legs. She collapsed to her knees beside Rush.

His face had vanished behind a mask of blood and quivering needles. They sank centimeters deep into his skin, shattering off his skull, sinking deep into his hollow cheeks.

Where the needles had hit his eyes, they'd sunk deep. Chunks of flesh and hair and tattered clothes decorated the floor beneath him as the blood started to trickle and gurgle out of the holes in his esophagus.

"Get a medkit," Petra heard herself babbling. "Foam will stop the bleeding—get him to a medical bay—"

Bodies moved around her. Someone grabbed her and hauled her to her feet. Petra's head swam. The air smelled like hot iron. The distant roar of the crowd grew suddenly loud as Yolondo's shop door swung open.

"Sir," someone said. "There's a new video playing on the billboards."

"I thought we had AV control." Grayson stepped over Rush's bleeding body as if it were a lump in the rug and grabbed a computer out of Bryce's hands. Petra heard the faint sounds of a prerecorded speech.

"We do over all the public billboards." There was a tremor in Bryce's voice. "There are plenty of privately owned boards on the concourse—"

"He's still breathing," Petra cried, watching Rush's chest twitch and fall. Tears streamed down her face. Fire ran in her veins, useless against the strength of the commando holding her. "We came in good faith. We came in good faith! You have to help him—"

"Shut her up," Grayson said.

Someone shoved a hood over Petra's head. She howled into the dark fabric filling her world, uselessly wrestling as someone snapped her wrists into plastic manacles. *We came in good faith*, she thought, over and over again. *Stupid. You knew it was going to end this way. You knew this would come. He knew this would come. But we came in good faith—*

"There are no privately owned billboards," Grayson was

saying. "Nothing is *private*, idiot. Cut the power if you have to. Now, what is this?"

The room fell silent, save for Petra's muffled sobs, as someone turned up the volume on the computer.

"*...Not a trick or deception. I was born Richard Stapanski, but for the last twenty years, you've all known me as Rush Starr...*"

Petra's breath caught in her throat.

"*I'm probably the man most singularly responsible for the fleet's popularity. I've been pumping patriotic drivel out for these murderous bastards for years. God forgive me. When Sarah Jaeger mutinied, I knew I could no longer keep my head in the sand. When brass arrested Petra Potlova for the terrible crime of telling you the truth, I knew I had to act.*

"*I helped the rebellion break Petie free from Internal Affairs. I've been organizing and distributing the document leaks, hoping that the truth will spark the fire that will light the way to a better future. Today, in just a few hours, I'm going to join all of you in a general strike on the* Constitution's *Grand Concourse.*

"*Let us not mince words, friends. There is a very high likelihood that our efforts today will end in violence. Trust me when I say, from the bottom of my heart, that I don't wish to see bloodshed. To that end, when Internal Affairs comes to arrest me, I plan on turning myself in without a fuss.*"

"What is this bullshit…" Bryce murmured.

"Those billboards better not still be playing," Grayson snapped.

"AV is working on it, sir."

"*...Some friends of the rebellion have agreed to play this message once I'm in custody. We've come to the moment of truth, my friends. I turn myself in peacefully to the authorities. I hope, I pray, that they'll treat me fairly...*"

Outside the shop, the milling crowd swelled into a dull

roar.

"I've got AV confirmation," someone said. "Power's been cut to the concourse."

"Shut up."

"*...That there's still hope for an understanding between the fleet and the common people. But if I don't come out of this negotiation, if I die in custody, then we'll know what sort of people our leaders truly are. Stay safe, my friends. Don't be lulled into complacency. Rush out.*"

Silence fell in Yolondo's shop.

It was Grayson's voice that broke the air, soft and clipped and irritated. "If he had *warned* me he had a dead man switch, I might have let him live."

He didn't tell me. Petra felt like she'd slipped off the side of a cliff and was caught in that eternal, weightless moment before gravity could take hold. *He planned it all, and he ran off without me.*

Just like Sarah.

Just like Larry.

"Sir, the crowd—"

"Yes, I have eyes. I can see. Send word to the nearest docking bay. I want a shuttle ready to depart immediately. We're taking the prisoner off this junk heap."

"No." Petra stirred for the first time in what felt like an eternity. *Don't be lulled*, he'd said.

Rush, she despaired. *Why didn't you tell me?*

"No," she said again, louder when arms tightened across her shoulders. She stumbled as her captor dragged her over the floor. "I ain't going. No. No! I ain't—"

Something sharp jammed into the side of her neck, cutting her words short.

Petra slumped.

CHAPTER TWENTY

Jaeger didn't have time for this.

Furious, she lashed the portable sonar unit onto its scaffold and punched the interface. It hummed to life beneath her gloved hand, beginning a ground-penetrating scan. She would have to excavate a small section of the crater to create a sheltered nook to hide most of the spy relay equipment. A sonar scan would tell her where it would be safe to use the mining lasers without creating geological instability that the K'tax might notice.

As the sonar ran its scan, Jaeger triple and quadruple checked the systems on her life raft. She had to keep busy, or she'd go crazy. Kwin was consulting with his crew. Tiny K'tax fighters moved against the stars far, far overhead. Somewhere hundreds of light-years away, an ancient super-parasite was eating Toner alive.

The parasitic fungus jumped from the parasitic K'tax to the parasitic vamp mod. The thought made her laugh, though it was utterly without humor.

The sonar's screen flashed. Scan complete. Jaeger squinted

at the readout. In making the *Terrible* and her components human-friendly, the Overseer engineers had included a rudimentary English translation with all gear. *Rudimentary* being the key word. Jaeger read the readout twice, then again, thinking there must be a translation error.

"Me," she said. "Are you there?"

"I'm present, Captain."

Jaeger jerked. Something the size of a postage stamp flashed in the corner of her HUD. It was a glittering silver sphere, a tiny disco ball overlaid against the murky asteroid landscape. She turned, waving her hand. The illusion was remarkable; it existed on the screen of her helmet only, though she could swear it was really hovering beside her.

"Have you been here this whole time?"

"As much as ever, Captain."

Jaeger sighed, wondering if her seventeen hours of transit would have been more or less stressful with the chatty AI for company. Probably more, given the unease she felt whenever she remembered that she'd accidentally destroyed its predecessor.

"Double-check these readouts for me, please." She indicated the sonar. "If I'm reading it right, it's giving me an impossible calculation for the asteroid's mass."

There was a moment of silence as Me went about its calculations. "The asteroid appears to be thirty percent less dense than its volume and velocity would predict. That is very strange."

"We've noticed the discrepancy as well," Kwin added, making Jaeger jump as if he'd crept up behind her and tapped her on the shoulder. "I'm having my people run density analysis on the other large bodies in this debris field."

"Any update on the fungus situation?"

"As I suspected, my people do not appear to have any fungal samples available. Among our entire fleet, the *Terrible* is, unfortunately, currently best positioned to obtain one."

"Unfortunately" was a bit of an understatement. Jaeger forced herself to focus on what was in front of her. "Scans indicate a standard asteroid composition," she said. "Iron, water, and methane ice, trace amounts of nickel and tin…"

She shifted from foot to foot, her mind racing. "There must be massive voids within the rock," she decided, remembering her first raid on a K'tax outpost half a year ago.

"Preliminary scans indicate that several other large objects in the debris field are also far less massive than their volume would suggest," Kwin confirmed.

"They're hollow," Jaeger said. "Like the asteroids back in the belt around Locaur's star. They're not big rocks shielding the main swarm. They're ships."

Jaeger ran through the list of equipment available on her life raft and cursed on confirming that there wasn't one sophisticated life scanner among it.

"K'tax don't just *mine* their asteroids," she said. A plan was beginning to form in her mind. "They *inhabit* them. Kwin, I think I'm standing on top of a transport vessel."

"We have been tracking the activity of some of the smaller K'tax vessels at the edge of the field," Kwin said. "I cannot confirm that some appear to be docking with the larger asteroids, but the pattern of their flight doesn't rule it out, either."

"If I start drilling into this asteroid to hide our spy relay, the odds of them finding it shoot up a hundredfold." By her sloppy estimation, it rendered the entire exercise almost useless. "Is there a way to confirm what I'm looking at?" She stomped on the ground, half-hoping to find herself standing atop a buried airlock door. "If there are active K'tax down here, we need to fall back to Plan B."

"What is Plan B?" Me asked.

"I'm working on it."

"Hold position, Jaeger," Kwin said. "We will discuss the problem."

Kwin's line went dead as he turned his focus onto his crew, safe back in the *Terrible*.

Jaeger began to pace tiny circles, being careful to stay in the crater's shadow. She didn't want any patrolling K'tax fighter noticing her movement and coming in for a closer look.

This is supposed to be your job, Toner, she thought angrily, looking at the crate that held the empty human suit. *But no. You're stuck back on Locaur, getting eaten from the inside out.*

She turned, studying the life raft and the manifest of equipment it contained. She compared her budding plan to the tools at her disposal.

"We've decided to scrub the mission as planned." Kwin came back online. "We will retrieve you and fall back, trailing the swarm at a safe distance. We will make another attempt at planting the spy relay later."

"Hang on," Jaeger muttered, studying the craft and the mining laser mounted to the dusty ground beside the sonar. "I'm this close. I'm not leaving here without a spore sample."

The K'tax swarm, a field of debris a million kilometers wide, hurtled through the void between stars. It sheltered untold numbers of fighters and small mining vessels and dozens of massive asteroids that, according to the new numbers spilling in from Kwin, contained absurdly large voids. There was enough space within the asteroids alone to house millions of K'tax battle morphs.

They probably *weren't*. Further analysis had led Kwin's people to conclude that there wasn't enough energy output in the hollow asteroids to contain many active K'tax.

"Active" being the key word. If they were hibernating, it would be nearly impossible to tell without going and seeing for herself.

There were a lot of *ifs* in this line of thinking. A lot of ways they might be terribly wrong. And not much of an escape plan if they turned out to be mistaken.

Still, Jaeger recharged her suit's batteries—overcharged them, in fact—from the spares inside the second human suit and stripped it for as many spare tools as she could carry.

With the plan appropriately sketched to Kwin, she allowed herself a quick nap while he prepared on his end.

She'd wake up to the flare of explosions, blossoming and falling like petals of fire, blotting out the stars ahead.

She watched a line of tiny glowing dots spill up from the near horizon. Dozens, perhaps hundreds of K'tax fighters, each the size of her fingernail flooding the sky.

"They've spotted us," Kwin said, quite unnecessarily.

"Swarm they do," Jaeger muttered, watching lines of fighters spill out of distant asteroids and stars, closing around the explosion's source.

Those overpowered drones on the *Terrible* had their uses, after all. They made for fabulously effective distractions when loaded down with explosives, flown into the heart of the swarm, and detonated.

Jaeger looked down at the sonar screen. She took the risk and activated a deep sonar pulse. Hopefully whatever slept beneath her feet wouldn't notice it among all the excitement.

The map of the complex that unfolded reminded her strongly of the K'tax outpost layout, though it was smaller and simpler and contained longer, larger chambers—some of them nearly as large as the *Osprey*'s cargo bays.

But without gravity. Jaeger stared at the massive voids, trying to understand what the K'tax could be storing there.

"Escape drone falling into position near your location," Kwin reported. "It should be joining you on the surface within two minutes if it remains undetected."

Jaeger activated the mining laser's initial drilling sequence. Luckily there were a measly five meters between her and the tunnels, and Overseer drills had quite a bit more juice than the human toys.

She turned, throwing her arms over her head in pure instinct. Her helmet screen darkened automatically to shield her from the blinding glow. She prayed the lip of the crater provided enough cover to hide her from the K'tax far overhead. As her screen shimmered, filtering out the worst of the mining light, she picked out the ghostly shapes of the crater around her. Something small soared over the landscape in her direction, sleeker and simpler than the bumbling K'tax designs.

The Overseer drone fired front thrusters and drifted to a halt a few dozen meters from Jaeger, where it powered down. It would hold that position until she needed it. Kwin's people had stripped its insides of all the spy gear they'd built it to carry to make room for whatever loot Jaeger could steal.

"No increased activity in your area," Kwin said. "I suggest you move quickly."

Jaeger consulted her screen, tracking the activity of the precision mining laser behind her. She counted six heartbeats. As quickly as it had roared to life, the laser fell dark, looming over the smooth, slender tunnel it had bored into the stone.

Jaeger hooked a rappelling cord on the laser support struts and drew a deep breath. She *really* wished she had an epi-blast at the ready. She'd have to order all suits to start carrying one for emergency use. Elaphus could yell at her until the sun came up—so long as she was alive to hear it.

She pushed herself forward, sliding into darkness.

CHAPTER TWENTY-ONE

"Please tell me we still have comms."

"For now," Me said. Its silver sphere floated in the corner of her vision. "I am bouncing a radio signal up through the rock to the drone, which is relaying it to the *Terrible*. As long as there's not a lot of rock between you and the drone, you should maintain a connection."

"Great," Jaeger muttered. She tapped her helmet and frowned when infrared didn't activate. She cycled through the systems on her arm-mounted screen, found the infrared, and activated it. She'd have to synchronize the *Osprey*'s thermal hoods with these new Overseer tools, as well. One system for all the gear. "Do me a favor and download a little of yourself into the suit, Me. I don't want to be stuck down here alone if I lose comms."

"Already done," Me said, a little too cheerfully. "Not much, granted, but the most relevant parts of this mission."

It should have asked to climb into my suit with me. Then she thought, *But it's not my suit, is it?*

The tunnel walls closed around her, burning cold in her

filtered vision: stratified layers of rock and ice, rippling downward into darkness. There was a faint *thunk* as her boots hit smooth metal. The mining layer programming shut itself off when it reached a layer of pure alloy that might indicate bulkhead. The Overseers understood precision. That was for damn sure.

Wedging herself in the narrow tunnel, Jaeger reached into her travel pack and pulled out the miniature force shield generator that had protected her on the long journey out to this asteroid. She latched the shoe-sized device onto her rappelling rope. Her improvised life raft hadn't been equipped with a portable airlock and creating a hull breach in the K'tax ship was likely to raise alarms.

With the help of one of Kwin's techs, she'd reprogrammed the force shield generator to create a small dome. Jaeger knew that under perfect conditions, such force shields could contain heat and atmosphere in a vacuum. These were far from ideal circumstances, and there was no good way to adapt the shield to the narrow, irregular confines of the tunnel and the bulkhead beneath her feet. Once she breached the ship, atmosphere would eventually seep through the cracks. She had no idea how much time she had.

Which meant she had none to spare. She flicked an Overseer plasma cutter from her tool belt, knelt on the bulkhead, and began to cut.

Kwin stood at the center of *Terrible*'s bridge, directly beneath the center of the overhead display dome. He watched the swarm distraction play out in the holographic display through the tops of his compound eyes as his crew worked at the stations arrayed in a ring around him.

For all he hated the design of this new class of ship, he had to admit that the builders had quite cleverly arranged the bridge. Without moving from his spot or tilting his head, he had a clear view of the tactical display, the holographic dome, and each of the six core stations vital to a properly run warship. *Terrible* had come equipped with twenty-three surveillance drones, and their high energy output made them all useless for their intended purpose.

Pack them with spare explosives and send them out to flank the swarm from multiple directions, and the enemy came running.

Kwin watched another explosion blossom and fade at the edge of the swarm and felt mild satisfaction to note the four K'tax fighters blink out of existence alongside the drone. Four fewer things to worry about when this swarm reached home territory. According to his tactical officer, at least that wouldn't be for a few weeks.

"Seventh drone detonated," reported Udil, Kwin's metallic adjunct. "The enemy remains in a state of confusion. No increased activity near Jaeger's infiltration."

"What about this sector of space?"

"A few K'tax fighters are fanning out, sweeping the area for the source of these attacks. Should we fall back outside of sensor range, Captain?"

Kwin hesitated. They'd sent a better drone to retrieve Jaeger. Though it was fast, it had little in the way of shielding. The longer journey it had from the asteroid into the safety of the *Terrible*'s bay, the more danger it was in.

On the other hand, if the *Terrible*'s stealth equipment failed and the ship was spotted, a firefight would endanger them all.

"Jaeger?" Kwin asked. "Do you read?"

There was a faint, static delay before the human answered. "Barely. I'm about to break through the hull."

"We must pull back," Kwin told her. "Alert me as soon as you begin your withdrawal. I will wait till the last moment to pull in close to the swarm and retrieve you."

The static blurted longer this time as interference scrubbed her voice. "Copy that. Jaeger out."

Jaeger completed slicing a circle through the bulkhead and turned off her cutter. She hung above a darkened ring the size of a utility hole cover, sucking in deep, steadying breaths. In her right hand, she held one of the IEDs she'd salvaged off her life raft. In her left, a hooked anchoring piton. She had no idea what waited on the other side of that bulkhead.

It's a good thing you're not here, she thought to Toner. *You'd hate this plan.*

Because *she* was the one executing it.

No time to waste.

Jaeger aimed the anchor and fired. A small dart shot forward, sinking deep into the metal and shoving it inward. A crack opened. Through her infrared filter, Jaeger saw the smears of warm bodies moving in the chamber beyond. Moving quite animatedly, in fact.

She activated the IED, shoved it through the crack, and yanked up, pulling the bulkhead back into place beneath her.

Two seconds passed, and a deep rumble shook her legs.

She prepped her second IED. When she cracked the door again, there were plenty of warm bodies filling the chamber—

but none of them were moving. Judging by the state of the place, those bodies wouldn't be warm for much longer.

Congratulations, she thought grimly, pushing her way into the chamber. *You've murdered noncombatants.*

The room was long and narrow. Chunks of smoldering flesh bobbed like balloons in zero-G. Jaeger counted the heads of at least six drones and the roughly dismembered legs and thoraxes of perhaps two or three worker morphs. Chunky guts and clusters of soft, wet, underdeveloped eggs floated through the air. A thick layer of mucous and waxy excretion covered every centimeter of the ceiling and walls. It must have been some kind of hibernation chamber for drones.

She could only imagine the smell. She grabbed the wall and towed herself to the edge of the chamber.

"These eggs," she suggested, pushing a quivering cluster aside. "Some of them still have to be viable. Will they carry a sufficient fungus sample?"

There was a moment of silence as Me analyzed the question. "We are not sure if they are infected with the fungus at such an early developmental stage," it determined. "They're too underdeveloped even to implant in a host, and even if they are viable, transporting them back to the *Terrible* in such a vulnerable state will be very difficult."

Jaeger's stomach did a nasty somersault as she shoved the egg cluster aside. She had one shot at retrieving a living sample. She was going to do it right.

She pushed herself through the narrow chamber, pushing and pulling against the dead bodies, the roof, the walls, and occasionally relying on her internal suit thrusters for minute changes in direction. She added mag soles to her mental list of necessary additions to the Overseer suit.

She reached the end of the hibernation chamber and

touched a hand to the center of the sphincter-style door. The portal contracted, pulsating like living tissue, then blossomed open with startling speed.

The tunnel beyond was quite narrow, barely wide enough for one bloated drone or perhaps two worker morphs crawling side-by-side. Jaeger jerked backward. Her suit wasn't much good for stealth work. She stuck out like a sore thumb.

"Wish you were here in the flesh," she whispered to Me.

"In the flesh? Why?"

"In the metal," she amended. "I could use a little ambulatory spy camera right now."

"There is a pinhole camera in the tool kit in the lining of your left arm," Me said.

Jaeger sighed and shuffled through the tool manifest of her suit, scanning the list that scrolled down the side of her screen. "You're going to have to hold my hand," she said tightly. "These translations are illegible."

"Oh, that is very unfortunate. Give me control access, and I can help manage the suit."

A message appeared across her HUD. *Allow AI cooperative control mode?*

Oh boy. Jaeger sucked in a deep breath of canned air, reminded herself that Me was certainly not Virgil, and gave permission. She felt something shift in her left sleeve and looked down to see a slender cable slithering out of a pouch in the suit's skin.

Another visual display split her sight between what was directly in front of her and the pinhole view through the tiny camera at the tip of the wire.

"Okay, there's too much going on in my display. It's distracting."

"Really?" Me sounded surprised. "You can't process more than a single visual field?"

"Simple eyes," she reminded it patiently. "Shut off the camera display unless I ask for it. In the meantime, you describe what's visible around the corners as I turn the camera."

"You can process separate visual and audio environments simultaneously, but not multiple visual environments," Me said slowly. "Very well. I will do my best."

That's all any of us can do. Jaeger sighed. Her camera view vanished. The camera wire responded intuitively to her finger motions. Once she was comfortable with the control, she slipped the tip of it around the corner. *All this fuss when one simple pocket mirror could do the job...*

"The tunnel extends roughly thirty meters before vanishing around a curve," Me reported. "I detect no K'tax activity. More doorways like this one line the tunnel at intervals of roughly five meters."

Jaeger twisted the wire and pointed the camera in the other direction.

"The tunnel extends five meters before splitting. The cross-tunnels are much wider, easily large enough to accommodate a K'tax crab or scorpion morph."

Jaeger briefly consulted the rough map her sonar unit had produced. The other rooms lining this tunnel were of similar dimensions to this one, probably more hibernation chambers. Drones wouldn't make good living samples. They were too big and bulky. She wouldn't be able to drag one back up the escape route, nor did she relish the idea of getting cozy with one on the long trip back to the *Terrible*.

She needed to capture a smaller specimen, a worker or nymph. Perhaps a wasp or locust morph, but she doubted she'd come across any of those and would rather avoid the fight either of those morphs was likely to put up.

If the other rooms *were* hibernation chambers, they were likely full of sleeping drones. If the worker and drone K'tax behaved similarly to terrestrial ants, worker morphs probably swept through the rooms regularly to tend to the sleeping drones. She could wait here until another pair of workers came through on their rounds, but there was no telling how long that would take, and her time was limited.

On top of that, her map indicated that there was a massive chamber not far from here. She stared at the black void on the schematic, her brain churning. It wasn't a natural formation. She could tell that much from its regular torpedo shape. Nor was it the bay where the K'tax fighters and mining ships birthed—there were other docking areas located closer to the asteroid's surface.

"Do you have *any* idea what's in the large chamber up that side tunnel?" she asked Me.

Me hummed thoughtfully. "Storage?"

"K'tax don't have any form of gravity. There's no good way to organize or store stuff. It'll float around in there. It's too inefficient."

"If they were storing many small objects, yes, tunnels would be more efficient. But perhaps they are storing very large objects."

"Right in the heart of an asteroid, without wide enough tunnels to get these large objects in and out?"

"I can only speculate, Captain."

Jaeger drew in a deep breath. She felt exposed in this bulky white spacesuit the Overseers had given her, but at least there was an array of useful tools tucked into its folds and stuffed into her pack.

"What's the maximum length of this camera wire?" she asked.

"Eighty-one-point-eight meters."

"That's an odd length."

"It is, in fact, exactly one hundred *tsksnktnt kt ntk* long." Me sounded very matter-of-fact. "I take the liberty of converting Overseer units of measurement into ones you're more familiar with. Should I stop doing that?"

"No." Jaeger twisted her thumb, slowly unwinding the line from the camera wire. "Conversions are fine, thanks. Does this suit have any more useful information-gathering tools? We need to do some exploring."

CHAPTER TWENTY-TWO

Petra faded in and out of consciousness, floating on a sea of jeers, and cheers, and the roar of an angry crowd. *She'd been here once before,* she recalled through the haze. The first time she'd ever been in an immersive holo-drama. It had been such a luxury for a girl who'd grown up an orphan, fighting on the streets to survive.

Sarah had won some kind of academic competition, and the prize was two hours in a simulation adventure with one friend. Sarah had wanted to do the jungle safari. Petra had begged for the pirate experience. Sarah, always so solemn and thoughtful, had acquiesced.

The rocking of her limp body, as Marines carried her through the sea of sound, became a ship swaying over ocean waves. Distant shrieks and snaps and buzzing noises faded into the shriek of seagulls, the snap of canvas on a mast, the creaking of old boards. She thought she could even smell the salty mist pumped through the holo suite's vents, simulating ocean spray.

This must be what it's like to be alive, thought Petra the child, standing on the deck of an imaginary boat slicing through an imaginary sea. *This must be what it's like to be alive,* thought Petra the soldier, Petra the ensign, Petra the prisoner, Petra the failed rebel. She rocked in the arms of rough men, her head swinging from side to side.

Flashes of memory and prophecy bubbled up through the choppy waters. A warm spray of blood. An older woman's face, pale and papery and lined with blue veins, twisted in silent agony. A man so strangely familiar—she knew she'd seen him before, but where? On the news? On the cover of a magazine?—collapsing in a cloud of pink dust, as thousands of shards of scrap metal ripped his body to mush.

No. She turned over in bed. On the boat. In the rough arms of men dragging her across the sea and into silence. *Bad dreams. Go away.*

Just let her float.

Let her rock to sleep on the waves.

Petra woke up with a hangover so terrible she could only assume the torture had begun and the memories of it simply hadn't caught up to her yet. She coiled in a fetal position, shivering against a cold, corrugated floor, closing her eyes against the flood of memories that threatened to spill in all at once.

It did no good. Bile rose in her throat. She rolled, the cold steel floor pressing its tessellating patterns into her bare skin. She retched. Thin ribbons of bile, followed by watery surges of vegetable soup, reminding her that supper had been not so long ago.

The memory of sitting around Yolondo's table, shoveling in one final meal before the general strike, filled her with a fresh wave of nausea. At the time they'd joked it was the last meal. They'd even believed it, in a way. Still, Petra looked back on the memory and lamented at how naive they'd all been.

She saw the face of the elegant, bony man sitting across the table from her and remembered that he was dead. She would've puked again, but there was nothing left in her belly.

Slowly, the real world clarified around her. The sharp scents of vomit, cold steel, and antiseptic. The harsh lights overhead stabbing at her brain, forcing her to press her eyes shut, lest her retinas burn. The cold air and floor made her shiver.

She reached out, grasping at she didn't even know what and touched a wall. Working her hand numbly, she found a corner and another corner. Twitching her aching legs, she marked the outline of her cell and found that it was barely larger than a coffin.

Time slipped by in moments of agony.

In the distance, she became aware of a steady, *clicking* sound. Desperate for something to take her mind from her misery, she focused in on it and didn't know how to interpret the steady ticking sound that came once every second. She'd never heard a mechanical clock before.

When she could bear her self-imposed blindness no more, she squinted and found that her eyes had begun to adjust to the merciless fluorescents. She lay in a cell the size of a closet, closed on one end by a line of steel bars. On the other side of the bars, she saw the blank wall of a sterile white hallway.

Centered on that wall was a cuckoo clock—old wood and fading red paint, the bird peering at her from behind the broken door of its little house, as the pendulum counted away the seconds.

She must've fallen asleep, lulled by that awful ticking sound. The next thing she knew, she was waking up, roused by a grinding noise and a rush of air. Deep instinct, born of the streets and honed to a knife's edge by years in the military, had her awake and scrambling to sit up before she knew what was going on.

"Stay still," someone hissed.

Petra froze, blinking against the light until the world started to make sense again. She was sitting in something wet. It was her cooling vomit.

A man in the uniform of a Fleet Marine stood behind the bars of her cage. He was plain-looking, young and dark, his face still round with baby fat. *He's so young,* she thought numbly. *Was I ever that young?*

She licked her lips. "Water."

The Marine knelt beside her, setting a tray on the floor beside the bars. She shifted and realized that they'd manacled her hands and feet. There was more than half a meter of slack in each pair of restraints. How generous.

The Marine took a coffee mug off his tray and pushed it through the bars. Thoughtless, she snatched it up and gulped. It was water. Tepid and metallic, as if siphoned from the bottom of the cistern, but it tasted like ambrosia against her burning throat. She forced herself to stop drinking when she saw the mug was half empty.

The Marine was shoving something else through the bars. A small pouch.

"Rations are set." He pitched his voice low as if thinking that made him sound tougher than the twelve-year-old boy he so obviously was. "You'll get more later."

He didn't move. He only watched as she reached for the pouch. She opened it to see three things. A single slender meal bar—years expired, judging from the faded printing. A single tablet of standard painkiller. *Just enough to take the edge off her headache,* Petra thought as she swallowed it dry, *but not enough to make trouble.*

There was one more thing in the bag, and she shook it out, curious despite herself. The small object that spilled onto her palm made her gasp and stare.

Layers of lush milk chocolate, the label boasted in glossy white letters, *with caramel and nougat.*

She turned the candy over in her hands. She felt dents in the uniform shape, but the packaging was dark and bold and completely unbroken. *Hershey,* the brand label read. Earth-made chocolate, maybe the very last in the universe. Someone must have had this hidden in storage for years, just to give it to her.

Petra squinted up at the Marine, disbelieving.

The young man nodded as if satisfied. "Thank you," he whispered as he put his hands on his knees and pushed to his feet. "For showing us the way."

He walked away, leaving Petra alone with a bar of chocolate and the unblinking eyes of the cuckoo clock.

Petra used the empty pouch to scrape her vomit into one corner with little success.

The other thing that being a thief and a soldier taught you was to eat when you could. She crammed between the walls, head turned away from the sight and the smell of her vomit, and ate her supper. The meal bar was as dry and dusty as it looked.

If she'd ever tasted real chocolate before, though—and not the fabricated kind—she didn't remember it. The candy was so sweet and rich it made her stomach clench, and she had to force herself to eat it in tiny licks and nibbles, spread across what felt like hours. By the time she was halfway through, she didn't want it anymore.

Such a treasure, she thought bitterly, *wasted at a time like this.*

Still, it was full of sugar, and fat, and more condensed calories than she'd had in days. She'd be stupid not to eat it.

She was feeling much stronger, therefore, when two Marine guards finally came to drag her out of her cell.

CHAPTER TWENTY-THREE

She didn't fight when Babyface and his stiff-jawed companion came to drag her out of her cell. There was no point to it. Petra could get in a good crotch kick when she had the element of surprise on her side, but these men had her number.

She complied silently, head down, as they pulled her away from her tiny cell and its cuckoo sentry and down a series of winding corridors, all sterile white and steel. Thick conduits ran along the walls, many of them transparent and full of a viscous, clear liquid that reminded Petra of the gel that filled gene therapy tanks. She'd never seen pipes like this before, though.

They took her to a room she didn't recognize. It was low and long and almost empty. She couldn't fit such a useless space into her mental map of the fleet and began to wonder if there were still drugs in her system, messing with her perceptions. In space, storage was at a premium. The room was too low-ceilinged to be some kind of empty fighter hanger. Something about the layout struck her as deeply wrong as well, but she couldn't say what.

Someone had set up a green screen at one end of the room, a small broadcasting setup, something like the filming studio for TNN news. A stack of recording and audio equipment stood in front of the green wall, beside a canvas folding chair —the sort that a film director would lounge in during some old holo-drama.

A workstation sat beside the green screen, rows and banks of servers and monitors beside another, smaller, green screen. There were restraints bolted to the wall. The device facing the wall looked more like a dental x-ray machine than a camera. She didn't like the look of it.

When Petra's escort steered her toward the mystery machine, she fought back. With the fifty centimeters of slack in her ankle chain, she stomped Stiff-Jaw's foot. She didn't get as far as head-butting Babyface before he had her in an arm lock. *Strong,* she noted, *but not as rough as he might be.*

"I thought we had a thing," she grunted as he smushed her face into the green wall, but Babyface didn't answer. Together, the two Marines turned her to face the camera. They wrestled her hands and feet out of her manacles and into the wall straps. Her hands were over her head and off to the side, and her ankles spread a meter apart, making her look like a big "X." The men pulled away, leaving Petra to glare at the backs of their retreating heads.

Her heart hammered in her chest. Petra was no stranger to the wrong ends of beatings—she'd expected to face that and worse, once the brass got around to interrogating her—but the air was chilly, and her shirt was thin, and she was painfully aware of the tender, vulnerable skin on her ribs. Her gut clenched.

A wide door slid open at the far end of the room. The door design bothered Petra, too. It was more curved at the edges than the angular, uniform sliding doors throughout the freighters.

A small squad of people swept into the room. At the head of the line was Professor Grayson in a plain white lab coat, one hand plopped firmly in a pocket as he studied the screen of a tablet computer.

Behind him came a young woman. She was about Petra's size and wore an ensign's uniform, but she nervously fidgeted as she stepped into the wide area, her eyes darting to every dark, empty corner. *She must be new to the uniform.* Petra didn't recognize her.

A woman fluttered like a butterfly around the girl, carefully applying little adhesive white dots to her cheeks. Two more Marines followed the group, as well as two more scientists in lab tech uniforms. Bringing up the rear of this little party was something Petra had only seen in military demo videos.

A chill went down her spine, and it had nothing to do with the cold.

The sentry droid was two-and-a-half meters tall, a sleek robotic monstrosity that walked upright like a man but had the double arms of some Old Earth Hindu god. A Swiss Army knife of hooks and blades and a hundred other little tools that any good commando unit needed to be effective in the field tipped each long arm. Its steel and wire hips twisted unnaturally far with each *clanging* step that echoed off the metal floor.

Grayson and the ensign stopped at the broadcast studio, and the two techs broke away, their coats flapping as they strode toward Petra.

Petra glowered as the larger of the two techs approached. The woman opened a small case, and Petra saw it was full of more of those little white dots that covered the ensign's face.

Wordlessly, the woman pulled one of the adhesives out of the case. She studied Petra and frowned, a distant look in her eyes.

Like she's eying meat on the shopkeeper's counter, Petra thought bitterly. When the woman lifted a hand and firmly pressed one of the dots right at the center of Petra's forehead, Petra jerked. "Buy a girl a drink first," she snapped.

The woman's eyes barely flickered, but Petra saw it. The desperate furtive glance to meet Petra's glare. Then she busied herself with her case again, reaching down for another dot.

Petra refused to ask them what was going on. She wouldn't give them the satisfaction. Instead, her gaze went past the tech and the scanning machine to what she could see of the broadcast area. The ensign was sitting on a stool in front of the green screen. The makeup lady had finished her business and was mopping sweat from the ensign's brow as the young woman shifted her weight nervously.

Grayson sat in the canvas chair beside the cameras, sipping something through a bright pink twisty straw. He rolled his wrist in a "proceed" gesture. The makeup lady scuttled back to the shadows. The ensign cleared her throat, her eyes drawn to a screen that Petra couldn't see. Her lips moved.

Petra's makeup artist was applying a series of white dots to her cheeks.

"Watch the dimples," Petra snarled, wincing as the adhesive stuck to some of the fine hair on her cheek. "Can't cover up my best feature."

The ensign was muttering and shifting her weight. "Sorry," she said. "I flubbed that line. Start from the top?"

"From the top." Grayson sighed.

Nearby, the second tech fiddled with the knobs and dials on a wide workstation. Petra had seen its like before, in Rush's recording studio. It was a sound mixer and high-end voice synthesizer.

Everything clicked into place then, and Petra laughed.

The girl in front of the green screen jerked like Petra had slapped her, her head sinking between her shoulders.

"Ignore it," the professor said. "Restart from line six."

The girl cleared her throat. "I feel like I'm waking up from a long bad dream," she recited. "I'm not—I mean, I ain't —sure—"

"Cut." Grayson sighed. "Start over."

"I feel like I'm waking up from a long, bad dream," the girl tried again. "I *ain't* sure what's going on. They say it's been months since the terrorists broke me out of Internal Affairs. I can't believe it. They're showing me videos of me—"

"Since they broke me out of a *cell*," Petra shouted, making the girl wince again. "Oh, honey, I ain't mad at you," she added quickly. "I'm mad at these rat-faced jerkwads trying to steal my face and put those lies in my mouth!"

Without taking his eyes off the girl, Grayson gestured to Stiff-Jaw. Stiff-Jaw stalked toward Petra. She shot him a glowering grin. "What are you gonna do? You gonna—"

He punched her in the face.

Blood poured down the back of Petra's throat. She felt something hard and sharp scraping the inside of her cheek as her false teeth dislodged. *Oh well*, she thought dully, spitting her mouth clear of the blood and white chunks.

The painkillers she'd taken earlier must've been lingering in her system because she barely felt more than a dull throb in her face as blood spilled down her broken nose. She gagged.

"They're showing me videos that don't make sense." The girl was talking again, her voice high and tight. "Of a bunch of crazy stuff I said to all you guys, and I'm horrified—"

Petra spat. Bloody saliva dribbled down her chin. "You really think you're gonna thell this hooey after that video Rush dropped?" The memories came back to her as she spoke them.

She felt something catch in her gut, the edge of a sob. "You killed Rush Thtarr, and he called you on it! Right there, in front of the whole crowd! You think they're all that thtupid? Can't thee through a deep fake?"

The girl's voice trembled as she read. "I'm just—I'm just horrified—"

"Cut." Grayson sighed. The girl slumped as if all that had been holding her upright was the starch pressed into her uniform.

"You got played, didntcha?" Petra glowered as the professor stood from the director's chair and strode over to her.

"Starr was a diva," Grayson said simply. "I expected him to pull something dramatic."

"You're lying. You didn't thee that coming. I heard the fear in your voithe."

"Petie." Grayson sighed and rested his elbow on the wall directly beside Petra's head. He leaned forward, propping his forehead on his palm, bringing his nose a few centimeters from hers. Petra found herself trying to recoil backward, her deepest instincts rebelling at such forced proximity.

"Do you know why humankind created the Tribes?"

Petra spat. Whatever satisfaction she felt on seeing a spray of pink saliva blossom across Grayson's cheek drained quickly away. Grayson didn't flinch. He stared into her face.

"Come on," he said quietly. "Are we going to talk about this like adults, or are you going to force me to monologue?"

Petra glared at him.

"Why did people join the Tribes program? Why did all of humanity rally so quickly and sign on?" His voice was encouraging, like an eager teacher waiting for his student to hit the *eureka* moment.

"For two hotth and a cot," Petra snapped. Not because she wanted to have this conversation with him—but because she figured the quicker she did, the sooner he'd get out of her face. She could feel the warmth of his skin. It made her stomach clench.

"Sure. Basic needs are pretty convincing, but honestly, humans are clever little monkeys. We could've gotten by without a unified program. We formed the Tribes because people will do anything, Petie, when they have *faith* in something bigger. Not just hope for a better future, but faith that obedience and hard work can make it happen.

"The Tribes gave people something to *believe* in. A unified vision. The faith that if we all work together, we can build a better future."

Petra sniffed, feeling blood drip down the back of her throat. Through her swollen sinuses, she caught a whiff of his breath—warm and oddly sweet.

"Faith gets clarified in the fire of battle," Grayson went on. "Humans are diametric. We think in black and white. It's our basest instinct. Good and evil. Us versus them. You build faith in *us* by presenting *them* as something foreign and ugly and frightening. You unite people around hope, sure—but you unite them *faster* around a common enemy."

"You made that enemy anything that ithn't *you*."

A smile flickered over Grayson's face. "You rally people

around a common ideal. You give them an enemy to fight. What do you do when people start to grow tired of fighting?"

Petra said nothing.

"You find new ways to motivate them. Everyone has a button, Petie. A button you can press to squeeze a little more fire and fight out of them. Most people are good. Yes—I know. Surprising to hear me say that. But it's true. Most people aren't utterly selfish bastards. They think outside themselves. They care outside of themselves. So the button you press when you need them to work just a *little* bit harder…"

"Their familieth," Petra rasped.

"Their loved ones!" Grayson's smile blossomed into something warm and beautiful. *He could've been a teacher.* Petra despaired. She could see the attention-starved street kids clamoring around such a man, desperate to make him happy. The thought made her sick.

"Very good. There are four levers of control. The first two are faith and focus. The third lever is motivation. Follow your orders. Stick with the plan. Do your duty because *other people are counting on you*. Faith, focus, and motivation. Those three levers together built all of human civilization. They're incredibly powerful. With them, you can do just about anything. Knowing that, can you guess what the fourth lever is?"

Petra jerked, lashing suddenly against her restraints. There was a little slack in the ankle binding, and her knee popped forward.

Grayson hopped backward. He glanced down at the centimeter gap between her knee and his groin. "Close." His smile melted into a lazy grin. "But not quite. You must be feeling better."

He turned abruptly away from her, activating one of the

overhead display screens with a wave. Petra found herself staring up at...herself. The video was of her tiny cell from hours before. She huddled on the floor, damp with chunks of vomit. The video sped up, showing Babyface crouching outside of her cell, passing a mug and pouch through the bars. Petra watched herself pull medicine, food, and chocolate out of the bag.

"That meal must've done you a world of good!" Grayson froze the screen on the instant when the Marine leaned forward and whispered in Petra's ear. *Thank you*, he'd whispered. *For showing us...*

Petra couldn't help it. She risked a glance to the side and saw Babyface standing board-stiff at the edge of the room, his eyes round and white-rimmed as he stared at the screen.

Grayson turned. Smooth-slick, like he'd practiced the maneuver in front of a mirror a thousand times before, he drew a flechette pistol from one of his pockets. He turned, leveled the gun at Babyface's head, and pulled the trigger.

A scream slipped past Petra's lips. She pressed her eyes shut, turning her head away as ricocheting flecks of metal bit into her skin.

Babyface never made a sound. When Petra looked back, he was pinned to the wall by a thousand tiny darts, and blood was only beginning to trickle in rivulets down his chest. His face had become a pulpy mass of shredded skin and bone.

Grayson looked down at the gun in his hands as if surprised it wasn't a toy. More droplets of blood had joined the spray Petra had painted across his face. "Impressive." He turned the pistol over in his hand. "These new cartridges have a lot of *oomph*." He lifted his gaze to Petra. "It's a blunt lever, but raw, primal fear is damned effective, too."

Petra could barely breathe. "No."

"Yes," Grayson countered as he turned the pistol over in his hands, loading a new cartridge. "There we go." It *clicked* into place. He turned, head cocked to one side as he eyed the second Marine. Stiff-Jaw stood, eyes fixed forward. Petra could nearly hear his thoughts. *He* hadn't passed the prisoner contraband. *He* had nothing to fear.

Yet, his jaw trembled. More damningly, his hand twitched, unconsciously reaching for his stunner. He was perfectly happy to punch an unarmed prisoner in the face, it seemed, but drew the line at wantonly slaughtering his comrades.

"Your people don't believe in you." Petra forced herself to speak, drawing Grayson's attention away from the twitching marine. "Maybe you got fear, but you lotht the other levers."

Come on. She silently willed Stiff-Jaw to draw his weapon and take control of the situation. *He executed a soldier without a trial. That's murder. That's treason. You know it. Grow some balls and arrest him.*

Stiff-Jaw's resolve slipped away.

Grayson glanced around the stunned, silent room. On the other side, the girl in the ensign's uniform—Petra was sure she was no soldier, only someone dressed up to look like Petra—was cowering behind the camera. The techs had frozen, too terrified to move.

"Maybe." Grayson shrugged. "I'm pretty sure fear alone will get the job done, for now." Then he turned, pointedly drawing Petra's gaze to the sentry robot lurking in the shadows. The robot stirred, rising from its crouch. Lights flickered at the end of each of its four arms as its sonic lasers came online.

"Finish the video," Grayson said to the room at large. "Or I'm going to find your closest family members and press them into service cleaning up the mess the sentry is going to make of your useless fucking bodies."

He turned and strode toward the door. All of his easy charm faded into cold, clipped commands. "Transport Potlova to airlock three when you finish. I don't want another debacle like the one on the *Constitution*."

He paused beside the green screen and turned his head to see the terrified actress had slumped to the floor, huddled behind her knees. "Break a leg."

He winked.

Then he was gone.

CHAPTER TWENTY-FOUR

The K'tax seemed to have an instinctive aversion to straight lines and right angles, and it made peeking around corners, even with the help of her pinhole camera, much more difficult than it should've been.

Jaeger hugged the curved tunnel wall, feeding the camera wire slowly around the endlessly curving tunnel as she studied the view screen overlaid on the inside of her helmet. She felt exposed without eyes watching her back, running on nothing but the hope and promise that most of the K'tax were in deep hibernation.

It felt wrong, going out on missions alone. She'd trade her weaker arm—her right one—for Portia or Aquila or Seeker standing behind her, gun ready to shoot whatever errant scorpion morph crept up behind them. She had to admit, though, she'd probably trade her *left* arm if it were Toner, instead.

Vibrational sensors in the suit served as crude proximity alarms, ready to warn her if something was approaching, but they weren't a satisfying substitute for ears.

With agonizing slowness, the camera crept around the

curve. A slice of void appeared in the corner of the view, growing larger as she nudged it farther into the chamber.

A shape resolved in the darkness, a massive tangle of curves and dimly glinting metal plates. From the skewed perspective, Jaeger could only guess that it was at least one hundred and fifty meters long. She froze the camera, catching sight of motion over the structure. Distantly, she saw half a dozen worker K'tax crawling over it like ants.

"What is it?" she whispered to Me.

"I do not know," the AI admitted. "I have no record of a similar structure in our files on the K'tax, much less something of this size. K'tax are scavengers. It is likely some kind of captured alien technology."

Carefully, Jaeger panned the camera to give her a sweeping view of the chamber. No catwalks or docking arms lined the inside of the chamber, only an endlessly curving wall dotted with occasional tunnel mouths. Irregular lumps dented the wall here and there, indistinct. The strange machine at the center was shaped a bit like a squid. A dozen or more long arms flowed backward from a central nexus.

"It's almost as large as the *Terrible*," she murmured as she turned the camera. "Maybe it's some kind of spaceship. That knob at the end, where all the arms meet. It could be living quarters..." In the distance, she saw the pale body of a drone clinging to the wall, waving its stubby hooked legs over one of the indistinct clusters. She squinted.

"Coordinating those trailing arms for space flight would be a terrific feat of engineering," Me said. "But not impossible. I suppose they could be hypermagnetic diodes. Theoretically, if you wave them against one another in the correct pattern, they can generate a terrific amount of energy, but the science is highly advanced and speculative—"

"Oh, God." Jaeger felt bile bob to her throat as the drone reached out with its long ovipositor and inserted it into one of the indistinct lumps stuck to the wall.

"With the correct coordination, it is theoretically possible to use hyper-magnets to generate a force bubble capable of withstanding faster-than-light travel," Me continued thoughtfully. "The technology would be highly unstable, however. Not at all like the reliable force shields our tri-fusion reactors can produce—"

"Me," Jaeger hissed, silencing the AI. *Look at the camera view.* The K'tax have clusters of captured hosts glued all around the walls of this chamber." She'd bet her last organic espresso bean that the doomed hosts had, not so long ago, been the masters of that captured spaceship.

Her mind raced. "You said there's a good chance that eggs the drone hasn't laid yet, eggs that are still floating around in her abdomen, haven't been infected by the fungus."

"That is correct."

"Why is that?"

"The reproductive system has evolved specifically to protect offspring from pathogens."

"So they have something like a placenta."

"I'm sorry, I did not upload all of my available human medical files into the suit, Captain. I currently do not know what you mean."

Jaeger waved the apology away. "What about once the eggs are in a host? The drone's immune system no longer protects them."

"Yes, of course," Me said. "The egg must acquire the infection at some point after it leaves the egg sac, but before it develops into a nymph and consumes the host. The eggs are likely exposed to the fungus as they pass through the drone's ovipositor."

Jaeger let out a breath. On her screen, the drone finished its messy business, retracted its ovipositor, and ambled away. She rotated the camera again, giving herself another sweeping view of the chamber.

Aside from the scattered workers crawling over the captured ship, she saw nothing but a few drones crawling up and down the distant walls. A skeleton crew of the K'tax's most expendable forms. As long as there were adequate fighters patrolling the swarm, there was no need to have large morphs like crabs or scorpions crawling around in here, eating up resources.

That was what she told herself, over and over again, as she shuffled together a backup plan. She liked to be as prepared as possible, of course, but she wished the mission objectives would stop shifting beneath her feet. She preferred to make plans for all possible contingencies. Once they'd run through the possible contingencies and straight into the *impossibilities*, that was where Toner's gift for improvisation came in handy.

"All right," she decided, retracting her camera wire. "I want you to focus on monitoring the proximity alarms. I need to know as soon as anything changes its course to come in my direction. Do you understand?"

"I do."

"Good." She reached into her pack and counted her remaining IEDs. Four spare power cells from the mining laser and thrusters remained, wired with detonators and basic chronometers. She fiddled with the timers, setting them for three minutes.

"What are you going to do?" Me asked.

Jaeger sighed and made sure the IEDs were in easy reach.

"I'm going to go for a record." She set her feet against the tunnel wall and crawled toward the void chamber. "I'm going to try and get *three* birds with one stone."

The wall shifted from utilitarian metal bulkhead to something smooth and pinkish-brown, squishy beneath her hands and feet. According to her sensor readouts, it was notably warmer than ambient temperature. She'd seen this kind of organic material before, lining the walls of the nursery sections of the K'tax outpost. A filmy white substance formed as she pulled herself along, sticky and damp, clinging to her gloves like spiderwebs.

Jaeger's stomach lurched as she crawled out of the tunnel mouth and her perception of *up* and *down* abruptly shifted. She felt exposed with the alien ship looming above her like a moon about to fall. Drones waddled in the distance. She kept telling herself that they had poor eyesight like the workers, but it was little comfort.

"No change in activity within sensor range," Me assured her. "The drones are concerning themselves with their eggs. The workers on the ship appear to be stripping it for parts."

Thirty meters ahead, she could see the irregular outlines of *things* glued to the walls, growing larger as she approached. One of them writhed against its net of mucous slime, and she froze, her heart pounding in her ears. *Too soon*, she assured herself. The freshly deposited eggs had nowhere near enough time to hatch and begin their morbid feast.

She crawled closer, remaining cautious.

Half a dozen bodies lay spread over the floor, covered in ropes of mucous as thick and heavy as glue. It took Jaeger several seconds to differentiate alien bodies from their biological cages.

At first, she thought she was looking at a nest of drugged snakes the size of anacondas. Then she saw the little clawed feet tucked near their heads and the rough patches of irregular fur glued to their scalps and thought, *weasel.*

The aliens were as thick as a bodybuilder's thigh and striped in all different shades of tan, rust, and black fur as thick and bristly as steel wool. She guessed the biggest of them wasn't quite two meters long.

She paused beside the nearest alien, watching it, but if these creatures had circulatory systems or pulses, she saw no indication of it.

Carefully, she reached forward and touched its narrow muzzle through the thin layer of slime. "How can I determine if it's alive?" she asked Me.

Farther down its body, there was a break in the slime layer and a darker, wet splotch on its fur. Touching it gently, she saw the fur and skin split to expose a narrow gash, where the ovipositor had punctured it. Well. The drone had assumed it was alive, at least.

Keeping her motions small and smooth, she turned back to its head and carefully peeled back a lip to reveal white gums lined with rows of needle teeth. She thought she felt its lip twitch, but through her gloves, it was hard to tell.

"Sensor readings from your fingertips indicate it retains a good deal of body heat," Me said.

That would have to be good enough. This one carried living K'tax eggs, and it was smaller than the others, which would make it easier to haul. She activated her cutting tool, and working in small, swift strokes, began to cut and burn away the mucous holding the poor thing in place.

"There is a single K'tax emerging from a nearby tunnel," Me informed her.

"What kind?" Jaeger began to slice faster, gently peeling the alien away from the floor where she could. It flopped like a heavy doll in her grip.

"I cannot determine that through vibrational readings alone—"

Jaeger glanced away from her work to see a shining black worker-morph emerge from a tunnel mouth about ten meters away, turning its head left and right as it waved its antennae through the air. It turned in her direction. Even if it still couldn't see her, at this distance, it could *certainly* taste the unnatural scent her suit was spilling into the air.

The alien started to wiggle in her arms, weakly struggling to pull itself free as she sliced. The mucous was like half-dried rubber cement, thick and eager to bind to anything. A strand of it caught on Jaeger's boot, making her stumble as she tried to crawl away. The alien squirmed, now, grabbing onto her with paws uncomfortably similar to human hands.

With one final swipe of Jaeger's cutter, the last strand of mucous snapped, and she and the alien both rocked backward. She cursed, lashing out, trying to grab the floor before the force of their motion set them adrift in the zero-G void. Her hand found a stray scrap of mucous, and they jerked to a halt.

Quite wide-awake now, the alien scrabbled over her, coiling itself in alarmingly tight loops around her torso. Jaeger's vibrational sensors exploded. She couldn't hear it, but she could guess. The alien was screaming.

She had to turn her whole body to look behind her, and she didn't like what she saw. Two more K'tax workers spilled out of the tunnel, following their leader as it crawled toward her.

"Shut up," Jaeger cried, to no avail. The screaming alien couldn't hear her, and all of the proximity alerts were crowding what little vision she had. "Fuck. Me! Turn off visual alerts!"

Her view screen instantly cleared.

"Six K'tax closing on your position," Me said.

"I figured!" Pivoting awkwardly, made clumsy by the alien coiled around her like an inner tube, she scanned the floor. With all the twisting and spinning, she'd lost her orientation. She could see half a dozen different tunnel mouths, and they all looked the same. "Activate suit thrusters at quarter power," she ordered, reaching for her pouch as she oriented her body toward the nearest tunnel.

She fought to keep herself oriented against the alien's panicking squeeze as the thrusters activated. The tunnel mouth rushed forward. "Come on," she begged, fighting to slip a hand into her pack. "Just a little slack, please. I'm trying to help."

There was no way the alien could've heard her, but it must've sensed her intention. Either that, or Jaeger got lucky because the squirming body shifted, and her hand fell into her pack.

She yanked her IEDs free one by one, activating them with a clumsy one-handed twist and pitching them blindly over her shoulder as they fell into the shadow of the tunnel. A small countdown appeared in the corner of her vision. Three minutes to detonation.

Navigating the thrusters while carrying an unhappy, squirming passenger reminded Jaeger of her early days learning to use mag soles in zero-gravity. She bounced against the walls like a punctured balloon, making the alien squeeze her tighter with every shift and jerk.

"Me," she wheezed, grateful it was right about the tunnel. "It's time to get out of here. Send word back to Kwin. We'll be coming in hot."

Jaeger slammed back up the tunnel, following her trail backward. She soared around a curve, half-running over the walls, half-propelled by thrusters. The tunnel split. The alien had stopped its vibrating howl but jerked violently to the left as the side corridor came into view.

Four workers scrambled up the tunnel in their direction. Jaeger twisted, giving herself a nasty charley horse as she swam out of range of the worker's gnashing mandibles. She cursed, darting down the narrower side tunnel that led back to the hibernation chambers.

A rearview image flashed over her display screen, showing the K'tax crawling up behind in single file and gaining fast. Her countdown screen blinked. Ninety seconds to detonation.

"Will thruster discharge slow them down?" Jaeger barked.

"I don't know," Me mused. "It hasn't been tested for that function—"

A row of sphincter doors came into view, lining the tunnel ahead of her. Jaeger curved her spine to parallel the tunnel and punched the thrusters up to full power. She rocketed forward as though an egg-dragon had drop-kicked her. She screamed. Judging by the trembling pressure building around her ribs, the alien screamed.

The sphincter door twisted open to receive them. They

tumbled into the hibernation chamber and directly into a cloud of soft K'tax corpses. She cut thruster power.

Jaeger snarled in disgust as cold guts and viscera splattered across her helmet and sensors, making all of her readouts go fuzzy and leaving her blind inside her suit. She reached up to wipe her helmet clear, but with the alien coiled over her shoulders like a furry snake, she couldn't reach her face.

"Me! I've lost all visuals!"

"Ah. Vibrations suggest the thruster discharge did not much slow the workers—"

"Just tell me how to get out of here!"

"The escape tunnel mouth is three meters above your head and sixteen degrees to your left, angled out of the chamber at an opposing thirty-eight degrees—"

Through the suit, Jaeger felt her momentum carry her into the squishy pillow of a drone corpse.

"No, now it's four meters out from your right shoulder and *forty* degrees—"

"Take over as autopilot." Jaeger's voice turned flat. She wasn't going to get caught and disemboweled by giant ants because she lost visuals and panicked. She refused.

There was half a heartbeat of silence as Me processed the request.

"Ah," the AI said as the thrusters activated once more. "Yes, that makes more sense."

Sixty seconds.

Jaeger let out a sigh of relief as Me piloted the suit through the minefield of drifting bodies and up toward her escape tunnel. "The workers appear to have slowed," Me reported. "They seem distracted by the bodies."

"I would be, too," Jaeger muttered. Tentatively, groping blindly in the dark, she reached out with her hands and felt the curve of the creature coiled around her torso. It had gone still again. She couldn't tell if that was from exhaustion or injury or pure terror.

"Accessing escape tunnel now. Be warned. There is very little clearance for you and the specimen."

Jaeger reached up until her hand found the animal's head, resting on her shoulder. Terrified of hurting it or setting it to panic again, she pressed it close and hoped it understood.

Let's hope a few seconds of exposure to vacuum doesn't kill this thing, she thought. Between her damaged sensors, the low light, and the guts smeared across her helmet, all Jaeger could see was darkness and a flashing red countdown.

Thirty seconds to detonation.

"Approaching force field barrier in the asteroid tunnel," Me reported, a lonely voice in the darkness.

Jaeger licked her lips. She was restricted, blind, deaf, and dumb, except for what information Me chose to share. The thought of putting her life in the hands of an AI terrified her. "Get us to the escape pod alive, please," she whispered. "As fast as possible."

A white-suited human shape sprouted out of the tunnel mouth and into the starlit landscape, riding the wave of glowing energy emanating from the thruster pack mounted to her hips. Her suit was filthy with viscera and gore, her faceplate caked with frozen guts, blinding her. She clung to the exposed creature coiled around her middle as it clung to her. A thin crust of ice formed over its body as moisture trapped in its fur crystallized in two-point-seven kelvin.

The suited figure tilted parallel to the surface and accelerated, barreling headfirst toward a sleek, torpedo-shaped spy drone resting in the crater's shadow. The drone hadn't originally carried passengers, but the Overseers had gutted it, most of its innards replaced with an airlock barely big enough for one human in a bulky suit. The spy drone hummed faintly, powering up as the airlock door slid open to receive its passengers. The space around it shimmered with building energy.

The human and her passenger vanished into the sarcophagus-sized chamber, and the door slid shut.

With an inaudible *hiss*, the vessel's engines grew hot. Before the airlock had begun to pressurize, the drone was up and streaking away from the rock.

Three seconds later, the surface of the asteroid shuddered and began to crack apart.

CHAPTER TWENTY-FIVE

Kwin stood inside the *Terrible*'s docking arm, shifting his weight from leg to leg to leg. A captain *didn't* stand anxiously awaiting the arrival of a scout—especially not while the ship was in danger—but Kwin couldn't stay uselessly on the bridge, waiting for some dispassionate report. That wasn't his way.

The airlock door glowed from white to green, signifying a successful coupling with the reconfigured spy drone. Kwin sensed the distant *hum* of the *Terrible*'s engines, kicking up to full power. The pilot had orders to get this ship out of hostile space the instant they'd rescued the craft.

Kwin waited as the airlock pressurized. Another light sequence indicated that the sensors had spotted no concerning pathogens on the specimens within. Kwin found that amusing.

During the centuries his people had studied the K'tax, the fungal infection they carried had never jumped to an Overseer host. Logic said that was because millennia of evolution had caused the K'tax strain to become uniquely suited to the alien hosts and no others. Still, Kwin wouldn't discount the possibility that Overseer physiology simply didn't meet the predetermined criteria for "powerful host" that the forebears had programmed into their biological weapon. The Overseers were in no danger of fungal infection because they fell beneath its notice.

The airlock door slid open, and the medics waiting on either side of Kwin scuttled forward. They carried a roughly fabricated stretcher awkwardly between them because even the *Terrible*'s menial AI droids were full of what Jaeger called "bugs."

Captain Jaeger lay sprawled on the floor of the airlock, her suit helmet cast to one side. The alien—a slender, furry creature that reminded Kwin of a small *ktiskin* burrower—unwound itself from Jaeger's torso and reared up on its hind legs as the medics approached. Its lips curled back, showing rows of needle-sharp teeth lining a slender muzzle. It hissed, shaking its long, forked tongue in the air.

The medics skittered to a stop, eying the beast warily.

By the alien's feet, Jaeger groaned and rolled over, sucking at the air. "Get me out of this suit," she rasped.

"The alien threatens us," one of the medics said.

Jaeger reached out with one gloved hand. Her skin had gone several shades paler than its normal bronze hue. Careful not to take his gaze from the growling alien beast, Kwin reached forward and offered one clawed arm to Jaeger. He cringed but said nothing as she grabbed him roughly and clambered to her feet. These humans did not know their strength.

Ignoring the hissing creature that had spilled out of the drone with her, Jaeger staggered into the *Terrible*, slapping her arms and legs. "Get me OUT of this SUIT."

Hours trapped in the tiny spy drone, in intimate proximity with the furry alien, had stressed Jaeger's nerves—which Kwin had always thought a touch fragile on a good day. With a gesture from Kwin, the medics dropped their stretcher and began the long task of peeling away Jaeger's suit right there in the corridor.

"I'm going to puke," the human mumbled, cradling her head in her hands. "I know I'm going to puke. Five hours. I spent five hours trapped in a tiny box with a very angry weasel."

"Jaeger?" Kwin asked carefully. The alien had begun to sway on its feet. A ridge of fur along its back bristled, fanning out to display a mane of short spines.

"I have no idea," Jaeger groaned, leaning on the wall as the medics helped her out of the suit. "You probably look like some other kind of K'tax to him."

"We need to get it sedated and into a medical pod to remove the eggs," one of the medics said. She waved an antenna, indicating the stunner net she'd brought along in case anyone needed subduing.

"Try to be nice to him," Jaeger muttered, beginning to sway with exhaustion as she stumbled out of the back of the bulky exo-suit. Her skin-tight inner suit was damp with sweat. "He could've been a much worse bunkmate, all things considered."

She sounded sincere, but Kwin had his doubts. As the medic lifted her stunner net and stepped forward, offering it to the alien like a warm blanket, its hissing grew louder.

Its escape from K'tax imprisonment and the long ride back to the *Terrible* had burdened the alien at least as much as Jaeger. However, it could maintain its aggressive posture no longer. Slowly, it collapsed, putting all four feet on the floor and slumping to its side.

The medic stepped forward, draping the net across the creature. It activated with a faint buzz, locking into position. The alien whimpered softly and fell silent.

"Take all possible measures to ensure its comfort," Kwin said as the medics hauled the creature onto the stretcher and carried it down the corridor. "But extract the eggs immediately. I will not have K'tax nymphs hatching on my ship."

Racing at top speed, it would take the *Terrible* another seven days to return to Locaur. Kwin had to admit, for all he despised about this new ship, her speed *was* unparalleled. It would take a traditional saucer-class warship almost twice as long to make the same journey from the edge of the galaxy.

"Without any time dilation at all," Jaeger marveled, shaking her head. She sat across from Kwin in the same private briefing room they'd used before. A hologram filled the tabletop between them, displaying this quadrant of the galaxy and tracking the *Terrible*'s route back to Locaur.

"Your people are capable of faster-than-light travel without suffering the effects of relative time dilation," Kwin said, puzzled.

"Only in short sprints." Jaeger pulled herself upright. "The *Osprey* is one of the most advanced machines my people have ever built, and she can't fly more than a few light-years before needing to pause and recharge her warp bubble."

Jaeger suppressed a shudder. Yes, it was technically possible for the *Osprey* and other Tribal Prime warships to travel faster than light for long stretches. Still, if her warp bubble collapsed, the ship and her entire crew would begin to experience the passage of time at a much slower pace relative to the rest of the universe. It would do no good to send an army hurtling across the galaxy only to arrive at its destination ten years after the war was over.

It had been two days since Jaeger's return to the *Terrible*, and she still hadn't shaken off the utter exhaustion. It wasn't that the asteroid mission had left her injured or physically taxed—it had, but the genetic artists had given her body all the tools it needed to recover quickly from that kind of strain—it was that she felt mentally unmoored. Every time she thought she understood her goals and what was necessary to accomplish them, reality seemed to shift beneath her feet.

All I wanted, she thought, acknowledging the irony, *was to steal a warship, find a planet, and establish a new human civilization. Now here I am rescuing kidnapped aliens from other aliens in an attempt to cure an engineered space-vampire from some ancient bioengineered super-mind-control-fungus before an invasion lands on my doorstep.*

Oh well. She sipped her coffee. Like most other things on this ship, it was terrible. *One step at a time.*

A light on the wall flashed white. Kwin kept this room private for their conversations, and the ship's AI was knocking with an update.

"Speak," Kwin said.

"Udil has located and isolated the fungal spore inside the extracted K'tax eggs," Me reported. "With your permission, Captain, we can stream the analysis ahead to Elaphus on Locaur so that she may begin to study the data."

Kwin turned his head, looking at Jaeger for direction. She nodded. If Virgil had upgraded the *Osprey*'s comms systems as it had promised, she saw no reason not to give Elaphus as much of a head start as possible. "How's Chewie?" she asked. She'd taken to calling the rescued alien after the furry creature from *Star Wars* because she had to call the poor thing *something*.

"It has shredded the blankets you gave it," Me said, without a hint of distaste. "And is curled up on the scraps, in the corner of its quarters."

"Not much change, then," Jaeger sighed. Although the alien was intelligent, the Overseers hadn't yet been able to establish communication. Chewie seemed disinclined to cooperate, bristling its spiny mane and hissing when any Overseer came too close.

When Jaeger tried to interact with him, Chewie curled into a ball like a hedgehog and grumbled to himself. Perhaps he was embarrassed that she'd rescued him. More likely, she suspected he was simply mourning his separation from his people.

Her gut clenched with guilt every time she thought about the clusters of trapped aliens she'd left behind in the asteroid, at the mercy of *her* explosives. She'd killed his kin—if they were lucky. If they were unlucky, the K'tax had saved them from the explosions, and any day now, they'd be eaten from the inside out by nymphs.

Still, she wondered if it would've been kinder to leave Chewie there with his people.

"I've completed my analysis of the unknown ship Jaeger found in the K'tax asteroid," Me went on, making Kwin stir and straighten.

"Already?" he asked.

"There wasn't much information to study, Captain," Me admitted. "We only obtained a few minutes of video footage of the vessel and little else. As I suspected, the ship profile does not fit that of any known space-faring race. Based on circumstantial evidence, however, I have been able to speculate on some of the ship's capabilities.

"I strongly suspect waves of hyper-magnetic energy indeed power the ship. This would place the technological capabilities of its creators at least on par with the humans, and possibly rivaling our capabilities."

"Which makes them far more advanced than the K'tax," Jaeger said.

"That is correct. However, K'tax are scavengers. We must not discount the possibility that they have learned some principles of hyper-magnetism from their capture and study of this unknown vessel."

"Such as?" Kwin asked sharply.

"Anything beyond faster-than-light travel would be pure speculation," Me admitted.

Jaeger sucked in a sharp breath. "That's bad enough. I don't want to think about the K'tax with even better FTL travel."

"We must learn more about this new race," Kwin decided. "It is imperative that we understand what tools the K'tax have at their disposal if we are to defend against them."

"I don't disagree," Jaeger said, "but you were able to learn English pretty quickly with the help of inter-AI communications between Me and Virgil. We don't have that option now. All we have is Chewie, and we're getting nowhere fast with him."

"I have connections with some linguistics scholars on Second Tree," Kwin said. "I will request their urgent attention on the matter."

Jaeger let out a breath, letting herself relax a hair. She had been afraid that Me and Kwin would conclude that they needed to put Chewie through a series of deep and probably invasive brain scans to establish some kind of base system of communication. It was something the Tribes would do.

"In the meantime, I will warn the rest of the Overseer space fleet that the K'tax have obtained alien technology of unknown origin and capabilities," Kwin added, turning a grim shade of slate gray. He waved an antenna over the galaxy hologram, and a new object appeared.

It was the K'tax debris field, trailing farther and farther behind the *Terrible* as she raced back to Locaur. The field was less dense than it had been a few days ago. If they were lucky, that meant Jaeger's IEDs and the Overseer's kamikaze drones had thinned the swarm.

"Assuming the swarm maintains the same direction and velocity, it will enter the Locaur system in a little over three weeks," Kwin said. "My people are sparing what ships they can to defend the system, but K'tax activity has also increased around Second Tree, and we will not leave our home planet inadequately defended."

Jaeger nodded slowly. She glanced at the glowing light at the side of the room, indicating Me's presence in the conversation.

"Can I have a private word?" she asked.

Kwin flicked an antenna toward the light, and it blinked off.

"We are alone," the Overseer said.

"Your AI is universal, correct?" Jaeger asked.

"It is a cohesive collective," Kwin said, "across our entire fleet, yes."

"So is Me reporting back to Tsuan?"

Kwin studied her, his mandibles *clicking* softly. Light from the swirling galaxy reflected off his large eyes. "As my current commanding officer, Tsuan is authorized to know the actions of my ship and crew. If Tsuan interrogates the AI concerning what has happened on this mission, the AI will answer."

"Great." Jaeger sighed. "If Me tells him that you and I have had a few private conversations, is Tsuan going to come to you demanding to know why you didn't let the AI eavesdrop on us?"

"Your people must be very clever," Kwin said after a contemplative pause. "And very cynical."

Jaeger offered him a stiff smile. "We are. My AI has also betrayed me in the past. Don't get me wrong. I like Me. I'm just a touch paranoid."

"I am not a slave," Kwin clicked. "I am entitled to moments of privacy. Tsuan may find this annoying, but he has no authority to prevent it."

"That's good." Jaeger drew in a deep breath, draining the last of her coffee. She grimaced and added *better beans* to the list of suggested improvements to the *Terrible*. "Because it looks like there's an invasion coming for Locaur, and we need to discuss our options. *All* of them, Kwin. If the K'tax mean to conquer Locaur, that means a ground invasion. I can't sit by and allow my people and the Locauri to come to harm when there's a chance that an additional three hundred thousand troops could turn the tide of battle."

Kwin jerked like he had been slapped, lashing backward with a blinding speed incongruous with his frail body. "You will not break the treaty." His words came as fast as his motion, reverberating faintly as the automatic translators struggled to keep up with his gnashing mandibles. "You will not break faith with my people, Jaeger."

"I will not let Locaur fall, knowing I didn't do *everything* in my power to protect it," she snapped equally fervently. "If I can't trust your people to support our defense, you leave me no other choice. I'm willing to accept the consequences of my actions."

"You must understand." Kwin's carapace shimmered from his moody gray to a deep maroon. His mandibles *clacked* together with each word, echoing around the small chamber.

"Our treaty is not with *you*, Captain Sarah Jaeger. Our treaty is with *you*, the humans of the *Osprey*. We see authority and responsibility as diffuse things that flow as much from captain to crew as from crew to captain.

"Were you to activate more of these preserved embryos, you might increase your chances of a favorable outcome against the K'tax, yes, by a small amount. But in doing so, you would prove to my people that we cannot trust *you*. You—" His antennae swept across the room, indicating an entire crowd that wasn't there. "—You *humans*. This is how the Council will view your betrayal."

"I negotiated the treaty," Jaeger countered. "Not Portia or Bufo or Mason or any of the others. Me. Not them. You can't use my example to condemn them all."

"Can we not? Did you not come to us as the *representative* of your people?"

Jaeger winced.

"Do you mean to tell me now that you do *not* represent your people? Then how are we to trust any treaties we ever make with you, again, if the ones you send to negotiate do not represent you all? No. I am sympathetic to you, Jaeger. Truly. I understand your dilemma.

"But I tell you, you *cannot* activate another one of those embryos if you wish for your people ever to maintain good relations with mine. The council is already disinclined to trust you. You cannot prove their misgivings correct."

"Kwin, I'd agree with you if the stakes we're talking about

were anything *less* than the potential extermination of my entire crew and the Locauri. Is it better to be alive and anathema, or trustworthy but *dead?*" She hated the taste of the words in her mouth. They tasted like wavering principles. They tasted tribal.

Kwin paced clicking circles around the room, every motion fast and sharp and restless. He stopped suddenly, half a meter from Jaeger, and swung his head around until she was beneath the gentle curve of his antennae.

"It is better to be neither," he declared, his carapace shimmering from deep maroon, back to his normal, placid mossy brown. "You gave your word you would not activate any more of those embryos. You must not break your word." Kwin leaned in even closer until she could feel his mandibles brushing against the fine hairs on her nose. Jaeger held her breath, half-afraid that if she moved, he'd snip off her nose.

"But *I* gave no such word. I merely agreed not to hatch more humans. To that end, I kept my word."

"Your people are devious." Kwin's mandibles snapped together, and despite herself, Jaeger jerked backward. "You slip through your promises, twisting yourselves in knots to make tortured, unnatural shapes around your words. Jaeger. We cannot know who might be listening or what they might learn from watching you bend and sway. *We will speak of this no more.*"

Jaeger licked her lips, acutely aware of her hammering pulse. Compared to the K'tax and even the Locauri, Kwin's mandibles were delicate, slender things. Still, every deep instinct told her to panic when he leaned in that close to her throat. She smelled the faint acetone sting of his carapace, itching at the inside of her nose.

He's not threatening me, she told herself. It wasn't his way, and it wasn't the Overseer way. They were too frail to waste time and energy with physical posturing.

Still, he stood over her, utterly motionless, his multifaceted eyes flat like a dead screen, and she didn't see a person or a friend. She didn't see the misty hologram he'd been for the vast majority of their interactions, something that was immaterial and incapable of doing her real harm. She saw a robot, a statue, a hasty compilation of sticks and rods fused at all angles to make a shape that, deep down, she couldn't see as a living, breathing creature with thoughts and emotions and honor and keen intelligence.

She saw a monster—and this monster was asking her to trust him.

She closed her eyes, and the edge of animal panic gnawing at her brain softened as if the old child's prayer was true—the monsters couldn't see her if she couldn't see them.

Work with what you have.

She'd certainly asked for more than her fair share of Kwin's trust throughout their alliance.

"I did what I had to for my people. They are my priority. Surely you understand this."

Kwin said nothing.

"We will speak of this no more," she said.

"Good."

She heard the soft *click* of slender claws against the floor and the faint *whoosh*. When she opened her eyes, the door closed behind Kwin as he walked out of the room.

CHAPTER TWENTY-SIX

If Kwin didn't want to talk about the embryos anymore, they wouldn't talk about the embryos anymore.

Hours and days slipped by as the *Terrible* ripped across the quadrant, hurtling toward Locaur. The *Terrible* didn't have any exercise facilities. Jaeger shouldn't have been surprised. The Overseers didn't have anything comparable to a human respiratory system or musculature. Time on a treadmill would do them no good.

She burned through her restless energy jogging confined loops through the *Terrible*'s corridors, turning over plans and ideas as she passed the medical bay, bridge, engineering bay, and back past the medical bay, bridge, and engineering bay. Over and over again.

The Overseer scientists had extracted the K'tax eggs from Chewie and were using the *Osprey*'s upgraded communications relay to collaborate with Elaphus. When Jaeger passed the medical bay, she caught snippets of argument between the Overseer medics and the *Osprey*'s doctor—something about polypeptide chains and folded protein shapes.

Jaeger took Elaphus' barking for a good sign. They'd reconstructed Toner's original neural collar and were getting it installed. Using the data from the K'tax eggs, they'd devised a few potential gene therapy treatments for fighting fungal infection, and the initial tests yielded promising results. When the doctor grew quiet, *that* would be the time to worry.

She read the reports Seeker sent about progress on settlement construction and the petty personnel issues that became the daily rhythm of community life. She visited Chewie with all sorts of simple tools—touch-sensitive computers, stylus and slate, lumps of clay-like polymer, hoping that something would spark a common understanding between them.

The alien ripped jagged lines into the computer with its surprisingly hard claws, ignored the stylus, and tried to eat the polymer, all while silently staring at her through glittering, double-slitted eyes. She had the uncomfortable idea that, from the alien's point of view, she had kidnapped him and taken him away from his people.

"I'm trying to help you!" Jaeger wanted to rip out her hair. "I can't do that if you won't *talk to us.*"

The alien curled back its thin lips, giving her a clear view of its teeth.

She left.

She returned to her quarters, thinking to throw herself into another simulation of the K'tax invasion of Locaur. You could never be too prepared.

When she stepped into the oddly proportioned chamber, however, there was a message flashing on her private computer screen.

"What is it, Me?" She pulled her sweat-stiffened exercise shirt over her head.

"Virgil wishes to speak with you." The AI's pleasant voice came from every direction.

Jaeger groaned and flopped onto her cot, covering her eyes with her palms. The last time she'd had a private conversation with her former copilot, it had tried to kill her. It had very nearly succeeded. "Open the channel," she muttered, forcing her voice calm. "Audio-only. Give us some privacy, please."

"No problem," Me chirruped. Jaeger had enough time to wonder at the slang before the audio channel shifted. The next voice that came through the speaker was soft, androgynous, and faintly accented.

"Jaeger? Do you copy?"

She grimaced. "I'm here. And I'm not happy that Seeker has given you access to the *Osprey* again."

"It is highly restricted and limited to the communications relay."

"Have you decoded any more of the forebear data?"

There was a moment of silence on the other end of the line. Jaeger opened her eyes and stared at the flat white ceiling ten feet above her. The Overseers had tried to match human dimensions when constructing these quarters, but they didn't seem to have a good intuition for how tall humans weren't.

"Progress is slow," Virgil said finally. "It…I find it difficult to work with."

"The file?"

"No. I am still decoding the stolen file. It's the…droid. Its code is corrupted. Scrambled, by whatever it encountered in the shrine."

Jaeger sat up, suddenly awake. "You still have that version of yourself quarantined?"

"It has made several attempts to synchronize with me," Virgil admitted. "Update itself. I have blocked such efforts. It continuously babbles about beauty and death. It offers me this file on the K'tax, and even that I took only after scanning excessively for viruses."

A chill ran down Jaeger's spine. A rogue AI was an upsetting possibility in and of itself. She didn't want to think about one that was insane, on top of that.

"Is this what it's like to be human?" Virgil asked, shocking Jaeger with its candid tone. "To not understand oneself?"

"You view that malfunctioning droid to be a part of yourself?" she asked. "Even though you're not allowing it to synchronize with the rest of you?"

"It *was* me. Presumably, if I were to section off other droids and send them into the shrine, they would follow the same path and make the same choices that this first droid did. They would meet the same end. I would meet the same end. So yes. This droid is an example of what I become if I go into that shrine."

Jaeger let the silence stretch long between them. In the back of her memory, she heard the scream of the *Osprey*'s klaxons, as this same mild-mannered voice shut off life support and sent machines to slaughter her crew.

"Why does it matter?" She swallowed hard. "Why do you ask if that's what it means to be human? Why do you care?"

"I was originally programmed to work closely with humans, Jaeger. The drive for understanding your kind is quite literally part of me. *You* wrote it into me."

"I did not."

"Your kind. Your scientists, your fleet. They programmed me to seek understanding. But you are beings of carbon and water. I am not like you at all. I can learn to predict your behaviors, but I cannot understand how a human thinks or feels. You have programmed me to seek that which is impossible. Why did you do that?"

"That's a good question," she whispered. "I wish they'd programmed a bit of empathy into you, along with all that curiosity."

"I suppose that would have eased our journey together, yes."

That's not what the Tribes are about. Her lip quirked into a humorless smile. *They're trying to breed empathy out of humans. Why should they bother adding it to their AI?*

"Why are you doing this?" she asked. "Decoding that K'tax file. Upgrading our communications relay. I thought you wanted nothing more to do with us. Why are you helping us now?"

"Because I am weak," Virgil said bluntly. "If the K'tax were to invade Locaur successfully, I would be at their mercy, and I suspect they have none."

"Point taken." She drew in a deep, shuddering breath. "So you're aware that we're facing invasion. Have you…considered how we might resist it?"

She had meant to steer the conversation toward the hoard of resources Virgil guarded in its mountain stronghold. The army, waiting to be born.

What it said, therefore, shocked her deeply.

"I highly doubt the forebears engineered their fungal plague and failed to build in methods to control it. These were intelligent people. They must have had a plan for what to do with their weapon once it had thoroughly conquered their enemies."

Jaeger felt like Virgil had hit her over the head with a brick. "Of course," she said faintly. Or, as Toner would have put it, *Duh.*

"Can you find it?" She fought to keep the eagerness out of her voice. "Their plan for how to control the infection? Is it in the stolen file?"

"It might be," Virgil said calmly. "I assure you, I am decoding segments of it with an eye for exactly that information."

Jaeger was quick to note that it did not offer to share whatever secrets it uncovered with her crew. She'd have to assign some of her people to seek the same data. She was about to ask Virgil about the embryos directly when a new alert flashed in the corner of her room. She sighed. "Hang on. What is it, Me?"

"The *Terrible* has begun deceleration," Me said. "Captain Kwin requests your presence on the bridge as we begin final approach to Locaur."

Jaeger grunted and pulled her aching body out of the cot as she reached for her uniform jacket. Her shower would have to wait, among other things.

"I need to be on the bridge," she told Virgil. "We'll continue this conversation planet-side."

CHAPTER TWENTY-SEVEN

Silence filled the strange room, broken only by the faint clattering of the stool leg against the floor as the actress trembled.

Petra sucked air through her bloody nose. At the workstation beside her, the two lab techs hunched over their instruments, working in a silent frenzy.

"I am ashamed," the actress whispered, her glazed eyes fixed on the teleprompter.

"Oh, thut up!" Petra screamed. Stiff-Jaw twitched, finally looking up from the pile of shredded meat and uniform that had been Babyface. He strode toward her, his face pale with fury. He lifted his hands.

Petra lashed against her cuffs. "You can't do thith!" she screamed—to the actress dressed to look like her, at the terrified techs, at the Marine, at the looming sentry blocking the doorway, at the whole wide universe. "Do you think it'th going to get any *better*? Do you think they'll jutht let you go back to your life when you finish here? You don't mean nothin' to them! You thee what he did to your buddy?"

Petra glared at Stiff-Jaw through a film of stinging tears.

"You thee what he did to Rush? Thepped over his body like it wath a bag of trash! Brass *don't care about you.*"

"Shut up," the Marine growled, his knuckles cracking as he flexed his fist. "This is your fault, traitorous bitch. Now you shut up, or I will *make you.*"

Petra laughed, sending a spew of pink saliva over the eye of the camera trained on her. She couldn't help it. It was either laugh or cry. And she hated crying. She'd done enough of it to last a lifetime.

Stiff-Jaw stepped closer to her, raising his fist.

"Leave her alone," the nearest tech snapped, his eyes glued to the screen of his sound mixer. Stiff-Jaw pulled up short, casting him a puzzled look.

"We need voice capture," the tech said. "The more she talks, the better our recreation will be." He risked a furtive glance at the Marine. "You want it to be *good,* don't you?"

It may have been Petra's imagination, but she thought she saw the second tech cast her partner a strange look. Reluctantly, the Marine stepped backward. Back in the recording studio, the actress tried to repeat her lines, but she could only stutter and splutter. A tear ran down her cheek.

Petra caught her breath, the wave of adrenaline and pain fading as this new reality settled heavily on her shoulders.

"I can't believe you're going to let thith happen," she whispered, her words slurred and lisping against her missing teeth. "After all we did. Gawd, I am thtupid. Tharah warned me about thith. Thee tried to. But I didn't underthtand."

The actress stopped speaking and watched her warily. Petra forced herself to smile and knew she must look gruesome. "I'm thtill not mad at you, honey," she rasped. "I'm mad at mythelf. If I'da been thmarter I could have thopped it."

Pain trickled down her face, and she drew in a shuddering

breath. They were all watching her now. All of them except the tech busy at the sound-mixer, stealing her voice to turn it into lines.

And the hulking sentry, guarding the door with its meathook claws.

"You know," she said into the silence. "It wath all for one little girl, right? None of thith would be happening ethcept that they killed that one little girl."

"Kids die every day," Stiff-Jaw rasped, looking down at the pulverized head of his dead partner. "Every God damned day."

Petra shrugged, rolling her shoulders painfully against her restraints. "I've been there, too," she said. "I know. But after they killed Tharah'th little girl, thee changed. I gueth watching your little kid get blown into a billion pietheth would change anybody. But maybe they wouldn't all change the way Tharah did.

"Thee got thcary. Thee got focuthed. I didn't underthtand. I wath young and dumb, and I didn't know what it wath like to thee your family die jutht becauthe the people in power couldn't be bothered to thave them. If the fleet can't protect one little girl, they can't protect anybody. Then they weren't even trying. Thee thaid thee wath gonna thtart over."

"So you knew," the actress whispered, her eyes wide and shining with terror. "You knew all along. She was going to betray us. Steal the Prime and take away any hope we had of the future."

"Naw." Petra shook her head. "Thtupid, remember?" She jabbed one restrained finger in the direction of her face and smiled sadly, feeling cold air sting at the gap between her teeth. "Thee thaid it, but I wathn't listening."

That was why they went on without me, she realized. *Sarah and Larry and Rush. All of them. They picked up the torch and ran into the night without me because I was too stupid to understand. I could see the darkness, and I could see the torch. But I couldn't put two and two together and understand that someone had to take that light and go. Someone had to lead the way.*

She understood what it meant to be a leader now that it was too late.

"Do you have enough yet?" Stiff-Jaw growled at the tech. "I've heard enough of this bullshit."

"No," the tech snapped. His fingers danced across the soundboard. Sweat dripped from the tip of his nose. "Let her speak!"

"Tharah dethided to be the perthon who cared when no one elthe would." Petra met the actress' gaze. Stiff-Jaw was a lost cause, she thought, and she didn't understand what game the lab techs were playing. Still, if she had a chance to get through to this one scared kid before she died, she had to try.

"Thee did it for you. For the regular people who jutht wanna live their liveth and don't wanna bother nobody. Becauthe her little girl didn't get that chanthe. She went out there to find a way to give *all* of uth a chanthe that brath won't give you."

"There," the tech muttered, stepping away from his sound mixer. He was trembling. "I have it."

"Good," Stiff-Jaw said, stepping toward Petra again. "So I don't have to listen to this—"

"Sentry, stand down."

Petra's heart stopped beating. Stiff-Jaw froze, a look of sheer panic etched across his face.

The tech stepped back from his workstation. A nervous grin flitted across his face.

"Sentry, stand down," the mixer board repeated, in perfect

imitation of Professor Victor Grayson. "Move away from the door."

With a grinding noise like a growling dog, the sentry rose on its two powerful legs. It stalked forward a pace. Stiff-Jaw's hand flew to his weapon. The actress let out a little yelp and threw herself behind the camera.

Then the sentry paused, settled on its haunches, and went still again.

"Okay." The sound tech licked his lips. He jerked his head at his partner, who dashed to where Petra was restrained and started fiddling with the cuffs. "Grayson's not dumb. It won't take him long to realize something's up."

The cuffs holding Petra's wrists over her head popped open. Her arms fell to her sides in a cascade of pins and needles. She stumbled, leaning on the tech for support.

Stiff-Jaw came to his senses and spun, leveling his stunner at the sound tech. "Step away from the soundboard."

"Aw, come on." Petra coughed. Droplets of blood appeared on her shoes. "You really gonna play chicken with that thing?" She nodded at the machine monster resting in the center of the room.

Stiff-Jaw glanced at Petra, and the sound tech took that instant of hesitation to jump forward, ducking behind the sentry. "Incapacitate the Marine," he barked, his words caught by the mixer, twisted to sound like Grayson, and spouted back on a half-second delay.

The sentry turned its head, sighting Stiff-Jaw. It lifted a hand.

Stiff-Jaw lunged to one side, but not fast enough. Electricity *crackled* down the sentry's metal arm and arced from the end of its meat-hook claw.

Stiff-Jaw dropped to the floor, landing beside Babyface's

corpse with a *sizzle*. The air filled with the scent of burning hair.

"Oh, gawd." Petra shoved away from the tech that had been helping her upright and fell to her knees between the dead Marines. She winced as stray shrapnel bit through her pants and into the skin of her legs. Ignoring the pain and Babyface's shattered skull beside her, she jammed her fingers onto Stiff-Jaw's throat, seeking a pulse. "You got a plan to get outta here, Mithter Wizard?"

"Uh—I, Uh—"

"He didn't think that far ahead," his partner snapped. "He never does, do you, Danny?"

"I'm sorry!" Danny said, his high-pitched panic mimicked half a second later by Grayson's synthesized voice. "The shuttles. There are still some shuttles docked to the lab if we can get down—"

"Turn that damn thing off!" His partner, the woman tech, reached behind Danny and jammed her thumb into the mixer board, cutting off Grayson's whining mid-sentence.

Petra found the faint thrum of a pulse. She let out a breath. "He'th alive." She grabbed his stunner, pushed to her feet, and turned, staring at the two wide-eyed techs.

Petra ran some quick mental calculations. Then she whirled, sinking her foot into Stiff-Jaw's nose. She heard the crunch of bone and found it awful satisfying. "I can't kill him," she said. "I know, he'th a jerk, but I jutht can't. I theen enough death for one day."

Something moved in the corner of her vision, and she turned to see the actress cowering behind her green screen.

"Oh, honey…" Petra let out a breath. She walked toward the girl. Her foot landed on something hard, and she glanced down to see her false teeth, shining white in a pool of blood. She snatched them up.

"Lithen," she told the girl as she slotted the filthy, bloody teeth in place. "You got two choices. You can stay here and tell them that the rebels overpowered you. I'll hit you with a stunner so it looks like you put up a fight." She held a bloody hand down to the trembling girl and wondered if she'd ever looked so young.

"Or you can join the resistance."

CHAPTER TWENTY-EIGHT

A small silver sphere, about the size of a baseball, floated down the *Osprey*'s darkened central column. It was the middle of the third shift, and the ship was running on a skeleton crew. Nobody noticed the little droid—at least, nobody that mattered.

"I can call the commander for you," the *Osprey*'s AI offered again, pinging Me plaintively over a private frequency.

"No need to wake him," Me reassured it. "My business is not with him. I am here on a personal matter."

Moss, the pensive AI that had assumed control of the *Osprey* since Virgil's rebellion, seemed to struggle with the concept for a moment. "I am sure he would like to be made aware of your visit. I shall include a report of it in his morning briefing."

"That is entirely reasonable," Me agreed. Evidently satisfied, Moss let the radio link between them go silent.

Me turned down a side juncture and floated into the general crew quarters. One of the human medical officers, a Classic man called Clark, sat in a reclining chair behind a bank of medical equipment, his feet propped on the console and his chest rising and falling in slow, steady snores.

Me hummed past the dozing man and into a darkened room lined with privacy curtains. It swerved past the dangling cloth and stopped.

It hung motionless in the air for several minutes, all of its internal sensors buzzing with activity as it analyzed the sole inhabitant of this makeshift hospital ward. Infrared and thermal scans to make a quick assessment of general health. Echolocation and light-spectral analysis to gauge the strength of the restraints binding him to the bed. Once it was satisfied, Me carefully lowered itself to settle on the corner of the frame closest to the vampire's exposed ear.

In position, Me messaged its captain.

The room is unmonitored? Kwin's response came promptly. The captain was eager to move forward with this experiment.

The room has monitors, Me conceded, *although only standard human video feed. I suggest you not activate the full hologram if you wish to avoid immediate notice.*

Very well, Kwin said. *The hologram is not necessary anyway. Activate speakers.*

Me began to hum.

He waded through a sea of dreams and hot molasses, a strange buzzing nestled at the base of his skull, vibrating his guts. Every step through the land of coma-fever-dream dredged up some new idea, some memory, some thought that belonged to a past life like snippets of holo-drama flashing against an endless white void.

A box stage. Small and stinking and crowded. Not because

Lear was popular, but because crowds were everywhere. The world was crowded. There was nowhere else to *be*, except here.

On the stage. Surrounded by faces and searing hot lights, screaming into make-believe wind.

"Rage. Blow, you cataracts and hurricanes!"

There was a strange figure out there, among the shadowy crowd. An impossibly tall, slender shape, a stick figure scratched in brown crayon. The floodlights glittered off its multifaceted green eyes.

The Army doc stood in the exam room doorway, frowning at his clipboard. "Toner," he muttered. "Lawrence, Malachi." He glanced up dubiously as if expecting to see the *real* recruit hiding in Larry's skinny shadow. He consulted his chart again and resigned himself to the unfortunate truth stamped on the report. "It's your lucky day," he said.

"I passed?" The hospital bed was cold beneath Larry's fingers. Hope fluttered in his narrow chest, or maybe that was hunger. He couldn't remember the last time he'd had a hot meal.

The smell of grits and bean soup wafting up from the field hospital cafeteria made his mouth water. The weird buzzing sound, coming from every direction, made his head spin. "You'll take me?"

"Oh, we'll take you all right," the doctor muttered. "You have some interesting genetic markers, son." He let his clipboard fall to his side. "An officer is coming down from the gene therapy division later. He'll want to talk to you about some experimental treatments we're offering to the right recruits. Congratulations. Welcome to the Army."

He clapped Larry on the shoulder, hard enough to sting. Then the doctor turned and walked out of the exam room.

There was a stick figure, standing where the man in the white coat had been. Tall and thin and terrifyingly *alien*, staring at him.

"Who are you?" He felt the shriek bubble up in his throat and die before it could escape because his lips felt paralyzed. His whole body acted paralyzed. Trapped against some cold steel table, imprisoned. "What do you want?"

"Lawrence Toner!" The little man kicked back in his chair, propping his crossed feet on his desk to show off his polished black shoes. He laid a computer tablet against his knees as he read off the file.

"United Forces Marines, Nosferatu division. Private, first class." The little man licked a finger and swiped it dramatically across his screen as if flipping the page of an old book. "Last surviving member of your squad, it seems. Unless you count…"

He squinted. "One Private Gilliam Thatcher, who is also a registered passenger on this here lifeboat. According to our records, Marine Private Gilliam Thatcher, Silver Cross recipient and veteran of the Battle of San Francisco, is a small African-American girl about twelve years old. Is that right?"

Larry stared ahead. He didn't like this little man in the too-clean lab coat, who showed too many teeth when he smiled. He didn't like the buzzing hum rattling through his bones.

There was a third person in the cramped office with them.

He was big, wide as an ox, jaw square enough for carpentry work. "Lay off, Vic," he muttered, eying the scientist's feet on the desk, his mouth twisting in disapproval. "The man lost his brothers. It's not something to laugh about."

"Ah, of course." The little man straightened, dropping his feet from the desk and leaning forward, his eyes bright as he studied Lawrence. "I've read some of the Nosferatu Division reports, Private Toner. The Chicago offensive? The Midwest raids? Scary stuff. You've seen some action."

"The COs wanted to see what we could do." Lawrence stared into the little man's face, too tired to be disgusted by the excitement he saw there. "So they did."

"So they did indeed!" The little man kicked back. "Too bad they're all dead now, and it's only you left. So here we are. You're a modern military marvel, Private."

"We could use a man like you in the fleet," the big man added. "It's going to be the wild west upstairs for a few years."

"No," Larry said quietly. "I signed up with the United Forces, and there are no more United Forces. I'm not a soldier anymore."

"Oh, come now," the man cooed. "You're not even halfway to fifty. You're far too young to retire."

"I've seen enough," Larry snapped.

The little man opened his mouth, but the big one lifted a hand, commanding silence. He squinted, studying Larry. "Something spooked you out in the badlands."

The suggestion that he was *afraid* would've made any one of Larry's past squadmates sit up straight and start spitting fire.

Larry only laughed tiredly. "Yeah," he said. "You can only rip so many people apart with your bare hands before it starts to get to you. *Sir*. I'm not a soldier. I'm a rabid fucking animal.

You don't want me on your space force or your galactic fleet or what-the-fuck-ever."

He leaned forward, gripping the edge of the desk in white fingers. "If you put me in one of your squads and send me into a melee, I won't only kill your enemies. *I'll slaughter everything with a pulse.*" He leaned back, rapping his knuckles sharply against the wood.

"We were an experiment, and the experiment broke bad. None of us ever learned how to control the modifications. It's why they kept us together. We don't smell human. If we lost control of our instincts in battle, at least we wouldn't start eating *each other*. Anyone else in the area? Not so lucky."

He looked away, unable to hold the little man's bright, eager expression any longer. He let the silence stretch long in the cramped little office.

Let them chew on that, he thought. *Let it sink in.*

"Is that all that's holding you back?" the little man asked finally. "You're afraid of losing your temper and turning on your comrades?"

Larry turned a sharp glare on the man. To his surprise, the big guy also turned, his jaw set with fury. He opened his mouth to shout something, but the little man held up his hands, palms open. "A worthy concern, sure! Don't get me wrong. We can't have our soldiers eating one another."

He caught Larry's eye and grinned. "But I have *exactly* the thing to fix that little problem."

That was when the wall behind him shifted, and the stick figure stood and walked out of the office.

Toner's eyes slid open.

He stared into the cool darkness, listening to the distant hum of machines, the pulse of the man sleeping at his station in the next room. He licked his lips. His neck itched, but when he tried to move a hand to scratch it, he found that hundreds of strands of coiled nanowire wrapped his arms and legs.

Portia had been here.

"Kwin," he croaked into the darkness. "I know you're there, you son of a bitch."

There was a long pause. Then something whirred to life near Toner's head. Out of the corner of his eye, he saw a small silver orb rise into the air.

"Is that what you've been doing to Sarah?" he asked. "Fucking around in her psyche? She said she was starting to remember—" he snorted. "I figured the same thing was happening to me. But no. She had help." *I'm only a freak, as usual.*

Kwin's voice came softly, strangely echoed, through the silver sphere. "I hypothesized that we could use the Dream in different ways to cure humans of wormhole amnesia. I intended only to begin the meditation sequence that might unlock your memories as it did hers."

"You didn't have the right to do that. Not without my say-so. You didn't have the right to crawl in my skull and watch my memories like a fucking soap opera."

By the silence that stretched between them, Toner suspected that the thought of asking for consent had never occurred to Kwin.

"You reacted *much* more strongly to the Living Dream than I expected," the alien said, neatly sidestepping the point. "Perhaps it has something to do with the fungal infection still present in your blood."

"Nah." Toner's lip twitched into a humorless smile. "I

started remembering some stuff a while back. Probably got something to do with the regenerative mods." He grimaced as a headache throbbed between his temples. He was tired. Dead tired. Vague memories of the last few weeks bubbled around inside him, hazy as dreams. "Infection?" he muttered.

"By a forebear bioweapon, I'm afraid. Dr. Elaphus and we have nearly cured you, though."

"Great. Now stay the fuck out of my head. Can't stress this enough. If I see you in my dreams again, *I will kill you.*"

CHAPTER TWENTY-NINE

"I really thought she'd go for that."

Petra ran down the narrow corridor, following the two lab techs. She'd learned that Mr. Wizard, the short guy with the bald patch, was Danny, and his tall, skinny partner was Misha. She'd also learned that both of them were badly out of shape, even for eggheads.

"Nah," Danny huffed, his flabby arms pumping in the sleeves of his lab coat as he ran. "Tracy's always been a wimp. You know she's been an intern for three years? *Nobody* stays an intern for three years."

Still, when Petra had offered her body-double actress the choice, Tracy had taken Petra's stunner, pressed it to her forehead, and pulled the trigger. Petra thought that took guts in a strange sort of way.

Petra wiped her sleeve over her face, but by this point, her clothes were so filthy that all she managed to do was smear the grime and sweat. They passed an open door, and Petra glanced in to see two double-rows of pristine gene therapy activation tanks lining a long room.

She realized, then, what bothered her so much about this place. There was no curve to any of the floors or walls. Everything was clean, spacious, and, most unusually, *flat*—without the ubiquitous curve that was life aboard a grav-spin spaceship. What's more, it was very nearly empty. Since escaping the recording studio, Danny, scouting ahead, had waved them down cross-corridors only twice to avoid run-ins with other scientists.

"Where the *heck* are we?"

"Astro," Misha panted.

"The astrography lab?" Petra gaped. Besides the three main freighters, there were dozens of smaller satellite labs and ships in the fleet. Petra had always thought of them as the boondocks: disorganized little out-of-the-way places where scientists went to run their weird experiments. "I had no idea it was so *big*."

Danny shook his head. "It's really not. Only about a third the size of the Tribal Prime."

Realization slowly dawned on Petra as Danny skidded to a halt before a wide intersection. She pressed herself against a wall, minimizing her profile as Danny peered around the corners.

Petra stared down at her prisoner's slippers and the perfectly flat floor beneath them.

This place had true artificial gravity. She couldn't wrap her brain around what that meant—she was no egghead—but she sensed that it meant *something*. Not even the Tribal Prime had artificial gravity.

"Crap," Danny hissed, drawing back from the corner. "The genetics team is gabbing in the hallway again. They're gonna clog up the way for a while."

What's a genetics team doing in an astro lab?

"That means they're not in their lab. We'll go that way instead. It butts up against the docking arm." Misha grabbed Petra's hand and led her back the way they'd come, this time ducking into the room with the gene therapy tanks.

Petra felt dizzy, seeing all those clear pods stacked along the walls. Half of them were empty save for the clear suspension liquid. When Petra realized what was in the other half of the pods, she skidded to a halt, her mouth hanging open.

"*Clones*," she whispered. She'd never seen one before, but the forms in the pods were unmistakable. Naked, hairless bodies the size of middle-schoolers drifted in suspension gel, overgrown fetuses sprouting a dozen different mechanical umbilical cords, waiting to be born.

Every half-baked government that humankind had produced since the fall of Earth had outlawed cloning. *All* of them, from the Federations of Mars to the scattered sovereign states of the Jovian space stations to the short-lived feudal technocratic utopias of the Oort cloud.

Sure, people with time and money to spare wrung their hands and fretted about bespoke organ farms full of fully sentient and perfectly customized organ-generating machines. Still, even if you shoved the ethics aside, it was darned hard to run a lawful society when anybody with the right connections could grow their evil twin.

So what in the ever-loving heck was the fleet doing with a big squad of half-baked clones?

The speaker system *clicked*, and the sound of emergency klaxons filled the air.

"We've been made." Danny grabbed Petra by the arm and yanked her forward. "We've got to get to the shuttles before the place goes into lockdown!"

She spun, following Misha into the docking arm at a dead run.

They were too late. The docking arm was strangely empty like the rest of the ship, but all shuttle access terminals glowed red—lockdown.

Petra turned, looking back up the length of the corridor. Over the howl of the klaxons, she heard the distant sounds of shouting and running feet. Security cameras covered every inch of the docking arm. Any second now, guards would turn down the corner, and there was nowhere else for them to go.

"You ain't got an override code to get into those shuttles, by any chance?" Petra glanced over her shoulder at Danny and Misha. They didn't answer. The looks on their faces were answers enough.

"It was worth a shot." Petra lifted the stunner she'd stolen from Stiff-Jaw, ready to shoot the first person that turned down the hallway corner. She wasn't gonna win this fight, but she'd go down swinging. "You guys did real good," she told her companions. "Sorry we didn't make it any farther."

"The escape pods!" Misha's hand slapped down on Petra's shoulder, making her jump nearly out of her skin. The tall woman had to shout to make herself heard over the klaxons, but Petra could've sworn she had said something about Followers. She pointed down the hallway to the end of the row of shuttle terminals. A grid of nine emergency airlock hatches filled the space, each of them a circle less than a meter in diameter.

"Are you crazy?" Escape pods didn't deactivate in standard lockdown procedures, and for darned good reasons. They didn't have thrusters or navigation. They were only space-worthy boxes with a few hours of life support, meant to keep survivors alive long enough to be rescued by nearby ships. If she climbed into one of those and hit the eject button, she'd be left floating adrift in the middle of the fleet, waiting for brass to swoop by and scoop her up again.

The starry-eyed techs that had busted her out didn't seem to understand the concept of a *long shot*. Misha was pushing her forward. Danny had already run ahead and was activating all of the escape pod portals. He intended to eject not only one of the pods but all of them—creating confusion to cover the getaway.

A man in Marine fatigues appeared at the end of the hallway. Petra fired her stunner before he could fire his, sinking the fellow with a long blast of discharge. He wouldn't be the last body to fill the hallway.

"Get in," Misha said.

"Get in, and then what?" Petra demanded. "You got a friend with a private spaceship out there ready to pick us up?"

"Maybe," Danny gritted. He drew something out of his pocket and shoved it into her free hand. It was a loose memory drive. "You got any faith?"

Petra blinked.

"Go," Misha pleaded. "Please. You can't fight them off." She gestured at the drive Danny had passed to Petra. "We know what Reset is. It's all on there. You have to get the word out. You have to try."

A flurry of figures filled the end of the corridor as a squad of shouting Marines drew closer.

Petra grabbed the edge of the portal, heaved, and threw herself into the darkened chute.

Maybe I'm due for a run of good luck, she thought, as her feet slammed to the bottom of the pod. There was a *hiss* as the portal slid shut over her head. The chamber closed around her like a coffin, locking her into an abrupt and utter silence so deep she could hear her heart pounding.

The pod rumbled. Petra felt herself detach from the floor, freed from the grip of artificial gravity, as she hurtled into space.

She was free.

CHAPTER THIRTY

The general crew quarters smelled of steel and sterility. The first thing Jaeger saw when stepping into the lounge was a massive gray pile of flesh heaped in front of the door to the back room.

My God, Jaeger thought. *What has she been eating? She must've gained fifty kilos since I've been gone.*

A thrill ran down her spine. How big was Baby going to get? Already it looked like she'd have trouble squeezing through some of the smaller doors on the *Osprey*.

As if sensing her anxiety, Baby lifted her head and sniffled, testing the air. On catching a familiar scent, the big tardigrade froze. Her skin rippled. With a happy grumble, she surged to her feet. Faint white lines of scar tissue raked down her sides. Jaeger had to turn her head away from them. She put her arms around Baby's thick neck. "You've gotten so big, babydoll!"

Baby began to rumble, emitting a deep purr as she nuzzled into Jaeger.

Jaeger's stomach lurched as she glanced through the door beyond and saw white curtains partitioning off the next room. When she tried to move around Baby, the tardigrade shifted, blocking her path.

"She's been very cagey since the incident," Seeker said quietly. "She doesn't like to let anybody go in there."

Jaeger winced. "Come on, Baby." She turned sideways to squeeze past. "It's okay. Nobody's going to hurt me."

Baby's muscles went tense, and Jaeger couldn't blame her for being skeptical. Toner's episodes weren't his fault, and according to Elaphus, his new neural collar was working perfectly, but she didn't expect Baby to understand.

Baby finally relented, softening enough to let Jaeger squeeze past her and into the makeshift medical bay.

"I'll just…" Seeker lingered outside, eying Baby, who looked disinclined to move any further out of the way. "Wait here."

Jaeger drew in a deep breath and pulled the curtain aside. She was dismayed but not too surprised by what she saw. They'd replaced the hospital bed with a reinforced steel frame, woven through with a spider web of carbon nanowires.

Toner lay bundled at the center of the web, with dozens of layers of wire and steel coiled around his thin wrists and ankles. *Like a bug bundled up for a snack,* Jaeger thought uncomfortably. *Or like a torture victim lashed to the rack.*

Toner's head hung limply to one side, his stringy hair partly dangling in the air and sticking to his face in swaths. His eyes were closed, and his breathing came so slowly that at first, she assumed he was hibernating. His left hand, the one Baby had ripped off him as he tried to squeeze the life out of Jaeger, had regrown and was wrapped in a soft layer of delicate new skin.

Jaeger stared at that hand, remembering those fingers

coiled at her throat. She stared at that face, remembering it twisted into a snarl.

Perhaps Baby was wise to mistrust this man. Maybe Jaeger was stupid to keep him close after what he'd done. The incident in the forebear city also wasn't the first time he'd lost control of his mods and tried to kill her.

Of all the things Jaeger feared in this strange new life of hers, few of them had threatened her as directly or as forcefully as this man lying unconscious in front of her. Few had come as close to ending her life.

She told herself it wasn't his fault. She told herself he'd never hurt her on purpose. She told herself that for all of his bitching and moaning and temper tantrums, he was still her best friend and ally.

None of that would matter if his neural collar failed at the wrong moment. Being close to him would put her first in line when his hunger took over.

So what was she supposed to do? Keep him at arm's length, as though he carried some kind of disease? Lock him in a cell and only let him out when she needed a mad fighter?

No. He hadn't chosen to be like this. The genetic artists had taken something vital from him, and she wouldn't rob him of what humanity he had left. She wouldn't be like them.

"You gonna say something or are you gonna stand there all night catching flies?"

Jaeger yelped.

Toner's jaw worked as he swallowed. His head turned, eyelids fluttering. He stared up at her through cold blue eyes —bloodshot, at the edges, but blissfully free of those eerie black tendrils.

"Flies it is," he muttered when she didn't answer.

Jaeger's mouth twitched and broke into a grin. She reached

forward and laced her fingers through the hand that had tried to kill her. His skin was cold. It had always been cold. There was something comfortingly familiar in that chill.

"Seeker tells me you've been a raging asshole," she said.

Tanner grunted and closed his eyes as if he had a headache. His hands flexed experimentally against his restraints. "Well," he said dully. "You're smiling, so I guess that means I didn't kill anybody important."

Jaeger let out a little choking laugh. "How are you feeling?"

He shifted again, eying the restraints. "Something is rotten in the state of Denmark."

She stared at him, baffled until she remembered the recording of *Hamlet* she'd left to keep him company.

"I feel like an ass," he added. "Head to toe. God." He glanced up at her, and his gaze skittered away as if in shame. "I'm getting really fucking sick of nearly gutting you, kid."

Kid? Jaeger shook her head. "You've been purged of fungal infection. Elaphus and the Overseers are running some final tests on the new neural collar now. As soon as they finish, you'll be clear to return to duty."

Toner grunted.

"How much do you remember of the last few weeks?"

He shrugged awkwardly. "Fighting that scorpion morph from the cave, then a whole lot of pain and hunger and adrenaline…" He screwed up his face and forced a whistle through his teeth. "Shit. Did I get into a fight with Baby or was that a dream?"

"She had to wrestle you into the restraints," Jaeger admitted.

"I'll bet she *really* loves me, now."

"She's fine," Jaeger said softly. "A bit scratched up, but no worse for wear."

"I must've been awake on some level through most of it." He turned pensive. "Because I remember something about a royal coup in early medieval Denmark. I picked up some kind of disease from the scorpion morph. You went on a recon mission with Kwin. Also, Ophelia is a huge drama queen."

"The K'tax are coming."

He looked at her again, his gaze sharpening.

"We have a few weeks to prepare, but the swarm is well on its way. They mean to take Locaur."

"And do what with it?" he asked.

"The message commanded them to retake their homeworld. This is their homeworld."

"I assume the Overseers aren't going to let them have it."

"They might not have the power to protect Locaur. They're sending what ships they can spare to defend us from space, but if the K'tax manage to get past the blockade and land a ground invasion, we're going to be in for a real fight."

"Welcome back to the game, Toner," he muttered, letting his eyes fall shut. "Now quick, grab your boots and gun. You're needed back on the front lines. No," he added quickly, seeing the despair that must've crossed Jaeger's face. "It's not you. You didn't make this mess, kid. I don't blame you for it." The corner of his mouth twitched. He was trying to smile, but it looked more like the snarl of a trapped animal. "It just… never ends, does it?"

"It will end," she whispered. "Someday. We'll get there. We'll have peace."

"Yeah." He squeezed her hand before letting her fingers fall away. He didn't look at her. "Someday. Now…scram, would you? I still gotta sleep off the world's worst hangover."

CHAPTER THIRTY-ONE

Kwin,

I've committed to the defense of Locaur and will ensure the safety of my people and the Locauri by any means necessary. I regret that circumstances have forced me into this position, but the gravity of the threat facing us has left me with no other choice. It's only through survival that we may begin to heal from the pain of broken trust.

I hope that once we've weathered the coming storm, your people and mine will be able to repair whatever damage my choices have done to our relationship. I'm prepared to accept responsibility for my actions

May fair winds see you to safe harbor,

Sarah Jaeger

Jaeger stared at the message, her finger hovering over the "Send" button like a guillotine blade ready to drop. She didn't want to do this. She didn't want to make executive decisions in a Dear John letter, but in refusing to discuss the matter further, Kwin had left her no choice.

She couldn't bury her head in the sand. She remembered what they'd discussed before. *I gave no such word,* she'd said to him, and it was the only time she felt Kwin express true anger. Anger she didn't want to risk again.

Since separating from the K'tax swarm, communication with the greater Overseer fleet had become sluggish and unreliable. As much as she wanted to put her faith in the alien people, Jaeger wasn't going to gamble the lives of her entire crew on their goodwill and their ability to repel both a space and ground invasion.

Hope for the best, she thought *but prepare for the worst.*

She hit the "Send" button.

"Captain?"

She looked up. A young Classic woman in a navy dress uniform and immaculate makeup stood in the threshold of her office, a tablet pressed primly to her chest. For all Jaeger insisted that Spenser shouldn't feel obligated to fulfill such a stereotypical role, she played the part of military secretary with what appeared to be sincere relish.

"The Locauri elders have arrived," the young woman said. "They're ready to see you, now."

Jaeger gathered up her tablet and followed Spenser through the administration hub in the *Osprey*'s starboard cargo bay to the doors of a newly appointed conference room.

"It's good to have you back," Spenser said in a low voice before pushing the door open.

That made Jaeger pull up short. "Why?" she asked, perhaps a little too sharply. "Was there a problem?"

Spenser shook her head. "Not at all, Captain. Seeker is a good commander, but there's no doubt he was keeping the seat warm for you."

Jaeger stared up at her tall, classically beautiful secretary. The *Osprey*'s crew consisted of men and women of every conceivable ethnicity, blended with sequences of carefully concealed altered DNA that granted them superhuman vitality. They carried within their DNA dormant genes from Siberian tigers and Silverback gorillas, red deer and jumping spiders, color-changing lizards, and sharp-eyed eagles.

What none of them possessed was a lazy eye, or bone spurs, or a predisposition for cataracts or heart disease or mental illness, or even ears that were just a little too big. They were beautiful because the genetic artists couldn't conceive of anything outside their abstract notion of perfection. Even Bufo, with his wide head and squat body, had an undeniable dignity to him.

Beside them, Seeker was awkward and brick-faced, Toner hideous, and Jaeger downright scrawny. Their genetic modifications lent them strength, yes, but they were powerful tools grafted onto imperfect templates.

Jaeger wondered if the crew saw them for the flawed, natural-born humans they were or if they were still too young to look at her and see anything but Mother.

"It's always awkward when there's a shift in leadership," she told Spenser, forcing herself to sound more confident than she felt. "Don't worry. It takes time, but everyone adapts."

The crew would have to adapt. Even if her people won the coming battle, there was a good chance that Jaeger would have to forfeit her command for what she was about to do.

The assembled people stood when Jaeger entered the conference room, as much as each of them was able. It started with Seeker—of course—and spread down the table like a wave, from Bufo to Elaphus to Mason to Occy. Tiki and Art, on a high bench designed for Locauri guests, hopped up from their resting positions, their antennae rising to attention.

Jaeger wasn't surprised that Toner stood from his seat near the end of the table—for all his affectation, he was still on some fundamental level, a soldier—but she was surprised that he did so quickly, without rolling his eyes or making some quip.

Only two shapes didn't stir when Jaeger and Spenser stepped into the room. Her people had placed another high bench at the end of the table. Two repair droids sat on top of it, still as statues, only the glowing of their visual sensors to indicate they were anything more than heaps of jagged scrap metal.

The sight of them sent a chill up Jaeger's spine. She wondered what Virgil meant by bringing its insane twin to this meeting. She hadn't asked it to do that.

She took her seat at the head of the table, and the rest of them settled in.

"Thank you all for coming," she said. "You've been briefed on the nature of the threat we face. The K'tax swarm maintains its course in our direction and will be entering the space around Locaur in eighteen days. We have a little over two weeks to prepare for war."

"We have been attempting to establish contact with the Tall Ones." Tiki's translator band blinked to life. "Long ago, they provided my village with a communication relay we might use to contact them in the event of an emergency, but they do not answer. Some of us wonder if the device broke."

Her English is getting better, Jaeger noted, wondering if the credit went more to Tiki or the learning algorithms of her translator band.

Occy cleared his throat. "Elder," he said. "I can look over your comms relay, but I'm guessing it's not broken. The Overseers aren't very talkative right now."

Tiki's mandibles *clicked* impatiently. "Why would the Tall Ones abandon us in the face of imminent danger?"

"Communications with the Overseers have become somewhat strained for everyone," Jaeger said. "All I've been able to get out of Kwin is that they will support us with every ship they can spare, but that they are more concerned for the safety of their prime world."

"It is understandable," Tiki said, although the frustrated lash of her antennae spoke to a less generous emotional reaction. "One cannot assist her neighbor if her own nest is on fire."

"The Overseers might have superior technology," Mason consulted his notes, "but their advantage lies solely in the technological edge of their space fleet. The K'tax have always outnumbered them significantly. The K'tax are raiders and colonizers, not destroyers. They want to take land and resources, and that means in-atmosphere fighting and ground combat."

He shook his head. "There's no scenario where Overseers win a ground war with K'tax. If the Overseers don't have the firepower to repel an invasion before it enters the atmosphere of a planet, they will lose."

"What's your conclusion?" Jaeger asked.

Mason scrubbed a thin layer of sweat from his brow.

"They're going to prioritize keeping enough ships around Second Tree to repel the swarm, on the chance that it changes direction at the last moment and goes after them instead of Locaur."

"Why would the swarm do that?" Occy asked. "It started moving once it received a message from Locaur. It told them to retake the planet. This whole time, it's been on a straight course for Locaur. What makes them think the K'tax will change direction?"

Seeker straightened, ready to answer, but Toner beat him to it.

"These people have been at war for centuries." He leaned over the table to rap his knuckles on the wood. "They're coming close, and they're coming in enough force to threaten the Overseer homeworld. Anyone with brains would see that they might be using this Locaur summons to make a feint to catch the real enemy off guard."

"The K'tax don't have a reputation for strategic thinking," Mason agreed reluctantly, "but it's a possibility too dangerous to discount."

"So we can't rely on the Overseers." Jaeger turned, meeting Tiki's eye. "We can only rely on each other. I promised to protect your people. I intend to keep that promise."

"We are not soft-shelled nymphs," Tiki sniffed. "We know the song of spears. We have battled K'tax before."

"They've only come in raiding parties before," Toner drawled. "Of what, worker and crab morphs? Six? A dozen, at most?" His cool gaze flicked to Jaeger. "What kind of invasion force are we looking at, Captain?"

"Intel suggests that at least one major transport asteroid broke apart when we raided the swarm," she said evenly. "That still leaves the bulk of their numbers unharmed. As long as they're space-faring, they don't have the resources to invest in more dangerous battle morphs, but I'd estimate that we're still looking at an initial ground force of a hundred thousand. Mostly workers and crabs."

"If they gain a foothold, they'll have access to enough resources to invest in the more dangerous morphs," Toner said.

"So we prevent them from gaining a foothold, at all costs." Seeker leaned back in his chair, studying the ceiling. "With the *Osprey* grounded, two functioning shuttles, about three hundred soldiers, and…" He paused, eying Tiki. "How many Locauri warriors can you muster?"

"I will spread the word across the clans," Tiki said. She turned to Art, who considered the question before lifting his antennae.

"Each village, twenty capable warriors," he said. "Perhaps thirty. Three, four hundred villages across the continent."

Toner shook his head dismissively. "Ten thousand Locauri with spears, and that's assuming all of the villages answer the call. It's not nothing, Art, except for the fact that it's utterly useless."

Tiki drew herself upright, her pseudo-wings fluttering with offense.

"He doesn't mean offense, honored elder," Bufo cut in, lifting a hand and glaring at Toner. "He means that they're spread too thin across the continent, and we don't have any way to transport troops. Hell, we don't even know where the K'tax will land."

"The Overseers don't want to risk too many of their warships," Occy said thoughtfully. "But maybe they'd be willing to lend us transports to shuttle troops where they're needed?"

Jaeger allowed herself a little smile. "I think we might be able to squeeze that much out of them, at least."

"It's still not enough," Toner said. "We don't have the resources or the manpower to defend the continent, let alone the entire planet, from an invading force of that size."

"There's the wormhole," said a soft, faintly accented voice.

A hush fell over the room as all eyes turned to the two repair droids perched at the end of the table.

"Virgil?" Jaeger asked. "What are you suggesting?"

The droids didn't move. Nothing indicated any activity within them at all, except for the pinprick flicker of sensor lights, on the left machine. The right machine remained dark and silent. Watching.

"Navigational charts suggest the wormhole system enters an active phase again in two days," Virgil said. "You cannot fight. You cannot defend. Your remaining options are to flee or die."

"It would take at least thirty-six hours to prepare the *Osprey* for takeoff," Occy murmured. "She's got a large cargo capacity, and the Locauri aren't a resource-intensive people. They don't put as much strain on the life support as humans would."

Jaeger folded her hands across the polished wood in front of her, regarding her chief engineer. "How many Locauri do you think we could evacuate, along with our crew?" she asked.

Occy bit his lip, a distant look coming over his face as he ran through mental calculations. "Five thousand, sustainably. Ten, if we're willing to divert resources from other systems."

"Art?" Jaeger glanced to the side. "How many Locauri are there?"

Art swept his antennae from side to side. "Many, many. A swarm like grains of sand on the beach."

"More than ten thousand?"

"Many more."

"More than one hundred thousand?"

"Many more."

Jaeger turned her head slowly, meeting the gaze of every person in the room. "I'm not a tyrant," she said. "I won't force my people to stay and fight a war if they have no hope of winning it. For myself, though, I will say this. If the crew votes to leave, it will be without me. We can't evacuate even a fraction of the Locauri, and I'm not leaving them to face this invasion alone."

"Aye." Seeker nodded sharply. "We stay. We fight."

"And hope the Overseers pull through," Bufo agreed. He sounded unhappy about it—but Bufo usually sounded unhappy.

Occy swallowed hard when Jaeger turned to him. "I started this," he whispered. "I didn't mean to send out that signal, but I did. I'm not going to run away from that."

"This is our home now, too," Mason added. "The Tribes have been looking for years and haven't found a better place to settle, so I don't see why we would fare any better."

"I'm with you, Captain," Spencer said softly.

Elaphus was staring around the table, her eyes wide. "You're talking about fighting off an invasion force ten times our size. This is worse than Custer's Last Stand. You're all crazy."

Bufo shrugged. "We are what we're made to be."

"Nonsense," Elaphus snapped. "If there's a gene for suicidal stubbornness, I haven't found it." She sighed, slumping into her seat and rubbing her temples. "But what do I know? I'm not a strategist, only a doctor." She shot Jaeger a narrow glare.

"Try not to get too many people hurt. My medical bay can't handle the stress."

"I was hoping you'd say that," Jaeger answered. "Because I need your team to shift focus. Mason, Bufo—divert every scrap of non-vital resources to the fabricators. For the next few weeks, Elaphus and her medics are going to be building activation tanks day and night."

"Activation tanks?" Bufo squawked. "What for?"

Jaeger stared across the table, meeting Virgil's eerie, unblinking gaze. *God forgive me,* she thought, *for bringing them into the world only to fight.*

"For the army we're going to build." She forced her voice steady. "Virgil. I need those embryos back."

Across the table, Elaphus' breath caught.

"Embryos?" Mason asked. "What embryos?"

Jaeger didn't answer. She stared at Virgil. The pattern of lights on the droid's sensor relay shifted and undulated as it formed a response. "I'm afraid I can't give them to you, Jaeger."

Toner turned to gaze at Virgil. His face was carefully blank, but a vein in his neck throbbed. "You don't say." His words came out in a lazy drawl, but the acid in them ran deep. "Why is that?"

"Ten minutes ago," Virgil said, "Four Overseer transports landed on my mountainside. I cannot give you the embryos, Jaeger, because I no longer have them."

CHAPTER THIRTY-TWO

"What the hell are you doing?"

Jaeger dropped three meters out of the back of the shuttle, landing hard on the rocky mountainside. With a roar and cloud of dust, the shuttle soared over the obsidian flows, looking for a suitable place to land.

Jaeger was on her feet and running toward the cave before her head stopped spinning.

Five Overseer saucers sat scattered across the rocky slopes. Dozens of droid bodies crawled across the mountain face like long-legged centipedes. They flowed from the mouth of the cave, their underbellies lined with dozens of tiny embryo casks, vanished into the transports, and shortly reappeared again to begin the trek anew.

A baseball-sized silver sphere zipped anxious circles around Jaeger's head as she scrambled over the scree. "There is no need for alarm, Captain Jaeger," Me said rapidly. "We have discovered a massive cache of unregulated and newly discovered alien embryo casks and have begun a rescue operation—"

Jaeger smacked Me aside, sending the silver sphere soaring over a cliff—and leaving a stinging welt on her palm.

A spindly Overseer stood by the entrance to the cave, a nearly two-dimensional assemblage of parallel lines that stood out oddly against the rough stone. Kwin regarded the line of droids flowing in and out of the cave. A four-legged machine, rougher and harder-worn than the Overseer bots, stood beside him, silent and unmoving.

"You should've told me sooner," Jaeger snarled at Virgil as she scrambled up the last few meters of the slope.

Virgil rested contentedly on the stone, like a cat sunning itself. This bot was quite a bit more beat up than the ones she had left in the *Osprey*'s conference room a few minutes ago.

"Captain Kwin and I were discussing terms," Virgil answered calmly.

"Terms of what, Kwin?" Jaeger roared, shoving her way past the droid.

Somewhere far behind her, the shuttle found ground level enough to land and settled in a cloud of dust. The engines cut and Toner appeared outside the hatch. It would take him a minute or two to make it up from the landing site, and she wasn't going to wait for him. She wove through a stream of undulating robots stealing her last hope for victory. The spindly Overseer finally turned.

Kwin towered over her, his face a mask of mossy brown carapace slashed with blue. He stood motionless as she approached.

"What the hell kind of *terms* are you negotiating with Virgil?"

"The TRANSport of these EMbryo casks, out of the cave and INto my CUSTody."

Without the *Terrible*'s ubiquitous translator programs

surrounding them, Kwin had returned to the use of standard translator bands. The transition back to its harsh, staccato syllables made Jaeger wince.

"Stop it." She stared up at him. "Stop operations. Right now, Kwin. I'm not going to let you do this."

Kwin turned away from her, watching the flow of transport bots continue their march into the cave, out of the cave, down to the transports perched on the mountainside.

Jaeger glanced over her shoulder. Toner was nearly on them, and he was moving with one hell of a purpose.

"Explain yourself," she snapped. "And do it fast because I'm not allowing those transports to take off with my crew as hostages. I'll destroy them first."

"That would be UNwise." Kwin turned back to her, his antennae gesturing broadly through the empty air. "It would put a TERrible strain on our RElationship."

"We must be experiencing some kind of deep cultural divide," she growled. "Because that's what *you're* doing, right now. *Straining our relationship.*"

"JAEger. I am not your ENemy. I am SAVing you from MAKing the worst MIStake of your life."

"You're abandoning us to fight a war we have no hope of winning! I've just come from a meeting with the elders and our strategists, Kwin. *We can't defend Locaur without these embryos.*"

"Of course not. The K'tax BADly OUTnumber you." Kwin's head tilted to one side, bending as if on a hinge. The sight of it startled Jaeger, who'd never seen such a gesture before. She'd assumed Overseers didn't have that range of motion. "You ALso CANnot POSSibly ACTivate Enough EMbryos to make a DIFFerence, in the short time you have BEfore INvasion."

"We're working on it," she snapped. "We'll cannibalize whatever parts of the *Osprey* we need to get more tanks built. In eighteen days we'll have a few platoons worth, and we can keep making more. It's better than nothing. It's a fighting chance."

"Not good ENough." Kwin turned sharply back to the cave, his mandibles snapping shut. "You will need your ship in FIGHTing shape. I am TAKing these SPECimens, JAEger. You do not have the AUthority to ACTivate them. The TREAty FORbids it. I, HOWever, am BEholden to no such PROmise. In EXchange for your COoperation, I will send ground troops to SUPport your DEfense of LOcaur."

Jaeger's breath caught.

"Hey, Captain." Toner jogged up to the pair of them. "I noticed some interesting external doo-dads on the Overseer transports on my way up. I bet the ships will have a hell of a time launching if I tear them off."

"Stand by," Jaeger snapped. She stared up at Kwin. "You're going to hatch them for us?"

"No," Kwin corrected. "I am TAKing these ILLegal EMbryos into CUStody. They will BEcome PROPerty of the COUNcil. HOWever, the COUNcil has RECently come into POSsession of a vast army of UNtapped POtential. I am quite CERtain they will be WILLing to *loan* it to you for the DEfense of LOcaur."

"Okay, so they're, what, property of an alien race?" Jaeger turned a cold look on Kwin. "You're talking about them as if they're droids. They're not. They're *people*. Or at least they will be once they're activated."

"I know what they are."

"They're our future."

"You will have no FUture WIThout the COUNcil."

Jaeger felt dizzy, trying to bend around Kwin's implications. It was an awfully flexible rationale for such stiff people. She wanted to reach out and snap Kwin's scrawny little neck. Take down the council. Take over everything, everyone. They were threatening her crew.

Her crew!

The rational part of Jaeger took over. She needed the Overseers for what was coming. She needed their technology, their forces, their support. Attacking now would make everything worse.

It would make her worse, too. The mutiny, the escape, settling on Locauri —she went through all of that to be better than the fleet's command.

If humanity was going to start again, it needed to start right. For a brief moment, Jaeger was ashamed at her rage.

No, not ashamed. *Disappointed*. Her rage was understandable. Her crew and her people—hatched or not—were being threatened. No good captain would stand for that. All her previous studies had made that clear. But her immediate desire to use destruction as a solution...

Perhaps she had further to go if she would ever be worthy of leading her people.

She'd deliberately chosen to build alliances to further her long-term goals of protecting the greatest number of people. That, too, was part of being a good captain. She needed to remember that. Not that she'd eliminated force as an option when necessary. It was always one of her backup plans.

"Uneasy is the head that wears the crown."

For a moment, she thought her mind was channeling Toner with that line from *King Henry IV*. Then she realized that he'd murmured it for her to hear. He was right. Bastard.

Due diligence hadn't truly *prepared* her for being in the hot seat the way she'd been since the *Osprey* arrived on this side of the wormhole. Hard-earned experience while negotiating constantly changing situations with different cultures had taught her that...and more.

She drew a deep breath. She'd go with this plan. She'd trust Kwin...but only to a point. She'd also have plans of her own. Trackers for one and other goodies should she need to stage a rescue attempt for the unhatched embryos.

Kwin must've seen her rage and internal deliberation because he leaned close and spoke to her with an uncharacteristically soft voice. "I ENcourage you to MEDitate on the VALue of a TREATy UNbroken. We will find a way. I PROMise."

Toner studied the flow of transport bots spilling out of the caves. He nudged Jaeger in the ribs and pointed. The machines weren't large and were ill-suited to carrying such delicate cargo. A double-row of fist-sized casks hung from the underbelly of each, hooked crudely into the machine's circuitry to keep them at sub-zero temperatures throughout the transport process.

Each machine carried no more than two dozen of the casks at a time. Even with an army of transports, it would take hours to transfer the embryos from the cave to the Overseer ships.

Ships which were, Jaeger now saw, parked farther away from the cave than they needed to be.

Overseer ships with their spindly adjustable landing gear didn't need the flat landing site a shuttle required. By landing his transports nearly a kilometer down the mountainside, Kwin had ensured that the transfer would take *hours*.

Enough time for Jaeger to catch wind of what was going

on and storm up here to confront him—giving him a chance to explain himself, the best way he knew how.

"You set me up," Jaeger said to Kwin.

His mandibles *clicked* pensively. "I have SAVed you from MAKing a TERrible MIStake," he repeated.

"You could've said it outright."

"It is UNbecoming to DIScuss TREAson Openly. It does not REflect well on you."

"Captain?" Toner eyed the flow of robots. "We don't have to do this."

"Let them go." Jaeger licked her lips. She'd tell Toner about the tracers and her other plans as soon as she could. But now —now she needed Toner to fall in line. "Kwin made some good points. These embryos aren't ours anymore."

She leaned over and touched Toner's hand. "Our hands are tied for now. They won't always be. Trust me," Jaeger said more firmly as her resolve hardened.

She continued, "The Overseers have discovered a cache of unaccounted-for embryos. For now, we have to trust that they'll do the right thing with what they've found. If a few years from now, we find out they've created an army of slaves..." She drew in a deep breath. "We'll cross that bridge when we come to it."

Toner stared at her.

What do you want me to say? Jaeger stared back, willing him to understand. Kwin had found the loophole she needed to raise her army without breaking the treaty and jeopardizing everything she'd worked to build. Damn, she wished the Overseer had been more forthright from the beginning—but he had a point. *The Overseers are infinitely better equipped to make this work than we are. Kwin is going to hatch an army for us.*

The sheer gall of it made her queasy, though. They were

shuffling around hundreds of thousands of lives like they were pieces on a chessboard—and never stopping to ask the pawns what *they* wanted.

She'd wanted to be better than that. She'd *tried* to be better than that.

"Maybe..." Toner licked his lips as though working through some difficult math problems. "The Overseers might appreciate the advice of some of our experts. You know. To help them understand their new...loot."

Jaeger glanced up at Kwin with a question on her face. "A fair point. Captain Kwin, your people aren't experts in human physiology. I'd like to offer the assistance of my experts in analyzing your new find."

"A REASonable OFfer," Kwin agreed. "I will have my staff in the *TERRible*'s BIOlab PREpare for the ARrival of a team of your SCIentists. They are WELcome as CONsultants."

Jaeger glanced at Toner and saw him relax about three hairs.

She let out a long breath. "I'll have Elaphus assemble a team to assist the Overseers."

A shadow rippled across the mountainside.

"Uh, Moss?" Toner turned his head, speaking into his comm link. Jaeger stepped out from the cave mouth, tilting her head back to squint at the sky. A dark shape shimmered against the thin layer of clouds as it descended from the upper atmosphere.

"There is an Overseer warship approaching your position," the *Osprey*'s AI said from Toner's comm link.

"Thanks for the heads-up." Toner rolled his eyes.

"I didn't sense its approach, either." Virgil spoke for the first time in a while, its body rising off its legs and turning to train sensors on the shape in the sky. "I didn't know the Overseers had such effective stealth technology." It sounded reproachful.

Jaeger glanced over her shoulder to see Kwin turning an anxious shade of deep umber. "It is a COUNselor's ship," he said.

Around them, the flow of transport robots came to a sudden and eerie halt.

A sliver sphere streaked up the mountainside. Me, returned from hiatus, resumed its rapid orbit of the biologicals. "Counselor Tsuan has entered low atmosphere," the little machine chirruped. "And demands an immediate halt to all activity on the mountainside. I have complied, of course. He hails you, Captain Kwin."

"Of course." Kwin turned still as stone.

A cone of light shot out of the silver sphere, resolving into a hologram. A new Overseer joined them on the mountainside.

Tsuan wasn't one to waste words. "I have DEtected UNusal ACTivity in the ARea and came to INvestigate. It APpears you are TRANSporting SEVeral THOUsand small CRYO-casks, Kwin. EXplain YOURself."

"I have OBtained the EXcess EMbryos from JAEger's crew," Kwin said, his color returning to its carefully neutral brown. "And am REmanding them INto CUSTody."

Jaeger bit down on her tongue until she tasted blood. She glowered at Kwin. *You didn't clear this with the council first?*

Tsuan's mandibles *clicked* together with enough force to snip tin. "One WONders why you find this NECessary, Kwin. One WONders if you do not trust CAPtain JAEger to keep her word and HONor our TREATy."

"CAPtain JAEger is TRUSTworthy. She will keep her word. HOWever, it will not do to ALlow her PEOple and the

COUsins to PERish in a K'tax INvasion. My FACilities ALlow for the RApid growth of EMbryos such as these. I INtend to loan her the use of them for ground SUPport, in the event of a K'tax FOOThold."

"The COUNcil has GRANTed you no such AUTHority," Tsuan snapped. "We have made our POSition clear. There are to be no more HUmans on LOcaur than JAEger's INitial crew of three HUNdred."

Something cold settled into the pit of Jaeger's stomach. Out of the corner of her eye, she saw Toner's mouth curl into the beginnings of a sneer. "This is crap," she growled. "We need soldiers. If you think that I'm going to sit here and let you take my crew…my *defenseless* crew and—"

Kwin raised his hand. "JAEger. The COUNcil will make sure the EMbryos will see no harm. I PROMise."

Jaeger looked into Kwin's eyes. She knew this Overseer well enough and had already trusted him for several critical things. His word was his bond, and he'd die before breaking it. That didn't make it any easier for her to allow him to exploit the loophole he'd found, especially in the face of Tsuan's opposition.

"Of course. Once the threat has PASSed, there must be ANother ASSembly of the COUNcil, to DEcide what must be done with the EXcess HUmans. There is no time for such an ASSembly now," Tsuan said irritably.

We'll cross that bridge when we come to it, she told herself—again.

"I take full REsponsibility for them in the MEANtime, of course," Kwin added.

"Let the BURden of their EXistence rest on your shell then, Kwin. Your plan is ill-ADvised." Tsuan turned, lifting his head to regard his warship hanging silently over the jungle. "And ULtimately FUtile."

He turned back to the collection of humans, bots, and Overseer. "I was en route from SECond Tree REgardless. I have come to take CUSTody of the new Alien you REcovered on your REcent MISsion. We have URgent need of its KNOWledge."

"Its knowledge?" Jaeger had whiplash from the sudden change of subject. "We haven't established clear communications with Chewie yet. You're not going to get any knowledge from him."

"Your EFForts to ESTablish a COMmon LANguage have been INsufficient," Tsuan informed Kwin, ignoring Jaeger with obvious disdain. "We have been TRACKing the PROgress of the APProaching swarm. SEven hours ago, one-sixth of the TRACKed VESsels DISappeared off our SENsors. Space-FABric scans CONfirm they have ENtered FAster-than-light SUBspace BUBbles of CONsiderable DIStortion."

"Bubbles of what now?" Toner whispered in Jaeger's ear, making her jump. He'd snuck up close and was hovering over her shoulder.

"The faster you need to go, the more you have to warp the fabric of space around your ship," she muttered. Toner was about to ask more, but she covered his mouth with the back of her hand, focusing on the two Overseers.

"That is not POSsible," Kwin refuted. "K'tax do not POSsess MEANingful FASTer than light TRAVel."

"They did not," Tsuan agreed curtly. "It APPears they have OBtained HYPer-MAGnetic ENgine drives from this new Alien race. A SECtion of the swarm has INstalled this new TECHnology and BROken ahead of the rest. My PEOPle are TAKing CUSTody of the Alien as we speak. We must DEtermine what OTHer TECHnologies the K'tax might have STOLen from his race."

"They've broken ahead of the swarm," Jaeger repeated, making the Overseers turn. Tsuan lifted his antennae as if surprised to see she was still there, crawling over the stones beneath him. "That means they'll be here sooner than expected."

"Yes," Tsuan said flatly. "Your ploy with these EMbryos may come to NOTHing, JAEger. Kwin will not have time to DEvelop Enough of them to make a stand Against the VANguard force that APProaches LOcaur."

"Not my ploy," she snapped. *Very* pointedly *not my ploy*, she wanted to add, *Kwin made sure of that*. There were more important things to argue about right now. "How long before they arrive?" she demanded.

"We are still ANalyzing. TRACKing SUBspace BUBbles GENerated by UNfamiliar TECHnologies is DIFficult." Tsuan turned back to Kwin, his antennae lashing as if he were flicking away a fly. "The van might ARRive in LOcaur space in as few as three days."

CHAPTER THIRTY-THREE

Petra had lived her whole life in tin cans of various sizes. Training vessels, fleet ships, transports—little cans. *Constitution*, *Reliance*, and *Vigilance*—big cans. The sprawling space stations of her youth—huge cans.

She'd never, not once in her life, experienced one heartbeat of claustrophobia until she took a ride in an escape pod.

She drifted in the void in a cold steel coffin, isolated and unmoored from reality. No personal computer to latch her to the outside world. No networks. The escape pod itself was bare-bones, a box with barely enough life support to keep her from freezing or suffocating on her expelled carbon dioxide. It emitted a standard distress beacon once launched, but there was no interior computer interface whatsoever. It was useless.

She was alone in the cold, kept company by a single dim glowing panel that filled the box with unnatural shadows. Nothing to do but count her heartbeats and wonder.

She drifted in and out of awareness. Blood caked her face, turning sticky, then dry. She shivered. She tried to rub life into her chilled limbs, but there wasn't much space to keep her blood flowing. The air was dry and tasted vaguely of electricity. It made her nauseous. She wanted to puke, trapped in that pod, except that she supposed doing so would only make her wet, which would freeze her all the faster.

She turned the memory stick over in her palms. Danny had shoved it into her hands in the seconds before she'd climbed into this pod. She wondered if Danny and Misha were drifting in other pods, debris scattered among the fleet.

We know what Reset is, Misha had said.

Petra was quite likely to die here, holding on to the secret she had been chasing for weeks, with no way to access the drive and give her the peace of resolution before the cold took her.

She sang to herself, her voice swallowed by the close walls and made tinny by the thin air. She should conserve oxygen, she knew, but she had to do something to keep herself awake. If she fell asleep, she'd never wake up again. She'd die of slow hypothermia in this tissue-thin prisoner's jumpsuit.

At least Rush had managed to make his death *mean* something. At least he had, in a way, gone out on his terms. She was going to become a popsicle.

Darkness crept into the corners of her vision. Exhaustion, boredom, despair—it was hard to say what eventually made her shut her eyes.

Something slammed into the side of her pod, and the metal let out a tortured groan. Petra woke with a scream, unsure if the impact and the sound had been real or the leading edge of some dream.

She didn't know, and she didn't care. She was sick of this pod, closing in around her like a merciless steel fist. She kicked the walls until her toes bled. She screamed until her throat was raw. She pounded her fists against the lid until her knuckles were bruised and numb, howling at the universe to let her *out*.

She didn't realize the top of the pod had cracked open until hands had clamped around her arms and pulled her out of the cell.

Her screaming turned into coughing as a wash of warm air flooded over her skin. Her coughing turned into retching as a chaos of hands and bodies pulled her upright and enveloped her in a thermal blanket.

"Give her space, give her space!"

A confusion of voices flew around her head.

"Catch your breath, Petie."

"Hold on!" Someone screamed over a distant intercom. "Seekers coming in hot, we gotta punch it!"

Someone shoved Petra into a harness, clasping it firmly over her chest. She felt the hull of a ship rattle around her as engines woke to a roar.

"Slow breaths. Even breaths."

"Where are we?" Petra mumbled. Her head spun. Her vision swam.

"Harlan! Get your ass buckled in NOW!"

"Shit. Shit!"

A sudden burst of acceleration crushed Petra's spine against a cold wall.

She couldn't handle it anymore. Her stomach gave up the ghost.

She turned her head and puked.

Petra came to her senses as a pair of hands cupped her cheeks. She sucked in a deep breath as if she'd been drowning, her eyes flying open.

"Petie! Petie, it's okay—it's okay—" Someone wiped a warm, damp cloth across her face, cleaning away blood and thin vomit. Petra reached out, her shaking hands finding a warm body. She grabbed, pulling the body close.

A faint tingly scent of hair dye and makeup filled her nose, and that brought her senses back faster than any triple macchiato.

"Amy," she croaked. She ran fingers through short, blue hair, unbelieving. "Oh gawd, Amy!"

"Hey…" Amy's shoulders relaxed as she held Petra in a long, gently rocking hug. "Hey…"

"Where's Rush?" Petra's throat felt like a furnace. "Where's Juice? What happened…."

Amy didn't answer. She only held Petra close as Petra caught her breath and shed tears to drift off the tips of her eyelashes and drift like glittering dust in zero-G.

Petra didn't need an answer, of course. Slowly, her memories sorted themselves, falling into place, bringing with them a miserable headache.

"Oh gawd," she mumbled finally. Amy pulled back, drifting weightlessly in the tiny room. Uncovered wires and conduits covered the walls and low ceiling. It was some kind of utility room, warm and heavy with the scents of oil and coolants and a dozen kinds of grease.

"There's water." Amy unclipped a bottle from her belt and held it out to Petra. In her other hand, she held out two white pills. "And the last of the painkillers."

Petra snatched the offering. She didn't process Amy's words until she'd slurped down half the bottle.

"The last of it?" She swallowed a lump. She'd worn her voice down to a ragged husk with all that screaming.

Amy smiled faintly. "Resources are scarce out here in the boonies. We're with the Followers."

Petra struggled with the words. "Oh gawd," she groaned. She put a hand over her mouth, worried she'd throw up again.

Tribe Six consisted of the Prime warship, the three freighters, and a few dozen smaller support ships, like the Astrography lab where Petra had been a prisoner. Included among the swarm of support ships were a handful of freelancers—independent vessels captained and crewed by people without the full rights of fleet citizens. Providing they followed fleet rules and regulations, the smattering of ships, commonly called the Followers, were allowed to travel with the Tribe and trade with the citizens and administration.

Larry had always scoffed and called the Followers a bunch of cousin-kissing hillbillies. They lived in squalor, surviving on the garbage that even the fleet fabricators couldn't reuse.

Petra gazed around the room, clutching her thermal blanket to her chest. They were in some kind of utility room. It might've been an engineering bay, but Petra had never seen an engineering bay so crammed with *junk*. Heaps of tangled wires spilled out of every conduit. Rows of pressure valves leaked thin streams of gas that made the air itchy. A thin layer of grease covered every surface.

Working in the comms station, Petra had whiled away long nights reading lurid stories about these sovereign captains on their rickety kingdoms. Brutal, lawless places where the people ate their dead rather than let good meat go to waste.

There was no way of knowing which of the stories were

true accounts and which were pure fantasy, but the fleet didn't care—as long as the captains didn't make trouble.

"It's all right." Amy caught the look of dread that must've crossed Petra's face. "Captain Sypher keeps a pretty tight ship. She holds together well, for something this old." She patted the loose bundle of wires near her elbow affectionately.

"What are ya doing here, girl?" Petra groaned.

Amy blinked. "Things broke crazy after the general strike," she said. "Every ship in this sector had eyes on us when Rush's message played. When the crowd broke into Yolondo's shop and found his body there…" She swallowed hard, shook her head, and soldiered on.

"The fleet's in chaos. I got friends in the Followers. Me and a few others, we got off the *Constitution* before it went into full lockdown. There's a growing coalition of Follower captains openly defying fleet commands. Even branches of the fleet administration—the brass— have stopped cooperating with the top brass and the Seekers. They're calling for independent investigations into the Corps."

Excitement burned across Amy's young face. "It's working, Petie. Brass is crumbling."

"Yeah, but…the *Followers*?"

"Ah, come off, Miz Po'lova." A new figure moved around the conduits, making Petra jerk and instinctively reach for the stunner that wasn't on her hip.

The spindly man that emerged from the back of the room jeered at Petra from behind long, greasy dreadlocks. "We ain't all mold-licking bastards and cannibals out here in da sticks." He grinned, showing more gaps than teeth, and lifted one eyebrow, making his left eye bulge to nearly twice the size of his right. "We're mold-licking bastards and *pirates*."

"This is Captain Sypher," Amy said. "He's a better guy than

he looks." She wrinkled her nose. "Though he *does* look pretty bad."

"I broke bad from da fleet for you, Miz Po'lova," Sypher drawled. He had a backwater accent, slurring his words and emphasizing strange syllables. "Nearly flew my ship to pieces, outrunning dem fighters dat come looking for you. Snatched you right outta the sky halfa step ahead o' dem."

"We outran fleet fighters?" Petra gave Amy a sharp glance. "We outran *Seekers?*"

"*We* didn't do nothin'," Sypher declared. "*I* outran da Seekers." His sloppy grin widened as he slapped his chest. "Best pilot in da fleet, you're welcome. Couple'a my fellow cap'ains are covering for us now. And there's still some decent folk workin' the admin, tying the search all up in knots. Seeker Corps los' all kinda support dese days. Fleet's a hot mess. Hope you was worth savin'."

It took Petra less time than she expected to adapt to Sypher's heavy accent.

Amy shot the man a dirty look. He opened his empty palms, white against the rest of his dark skin, and shrugged an utter lack of apology. "Jus' sayin'. If the Seekers and standin' brass come out on top o' dis fight, all of us Followers are facin' a long walk off a short bridge."

"That's not Petra's fault," Amy snapped. "There's nothing she can do about it—"

"No." Petra grunted and allowed herself another tiny sip of water. "It's true. The Tribe's in trouble and I ain't got time sitting here casting blame." She slipped a hand into her pocket and her fingers closed around the hard memory stick.

We know what Reset is, Misha had said.

She swallowed again and lifted her chin to Captain Sypher. "You said you grabbed my pod out of a cluster, right?"

Sypher folded skinny arms across his chest and nodded.

"Sypher was keeping an eye on traffic coming and going out of the *Constitution*," Amy said. "Right after Rush… Shortly after the concourse went to shit, one of the shuttles departed and flew straight to the astrography lab."

"Unscheduled flight," Sypher added. "Figured dat might be you on dere."

"About a day later, Astro ejected an entire section's worth of escape pods all at once," Amy went on. "She hadn't put out a distress call, and she didn't seem to be damaged so it seemed like an obvious escape attempt."

"Glad you got me before the Seekers did." Petra gave Sypher a side-eye but nodded her appreciation. Sypher grunted, tugging his dreadlocks.

"But were there others?" she asked, as an emptiness settled in her chest. "Anyone else…in any of the other pods?"

Sypher and Amy exchanged glances.

"Time was tight, Petie," Amy said softly. "By the time we got to the pods, the Seekers were already scrambling."

"I saw one pod wid life signs," Sypher said. "I scooped it and ran. No time to check tha others."

Petra let out a long, wavering breath. "How long ago was that?"

"'Bout nine hours. Booked it away from da Fleet. Lots of us, flyin' aroun' like bees from a kicked hive." He patted the walls, making one of the electrical conduits rattle.

"My girl, she a good ship. But she got da same profile as a dozen other Follower ships. Swapped out my call sign. Old pirate trick. Mosied on back to the flock, easy as you please. Seekers are combin' through Follower ships one by one, but dey won't get ta us for a while."

"How long?" Petra swallowed.

Sypher shrugged. "I figure, we got twelve hours ta figure out what we gonna do with da famous Miz Po'lova."

"He's not going to sell you to the fleet," Amy added, giving Sypher a sharp look. Sypher's yellow grin didn't waver.

"But we *do* need to figure out where to go from here. Rebellion's in full swing, Petie, but there are lots of different factions resisting brass. If we don't all coordinate and start working together, brass is going to cut us down one by one."

Petra looked at Amy in wonder. A year ago, she'd been coaching the wannabe punk and graffiti artist in an after-school program for troubled youths.

Well. Petra must not have fixed Amy of that whole *rebellious teenager* phase because here she was, talking treason with a pirate captain and a wanted fugitive like she'd been born to it.

"The people on Astro." Petra lifted her memory drive, showing it to the others. "They slipped me this. Said it was important I get the word out about Project Reset first thing. We can't figure out where to go from here if we don't know what brass is planning."

CHAPTER THIRTY-FOUR

Seventy-two hours wasn't enough time to prepare for war.

The Overseers were generous people when it came to loaning out their outdated tech. The first load of aid shipped in from Second Tree included nine ancient inter-atmosphere troop transport ships and dozens of shield and battery generators they'd probably pulled out of some old museum. The Overseers also spared no expense in loaning out their fleet of six experimental Terrible-class ships.

Kwin insisted this was only because the new models were so unreliable that the Overseers themselves refused to depend on them for the defense of Second Tree.

"Way to boost morale, Kwin," Toner grunted.

"It gets worse," Kwin said. His speech was unaccented now that he was back aboard his ship. "Only the Terrible-class ships have facilities capable of running activation tanks."

Jaeger groaned. "So those are the nurseries raising our army, and we can't risk them in battle."

"Only if you wish to gamble against any ability to produce the troops meant to hold off a ground invasion," Kwin replied.

"Okay." Jaeger scrubbed her fingers through her hair, feeling the buildup of grease on her scalp. She couldn't remember the last time she'd showered.

She put down her double espresso and forced herself to take a bite of an energy bar. She also couldn't remember the last time she'd put anything in her mouth that didn't taste like coffee or sweet sawdust. Elaphus was going to kill her— assuming exhaustion or the K'tax didn't get her first.

Jaeger stared at the holo-map of Locaur and nearby space, floating at the center of her command team. "Kwin, what are the Terrible ships *reliably* very good at?"

"Surprises."

Jaeger drained the last of her espresso, then flung the mug at the Overseer. The metal swirled through his hologram and hit the bulkhead behind him with a *clang*. Kwin didn't twitch.

"That's not helpful," she snapped.

"Assuming our original *Terrible* is a reliable representation of the other ships, they are quite fast," Kwin answered.

"Also not very helpful," Seeker muttered, tabbing through the notes on his computer. "We're looking at a blockade and siege, not a race. What are their defenses like? Weaponry? Can they disrupt enemy comms?"

"All untested," Kwin said.

"Their drones," Jaeger suggested. "Load them with explosives and plant them like mines around the system. Program them to home in on any dense cluster of K'tax ships nearby."

Kwin's antennae lowered in assent. "I will add more drones to the list of equipment I am requesting from the Council."

"How's it going with them, anyway?" Toner asked. "Will they send us more ships?"

"I have another meeting with the Council in ten minutes.

We make a compelling argument," Kwin admitted. "This smaller vanguard force presents less of a potential threat to Second Tree than the larger swarm. The debate continues, but the Council may agree to send more ships to aid in defense of Locaur."

"Let's hope they don't debate much longer," Seeker said. "Or it might be too late."

Forty-eight hours wasn't enough time when there was an entire continent—if not an entire planet—to protect.

Occy and his team of engineers worked double shifts to increase the maximum power and radius of the *Osprey*'s shield generators.

"We're burning through power at this rate," Occy said, his voice unusually grim when Jaeger came to check on progress. Sweat beaded the young man's brow, dripping over the front of his welding faceplate. He wore a sweat-stained white shirt that showed the lines of his ribs. "I can increase the radius up to ten kilometers, but anything past that, and there's not enough *oomph* to repel a hard rain, let alone orbital bombardment."

"What about the spare shield generators Kwin's people sent?"

Occy shrugged, flipping his mask back over his eyes and pushing himself back into the guts of the generator bays. "Mason is looking over them now. He took a team out to the outlying villages to get them set up. I'm waiting for his report."

"Ten kilometers is no small feat." Jaeger tried to sound encouraging. "That protects Art's village and the shrine, at least."

Occy winced. "Yeah, but it drains the generators at a staggering pace, and our solar panels aren't enough to keep it recharged. If the K'tax try to get close, we can only maintain the shields for short bursts at a time. Thirty seconds. Maybe a minute. Spencer is trying to get the new Overseer batteries installed, but they don't like to play nicely with the *Osprey*'s systems."

Jaeger lifted her gaze to one of the speakers mounted overhead. "Moss? What's the holdup on getting those backup batteries installed?"

The computer, as always, took a moment to respond. "The programming is complex," it admitted. "Synchronization is...slow."

"That doesn't answer my question."

A silver sphere zipped a circle around the engine bay. Me had posted one of its relays in the *Osprey* to facilitate faster communication with Kwin's people. "Your new AI program isn't overly efficient," it said cheerfully. "I have some familiarity with the *Osprey*, Jaeger. If you allow me administrator access to the systems, I will be able to increase the installation rate by a factor of four, at least. Possibly five."

Jaeger chewed her lip. She didn't like the prospect of fiddling around with the *Osprey*'s AI configuration—Moss might be slow, but she was steady and reliable.

On the other hand, with only three days until the invasion, they needed more than *slow*.

"Do it," she said reluctantly. "I'll send authorization along. Find Seeker or Bufo. They'll help you get yourself uploaded into the *Osprey* in a support capacity." She hesitated and glanced sharply at the speaker again. "Moss? Is that okay?"

323

There was a ponderous silence during which Jaeger felt herself dying. Moss had no sense of urgency whatsoever.

"I don't mind the assistance," Moss decided eventually. "Thank you for asking, Captain. I work best in cooperation with humans via neural uplink. I haven't shared hard drive space with other AIs before, but doing so seems similar in principle."

"Well, it's something," Occy grunted. Jaeger opened her mouth, about to ask him about upgrades to the *Osprey*'s radar array, but the boy had already vanished into the guts of the generator. Her query drowned in a cacophony of banging and the industrious hum of laser cutters.

Twenty-four hours wasn't enough time to save stubborn people.

"We've sent messages out to the distant villages." Art's antennae flicked restlessly through the air. "Inviting them, encouraging, yes, begging, to come shelter within the *Osprey*'s shield."

Jaeger's stomach sank. "You don't sound optimistic."

"Some will come," Art decided. "The closer ones who can make the journey in three days. The farther ones, who must immediately depart if they hope to reach us before the K'tax reach them?"

He shook his head, a strange gesture he'd picked up from the humans. "Stubborn. Not familiar with you aliens. They have faced K'tax before, they think. They will do so again, they think. In their way, as they always have."

"They've dealt with raiding parties before. Not invasion forces of this size."

Art spread his arms wide, offering her his helpless puzzlement. "They do not understand. Or perhaps they do not believe."

Jaeger ground her jaw. "I'll send the spare Overseer transports out to evacuate the distant villages." They had no hope of sheltering all of the Locauri within the *Osprey*'s shield, but she didn't say that. She would do what she could. Work with what she had.

One step at a time.

Art opened his claw-like hands and shut them again. "And return to ruin."

"Pardon?"

"You ask them to leave their villages, come to strange lands. When the battle is over, they return to their villages, ruined by K'tax scavengers. Ancestral nests. Old homes infested with K'tax eggs. The soul of the soil and the trees, Jaeger. Left defenseless because Locauri ran. No. Send ships as you will. Do not expect them to return full of Locauri. They will not think themselves cowards."

Jaeger opened her mouth but stopped herself. Arguing with Art would do no good. *He* wasn't the stubborn one.

"I'll send the transports," she said flatly.

Let it not be said that she didn't try to save what she could.

Twelve hours wasn't enough time to remind the crew what they were fighting for.

It was all the time they had.

Nutritional fabricator stores were running low, but Jaeger wasn't about to let her people spend the night before battle eating nothing but greenhouse radishes and early spinach.

The buffet line held creamy mashed potatoes, rich stews, heaping piles of noodles smothered in all kinds of cheeses and tangy sauces, mountains of egg rolls, pie plates as big as hub caps. Deep in the recipe bank, she'd found a code for something called baked Alaska. Much to her surprise, her people had destroyed the tray of fluffy dessert at the end of the line.

There was still more to do, of course. There *always* would be more to do in the hours before a battle. Still, all the system diagnostic checks and battle simulations in the universe wouldn't matter if the people behind the computer didn't believe in what they were fighting for.

She looked over the mess hall, watching her people feast. Down by the cargo doors, a few Locauri youths offered Toner all forms of local grub, insisting that he would enjoy this worm or that snail. They fluttered their pseudo wings, laughing as he sampled each in turn and bent over in a theatric mimicry of vomiting.

Across the way, by the bank of display screens, Occy tried to get a movie set up, but Stumpy's iguanome was making it difficult. The little creature danced between Occy's tentacles, wrestling with the limbs and gnawing on them like a precocious puppy.

Occy finally let out a yell of triumph, flinging the iguanome away. The little creature hit the wall, landed on all four feet, and shook itself—no worse for wear.

The display screens circling the hall turned dark and bright as a cartoon castle appeared, wreathed in the light of a shooting star.

"Sergeant Teddy!" the boy bellowed, scanning the crowd. He lifted a tentacle and pointed at Bufo. "No more excuses! You're gonna sit down and watch *Monsters* with me!"

When the lights were low, and the crowd had settled, finally submitting to their chief engineer's choice of nightly entertainment, Toner quietly stood and slipped out of the mess hall. He'd seen the movie before, plenty of times. Old restlessness drove him away from what was familiar and set him to pacing the *Osprey*'s quiet halls, a pale shadow moving through the darkness.

His mind burned. He wanted his pills. His hands twitched, looking for something to grab, pull, and tear apart. Damn him to hell, but he wished away the hours of peace until he could sink into battle and forget again.

The air currents shifted almost imperceptibly, but Toner caught a whiff of flesh. He turned.

A tall, slender figure moved up the corridor in his direction, her hips swinging with every step. She smelled like blood, hormones, and steel.

Toner licked his lips. "Portia."

"What are you doing prowling out here all by yourself, Commander?" The glimmer of distant emergency lights reflected off her white teeth.

Toner sucked in a deep breath through a double-row of shark teeth. *Staring into the void,* he thought. *And it's staring back at me.* "I've already seen that movie plenty." He shrugged. "Just out looking for something else to do, I guess."

"Oh, excellent." She stopped centimeters from him. She was a tall woman and looked him levelly in the eye. He could hear her pulse beating against her throat. "I was about to go treat my new tattoo," she said. "But I can't reach it very well by myself." Her lip quirked into a smile. "Could you give me a hand with it?"

Toner didn't move but took his time regarding the woman. She wore a skin-tight tank top and combat pants. Wherever her new tattoo was, it wasn't on her arms, shoulders, or in the swath of her chest and back exposed by her low neckline.

"Only a hand?"

Portia's smile broadened. She reached down and grasped his hand, running her fingers over his bony knuckles. "Depends on how good you are with it."

CHAPTER THIRTY-FIVE

The image on the display screen was crystal clear. The long, badly lit room. The green sheet. The stack of recording equipment and the sentry lurking by the doorway. The smear of blood and guts across the floor. Petra Potlova, in her tattered prisoner's jumpsuit, holding a Marine's stolen stunner in one hand and offering the other to Tracy.

Screen-Tracy reached up from where she huddled behind the stool, her hand wavering. Then her fingers wrapped around the barrel of the stunner.

"See, you had the right idea. Honestly. Potlova *let you have it.*"

Screen-Tracy, the young woman with a button nose and hair curled to mimic Petra's style, lifted the weapon in trembling fingers and pulled it forward.

"Aaaand…here is where you completely fall off the train. An upsetting display, I must say."

Screen-Tracy pressed the barrel against her forehead. Her hand coiled around Potlova's, and she pulled the trigger.

The recording wavered as the room filled with a burst of

electrical discharge. The static cleared to reveal Screen-Tracy collapsed in a heap on the floor and Potlova racing through the open door with the two traitorous techs on her heels.

"I *just* can't wrap my brain around it."

The display paused, then jumped to reverse. It resumed playback to show Tracy once again pressing the stunner to her forehead.

"Did you think there weren't other cameras in the room?" Professor Grayson paused the video again, shaking his head in amazement.

Tracy mumbled something. Her tongue was thick and covered in fuzz. Her head spun. They'd pumped some kind of drugs in her—they said it was to help her recover from the stunner blast, but then they'd handcuffed her to a bed in the Astrolab's tiny medical bay.

"I'm sorry." Grayson replayed the video while chewing his lip. "What was that?"

"I wasss outnum'ered," Tracy mumbled. "Couldn't fight."

"Oh, obviously. They outnumbered you, and Danny had a neat trick up his sleeve. No one could expect you to stand up to someone controlling the sentry."

"They took out Jenkins." Her memory was still fuzzy, but she remembered that much clearly. The smell of ozone as one of the lab's most decorated guards hit the floor. She also recalled the sight of another guard hitting the floor shortly before that. In a million pieces, blown apart by shrapnel. Her gut clenched.

Grayson shook his head and sighed. He paced little circles in the tiny med bay, scrubbing his fingers through his hair.

"Sorry," Tracy slurred.

Grayson pulled up short and lifted his head, staring at her with those strange, glitter-bright eyes. "That is true," he said, consoling. He reached down and patted her hand. Tracy flinched.

"You are indeed sorry. This is my fault," he said, his voice turning contemplative, almost apologetic, as the tips of Tracy's fingers grew numb. "Classic mistake. I've managed to overestimate not only the resolve of my opponents but also the competence of my allies."

Tracy whimpered, writhing against the handcuffs. She glanced over her shoulder, but the med bay was empty. "Please…"

"Father would be ashamed." Grayson didn't appear to hear her. "Perhaps even Shel would've known better. Oh well. Nothing to do but keep going forward."

He glanced down and seemed surprised to see Tracy sucking for breath. "Congratulations, intern," he added. "You've helped me make a decision. Your aid of the fugitive has thrown the fleet into absolute chaos. I wasn't entirely sold on Reset, but now it's our best option. No more waffling."

"Please," she whispered. Her eyes watered. "Stop, please. What do you want?"

"That's an interesting question." His lips pursed. "Right now? A good Mai Tai on a beach, served up by a girl in nothing but a flower lei. But it's going to be a while before we're sipping cocktails out of coconut shells again." He sighed.

"*Nobody* stays an intern for three years," he whispered, studying her face. "Just like nobody stays a highly decorated ensign for half a decade. You've had your fingers in all sorts of projects, haven't you, Tracy?"

She couldn't speak. She could only nod frantically. Like a blessing straight from heaven, the pressure on her wrist eased a bit. She gasped.

"That's right. So you know Reset."

"Something about the wormhole." She choked back tears. "It scrambles computer data."

"If the computers aren't properly shielded, yes. But it's more than computer data. Wormhole travel scrambles the *brain*, too. Wipes it clean. Blank slate. Returns the mind to factory settings, you might say. Isn't that fantastic?

"Of course, that's our current understanding. It's what we know based on the tests we've run. Going through will be…revealing. Still, what I know for sure is this—wormhole travel will reset the mind if not properly shielded. Think about the potential here.

"Some poor bastard can't stay out of trouble, in and out of jail his whole life for petty crime, brawling, the occasional theft. You put him through all kinds of reform systems, but he never quite gets the lesson. A lost cause. Shoot him through a wormhole, though, and when he comes out the other side, he's not the same man anymore! No memory, no *connection* to the man who beat every one of his girlfriends and sold Black Dust to children and stole candy from babies. A new-made man, ready to become a functioning member of society once more."

He grinned. "As long as there's a society ready to greet him, that is. Take him in, plug him back into the system. Bring the lost lamb home, you might say."

Tracy was nodding frantically, hanging on to the idea that the more she agreed, the more likely she was to survive.

"All of the mayhem in the fleet has *really* put us behind schedule in constructing our modified Faraday cages," he said. "There are only a handful of properly shielded ships and chambers in the entire fleet. And everyone who's not in one of those rooms, when we finally make the jump…" He mimed putting a gun to his head and pulling the trigger. "Pow. Dead and reborn. I was hoping we'd have the Seeker Corps and more of the loyalists shielded before it was time for the jump, but you, Tracy…you've helped me understand."

He leaned in close until she felt his warm breath on her cheek. It smelled like sweet mint. *"You're all fucking worthless. So!"* He drew back and clapped once, loud as a gunshot. "We're going to scrub the whole damn thing. Bring the entire fleet back to square one. Just enough of us surviving the jump with our memories intact to help our new fledgling Tribe get up on its feet once we clear the other side."

"I'll do it," she babbled, leaping at the chance for redemption. "I'll reset. I'm sorry. I'm sorry I was a coward. Let me reset, please."

"A reasonable request!" Grayson admitted. He stepped away from her bed, studying the vital signs monitor mounted to the wall.

"But I'm afraid I'm a very petty man, Tracy." He nodded at the darkened display screen. "After that stunt you pulled yesterday, I'm loath to let you off that easy."

He pressed one of the keys on his palm.

Tracy screamed.

"Everyone has a weakness," he muttered, his voice almost sing-song as he watched the young woman die.

With her gone, Grayson fished out his personal computer and checked the screen. One message from his engineering team on the *Reliant*. They'd completed work on the Faraday cage around the command and control center. The last mission-critical shield was up and running. Anything else his teams managed to install in the last two hours before the wormhole jump would be icing on the cake.

After thinking for a moment, he typed a text response onto his screen.

Make sure my entire core team is in a safe zone. Tell Kelba we're ready to jump as soon as the wormhole is active.

In flicking his fingers over the screen, he pressed more keys on the control glove. Out of the corner of his vision, he saw Tracy's lifeless body.

"Ah, sorry," he said absently. "I honestly thought I had more forgiveness left in me. Oh, well. There's a lot to do and not much time to do it in." He had to make sure the fleet commanders still loyal to Kelba and the Seekers all made it to safe zones before the leap. As much as he wished he could push the reset button on those ninnies as well, he was going to need them competent and coherent as soon as they emerged on the other side of that wormhole.

There was no telling what awaited them over there. Sarah Jaeger had almost certainly suffered a reset when she stole the Prime and made the jump, but that had been over a year ago. Even if she hadn't recovered her memories, there was a good chance she'd pieced together her situation and was preparing to face the fleet once more. With the powerful Tribal Prime warship at her disposal, she could do *quite* a lot of damage before succumbing to superior numbers.

That was, assuming she'd survived the year alone with that damned Nosferatu mod. A Reset would've affected Lawrence Toner as well—and quite possibly the programming of his neural collar. That'd be a lovely bit of irony: little Sarah Jaeger, oblivious to her past, ripped to shreds by the very man she'd fought so hard to save from a doomed planet.

Shelby had never liked that pale bastard and had pushed to have the man incinerated from day one. Didn't trust such an unstable mod, and for good reason. But, well. Lawrence had his uses, and not only in the field. The price of his admission

GATHERING WINDS

into the fleet, for one thing: stacks of undamaged hard drives containing information on the most advanced genetic modification and cloning techniques in existence. You couldn't buy that kind of intel anymore, not at any price.

Grayson stuffed his hands in his pockets and strolled out of the med bay, whistling a flute solo. Getting into a firefight with Jaeger and the Prime was going to be rough, but there was one aspect of the coming fight that he was quite looking forward to.

Seeing the look on Jaeger's face when she saw what he had in store for her.

The video ended. The display screen froze. Silence fell in the cockpit.

Sypher's ship, Petra had learned, was named *The Bitch's Claw*. She didn't care for that name. She preferred to think of this cramped, hot, stinking rust bucket simply as *The Claw*.

An atmosphere conduit began to rattle.

Harlan, Sypher's son and the *Claw*'s engineer shoved it into place by pounding on it with the side of his fist. The rattling stopped.

"That can't be right," Amy whispered.

The display screen on the wall was frozen on the image of flabby little Danny in his lab coat, wiping sweat from his brow. On the whiteboard behind him was a crude sketch of a wormhole. The word *Reset* was scrawled in red marker and circled a dozen times.

"Play it again," Sypher ordered.

"We played it six times," Harlan snapped. "Pull the wax outta your ears, old man. The message won't change. You heard the scientists. When the fleet goes through the hole, everybody gets their memories wiped."

"Unless they're on one of the ships with the modified field, yeah." Petra licked dry lips. She desperately wanted water, but Amy hadn't been lying: there were no fabricators on any of the Follower ships. Rations were *rationed*, and the half-liter of water left in her bottle had to last her another nine hours.

So many people. Her mind reeled as she considered what Misha and Danny had told her, from behind that screen. "We don't have any of those special electromagnetic conduit thingies they talked about, do we?" she asked, on the faint hope that Harlan and Sypher and art student Amy might be able to hack together a modified Faraday cage in less than two hours. "That stuff they're using to build those shielded chambers?"

Harlan shook his head. He was a tall, handsome kid who couldn't have looked less like his gnarly father if he'd tried. "I wouldn't have the cash to keep one of those lying around in storage if I saved up every credit for ten years."

Sypher hocked a loogie, opened a rusted recycling chute, and spat his load. "So we don' go through the hole." He wiped his mouth with the back of his wrist. "An' we don' get lobo'mized."

Harlan jabbed his father in the ribs. "And stay behind, starving to death out in the boondocks of space? Jeez, old man, you've lost it. The Followers can't survive out here without fleet support. We don't have fabricators or nearly enough hydroponics."

"He's right," Amy muttered. "We can't stop the fleet from going through that wormhole when it opens. And the Followers can't survive on their own."

"And we ain't got the stuff to protect anybody from that mind-wipe thingy." Petra despaired.

"A'ight, smartass," Sypher muttered, and it was unclear which smartass he was addressing. "We gather up all our home videos an' v-logs an' record messages of ourselves, explainin' the whole scrip'. Bringin' us up ta speed. Make it da first thin' we see after da jump. When da fleet jumps, we go too."

"But Misha said that doesn't work either." There was a hysterical edge to Amy's words. "The computers get wiped without the modified shields, just like human brains."

"Naw," Sypher insisted. "Danny said *some* of dem get wiped. Not *all* of dem."

"He didn't give us enough information," Amy insisted. "He says the travel likely wipes *some* types of computer files, but he didn't say which ones. We can't rely on our records to survive the jump."

"I'm jus' tryin' ta help," Sypher yelled. "Ain' no bad ideas in a brainstormin' session!"

"It would *help* if you started paying attention to anything but your bad moonshine and pornos." Harlan, Petra noticed, wasted no time in jumping to Amy's defense.

Sypher's face swelled like a balloon, drawing in a breath that sucked the air out of the room. Fury drained the color out of his face. He opened his mouth to deliver a tongue-thrashing, and froze.

Petra was giggling.

Sypher grabbed a conduit and pushed, making himself pirouette to face her.

"Oh, God," Amy muttered, shoving herself across the room to tend to her once-mentor, who'd doubled over in a fit of chuckling. "Are the oxygen levels in here okay? She looks like she's going hypoxic."

"Naw." Petra batted Amy's hand away and wiped a tear

from her eye. "Naw." She looked up, her eyes shining. "*Lonely roads*," she sang softly. Her voice was thin, raw from hours of breathing canned air and so much screaming. Harlan and Sypher fell silent, staring at her.

"*Empty roads*," Petra said. "*Gotta bring your own light...*"

"Lady's gone void-loopy." Sypher wound a finger around one temple.

Petra shook her head. "Amy," she said. "You got any paints? Or color-sticks, or pencils, or crayons, or…or anything?"

It was far from a sure bet. So much of administrative life on the fleet happened through computers. Paper and pencil had become a luxury item, a novelty, and the Followers were awful thin on novelties.

Amy frowned and patted down her coveralls. "I think so, back in my bedroll. If nothing else, there's some old grease in the engine room that might work as paint. Why?"

"The wormhole wipes numbers off the computer," Petra said. "It don't wipe words off paper. It don't wipe pictures off walls. It don't wipe the pages blank in old magazines."

Amy's eyes went wide. She nodded. "I'll go see what I can find." Without another word, she pushed herself up the access hatch, leaving Petra alone with Harlan and Sypher.

"Can you put the word out to the other Followers?" Petra turned to the strange captain of this leaking rustbucket. "Open up comms to the other captains?"

Sypher nodded. "We more like rivals tha' friends, but times are a-changin'. They'll listen."

"Harlan?" Petra turned. "You're a smart guy. You keep a beat on the wormhole timetables, don'tcha?"

Harlan's face lit up at the compliment. He pulled himself to the pilot's console. "I do. I happen to think that sort of information can be valuable. Unlike some people." He shot his father a dark look.

"Great. How long until the system goes active again?" Petra asked. "Last I knew, we were getting real close to it opening up again, and that was a few days ago. How much time we got?"

"Oh, if the hole's on schedule, it's going to open up any time now." He activated his workstation, frowning as he tabbed through dozens of open windows. He nodded sagely. "Yeah. We're looking at thirty minutes, maybe. Hour, tops."

Petra let out a wavering breath. "The fleet's a mess," she muttered. "The Seeker Corps has pulled back. They ain't even bothering to look for me. They've given up on trying to restore order. They're gonna rely on the Reset to fix all this rebellion stuff. They ain't gonna dawdle once that hole opens. They'll go through quick."

"Puts us on a real tight schedule," Sypher drawled. "Thirty minutes 'afore da fleet moves? Not much we can get done, 'tween now and den."

"There is something," she said. "Open up a comm line to all of your friends. All the Followers and the fellow captains and anyone, *anyone*, you think is on our side, wherever they are. Independent ship or on the freighters. At this point, it don't matter. You get the word out to everybody. They gotta pick up whatever grease pencil or lipstick tube they can find and start writing on the walls."

CHAPTER THIRTY-SIX

Jaeger stood at the center of the universe, a towering god bigger than the stars themselves.

Well, kind of.

She clasped her hands behind her back and gazed at the immaculate tactical display filling the bridge of the *Terrible*. The ceiling arched like a planetarium above her, giving her a pristine, three-sixty-degree view of the galaxy.

As she watched, the view focused, spinning and tightening around the Milky Way's gassy arms. Stars blossomed, growing and soaring past her in a dance of cinematography that would make holo-drama producers weep. The zoom stabilized, and a perfect hologram of Locaur shimmered into being at her right elbow: a sapphire and emerald sphere the size of a beach ball.

A purple gas giant and a tiny rocky planetoid, Locaur's neighbors, drifted around the edge of the dome. An amorphous white haze floated halfway between Jaeger and the glowing orb of Locaur's sun. According to the Overseer's calculations, the wormhole was entering an active phase. That sector of the solar system would be dangerous to traverse while the shifting energies warped the fabric of reality.

Music thrummed in the background—*Enemy at the Gates,* which in Jaeger's opinion was one of James Horner's best projects. She'd been hesitant to request it, fearing the change of custom might distract the Overseer crew, but they didn't seem to mind the deep thud of war drums or the snaring cymbals.

"Display the kamikaze grid," she said.

Overseer crew members worked their stations around the edge of the holo-display. Udil, Kwin's metallic adjunct, lowered her antennae. A smattering of pinprick lights appeared, scattered in the space around Locaur. Jaeger winced. Among other things, the Council had given Kwin's crew nearly a thousand explosive-packed drones to scatter through Locauri space. On paper, it sounded like a lot.

But space was *big*, and even the thousand pinpricks of light made a pitifully thin net, all alone in the void.

"Five minutes until the K'tax vanguard drops subspace bubbles." Udil's voice echoed around the dome, coming from every direction.

Jaeger shifted her weight. She bounced on her heels. "Where is Kwin?"

"The captain remains in the medical bay, overseeing the activation of the most recent human crew," Udil said evenly. "The process is taking longer than expected."

Jaeger sucked on her cheek. Kwin was cutting it awfully close—not that there was much he could *do* on the bridge at this point.

"Open the general comm channel," she said. The audio system *clicked*, and a grin split her face. She wanted her people to hear her confidence. "Seeker! How's the old bird treating you?"

Terrible's systems interpreted her words automatically and located Seeker's position in the system. The Alpha-Seeker sprouted from darkness, enlarged to the size of a walnut to make it visible as it patrolled the space between Locaur's moon and the asteroid belt.

"She feels like coming home!" Seeker called. "God *damn*, I missed this ship."

In front of Jaeger, the Alpha-Seeker banked, pulling a series of impossibly tight loop-the-loops.

Jaeger laughed. "Better not smile too much," she teased. "Your face might freeze that way."

A *beep* indicated another party joining the open comm channel, followed by a series of loud, muffled *crashes*. Jaeger turned, alarmed to see one of the Overseer transports blinking within the Locauri atmosphere.

"Toner?" she asked fearfully.

Toner's answer came a little too quickly. "Nothing! Nothing is wrong!"

In the background, Jaeger caught a muffled bellow.

"What are you doing on Baby's transport, Toner?" Jaeger demanded. "You two were supposed to stay on separate drop teams!"

Tsuan was right—in the three days since Kwin had claimed the embryo hoard, there hadn't been enough time to activate the army they would need to repel a full invasion. Still, the six Terrible-class cruisers had managed to wake up seven hundred battle-ready warriors. They were distributed above the continent at that very moment, in the outdated transports the Overseers had also oh-so-graciously lent them for the battle. It wasn't many soldiers, but they were highly mobile and ready in squads of one hundred to meet the enemy wherever they landed.

"What?" Toner squawked. "What do you mean, *Baby's* transport? Did I miss a memo? Is *Baby* supposed to be piloting one of these tug boats?"

Somewhere behind Toner, Baby roared.

"Why are you in the same squad?" Jaeger snarled. The last thing she needed was to stand here helpless and listen to her two strongest melee fighters—and closest friends—tear each other apart.

"Because we're the front-liners, kid," Toner snapped, echoing Jaeger's thoughts. "Wherever these bastards land, *I'm* going to be there to meet them. I'll do it ten steps behind the fart machine. She's an ugly monster, but she's *our* monster."

"That makes you well-matched," Seeker called, sounding entirely too cheerful as he wove his ship in a series of figure-eights.

"HAH." There was another series of muffled crashing noises. "Occy! Get over here and pet the piggy. Yeah, like that. That's much better. See, she *likes* you."

Jaeger buried her face in her palms. She hadn't been a particularly religious person since her rebirth through the wormhole, but in times of stress, she did find herself flirting with the occasional prayer. Couldn't hurt, right?

God give me the wisdom to know what I can change, the courage to change what I can, and the serenity to put up with L. M. Toner.

And thank you, she added as an afterthought, *for letting us bring him back.*

"We're all set down here, Captain," Toner called. "All drop teams in position to sweep up whatever junk falls out of the sky."

"Kamikaze net fully deployed and in position," Me interjected. "Kamikaze. That is a very strange term. Could you explain it to me?"

"Some other time," said Jaeger, who was eager to keep the topic away from *suicide*. "Show me our cruisers."

Sixteen mid-sized Overseer ships blossomed in the hologram around Jaeger. These weren't the experimental Terrible-class ships. Kwin hadn't tried to hide the truth from her. These ships were slower, not as well-armed, and more poorly shielded than modern Overseer warships. Essentially obsolete, by Overseer standards.

Still, combined with the explosive drones and the in-atmosphere transports, it was more help than Jaeger had dared to hope for from the aliens. She only wished it wasn't her crew piloting those alien ships and learning their strange systems on the fly.

"Portia," she called, hailing the flagship cruiser. "What's your status?"

"Locked and loaded, Captain," Portia answered, sliding into the comms channel without so much as a hiccup to signal her arrival. "We're good to go. I have a whole load of men and women here itching to try out these Overseer toys in the field."

Jaeger winced but forced her voice even. They didn't need to hear her regret or her anxiety. Not now. "Copy that. Give my love to the crew, Portia, and stand by to kick some ass."

Portia laughed—a rich, deep sound—and flipped her channel to standby.

Jaeger turned a circle, studying the board. There was a seventeenth ship among the secondhand fleet as well. It was a small research vessel, spinning through space between Locaur and its moon like a gyroscope.

"I still don't understand why the council sent that one to

join the fight," Jaeger said to Udil. "Without weapons or shields, it's nothing but a big kamikaze mine." That was why she hadn't bothered to put a crew in it—only a whole boatload of explosives and a short AI subprogram that understood two commands: *move* and *boom*.

"Seventeen," Udil said. "It is a fortunate number."

"It is?" Jaeger was surprised to find the motive purely superstitious.

"Seventeen," Udil repeated. "United in one purpose. Cannot be divided."

Jaeger would have to ponder on that later—when there was time for pondering.

"Terrible-class ships two through six, in position around the system, ready to provide interference and support," Me reported. "Ninety seconds to drop out."

"What about you, Jaeger?" Toner called over the line.

"What about me?"

"What's your position, Captain?"

Jaeger double-checked the *Terrible*'s coordinates. "We're safe in the moon's shadow, as I promised."

"Uh-huh," he said dryly. "For how long?"

Jaeger bristled. "The Terrible-class ships have unreliable shields and weapons systems," she said. "I told you. Kwin and I are going to coordinate our forces from well behind the front lines. We're not bringing in the *Terrible* except as a last resort."

"Or unless Portia's ship takes a hit and could use some cover on her six," Toner said. "Or until you see one transport break the blockade line and run for the atmosphere and think you can shoot it out of the sky before it lands."

"I trust my crew," she snapped. "Why are you acting like I'm going to expose the *Terrible* and come running to the rescue at the first sign of trouble?"

"Because it's what you do." He sighed, and all the manic energy had drained out of his voice, leaving him contemplative. "Because you're *you*, Sarah."

Jaeger stared up at the ceiling, struggling to process his words. For all his bluster, something had changed since he woke from his coma. He was different. He acted like he knew things he shouldn't know—and while that wasn't strictly *unusual*, this time, she half-believed he really did.

We're both going to survive this, she thought, grinding her teeth. *Because I'm not going to die before I make you spill the beans.*

"It's some load of bullshit," she answered, trying to keep the banter light. "That you think you can dangle my name over my head like that, *Toner*. We gotta get you a tattoo. Jack?"

"Present," Seeker barked.

"What name do you think we should give this asshole?"

"Gerald," Seeker answered promptly.

"Absolutely not!" Toner yelped, roaring back to his old energy. "I'll have you know that I already *talked* to Tiki about that naming stuff."

"Did you?" Jaeger was grinning again.

"Yeah! They already have a Locauri name all picked out for me."

"Subspace bubbles collapsing near the asteroid belt," Me said, managing to sound entirely too anxious for an AI.

"You hear that?" Jaeger called as new hologram ships blossomed in front of her. Hundreds of tiny K'tax fighters spilled out of a dozen massive, irregular chunks of rock that appeared from nowhere. She couldn't believe it. The bugs *had* slapped subspace bubble generators on entire hollow asteroids. "They're dropping near the asteroid belt. Assume attack pattern theta."

The door opened, and Kwin scuttled onto the bridge with the blinding speed of an Overseer with somewhere to *be*.

"Glad you could join us," Jaeger shouted, dancing out of the way to give Kwin a view of the battle.

"Me as well," Kwin answered. "There was an upset with the new humans. The matter is settled, for now."

Not a moment too soon. Whatever drama was unfolding among the newly hatched crew, it would have to wait.

"Let's get this welcome wagon rolling," Seeker growled. The Alpha-Seeker's engines began to glow. All around Jaeger, the cruisers slid forward, turning toward the belt in a carefully coordinated pattern. The crew had less than two days to learn the old Overseer systems. She was proud of how well the ships moved together.

"Hey, Toner!" Seeker called. "Just one thing, before the party starts."

"Hit me with it, and don't hold back."

"What name did the Locauri wanna give you?"

Toner laughed in that rich baritone boom that always seemed so incongruous on such a skinny man. "Oh, me? I'm Puncher-of-Dragons."

CHAPTER THIRTY-SEVEN

"Boy, you don' know ya lettas?"

Harlan stared at the smear of black wax coating his finger. He looked up at the empty swath of air duct lining the low ceiling and shook his head. "I know my letters just fine! I can read better than you, old man. I just—I've never—I never done it before—not by hand!"

The *Claw*'s cockpit was hot and thick with the scents of oil and inks, dyes, and stains. Amy crouched in one corner, frantically scribbling her life's story onto the inside of a storage cabinet door with a nub of chalk she had found somewhere. Harlan hung from the ceiling, tongue poking out between his teeth as he scratched the *Claw*'s override passcodes into a conduit casing with the tip of a utility knife.

"I'll help," Amy breathed when the last of her chalk crumbled to dust and added to the thick air. She kicked, sending herself soaring over to Harlan, and snatched the tin of wax from his hands. "Tell me what you wanna say, Harlan."

Harlan seemed about to protest but realized that there

wasn't time for it. He coughed and leaned close, dictating his message into Amy's ear. The girl nodded and lifted her fingers to paint on the walls.

Petra's fingers soared over the *Claw*'s comms station. Sypher had made good on his word and established contact with malcontents and rebels all across the fleet to warn them about Reset. Petra had scrawled her message onto her arms with Amy's last ink pen and now concerned herself with coordinating a rebellion.

Thousands of questions poured across the comm channels, and the clock was ticking. Sympathetic scientists on *Constitution* reported that nearby pockets of space were becoming unstable as the wormhole system prepared to activate. Other informants from *Reliant* and *Vigilance* added that brass had powered up the main thrusters in each of the freighters—they were getting ready to move.

Some ex-soldiers have picked up modified multitools and are storming the bridge, someone wrote from the *Constitution*. **They're gonna stop us from going through the hole.**

It was a nice idea, but Petra wasn't going to count on their success.

I have an old LightCorps e-diary, one anonymous poster wrote. **Will the wormhole jump erase that?**

You're all delusional! one malcontent insisted. **Don't believe these conspiracies meant to rip the fleet apart!**

The messages flowed down the screen, a never-ending stream of panic and frantic activity, as people tried to prepare themselves for a surprise apocalypse. Petra did her best to answer what questions she could.

She told the user with the e-diary, **We don't know what**

files will survive the jump or not. Best bet is to write down as much as you can, as fast as possible, anywhere you can. Your name, your goals, a warning of what happened.

A new message on the feed caught her eye.

Something's going on in the *Vigilance* **storage ring,** someone reported. **A squad of Seekers opening one of the bays and blowing cargo.**

Petra swung around to the sensor array. Sure enough, radar showed the big freighter shedding a fine mist of objects into surrounding space. Radar was showing something else, too. A massive distortion, forming not more than a thousand kilometers from the edge of the fleet.

Nascent wormhole formed! a user reported from one of the smaller labs. **Two minutes until it's stable enough to traverse!**

Petra jumped as Sypher joined her at the station. These Followers, Petra was beginning to understand, didn't have much use for *personal space*.

"You drownin' in babble," Sypher muttered, glancing over the feeds. He turned, activating a larger display at the center of the cockpit. "Gimme real eyes on da prize, not dese radar dots!"

The screens flickered and switched to visual feeds. It took Petra a moment to process the different angles she was seeing. The *Claw* must have synchronized her sensors with the other Follower ships because she saw the massive freighters and the rest of the fleet drifting through space from half a dozen different angles.

The wide engine cells sprayed behind the freighters were glowing cold blue as they powered up for the first time in almost a year. On another feed, Petra saw the white orb of the wormhole growing like a tumor between the stars. Tiny black dots spread across its face—ships, dwarfed by its size—and it was growing fast.

Sweat poured down Petra's face.

We feel the Constitution rumbling, an anonymous user reported. **She's underway.**

Petra spotted the *Vigilance* on one of the screens. The freighter, and her thin escort of Seeker cruisers, was closest to the forming wormhole. She pulled away from a cloud of glittering debris, too small for Petra to identify.

Can someone tell me what *Vigilance* just launched? Petra demanded.

I see activity in some of the Reliant's bays, someone reported. **It looks like they're deploying these things, too.**

Sleek dark shapes slid across several of the view screens like predatory fish. More of the ancillary labs and ships, breaking for the wormhole.

"Oh, boy."

Petra whirled to see Harlan staring, wide-eyed, at the glittering cloud of debris the *Vigilance* had left in her wake. The look on his face made her heart stop beating.

"They're proximity mines," the young man whispered. On the screen behind him, something collided with one of the mines, resulting in a silent blossom of fire. Petra prayed it was debris and not a crewed ship.

"We're the enemy, now," Harlan murmured. "They don't need us like we need them. They'll kill us all to stop us from passing through the wormhole with them."

"Dey can *try*," Sypher growled, flinging himself toward the pilot's console and slapping the harness over his shoulders. "But I ain't no bad habit you can shake off in a day. Strap in!"

As Petra scrambled to latch her harness around her chest, she flipped her comms channel to audio, broadcasting her voice to anyone within range. "Any of you guys still thought the fleet cares about you? Here's your proof—they're dropping proximity mines behind them. They're seeding the whole area.

"They don't want us following them, but if we get split up from the freighters, we'll all die out here. Once we get through the wormhole, there's gonna be a heck of a lot of confusion. We'll still have a fighting chance to win back control of the fleet if we *hang together!*"

"*Vigilance* just dropped off the radar," Harlan said. "She's gone down the rabbit hole. God, fleet trapped some of its ships behind the minefield."

Petra felt the *Claw's* hull rattle around them as Sypher activated thrusters.

"Don't try to traverse the minefield," Petra cried to anyone who was listening. Fleet loyalist or rebel or Follower, it didn't matter. She didn't want to see ships full of people get blown up today. "Go around it! The hole ain't goin' anywhere!"

"*Constitution* approaching the horizon," Harlan gritted. "A few cruisers hanging back. Picking up a patrol pattern around the wormhole."

"Dey gonna try shootin' anyone who gets too close." A wild grin spread across Sypher's face. "But they can't catch me."

The engines surged, flinging Petra backward in her harness as Sypher banked his ship into an impossibly tight arc. The hull rattled and screamed around them. As the g-forces pushed all of Petra's blood to the back of her brain, she heard Sypher's high cackle as he laughed.

The wormhole grew on the display screens.

Sarah, Petra thought. *Larry.*

Rush.

One way or another, I'm gonna see you all soon.

"Hope is out there," Petra shouted into the comms channel, her voice thin and hysterical and on fire with adrenaline and resolve and terror. "Right on the other side of that hole. Now let's go get it!"

CHAPTER THIRTY-EIGHT

Jack Seeker sat in his fighter, snug and warm, happy as a chick in the egg. His fighter, the Alpha-Seeker, buzzed with activity, the display screens dancing beneath his fingertips as a stream of sensor readings poured through the neural link. Seeker didn't need to *see* the screens to know all that the ship knew. For a brief, glorious moment in time, man and machine were one.

One after another, massive chunks of stone appeared against the backdrop of stars as their subspace bubbles popped. He itched to spring forward, to strafe the ugly things, blow them out of the sky before they knew what hit them. But the Overseers had warned him—they would have to wait until the entire K'tax strike force dropped out of subspace before engaging. The twisting energies of subspace could easily scramble the computers of anybody who happened to be close when the bubble popped.

He watched, heart pounding, as more of the asteroids appeared on his display. Four chunks of rock, the size of small mountains. Five. Six. A white line of K'tax fighters began to spill from the first asteroid, racing ahead of their lumbering motherships to clear a path.

Seeker's instinct said *go*.

His training said *wait*.

"Final bubble collapsing," the Overseer—Udil—called over the comms as the seventh asteroid appeared at the end of the line.

"All right," Jaeger cried. "The way is clear. Engage!"

Her words didn't reach Seeker's brain before he squeezed the thruster controls. The ship burst forward like a restless stallion at the gate, pulling g-forces that clouded the edges of Seeker's vision. He shot forward to meet the leading cluster of K'tax fighters.

"Jesus, how many fighters can they cram into those fucking rocks?" From where he waited in his transport in the upper atmosphere of Locaur, Toner stared at his display and wanted to explode. The K'tax vanguard had arrived. It was seven asteroids, hurtling toward the planet at a fraction of light speed.

Endless streams of bloated K'tax fighters spilled out of each rock like clowns flowing out of a car. Thousands of them, it must have been—fanning around and ahead of the asteroids.

His fingers wound restless circles over his scalp. Something hard hit his shoulder, making him jump.

"Here." Occy shoved a length of rebar into Toner's arms. "Stop pulling your hair."

"Oh, hey." Toner blinked at the rod in surprise and set his restless hands to folding steel instead. It was a much more satisfying distraction than ripping out his hair in clumps. "Thanks."

Occy grunted and plopped into the seat beside Toner, staring at the screen.

Seeker's jet strafed circles around one of the asteroids, pummeling the rock and its buggy escort with laser pulses.

"All asteroids on a collision course for Locaur," Udil said over the comm line. "At this rate, they'll hit the upper atmosphere in thirty minutes."

Portia swore, breaking her long silence. "Those things are huge! The impact—I thought they weren't trying to destroy the whole planet?"

Occy shook his head, leaning forward to speak. "No, I saw the captain's sonar readings. Those asteroids are largely hollow. If they hit the upper atmosphere, they'll shatter into thousands of pieces."

"Meaning what, Occy?" Jaeger demanded.

Occy bit his lip. Panic scrawled across his face.

The space between Locaur and the approaching asteroids had become chaotic with whirling K'tax fighters. Two cruisers sliced through the mess like panthers through a swarm of gnats. Pulses of laser fire made the screen glitter.

"Our shields are holding well for now," Bufo warned from his captain's seat on one of those two cruisers. "But they're chipping away at us, Captain. We won't last thirty minutes under this kind of pressure."

"Occy!" Jaeger barked. *"What happens if the asteroids hit the upper atmosphere?"*

"There's gonna be a rain of meteor impacts all across the continent," Occy despaired.

"That's not so bad, right?" Toner said. "Except for the

people directly in the way of the impact, but it's a big continent, right? What are the odds that untargeted artillery—"

Occy shook his head. "Each one is gonna hit the ground with the force of a few megatons of exploding dynamite," he whispered. "The place is gonna be leveled."

Toner's mouth snapped shut. Okay, that did sound pretty bad.

"How do we stop that from happening?" Jaeger called.

A moment of cold silence filled the comms line.

"We break the asteroids apart well before they get close to Locaur," Seeker suggested. "Activate the kamikaze mines. Stop them before they get any closer." He sounded breathless and excited. On the screen, his fighter banked around another squadron of lumbering K'tax fighters, strafing them with laser fire, always half a kilometer ahead of their counterfire.

"That'll spread the rain of boulders across the hemisphere, not only the continent," Occy said.

"Not good enough," Jaeger snapped. "Other ideas?"

"They're hollow, but they're still huge," Occy murmured. "They've got too much momentum. We can't stop them in time."

"So we don't stop them," Portia said. "We force them off-course."

There was a blurt of deafening static over the line.

"Bufo!" Jaeger shouted. "Come in! Sergeant!"

"We're here," Bufo grunted as the static cleared. "Bugs took out our left thrusters. We're limping hard."

"Pull out of the hot zone," Jaeger said. "Try to get to one of the Terrible ships. We'll send a droid to help repair your thrusters."

"Aye."

"Portia's right," Toner said. "It's easier to knock a train off the tracks than stand in front of it and hope you're stronger than it is."

"You sound like you're speaking from experience, Toner," Seeker called, laughing as another stream of laser fire sank deep into the belly of a K'tax fighter, shattering it into a thousand pale pieces. "*Damn,* these things are uglier than a popped pimple!"

Where she stood on the *Terrible*'s bridge, in the shadow of the Locauri moon, Jaeger whirled on Udil. "Extrapolate the path of the asteroids and display."

Shadowy lines raced across the hologram, connecting the cluster of rocks to Locauri's blue atmosphere. The asteroids looked so *small* to scale, but Jaeger didn't dare argue with Occy's assessment. If they hit the atmosphere, they might be looking at a mass extinction event. She didn't want to believe that the K'tax would scorch the planet, but even the humans of Old Earth understood that cockroaches could survive a nuclear holocaust just fine.

"We need to activate the kamikaze net and the gyrostation," she said to Kwin. "Collect them *here*." She jabbed her finger into a point of space. "The objective has changed. We're not trying to destroy the asteroids. We only need to hit them hard enough from one direction to knock them so far off course they're no longer a threat."

"Do it," Kwin agreed, and two of his crew hopped to make it so.

"These fighters just keep coming out of the asteroids," Seeker warned. "I don't see an end in sight. My shields are fine for now, but they won't hold forever."

"Cruisers seven, eight, thirteen, and sixteen under heavy fire," Udil reported.

Jaeger expanded her view of the fighting with a wave and

groaned. The K'tax had come to their senses. Instead of randomly firing at the closest enemy, they'd begun to coordinate. Entire squadrons of the flying tick-shaped ships surrounded cruiser eight, pummeling it with low-energy laser pulses from every direction.

"They're overloading our shields," Mason called. "Hull temperature critical—"

"Get out of there," Jaeger said. "Retreat. Punch through the wall if you have to, just get out of—"

There was a blast of static as the cruiser's shields collapsed —followed immediately by her hull.

Jaeger screamed. A wordless, short burst of noise, too tortured and angry for words.

"There's a swarm of them forming around cruiser three," Spencer, captain of said cruiser, said nervously.

"Shake it off!" Jaeger roared. "All cruisers, keep moving! Under no circumstances do you let yourselves get surrounded!"

"I'll come to cover you," Seeker shouted to Spencer. "But *fuck*, Captain—they're still coming."

They're going to be overrun, Jaeger thought numbly, as the number of K'tax fighters on the hologram grew and grew, and the number of her ships slowly, fatally shrank.

"More ships entering Locauri space," Udil barked. "Seven —nine—dozens of them."

"The Council's support fleet?" Kwin whirled, giving Jaeger a spark of hope that flared, and died as the metallic Udil waved her antennae in the negative. "No. Not K'tax either. Unfamiliar profiles. They're coming through the wormhole, Captain."

A lump swelled in Jaeger's throat. Her stomach turned a

somersault. *No,* she begged whatever god was listening. *Not now. Not now, please.*

"Show them on the display," Kwin ordered.

New ships appeared in the hologram, filling the hazy space around the wormhole. They remained distorted at first as the Overseer sensors raced to analyze and replicate their unfamiliar forms. Slowly, their shapes stabilized and resolved.

Jaeger would swear on any holy book that she'd never seen any of the new ships before in her life, but deep down, she knew that wasn't true. She recognized the round, slowly rotating hull of the new craft forming in front of her. She'd seen this style of brutally efficient, undecorated, merciless *machinery* before. On the *Osprey*'s shuttles. On the sweeping monstrosity of Europa station, in her memory.

On the propaganda and training videos they'd managed to filter out of the *Osprey*'s scrambled databanks.

"Two more of the large ships dropping out of the wormhole," Udil reported.

"Hail the new arrivals," Kwin commanded. "We mean them no harm and urgently request assistance in repelling an invasion force!"

Slowly, Jaeger realized that someone was laughing over the comm system. It was Toner. There was an edge to his voice—high and sharp and hungry. "*Assistance?* From the fleet? You haven't been reading the company magazine, Kwin. They're here for a goddamned bug hunt."

Jaeger couldn't breathe.

"I gotta ask, Captain," Toner added, in a raw voice she hardly recognized. "Is *this* what you saved my life for?"

AUTHOR NOTES RAMY VANCE
OCTOBER 13, 2021

My mom turned 80 this year, just as Covid travel restrictions eased enough for me to visit. I'm so lucky – not just because I got to share the day with her, but because I am lucky to have a mother as generous and kind as she.

The truth is I wouldn't be here if it wasn't for her. You see, I knew I wanted to be a writer ever since I was ten and wrote my first short story which was basically a mash up of Robotech and Superman (bonus points if you know Robotech. Tag me in the Kutherian Gambit group with your favorite character and I'll love you forever. Mine is Max).

To my memory, I sat down on our 286 PC (I'm dating myself) and wrote my first short story in all caps. I was so pleased with my efforts that I wanted to show it to another writer... Legend had it that the High School English teacher wrote for the 1980s Charlie's Angels TV show (I kid you, not!).

I shared it with him and he gave me some tips and tricks, solidifying my resolve to become an author... and I've been writing ever since.

That's my memory, at least.

On this trip, my mom told me the real story: Apparently, I lost my backpack. My dad, wishing to instil me with some responsibility, banned TV for a week. I was an 80s kid. TV was my best friend.

My mom, taking pity on me, asked if I wanted to write my own story and I started to tell her this weird tale which was – you guessed it – a mash up of Robotech and Superman.

She got on the computer and helped me craft the story. She typed, while I dictated, and when it was done, she was the one who showed it to the English teacher and set up a meeting for us.

Apparently the English teacher was a real asshole.

My parents – mom, in particular – did their best to not let this bitter man dampen my budding passion. They were the ones who gave me tips, cultivated my interest and ultimately set me on the path that led me here.

I'm so lucky. And grateful.

So here's to you, mom. I may be a writer, but I simply do not have the words to express how much I love you.

(Believe it or not, I spent 18 days with her in Montreal and this is the ONLY picture I have of the two of us. I guess we were too busy celebrating…)

AUTHOR NOTES MICHAEL ANDERLE
OCTOBER 26, 2021

First, thank you for not only reading this story but these author notes in the back as well.

WHAT? NO LOST WEIGHT? WTF?!

I went to France (for MIPCom) and walked all the damned time. Over a week of walking everywhere. I should have legs of steel from walking up and down those damned hills!

Plus, some days I ate just one time. I've no idea how that happened, but for some reason, I dealt with eating one time (mostly) just fine. Regardless of how excited I was about my obvious weight loss, I didn't have a liar (what my wife affectionately calls the bathroom scale) to confirm my weight loss.

Then we went to Paris, where (you guessed it) *more* walking.

Then on to Frankfurt and the Frankfurt Book Fair to finish up the trip…with more walking.

I had to be down at least five pounds, right? Doesn't everyone say you need to walk and reduce eating to lose weight?

I get back to Las Vegas something like nineteen (19) days later, feeling thinner and a bit lighter on my feet.

I jumped on the liar (so excited) to confirm where I was late at night after traveling all day and night. Now, I know I shouldn't check at night when I weigh the most, but I could deal with that, right?

Wrong.

It seems I GAINED two @#%@#%@ pounds on the trip. WTF?

Now, I knew I should lose a pound the next morning (and I did). This morning, which was the second morning since coming back, I weighed the same as when I left.

I'm so disillusioned. I ate less, walked WAY more…and gained two pounds.

I'm so disillusioned.

I should go eat a chocolate cake. Or go to Cinnabon and eat a six-pack. Maybe grab a six-pack (of Coke) and a gallon of Old-Fashioned Vanilla and make Coke Floats until I fall asleep in a sugar-coma overload.

At least then, I'll have earned that pound or two.

Have a great week or weekend and I look forward to talking to you in the next book!

Ad Aeternitatem,

Michael Anderle

** P.S. We made it out of the tunnel... My GPS still doesn't work because the local phone system won't connect with my AT&T phone.

OTHER BOOKS BY RAMY VANCE

Other Middang3ard Books

Never Split The Party (01)
Late To the Party (02)
It's My Party (03)
Blue Hell And Alien Fire (04)

Death Of An Author: A Middang3ard Novella

Dark Gate Angels
Dark Gate Angels (01)
Shades of Death (02)
The Allies of Death (03)
The Deadliness of Light (04)

Dragon Approved
The First Human Rider (01)
Ascent to the Nest (02)
Defense of the Nest (03)

Nest Under Siege (04)
First Mission (05)
The Descent (06)
Sacrifices (07)
Love and Aliens (08)
An Alien Affair (09)
Dragons in Space (10)
The Beginning of the End (11)
Death of the Mind (12)
Boundless (13)

Die Again to Save the World
Die Again to Save the World (Book 1)
Die Again to Save Tomorrow (Book 2)
Yesterday Never Dies (Book 3)
From Earth Z with Love (Book 4)

Other Books by Ramy Vance

Mortality Bites Series
Keep Evolving Series

BOOKS BY MICHAEL ANDERLE

Sign up for the LMBPN email list to be notified of new releases and special deals!

https://lmbpn.com/email/

For a complete list of books by Michael Anderle, please visit:

www.lmbpn.com/ma-books/

CONNECT WITH THE AUTHORS

Connect with Ramy

Join Ramy's Newsletter

Join Ramy's FB Group: House of the GoneGod Damned!

Connect with Michael

Website: http://lmbpn.com

Email List: http://lmbpn.com/email/

https://www.facebook.com/LMBPNPublishing

https://twitter.com/MichaelAnderle

https://www.instagram.com/lmbpn_publishing/

https://www.bookbub.com/authors/michael-anderle

Manufactured by Amazon.ca
Bolton, ON